T0283778

GHOSTSMITH

ALSO BY

NICKI PAU PRETO

THE HOUSE OF THE DEAD DUOLOGY

BONESMITH

THE CROWN OF FEATHERS TRILOGY

CROWN OF FEATHERS

HEART OF FLAMES

WINGS OF SHADOW

GHOST SMITH

BOOK TWO IN THE HOUSE OF THE DEAD DUOLOGY

NICKI PAU PRETO

MARGARET K. McELDERRY BOOKS
NEW YORK · LONDON · TORONTO · SYDNEY · NEW DELHI

MARGARET K. McELDERRY BOOKS • An imprint of Simon & Schuster Children's Publishing Division • 1230 Avenue of the Americas, New York, New York 10020 • This book is a work of fiction. Any references to historical events, real people, or real places are used fictitiously. Other names, characters, places, and events are products of the author's imagination, and any resemblance to actual events or places or persons, living or dead, is entirely coincidental. • Simon & Schuster: Celebrating 100 Years of Publishing in 2024 • For information about special discounts for bulk purchases, please contact Simon & Schuster Special Sales at 1-866-506-1949 or business@simonandschuster.com. • The Simon & Schuster Speakers Bureau can bring authors to your live event. For more information or to book an event, contact the Simon & Schuster Speakers Bureau at 1-866-248-3049 or visit our website at www.simonspeakers.com. • The text for this book was set in Ten Mincho Text. • Manufactured in the United States of America • First Edition • 10 9 8 7 6 5 4 3 2 1 • Library of Congress Cataloging-in-Publication Data • Names: Pau Preto, Nicki, author. • Title: Ghostsmith / Nicki Pau Preto. • Description: First edition. | New York : Margaret K. McElderry Books, 2024. | Series: House of the dead duology | Audience: Ages 14 up. | Summary: Wren grapples with the revelation that her mother is the Corpse Queen and must navigate treacherous alliances and the return of her long-lost twin brother in order to stop her father and mother and prevent war in the Dominions. • Identifiers: LCCN 2023059676 (print) | LCCN 2023059677 (ebook) | ISBN 9781665910620 (hardcover) | ISBN 9781665910644 (ebook) • Subjects: CYAC: Fantasy. | Ability—Fiction. | Siblings—Fiction. | Magic—Fiction. | LCGFT: Fantasy fiction. | Novels. • Classification: LCC PZ7.1.P384 Gh 2024 (print) | LCC PZ7.1.P384 (ebook) | DDC [Fic]—dc23 • LC record available at https://lccn.loc.gov/2023059676 • LC ebook record available at https://lccn.loc.gov/2023059677

TO CLAIR MARSLAND,

Tarot reader, crystal carrier, storyteller—
and the closest thing to a real-life ghostsmith I know.

Marrow Hall
BONELANDS
Severton
Landon Point
Astoria Peninsula
The Bonewood
North Road
Aspen Ridge
SPEARHEAD MOUNTAINS
HIGHLANDS
South Road
Brighton
Stonespear
Westway
Granite Gate
Southbrook
RIVERLANDS

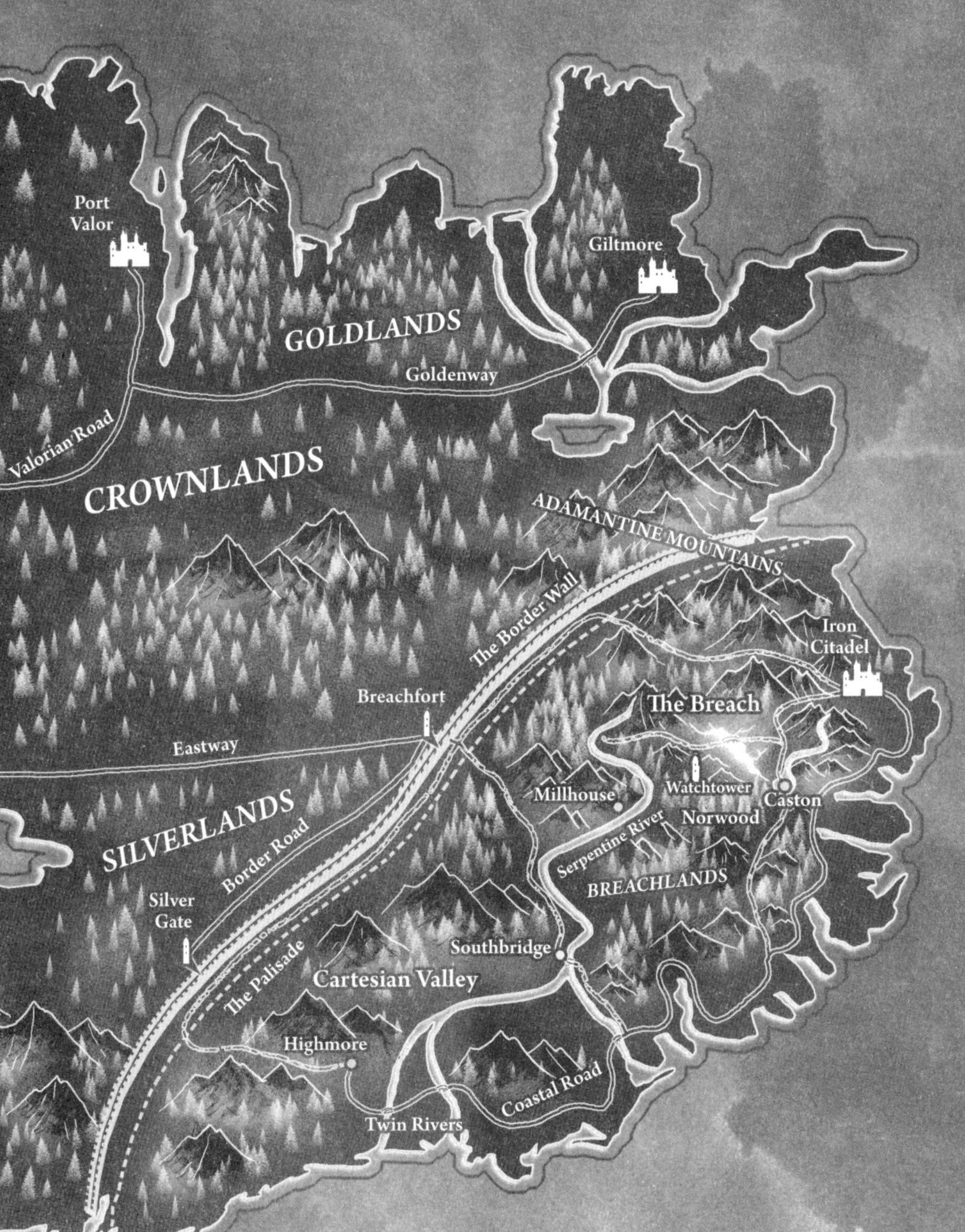

Port
Valor
Giltmore
GOLDLANDS
Goldenway
Valorian Road
CROWNLANDS
ADAMANTINE MOUNTAINS
The Border Wall
Iron
Citadel
The Breach
Breachfort
Eastway
Watchtower
Millhouse
Caston
Norwood
SILVERLANDS
Border Road
Serpentine River
BREACHLANDS
Silver
Gate
Southbridge
The Palisade
Cartesian Valley
Highmore
Coastal Road
Twin Rivers

ONE

The rumble of horses' hooves echoed in the night, an unseen foe riding hard on their heels.

Unseen, but not unknown.

"There they are again," came Leo's strained voice from Wren's right.

"Another Breachfort patrol," said Julian from her left.

They'd been chased from virtually the moment they'd set foot beyond the Border Wall, the gate creaking open behind them as they'd neared the palisade. Apparently, Wren's father had chosen to ignore her when she told him not to follow.

It wasn't entirely unexpected. She *had* just blown up his plans, exposed his betrayals, and robbed him of two high-value prisoners—a prince of the realm and the heir to the House of Iron—not to mention *herself*, a tool he was all too eager to use.

Anger flared in her stomach.

She would have to make him regret it.

As they crouched behind a tangle of scrub brush, Wren fingered the ghostsmith ring, the amplifier that gave her magic beyond her wildest imaginings. Magic that controlled ghosts and shattered bones.

Her ears filled with the remembered sound of a living bone being broken with a sickening crack. She squeezed her eyes shut, but the image of the guard's face inside the dungeons, the look of horror and confusion on his features as he clutched his arm, remained before her darkened eyelids.

She could do it again. Mow down her pursuers. Show her father what happened when he refused to heed her.

But knowing him, such a show of power would only make him want her and her connection to the well even more.

No, they would do what they had been doing all night.

Hide.

"Perhaps we should have taken the time to warn the commander," Leo said softly, catching his breath. "Told him that Lord-Smith Vance Graven, heir to the House of Bone, is a liar, a murderer, and a traitor. He might not have offered up his soldiers so willingly."

Wren had had the same thought herself. They could have saved themselves from pursuit, or even secured aid and allies, not to mention justice.

But trust in those in positions of power was thin between the three of them, and while they *might* have gained help in their quest to destroy the well and stop a second Iron Uprising—or an *invasion*, as Julian had called it—they might also have wound up questioned, imprisoned . . . or worse.

The complex plot Wren had discovered between Vance, the regent of the Iron Citadel, and the Corpse Queen ran deeper than she'd known, and she didn't relish the thought of finding out it ran deeper still.

"It wouldn't have mattered," she said grimly. "My father would have just ridden roughshod over him anyway, lying and manipulating until he had what he wanted."

"Sounds familiar," Julian said, whisper-soft, but they were inches apart, and Wren heard him.

She gritted her teeth. He'd not spoken a word all night; she'd thought the silent treatment was bad, but snide remarks under his breath were definitely an unhappy development.

She glanced his way but got nothing except his cold profile, as pale and distant as the moon. He cut an intimidating figure, helmet atop his head, gleaming black armor covering him from head to toe, making him untouchable—except she *had* touched him, had kissed his lips and raked her hands through his hair, though it felt like a lifetime ago.

The far-off thunder of the patrol, echoing in the night like an oncoming storm, changed direction and grew louder.

Next to her, Julian tensed, noticing it too.

"We need to move," Wren said. They'd long since passed the palisade, and though she'd secretly hoped the barrier would prove a line the patrol wouldn't cross, they had, which meant this chase could go on for hours still.

Even days.

"Where?" Leo asked, surveying the bleak landscape.

The copse of trees they'd hidden among when Julian and the other kidnappers attacked the Wall was too far away, and the fissures and caves that dotted the countryside were difficult to spot in the dark.

"There," Wren said, darting from behind the brush and forcing the other two to follow.

They skidded onto the ground behind a cluster of rocks that forced them to lie flat on their stomachs, and as Wren chanced a look back at the distant patrol, she saw something that made her heart sink.

There was a *bonesmith* with them.

Who they were was impossible to tell, but the bone armor was unmistakable.

Apparently, her father intended to follow them into the Breachlands. All the way in.

He intended to follow them for as long and as far as it took.

Stubborn fuck, she thought viciously. *Stubborn, ruthless* . . . reckless *fuck.*

She sighed. Of all the times to recognize herself in her father, now was *not* it.

The three of them remained like that, lying still and breathless on the cold, hard ground, for at least an hour before anything changed.

"Hey," Leo said hoarsely. "I think they're—yes, they're turning back."

The relief was plain in his voice, and even the tense line of Julian's shoulders descended from where they'd been hitched up near his ears. After watching the patrol slowly disappear into the darkness back toward the fort, he bowed his head and blew out a breath.

Wren, however, was not comforted. "They had a bonesmith," she said, getting stiffly to her feet and dusting herself off. "Probably more than one."

"Which means . . . ?" Leo said with a frown, moving gingerly as well.

"They'll be back," Julian said gruffly, standing upright faster than them both. As if it were a competition. "And they'll risk riding deeper into the Breachlands."

"They'll risk getting themselves killed," Wren said crossly. "They have no idea what they're up against."

Julian's eyebrows rose so high and fast, they disappeared under his helmet.

Wren scowled.

Yes, she had done the same thing mere days ago. And yes, it had been equally, if not *more* dangerous than what they were doing now, as she'd been traveling with *him,* a known enemy. But she had done that of her own stupid volition. These people were being ordered here by her father. For all Wren's flaws and shortcomings, she'd never have asked someone else to do something dangerous that she wouldn't do herself.

Here he was using people again, just like he'd used Wren. Like he would continue to use her if he had his way.

He wouldn't.

"If they intend to follow, then may I suggest we keep moving?" Leo asked, squinting after the patrol. "Perhaps we can gain some ground before they circle back—even lose them."

"Unlikely," Julian said, but he marched in the opposite direction all the same. "Not without horses."

"A horse or two would indeed expedite things," Leo said, speaking to Julian's back.

"I'm afraid you'll have to walk, Your Highness," Julian said without a backward glance.

Leo leveled a look at Wren. "Still angry with you, I see," he said grimly.

"With *me*?" Wren spluttered. "I'm not the only person who left him behind."

"True, but you *are* the only one to have stuck your tongue down his throat *first*."

Wren opened her mouth. Closed it.

"Hurry up, you two," Julian snapped.

Wren was *pretty* sure he hadn't heard them, but she hastened to keep up all the same.

TWO

Their immediate goal was to get to the relative safety of the Haunted Territory.

It was a truly ironic concept that stopped just short of being funny when Wren realized that thanks to her ghostsmith ring and the mess she'd made of things at the fort, her own damn family was a bigger threat than the undead.

But the truth of the matter was, with her and the ring, they'd be safer among the dead than the living.

Wren would prefer to draw her bone blades and do things the old-fashioned way, but she couldn't deny that walking through the violent ghosts and roaming revenants would be much more efficient than slicing through them.

Besides, the alternative was using the ring to slow the Breachfort guards that chased them instead, which would mean more splintered bones and cries of pain.

More looks of horror.

No, she'd rather face the Haunted Territory.

After an exhausting night of evading pursuit, the early hours of dawn were finally upon them. It brought with it a pale mist that clung to the ground before them, and the sight of that creeping fog put Wren in mind of the Breach. Tension knotted her shoulders, and she turned her attention to the dangers that lay ahead.

They had just crested a rise when a small group of figures materialized in the distance. They were Breachfort guards, stationed outside the mouth of the ravine that had seen Wren safely transported both into and back out of the Haunted Territory before.

"Get down," Julian said, dropping low to avoid being seen. Wren and Leo did the same, though they had enough distance and a higher vantage point, which meant they were unlikely to be spotted.

Still, she groaned at this new obstruction. *Of course* Vance wouldn't give up that easily. Rather than chase her around the countryside or deep into the Breachlands, risking walking undead and the wrath of the locals, he would simply bar her entry from the one place he knew she was trying to get to.

The same place *he* wanted to go.

All he had to do was block them from the Breach and wait for them to screw up and get caught. Despite how vast the region was, there weren't that many ways into the Haunted Territory, thanks to the Adamantine Mountains and the rocky foothills that surrounded it. There was the pass through the river gorge, the Coastal Road, and potentially some obscure route through the mountains, which would surely double or even triple their travel time.

Her father understood her well enough to know that taking such a detour would infuriate her, but he wasn't careless and likely had those places covered, too.

"Now what?" Leo whispered, somewhat desperately.

Even *with* the bonesmiths Vance had assigned to protect the Breachfort soldiers, this was a risky move on his part. She spotted a valkyr, bone armor glowing brightly in the rising sun, and a reapyr, whose robes stood out like a blot of ink on the barren landscape. They accompanied a patrol of around a dozen guards, which certainly wasn't enough to guarantee safety. Not in a place like this. And while the reapyr would be handy in ridding them of an undead permanently, they were little use in a fight.

"We can take them," Wren said. Leo gave her a pointed look. "Me and Julian," she clarified. "My father is likely trying to set up a perimeter around the Haunted Territory to bar our entry. This is a skeletal force, but he'll send more. We need to strike now. I can't—"

She stopped herself.

I can't let him beat me.

I can't fail.

Not again. Not because of him.

She cleared her throat. "*We* can't wait."

"Act now?" Julian repeated incredulously. "We've been running all night, and now you want to take on a dozen *mounted* soldiers armed with bows?"

"Well, if *you're* too tired . . . ," Wren said delicately, reserving judgment in her words if not her tone. "Then I guess—"

"I'm not *tired*," Julian bit out through clenched teeth. "But I'm also not *stupid*. As soon as they spot us, one of those riders will take off, raising the alarm and bringing more soldiers this way."

"That's if they *see* us, right?" Leo said thoughtfully, gaze roving the landscape. He darted a wary look at Julian. "Isn't there another way in? The shortcut you took when you . . . uh, followed us . . . after we, uh . . ."

Julian tensed at the reminder of their betrayal before jerking his head stiffly. "It only works coming out of the ravine. Going back in, scaling the scree would be . . ." His dark eyes raked over Leo before landing squarely on Wren. "Impossible."

He seemed to be suggesting that such a climb would be impossible for *them*, if not him.

Even if he was right, Wren resented the implication. She also resented being lumped together with the prince, as if she wasn't a trained fighter with more gall than both Leo and Julian put together. Plus, she was a good climber. Those library bookshelves had been nearly three stories high.

She bit down on a number of snippy comments, but apparently she had too many to muzzle entirely, because one slipped through her less-than-watertight self-control.

"Okay, *you* don't want to risk the climb and *you* are too tired to fight them. What other options do we have?"

Julian clenched his jaw, his nostrils flaring, and jerked his chin in the opposite direction. "We take the Coastal Road and try a different approach into the Haunted Territory. It'll slow us down, but the Breachfort guards won't pursue us there. They know they'd be met with hostility."

"Won't we as well?"

"*You*, without a doubt, but I have friends who could help us. These people know me and my family. They'll give us what we need."

"Oh, do these friends of yours happen to offer safe passage into the Breach?"

"You know very well that such a thing doesn't exist. Let's start with food and a place to sleep. Then we can try to come up with an actual plan instead of this chaotic free-for-all that you're running."

"If you'd rather return to the cell I sprang you from . . ."

"The cell you *landed* me in, you mean?"

"I was trying to *save you* from that, which is why I left you behind—"

"Tied up."

"—and told you not to follow."

Wren's chest was heaving, but the more riled she got, the colder, stiller, and *quieter* Julian became.

"Since when," he said, voice barely above a whisper, "do *you* give *me* orders? We were supposed to be a team. We were in it *together.*"

"I . . . ," Wren started, at a loss for what to say. His anger was a palpable force, rippling from him like heat waves, whereas hers had suddenly cooled off. "It was more of a suggestion," she finished meekly.

She couldn't meet Julian's eyes, so she found herself looking at Leo when she spoke. He scrunched up his face, shrugging slightly, as if to say, *Not your best explanation ever, but probably not your worst.*

"I think it's a good idea," Leo chimed in, speaking in that easy, confident way of his. "I doubt they'd expect it. Your father, he knows you to be . . ."

"Single-minded?" Wren offered, somewhat hopefully.

"Reckless?" Julian countered, not looking at either of them.

"I was going to say *determined,*" Leo clarified. "He won't expect patience or strategy from you. He'll expect you to fight. Look at them, just standing there out in the open. He's baiting you."

Julian shifted slightly at that, looking at the scene before them with renewed attention. "They could already have reinforcements in the ravine," he conceded, sounding impressed with Leo's observations. "Then it would just be a matter of luring us into a trap."

"It's decided, then," Leo said. "Julian, where are we headed?"

"Southbridge. I know someone who will take us in. We'll get some sleep, then strike out from there."

"Perfect," Leo said, getting to his feet. "I've always wanted to see Southbridge."

"Haven't you been there before?" Wren asked. She thought he'd mentioned passing through the coastal towns when he'd been kidnapped.

"Oh, I've *been* there," Leo said, "but last time, I had a bag on my head. I expect the view will be better this time around."

Smiling and shaking her head, Wren moved to follow him, but Julian's hand shot out, gripping her forearm.

"Let me make one thing clear. By taking you to these people, I am putting a level of . . . *faith* in you. If you betray me again—if you betray *them*—you will regret it."

Wren stared down at the place where his gloved hand wrapped around her wrist. She recalled that same hand without its glove, glimpsed for the first time inside that Breachfort cell. Flesh streaked with iron, every bone and fiber reinforced with enough metal and magic to crush a steel lock in its grip. A shiver ran through her.

Seeing her reaction, Julian released his hold at once, looking away. "Do we understand each other?"

Wren stared at the ground. Of course she'd never betray his friends. Of course she'd never betray him . . . *again* . . . but after what she'd done, she couldn't blame him for being suspicious. Though she'd already fought hard to earn his trust, his respect—his admiration?—as far as he was concerned, their relationship was back to zero. In fact, it was in an even worse position than it had been the day they'd met. At least back then, when they'd been trying to kill each other, they'd been enemies on *principle*. Now the things that divided them were decidedly personal.

And it was Wren's fault.

"Yes, I understand."

It was a long walk to the Coastal Road, made slower by frequent stops to check they weren't being followed and Julian's insistence on taking an indirect path that kept them out of the open.

They'd been walking all day and running all the previous night, which meant they were cold, hungry, and exhausted by the time the sun started to set and Southbridge came into view.

As they had done in Caston, Wren and Julian divested themselves of their unique and highly identifiable armor, putting it away in the packs they'd brought with them, and even Leo was forced to conceal his jewelry and wipe away his makeup, the same as Wren. She, however, also had her eyes to worry about. With the failing light, an ironsmith's or goldsmith's eyes could easily be mistaken for varying shades of regular brown, but pale white bonesmith eyes were far too distinctive. As such, Wren drew up her hood and was sure to keep her lashes lowered and her gaze downcast.

Unlike Caston, which relied on its walls alone, this town was heavily guarded—probably thanks to its proximity to the Border Wall. Sentries were posted everywhere, meaning they didn't have a chance of sneaking in.

"State your business," demanded the guard at the front gate.

"We're traveling on to Highmore, and we need a place to stay for the night," Julian answered promptly.

The guard's suspicious gaze roved over them, including their heavily laden packs. "What for?"

At this Julian apparently drew a blank, but Leo slid in smoothly, a bright smile on his face. "We're selling our homemade jams and jellies. All made with local fruit, of course. Would you care to try a sample? We have—"

"Your names?" the guard cut in, bored already. Leo was a genius.

"This is my wife, Winnie," Leo said at once, pecking Wren on the cheek. She did her best to look adoringly at him, while Julian—whose face was hidden from the guard's view—scowled. "I'm Reginald, though my friends call me Reggie. And this strapping lad is Olaf. He's the muscle!" He slapped Julian on the shoulder before leaning toward the guard conspiratorially. "Not good for much else, I'm afraid. Completely ham-fisted when it comes to preserves."

He said this last bit as if it were highly embarrassing, and it took everything Wren had not to laugh.

But the guard, despite appearing bewildered, seemed to think Leo's words were too outlandish to be anything but true. He waved them through without another question.

Frowning, Julian stooped to pick up their heavy bags, and Leo wrapped an arm around Wren's shoulders; together, the three of them entered the town.

They didn't make it far before they noticed the posters.

WANTED, DEAD OR ALIVE:
Julian Knight of House Iron
CRIME: Kidnapping of Prince Leopold Valorian
REWARD: 10,000 tokens

Wren gaped.

This was surely the regent's doing. No one else could be behind this.

The words "dead or alive" were drawn with red ink, and below was a rough sketch of what appeared to be a younger-looking Julian, probably based off an old portrait. His face was pale and his cheeks plumper, his hair curling boyishly around his face.

"Prince-*Smith*," Leo muttered, but he, like Wren, was staring at Julian. Thankfully, with his face dusty from the road and his dark hair slicked back, he looked little like the person in the wanted poster—but Wren doubted that would hold true in daylight. Besides, Julian was *known* around these parts. He'd said so himself. The locals knew him and his family. Did that familiarity and affection extend to his uncle Francis? And if it did, who would they choose? The future heir or the current regent?

Julian still hadn't spoken. His jaw was clenched so tight, Wren could see the muscles strain.

"We need to find your friends." She glanced around warily. "Immediately."

Julian's angry expression faltered. "I can't drag them into this."

"Either you drag them in, or we get dragged out of here in chains."

His broad shoulders slumped, and he nodded. "Come on," he said, leading the way off the main street and toward the nearest alleyway and, hopefully, to safety.

THREE

Dead or alive. Dead or alive.

The words echoed in Julian's head with every footstep, beating a taunting rhythm against his skull.

Dead or alive. Dead or alive.

He didn't know why it bothered him so much. Why it shocked him. The man had already tried to have him killed once. How hard was it to believe he'd try again?

Maybe it was the sheer hubris of it. The daring. To literally poster the Breachlands with lies and promise a reward in order to get regular folk to do his dirty work for him. To turn them into unwitting traitors, pawns in a game they couldn't begin to fully comprehend.

Or maybe it was the fact that his uncle was turning *the people* against him. It was one thing to understand his uncle had changed—or rather, had shown his true colors at last and had seen the potential in a world without Julian in it—and quite another to consider the possibility that the entire Breachlands would feel the same. That they could believe him capable of being the villain.

It wasn't just his mother who had visited villages with supplies and helped relocate families to safety. Julian frequently traveled the coastal towns, offering aid, free labor, and whatever surplus the Iron Citadel had in its stores—much to his uncle's annoyance.

He had rebuilt walls, planted crops, and fought off bandits.

He had shared meals, told stories, and passed wineskins around campfires.

He had even agreed to kidnap a prince in order to see their futures secured and their lives changed for the better.

And now Julian would learn what years of loyal service were worth in the face of the promise of the regent's favor and a fat purse.

"It's okay," Wren said, speaking at Julian's elbow, her breath coming in soft pants as she attempted to keep up with his longer stride. "No one saw you."

"And if they had?" he asked, glancing back at her but refusing to slow the pace. "Everything I've ever done—all my *family* has ever done—and now . . ." He shook his head, a hollow laugh escaping his lips. "First my uncle, and now everyone in the Breachlands wants to be rid of me?"

"That's not—" Wren argued, but he cut her off.

"Dead or alive," he snapped. "He doesn't even want Julian Knight. He wants a body."

"What he wants is a scapegoat," Leo said from Julian's other side. His tone was gentle, but the words were practical. He was trying to remove the emotion from the situation. Fat chance. "I told him his support in the Breachlands was at risk, and this is damage control."

"*Julian*," Wren said, taking hold of his biceps. She wasn't strong enough to stop him, and a part of Julian wanted nothing more than to fling away her touch, but it seemed his mind was disconnected from his body. He stopped on instinct, though when he rounded on her, it was with enough force to make her stumble, which felt like a small, petty victory—but a victory all the same. She released his arm. "This poster comes from the regent, not these people. If anyone here *is* looking for you, they're just looking for that reward. They don't know the truth. How can they? All they know is what they've been told by the people they trust."

Her brows were raised and her expression expectant, asking him to see the similarities.

Yes, she'd recently had her trust betrayed thoroughly and brutally. And so had he.

He expelled a breath and closed his eyes. He wanted to rage at her. The anger was still there, simmering, always simmering, because of course *she'd* betrayed him too.

Julian opened his eyes. Whatever Wren saw there, it caused her to rear back slightly.

He turned away.

Despite his anger, Wren was right, *loath* as he was to admit it. Anyone who saw that poster and leapt at the chance to kill him was clearly in a worse position than he was. Bandits and the like—the very people whose actions he had defended in the past. They didn't know the *truth*. They knew only what the posters papering the Breachlands told them.

Still. The thought rankled. If things went poorly, *this* was how he'd be remembered. At least his parents had died as heroes and would be remembered as good and honorable. If things went badly, Julian might not be remembered at all, and if he was, it would be as a traitor and a kidnapper.

He *had* to make sure things didn't go badly.

"Let's go."

They arrived at the building at the end of the lane just outside the old merchants' quarter. The houses were larger and grander as they climbed the hill to the north and smaller and squatter the farther down they went.

Julian moved past the front door, into the narrow lane alongside the three-story house, and knocked on the side door instead. He'd done this countless times before, and as usual, the comfortable din of voices and laughter within went silent, and then the sound of footsteps approached.

A latch slid back with a scrape, revealing a rectangular peephole. Familiar eyes scrutinized him, widened in surprise, then disappeared as the cover slid back into place. The lock clicked and the door opened—but just enough to reveal a middle-aged woman's face.

"Hello, Elsa," Julian said, but her attention wasn't on him.

It was on Prince Leopold.

"So it's true?" she asked, deflating slightly as though in disappointment.

"It's a long story," Julian said, glancing around uneasily.

"Believe it or not, I'm here by choice," Leopold said, flashing a dazzling smile.

Elsa's eyes narrowed, but eventually her tension melted, and she smiled too. Even Wren's wariness seemed to soften. Leopold had the gift of putting people at ease in an effortless way that made hot spears of jealousy stab Julian's gut. Nothing had ever been that easy for him, especially not when it came to him and Wren. After everything that had happened, he doubted it ever would be.

No, being around Wren was like tossing a blade into the air, end over end, the threat of injury working in tandem with the beauty and grace of the movement, the possibility of going faster, throwing higher, of becoming one with the blade a thrilling, tantalizing possibility—even though at any moment your grip could falter, the blade slicing your skin, reminding you that *no*, you are not as one . . . and you never were.

Julian shook the thoughts from his mind. "Elsa, we need a place to stay. Somewhere to lie low for the night. We'll be out of your hair first thing tomorrow." She pursed her lips, and his heart sank. Elsa was a good and kind woman, but she was practical, too, and would not risk those under her care. "Please," Julian added softly, hating himself. "Just for the night."

She sighed deeply. "Very well." Leaning back from the door, she whistled softly, and pattering footsteps announced the arrival of a young girl of around eleven or so. One of many under Elsa's care. "Millie, ask Arthur for whatever he's got left from dinner and bring it to the cellar. If he asks why . . ." She paused, waiting for the girl to complete the sentence.

"Tell him to mind his damn business," Millie answered promptly. Wren laughed appreciatively, and Julian caught the smile that threatened to spread on his face before it could take hold.

"Atta girl," Elsa said, pulling the door wider to allow Millie to slip out and dart through the night.

After reaching into the house for a lantern, Elsa led the way around back. There were several old barrels stacked there, and concealed behind them was a pair of double doors set into the ground.

She handed Julian the lantern before fiddling with a ring of keys, then unlocked the doors. Inside, stone steps led into the darkness.

"Go on," Elsa said. "Millie will be by with the food, and we'll lock up behind you."

"Thank you, Elsa," Julian said, giving her a quick peck on the cheek.

"Yes, many thanks," Leopold said, kissing her *other* cheek, the charming bastard. Elsa flushed, *giggled*, then swatted him away good-naturedly as he descended the stairs after Julian.

Wren chose to show her gratitude with a smile before joining Julian and Leopold in the cellar.

The doors swung shut, causing what little illumination the moon had provided to disappear, leaving them in the limited light of the lantern's glow. Moving quickly about the space, Julian located the two mounted lamps and lit them, bringing the cellar into full view.

The walls were cold, rough stone, and the floor was covered in old rugs to keep out some of the chill. There was a wooden table with a mismatched chair and a solitary, narrow bed on a rusted metal frame.

Julian sighed. He'd forgotten this place wasn't built for a single adult, never mind *three*. It was going to be a long night.

Wren and Leopold seemed to be having similar thoughts, both of them eyeing the space warily.

Spotting the cold brazier in the corner, Julian took up the lantern and used some of the oil and the flame to get the coals going again.

"What is this place?" Leopold asked, walking a slow circuit around the room. "It looks . . ."

"Child-sized," Wren supplied, coming to stand next to him.

It was true. Not only was the bed narrow, but it was low, just like the table and chair.

Before Julian could answer, there was a rattle atop the stairs, and one of the cellar doors swung wide again.

Millie appeared, arms laden with a wicker basket stuffed to the brim and a ceramic jug that sloshed and gurgled with every wobbling step she took.

"May I?" said Leopold, leaping forward to help, though all he did was take the jug and thrust it roughly in Wren's direction. She managed to grab it as it collided with her stomach and brought it to the table, while Leopold reached not for the basket but for the young girl's other hand.

She looked at him with all the confused wariness of an orphan servant not much used to kindness, but eventually she took the proffered assistance, though the frown never left her brows.

Julian grabbed the basket and started to unpack its contents on the table—stale bread, soft cheese, some cold chicken, and various bruised or overripe fruits.

As Julian worked, Leopold crouched down before the girl. "Nice to see you again, Millie. We've met before. Do you remember?"

When she stared uncertainly at him for several seconds, Leopold snatched a blanket from the bed and threw it over his head. When he yanked it off again, the girl was smiling. "I told you about my adventure. And if you can believe it, it's only gotten better since then."

He glanced up at Julian, who gave him a warning look. They didn't need this girl connecting any dots regarding Leopold's true identity.

"*But* I'll have to tell you about that some other time," Leopold said hastily. "Thanks for taking such good care of us."

"And for dealing with Arthur," Wren said. She was smirking in that familiar, mischievous way that made Julian's chest ache.

Millie smiled proudly. "He's too nosy for his own good and needs to be put in his place. Or at least, that's what Elsa always says."

"Elsa knows best," Julian said.

Millie nodded, mounted the stairs, then waved before she swung the door shut behind her with a resounding thump. The lock clicked into place, echoing in the silence.

"Is Elsa . . . She's not Millie's mother, is she?" Wren asked, likely making the assumption based on the fact that Millie called the woman "Elsa" and not "Mom" or "Mother."

"No. Elsa takes in orphans. She's got an orphanage upstairs."

"And downstairs?" Leopold asked, looking around the dark, cramped space.

"Some children can't stay. They might have been caught stealing, gotten into trouble with one of the local gangs, or be right around the age the bandits come collecting poor youths to swell their ranks. She keeps them hidden here until she can get them honest work or relocated to another town."

"You help her," Wren said. It was a statement, not a question.

Julian shrugged. "If I can. Whenever I'm in town, I test any of the new arrivals for ironsmith magic, just in case. And sometimes, well . . . it's not just the bandits that prey on the poor and the young. The regent recently lowered the age to join our standing military. Some youths show promise and seem genuinely interested, so I let them through. But others . . . They'd be better off here, working as stable boys or learning a trade. So I bring them to Elsa."

Wren looked at him so intently that Julian felt exposed. He hated that he was sharing more of himself with her, even if it was something he was proud of. It still made him feel vulnerable, like peeling off his gloves or removing his armor.

"And Arthur?" Leopold pressed, moving toward the food and delicately unearthing a cluster of grapes.

"He's the cook at the inn where Millie works. The orphanage is kept running from donations by several businesses in town, and the inn usually provides free or discounted food."

"Lucky for us," Wren said, unearthing a chicken leg and tearing into it with her teeth.

"Don't suppose that's wine in that jug, is it?" Leopold asked.

"Water, Your Highness," Wren said. "So unless you plan on waiting for those grapes to ferment, you're outta luck."

"The hardships of a life on the run know no bounds, it seems." Leopold sighed, sinking into the chair.

After Julian went for the bread and cheese, they ate in silence, but the meal didn't last long. The brazier was still much too cold for their basement room, and as exhaustion started to settle in, a shiver slipped down Julian's spine and his eyes itched.

He wasn't the only one. Wren couldn't stop yawning, and Leopold kept throwing longing, covetous looks over his shoulder at the bed.

Julian stood, busying himself with packing away the leftover pits, stems, and bones.

"You two get some sleep. I'll . . ."

"What, stay up all night?" Wren asked. Despite her heavy eyelids and slumped shoulders, her tone was sharp. Challenging. It was probably meant to be playful, but Julian was not in the mood to play with her.

He shrugged stiffly, turning his back to her as he continued to fuss with the basket. "I'm not tired."

"Liar."

He rounded on her. "Forgive me if I don't relish the idea of sleeping next to *you two* again."

Wren's expression—which had been smug and accusatory—was wiped temporarily blank, before guilt colored her features. She cast a look at Leopold.

"Julian, I—"

"Save it," he said, cutting her off. "I don't need to hear your weak apologies again." She'd already admitted what she'd done was a mistake, already explained that she'd been trying to protect him.

It didn't matter.

Right now they just felt like excuses. Empty words. No apology, no matter how thorough, how sincere, could ever make up for what had happened. Could ever undo the truth.

Julian had trusted her, and she had betrayed that trust. End of story.

"Sleep or not," Julian said, turning his back on the pair of them once more. "I don't care."

About you, he wanted to add but didn't.

She'd already called him a liar, and he didn't want to prove her right.

FOUR

"*Fine*," Wren said petulantly.

"Fine," Julian said back.

She stomped over to the bed, threw herself down on the rock-hard, straw-stuffed mattress, and started kicking off her boots. She gestured to the bed beside her. "I guess this is your lucky day, Your Highness."

"Yours, more like," Leo said, coming to stand before her with his arms crossed. Julian remained in the corner, fiddling with the brazier. "How many people get to say they've slept next to a prince?"

Wren looked up at him. "More than you'd like to admit to, I'll wager."

Leo grinned. "Fair enough."

He climbed onto the mattress, the threadbare blankets doing little to banish the chill as they shoved and shifted. The bed was narrow, which meant Leo's leg hung off the side and Wren's back was pressed firmly against the cold stone wall, but they fit.

Things got worse, however, once Leo fell asleep. The prince, obviously used to more *spacious* accommodations, sprawled and kicked, eventually yanking the blanket off her as he moved into a diagonal position.

While she was utterly exhausted, Wren found herself unable to succumb to sleep—and it wasn't because of the prince. Her attention was fixed on Julian's back, waiting, maybe, for him to look her way.

But he never did.

And all her usual tactics for getting attention—crude jokes or antagonistic words, black lips or flimsy attire—didn't work on him.

So instead she stared and waited . . . and hoped that if he didn't look her way, he'd at least let go of his anger long enough to sleep.

But when she jolted awake several hours later thanks to a knee from the prince, it was to see Julian seated on the floor, stubbornly upright, his silhouette hunched before the now brightly glowing brazier. He was holding his helmet, the firelight gleaming off the smooth metal, the dent that had so recently marred its surface now repaired. Perhaps the sound of it popping back into place was what had actually awoken her.

Whatever it was, Wren had the sudden urge to join him there. To curl up next to him, to take his gloved hand and beg him to accept her apologies, however weak. However insufficient. They were all she had . . . and they weren't enough.

A loud thumping stirred Wren from sleep a second time.

Gray light filtered through the cracks in the double doors. She turned to find Julian crouched before the bed, a finger pressed to his lips. Next to her, Leo's eyes were open.

The thumping came from upstairs, someone knocking forcefully on Elsa's door.

Shit.

Footsteps creaked on the floorboards above, moving in the direction of the front of the house. The sound of a bolt being thrown back. Low voices, their words muffled, though Wren distinctly thought she caught the name "Arthur." Too-nosy-for-his-own-good Arthur.

Julian's eyes fluttered closed for a second, and she knew he'd heard it too. Still, none of them moved.

More conversation, the voices getting louder. Sounding agitated. Then a cry of anger as heavy footsteps *thunk*ed across the floor—more than one pair. There was a riot of voices now, and then the sound of a young child crying as they were roused from sleep.

"Time to move," Julian said, leaping to his feet.

He backed away from the bed, gaze fixed on the double doors, which were locked—and their only escape.

Wren and Leo stood, joining him.

"Can you break it open?" she asked Julian.

"It's steel," he said before he caught on to her meaning. Not with his magic, but with his iron hand. He glanced down, then around the room, wavering. "If I do that, they'll *know* we were here."

"That ship's about to sail," Wren said, gesturing to the house above, where footsteps continued to stomp around. Wren recalled it was a three-story building, but even searching every floor would take only so long. "Imminently."

As they spoke, Leo had climbed the stairs as high as he could, crouching near the top to peer through the tiniest of gaps between the doors. He pressed, and the door rose an inch or so, the handles held together by a lock that dangled in the open space he'd just revealed.

"Can you bend it?" Leo asked, gesturing at the exposed metal. "Get me an angle so I can reach the mechanism?"

"I suppose," Julian said, rushing forward to have a look himself.

"And do what?" Wren asked, as Leo shifted onto his back and started fiddling with his belt. It featured beautiful gold filigree along the buckle, but Leo was prying the decoration off right before her eyes, peeling away the narrow strips of gold and molding them under his touch with hasty, repetitive motions that turned the swirling bands into a pair of narrow strips of metal.

Lockpicks.

Wren's mouth fell open, and Leo caught her expression, smirking as he finished his final touches. "I'm more than just looks, you know," he said.

Wren shook her head, still in shock. "Noted."

Now that Leo was ready, Julian pushed the door up again with his regular hand and used his iron hand to tug carefully on the lock, easily bending the steel until it was within reach.

As they worked, Wren darted about the space, removing all traces of them. She remade the bed, blew out the lanterns, and gathered the food basket and jug, before hovering uncertainly in front of the brazier.

The glowing hot coals had cooled somewhat, but there was no hiding that *someone* had been here.

While the commotion upstairs continued, Leo muttered to himself, a gentle clicking sound punctuating his movements.

"Leave it," came Julian's voice, and it took Wren a moment to realize he was speaking to her.

"Aha!" Leo said triumphantly, just as the sound of boots descending stairs thundered above, getting louder and louder by the second.

"Go!" Julian said, as Leo unhooked the lock and swung the door wide. Wren handed him the basket and jug, taking up one of their travel bags and following him out into the gray shadows of early morning.

Julian, meanwhile, tugged off his glove and scooped up the handful of burning coals in his bare hand, teeth clenched as he grabbed the second bag—the one carrying his armor—and followed them.

The second he was outside, Wren carefully closed the door and clicked the lock back into place. The metal was slightly bent, but surely they would attribute that to age and wear and nothing more.

Dumping the handful of coals into the water jug, causing the contents to hiss, Julian shook out his hand and pointed to a nearby shed. They climbed it, the shoddy structure shaking and rattling loudly, but they only needed it as a means to get to the roof.

No sooner had Leo's dangling foot been lifted over the edge than soldiers rounded the corner of Elsa's orphanage, scouring the alleyway. They were local militia, dressed the same as the guards that manned the gate last night, without matching uniforms or insignia, save for a deep blue armband tied about their biceps.

It took a moment, but they found the cellar and demanded its key.

Elsa was forced to open the doors with subtle trepidation, though she didn't fail to notice the bent lock. Expression fixed, she swung the doors wide to reveal the empty chamber below.

Soldiers poured into the darkness.

"Nothing," one of them called out. "It's empt—hang on . . ."

Wren's heart sank. The soldier who spoke, wearing a double armband that likely signified some sort of rank, emerged with a single piece of coal balanced on the edge of a dagger.

"Still warm," he said to Elsa.

"As I told you," she said, patience clearly fraying. "I sometimes use the cellar when we've got overflow. I thought we'd need it last night, so I came down to light the brazier, and . . ."

"And strangely, the brazier is entirely emptied this morning."

Despite her best efforts, Elsa's face flickered. "Yes, that's because—"

"No more lies, woman. He was here, and we will have him." He turned to half his soldiers. "You stay here and search the area." He squinted at the faintly glowing coal. "He can't have gone far. The rest of you, come with me."

"Well, that's our cue," said Leo, tossing aside the food basket and craning his neck to find a path over the roof. Like they had in Caston, the three of them scrambled over the tiles and leapt alleyways, pausing to listen to footsteps pass or to avoid residents as they poked their heads out windows, curious over the commotion.

Several houses over, however, the excitement died down, and the streets were calm and quiet, save for those who rose early for work, not for bounties.

They climbed back down to street level, taking refuge in the shadows between two buildings.

Julian appeared shaken. His glove was back on his hand, and though Wren knew it was mostly iron, there was flesh there too. He had surely scalded his skin, the metal potentially working against him, conducting the heat.

The scowl on his face was deeply etched, his lips forming a tight, straight line as he surveyed the main boulevard beyond their hiding place.

"If we move quickly, we might get past the gate before the entire town is aware of the manhunt," he said.

"The militia guard the gate," Wren said with a frown. "Surely they'll be looking for us."

"They aren't like a typical city watch," Julian said. "They'll hire anyone they can get, and there's a high turnover rate. That means there isn't a lot of internal loyalty. Southbridge has a good commander, but those men that showed up at Elsa's, they're likely from the night shift. I suspect they'd prefer to keep Arthur's tip—and the eventual bounty—to themselves and not share it with the day shift."

"A prize split ten ways is worth twice as much as a prize split twenty," Leo said, nodding. "This is good. This works to our advantage. They'll try to prevent us from leaving this quarter, but the search won't be town wide."

"Yet," Julian said.

"Even if we make it to the gate," Wren said, casting a skeptical look at Julian, "I don't know how you'll walk out of here without being recognized. It's broad daylight. Your features are . . . distinctive."

For some reason, Julian seemed to take offense to that. "And your bonesmith eyes *aren't*?" he shot back.

"There aren't *wanted* posters with my face on them!" Wren shot back.

"Will the both of you *shut up* and let me think," Leo said, and the obvious irritation in his voice was so out of character that Wren and Julian *did* shut up—purely from surprise. She'd never seen the prince lose his cool.

His fingers were pressed to his temples, while his golden gaze roved the visible street beyond.

"We need to get to the inn," he said.

"The inn?" Wren demanded.

"That's where Arthur works," Julian said, sounding as confused as Wren. "What do you want to do, talk to him?"

"Beat him?" Wren offered. Julian rolled his eyes, though Wren swore it was with less gusto than usual.

"I have no interest in crossing paths with Arthur," Leo said patiently. "I am more interested in the other guests, particularly *large groups* who might be packing up and moving on this very moment."

"We could hide among them. Maybe get through the gate?" Wren asked.

"That's the plan," Leo said. He adjusted his clothing, smoothed his hair, and hitched his winning smile into place. "Leave the talking to me."

Sticking to the dark alleys and avoiding the main road, the three of them edged nearer and nearer the town's inn. Southbridge was waking up around them, which provided more crowds to hide among, even if it made spotting the soldiers that were pursuing them more difficult.

As they arrived at the town's center, the inn came into view—but so did another, far less welcome sight.

More soldiers, these in matching uniforms with loops of chain mail and flashes of red enamel.

The Red Guard.

It was a small squad, a dozen at most, but they were not alone. It seemed every member of the local militia was also present, along with crowds of townspeople who milled around the square. There was no clear path to the inn, to the gate . . . or anywhere.

Not that they could take it even if there were.

Elsa stood captive in the middle of the increasingly rowdy rabble, and as soon as Julian laid eyes on her—with Millie cowering at her side—Wren knew his decision was made.

He'd never let her suffer for him. Never stand aside or let anyone else pay for his refusal to come forward.

"You two stay here," Julian said, gaze fixed on the scene before them. Elsa and Millie were standing atop some sort of stage that was likely used for town announcements—and possibly hangings—sandwiched between the captain who'd searched Elsa's house and two members of the Red Guard. An old, bent-backed man stood next to them with his head bowed, and Wren could only assume he was Arthur.

"Once they have me," Julian continued, "the town will settle down. You'll be able to get out of here."

"They're going to kill you," Wren said, taking hold of Julian's arm. When that failed to register, she reached for his hand instead. Finally, he turned to look at her and then down at their joined hands.

His expression wavered, and he glanced over his shoulder at Elsa and Millie. "I don't have a choice."

"Yes, you do!" Wren said, her voice bordering on hysterical. "You stay here, with us, and we figure out another way."

"There is no other way. If I stay here, they'll—"

"They'll *what*? Surely they're not going to harm a woman who runs an orphanage and her child ward! The crowd would turn on them. They're just . . . trying to scare them."

Right on cue, one of the Red Guard on the stage started shouting, demanding answers. Elsa flinched, and Millie turned her face into the woman's skirts. The crowd murmured and shifted, but nobody stepped forward. Nobody stopped it.

"Please don't," Wren said, seeing the resigned look in Julian's eyes. Panic seared her lungs, making it difficult to breathe. "Please."

"Sorry, Wren. You'll have to defeat your father without me."

Rage filled her in a sudden, hot rush. "Fuck my father! I don't—that's not—" she spluttered. As if *that* was what she was thinking of right now! Right now she was concerned with keeping Julian's head on his shoulders.

But he'd already turned away from her, making for the end of the alley.

She opened her mouth to argue some more when the press of a cold blade against her throat halted her movement. Next to her, Leo had a knife pressed to his neck as well.

The soldiers who held them wore the plain armor of the Iron Citadel military, but the soldiers that stepped in front of the alley, blocking Julian's path, were Red Guard. Julian whirled, saw that Wren and Leo were already caught, and cursed.

"You're coming with us, Lord-Smith Julian," said the nearest Red Guard. He smiled. "Don't worry, your friends are coming too."

FIVE

Kidnapped.

Again.

Leo would have been more indignant about the whole thing if there weren't a knife pressed to his throat. A knife pressed by a familiar hand: Jakob, one of the original kidnappers. Kind, earnest, and green-as-spring-grass Jakob. A glance to his left confirmed that gray-bearded Ivan had Wren.

"Be still, Your Highness," said Jakob, his words soft. Ivan communicated *his* request with more of a grunt, but it worked all the same. Leo and Wren froze in place, their empty hands lifted into the air.

Julian raised his hands without the need of a sharpened blade or a command, and together the three of them were pushed and shoved out into the open.

The reaction was immediate, starting from the back of the crowd to the front, a ripple of awareness that reached the distant stage like waves slapping against a dock.

The Red Guard members who stood there turned, and the people between them and Leo parted.

At least at first.

As their armed escort urged them forward, the crowd jostled on either side. There were sounds of shock and dismay.

Anger and disgust.

Outrage.

Leo wasn't certain to whom the reactions were directed at first—the posters *had* called Julian a kidnapper and a traitor—but it became clear when the first piece of rotten fruit splattered against red enamel that the crowd was on their side.

Shouts erupted. "Leave him be!" and "Let him go!" mixed with other words like "true heir" and "just a boy."

There were more cohesive arguments as well. "When was the last time the regent visited these parts? I'd take the Knight boy over him any day!"

Julian's eyes were wide, as if he'd not expected to see such loyalty from them, especially in the face of his uncle's soldiers. Still, there was fear in his expression, too.

The crowd started collapsing in on them, forcing their armed escorts to turn their attention outward with blades drawn.

Leo expected the captain of the Red Guard to call things to order.

Instead, it was Julian.

"Stop! Please," he shouted. The guards on either side looked ready to silence him, *forcefully*, until it became clear that what he was saying was working in their favor. The crowd settled.

What was Julian *doing*? They should be stoking the crowd's anger, not stifling it. They could use a riot to break free and slip away.

But then he saw where Julian's attention was leveled.

There were children in the crowd, already being pushed and knocked around. If things got out of control, they were likely to be trampled, to say nothing of the *deliberate* harm that would come to those who tried to rise up against the Red Guard and the Iron Citadel's military. Such a rebellion would be put down quickly. It's what always happened when unarmed civilians attacked soldiers with weapons.

The regent needed to keep the peace, yes, but he also needed to keep control. To ensure he appeared all-powerful, especially in the face of his nephew's alleged betrayal. To waver would be to leave room for doubt.

He'd crush all of Southbridge if it meant keeping the rest of the Breachlands in line.

The Red Guard captain smiled down at them all in satisfaction before seeing his opportunity to take the situation in hand. "We thank you for your cooperation." Soft murmurs broke out but no more. "Lord-Smith Francis, regent of the Iron Citadel, is merciful. He will allow his nephew to plead his case, and justice will be done."

Leo's brows rose, and from the dubious looks on both Wren's and Julian's faces, he thought they were thinking the same as him: this wasn't mercy; it was a necessary measure. They couldn't very well execute Julian here, in the midst of an angry mob, and expect to make it out without a fight.

This was their only course of action.

His statement done, the Red Guard captain gestured to the guard next to him, who produced a bag that jingled with its contents. The price for Julian. The captain tossed it carelessly at Arthur, while the local militia, Elsa and Millie, and the rest of the inhabitants of Southbridge rounded on the man, ready to unleash their anger or stake their claim.

Leo suspected that the trade tokens would not be worth the price he'd pay for betraying Julian Knight—if he even got to keep them.

Their group was led through the crowd toward the front gate, where horses were saddled and waiting for them. There was also a wagon, into which their bags, armor, and weapons were loaded.

They were bound and gagged and stripped of every scrap of iron, bone, and gold they possessed. The Red Guard who was searching Leo even found the gold on his back teeth after shoving his disgusting fingers into Leo's mouth. Leo was tempted to bite them clean off, but even if he'd had his fangs in place, they'd be no match for the man's hardened leather gloves.

Leo closed his eyes as the search took place, trying to focus on the mental fight. Trying to clear his thoughts of fear and frustration and impotent rage.

As a prince, Leo's life had been managed and supervised for as long as he could remember—by his teachers and tutors, his parents and his older brothers, not to mention the various stewards and wardens those people had put in place—but he'd always had *some* measure of control. Lately, all his autonomy had been stripped away, bit by bit, moment by moment, until his nerves were frayed beyond recognition and his good humor all but evaporated.

When he opened his eyes again, it was to see Jakob and Ivan ready to haul him onto a horse and tie him down.

It was all too familiar.

But as Leo was lifted and strapped into place, Wren and Julian treated similarly on horses nearby, he enjoyed one flash of blissful gratitude when he realized *this* kidnapping would not involve a sack over his head.

The rest of their party mounted up, and the horse beneath Leo lurched forward. They passed easily through the gate, albeit not in the manner Leo had originally hoped.

† † † †

Despite being the sort of person who tried to always see the positive side, the potential, Leo's anger continued. He tried to turn that energy to strategy, considering promises and threats, possibilities and posturing, but nothing held his attention for long.

Worse was Jakob riding next to him, *making conversation* as if they were old friends. Asking idle questions, commenting on the weather, the landscape, the temperament of the horse.

"She's used to novice riders, so she won't give you too much trouble."

"Novice riders?" Leo snapped. "I've been riding a horse since I was born. I used to *compete*—races, show jumping, even dressage. There's nothing *novice* about my riding."

"Oh," Jakob said. He rode in silence, failing to elaborate.

"Why would you think I was a novice?" Leo demanded. Despite the ropes binding him in place, his seat was perfect.

Jakob shrugged. "You fell so many times. Before," he said.

Right. *Before*, when Leo had been attempting to get the bag off his head and maybe the ropes off his hands and had only partially succeeded on the former. That had been back when Leo had felt actual *excitement* over what was happening. Back when he'd seen this whole thing as an adventure with a chance to prove to his family that he could get himself *out* of trouble just as easily as he got himself *into* it. A chance to prove that he had value beyond the twice-spare heir, and it couldn't be defined by a ransom price.

He sighed. "That was the bag," he said dismissively, though he darted a look at Jakob as he said it.

The boy smiled mildly. "Of course, the bag."

† † † †

As their party followed the coastline, crashing waves and rocky shores visible in the distance, Leo, Wren, and Julian remained hunched in their saddles, waiting.

Leo kept expecting them to pull to the side of the road and . . . finish things. He knew what that likely meant for Julian, but for Leo and Wren, it was less certain. The Corpse Queen wanted Wren, and so, if the regent intended to stick to their bargain, she'd be taken to her mother. But Leo? The idea that he might be meant for a simple ransom felt flimsy at best. The regent intended to march into the Dominions and *take* what he wanted . . . so what purpose could he fill? He was a weak tie to the throne and no more.

But perhaps a weak tie, when all other tethers were cut, was all he would need. . . .

A spare's spare he might be, but in line for the throne all the same—and certainly an easier target than his respected older brothers or his adored baby sister.

But as they kept up a steady pace, Leo found himself wondering if the "mercy" the Red Guard had extended to Julian wasn't *only* for show. Did they intend to keep Julian alive after all? If the regent needed him for something, they could be bringing him to the Citadel. There, he could force Julian to openly admit his guilt or actually put him on trial to give the whole thing an air of legitimacy and distract from the cold-blooded assassination it *actually* was. If that was the plan, it was sloppily done, with too many witnesses and too little evidence, but Leo had seen messier politics in the past few days—to say nothing of a lifetime in Port Valor.

With those thoughts in mind, he expected them to ride through the night, but their party started to slow before the sun dipped below the hills.

Leo's heartbeat kicked against his ribs.

They appeared to be entering a small roadside town, without the walls he'd seen at every other inhabited place so far.

Meaning, of course, that this place *wasn't* inhabited.

As they drew nearer, the dilapidated state of the buildings became evident, the windows dark and the roads overgrown.

It seemed an odd place to stop . . . until he spotted the temple. He glanced at Wren, who had seen it too.

It was a *bonesmith* temple.

It was a ruin, something that surely predated the Breach, back when these lands were a part of the Dominions. The characteristics were unmistakable, from the bone palisade surrounding the building and its adjoining graveyard to the inscription above the door:

Death is as certain as the dawn, and just as a new day will come, so too will the new dead rise. And we will be there. To find. To fight. To free. So the living may thrive, and the dead may rest in peace.

But then, carved beneath it more recently and in an unpracticed hand, was the addition:

There is no rest here.

With fear and anticipation thrumming through his veins, Leo kept his attention fixed on Julian as all three of them were pulled from their saddles and tossed unceremoniously onto the ground. Their rope bindings—better suited for strapping them to their horses—were quickly replaced with steel manacles. Julian's dark eyes flickered; his iron hand was relatively useless when it came to breaking free of a rope, but metal could be crushed and cracked.

Their captors thought they were tightening their hold on their prisoners, but they might just be giving them a chance to escape.

The problem was, manacles clanked and rattled loudly, so they'd be hard-pressed to make their escape silently—if they got the chance to make it at all.

The tiny bubble of excitement that had expanded inside his chest deflated somewhat.

Without any better plans, Leo did what he did best and watched every step their captors took, particularly the members of the Red Guard.

They dismounted. Gave orders. Spoke quietly to one another and unloaded supplies.

Then the Red Guard captain came into view. This was the man who would carry out the regent's order . . . whatever that order might be.

He sauntered up to them, removing his helmet to prop under one arm, completely at his ease.

His gaze roved each of them, smug and satisfied as he had been in Southbridge—even more so, Leo thought, as his mission appeared to be progressing as planned.

Around them was the hustle and bustle of a camp being set up, which included *tents* being erected.

Leo frowned.

Did they plan to *sleep* here? That seemed entirely unsafe and inadvisable, and the incredulous look on Wren's face confirmed his thoughts. They might be within the protections of a bonesmith temple, but the place was falling apart.

The Red Guard captain glanced over his shoulder, at the largest of the tents. He jerked his chin, and Julian was dragged forward into the darkened depths behind the canvas flap.

Terror pierced Leo's gut as he imagined a swift and silent execution, but when the captain followed Julian into the tent, a low rumble of voices reached them, one of them distinctly Julian's. An exchange of information, then.

That would at least buy Julian time . . . but how much?

Wren sagged into him, her body evidently weak with relief, but before they could enjoy more than a single moment of respite, another Red Guard emerged from the tent where Julian had disappeared and came for Wren.

She was hauled off, expression mutinous, and Leo could do nothing but stare after her, heart hammering. He looked around wildly, seeking some answer, and all he got was a glimpse of Jakob's pitying face as he stood watch over their last, lonely prisoner.

Apparently on the pretense of checking Leo's manacles, Jakob knelt before him and muttered, "They're, uh, questioning them."

Leo was desperate to drill him for information, but there was still a strip of rough fabric between his teeth, so all he could do was stare, bug-eyed, at Jakob.

They would come for Leo next. Any moment now, he'd be taken. He heard no shouts or cries of pain from within the tent, which meant they weren't torturing his friends for information . . . yet.

But time passed, and he remained there on his knees as fresh logs were piled onto an old fire pit, stew pots set over the flames, and horses and weapons tended.

Leo *should* be relieved. He was safe enough out here, on the hard, cold ground, his arms stiff and his jaw aching from the gag.

Instead, he was more panicked than ever. What was happening inside that tent? And what would happen to him?

His breaths started coming in short, sharp gusts of air. Sweat beaded his forehead, and his eyes kept darting around the darkening camp, unable to fix on anything.

Suddenly, Jakob's face loomed before him. "Are you all right?"

Leo's vision blurred, and he struggled to bring the soldier into focus. He thought he shook his head, but he couldn't be sure.

Jakob's face turned away. "He's not well. He looks like he's going to be sick."

One of the other soldiers nearby grunted. "So what?"

Jakob scowled. "You want him hurling all over you? Or maybe he'll choke on his gag and suffocate. Let me take him for a walk around camp. What harm will it do?" The soldier rolled his eyes, but Jakob persisted. "He's not going anywhere. And even if he did, how long would it take us to chase him down on horseback?"

A snort. "Fine. Be quick about it."

Then strong hands took Leo by the shoulders, pulling him to his feet. His legs were wobbly, due partly to the lack of oxygen his panting breaths were getting to his muscles and partly because his feet were asleep from being in an uncomfortable position for too long.

He leaned heavily on Jakob, who led him past the large tent that held Wren and Julian and toward a secluded part of camp. They passed under the tumbledown archway to the temple, and inside was darkness and quiet. Leo closed his eyes.

There was a pressure against the side of his face—his eyes flew open to see Jakob inches before him, his gloved hand raised. A second later, the gag around Leo's head loosened, and he spit out the fabric with a gasping breath.

He bent over, head between his knees.

When at last he could take a proper breath, Leo raised his head to find Jakob standing there, a silent companion. "Better?"

Leo swallowed. Nodded. "Yes, I . . . yes."

"You have nothing to worry about. You won't be harmed."

"*I* won't," Leo repeated, reading between the lines. "But my friends will."

There was no response.

Lifting his manacled hands to massage his jaw, Leo tried to gather his thoughts. The panic had subsided for now, but that didn't mean he was out of danger. It just meant that his body had forgotten it long enough for him to *think*.

He glanced out the door, the way they had come. "Don't they need to question me, too?"

For some reason, Jakob's gaze skittered away. "They don't intend to question you."

Leo's hands dropped, manacles clanking. He frowned. "Why?" Jakob just shrugged, but he was a terrible liar. "*Why?*" Leo repeated, though a part of him already knew the answer.

"They don't think you know anything of value. Being a third son and a known . . ."

"What? Rake? Reprobate? Good-for-nothing?"

"I was going to say *free spirit*," Jakob said carefully, and Leo laughed. He couldn't help it.

"That is a generous assessment, Jakob, and you know it."

"Here I was thinking it was insufficient."

Leo's eyes narrowed, but the words were guileless, delivered with simple, blunt honesty. Something pleasant tried to unfurl inside his chest, but Leo's anger quickly squashed it.

The soldier was right. It *was* insufficient. Leo was more than his face and his fashion sense. More than his quips and his charm—though those things certainly helped.

No one expected anything from him, not his family, not the people of the Dominions, and apparently not the people east of the Wall, either.

He had always known that and *thought* he'd accepted it.

But maybe he hadn't. Maybe he wanted to be more.

"They think I don't know anything? That I don't have eyes and ears? That I don't have power of my own?" Rage, hot and dark, pooled in Leo's stomach. "Here you are, *alone* with me. You'd never have dared it with Julian. With Wren. And your fellow soldiers would never have let you. But with me? The silly prince?" He laughed humorlessly. "Meanwhile, I'm the person who could kill you, right here, right now."

Jakob's expression faltered, his brow lowering. He was confused. Wouldn't be for long.

Leo nodded at him. "That necklace . . . family heirloom?"

Jakob's hand moved to his chest, where underneath his shirt—links just visible around his neck—was a thin metal chain.

A *golden* chain.

Leo raised his manacled hands and *yanked* on it with his magic. Jakob stumbled forward. "Bet you didn't know it was made of gold, tarnished as it is. But that's pure, and high quality, and all I'd need to wring the life from you." Leo twisted his hands, the chain mimicking his movements and tightening around Jakob's neck. His pale face reddened, and his eyes bulged.

Just as he was about to fall to his knees, Leo felt sick with himself and released his hold.

He was no warrior. No killer.

He was something else.

And he just wanted it to be enough.

"I'm sorry," Leo said at once. The boy was bent double, coughing and catching his breath, but the look he gave Leo wasn't of anger.

"Good to know it's worth something," he wheezed, glancing up at him.

Leo actually smiled, that thing in his chest squirming again. He just hoped the same could be said for himself.

A sudden shout cut through the night, followed by trumpeting horn calls.

Leo stared at Jakob, who looked in the direction of camp before turning back to Leo.

"We're under attack."

SIX

Wren was alone in a room when the horn calls sounded.

The Red Guard captain had already drilled her, the same stupid questions over and over again. He wanted to know about the Breachfort. About the garrison and about who was in charge. Wren gave the sort of non-information that answered the questions without telling him anything he didn't already know.

"The Breachfort is a fort along the Border Wall."

"It houses Breachfort guards, bonesmiths, silversmiths, and stonesmiths."

"The commander is in charge."

He grew irritated with her pretty quickly—surprise, surprise—and threatened a gauntleted fist to the face if she kept being "unhelpful."

Then he asked her about the Corpse Queen. At least there Wren didn't have to pretend ignorance. She didn't know what the woman wanted with her, not truly, nor her ultimate plans.

"Your regent's the one who's allied with her. Why don't you ask him?"

Wren got the gauntlet to the face at that, but it was more of a warning blow—enough to cut her lip inside her mouth but not enough to knock her unconscious.

The captain left her after that, presumably to go try Julian again.

The tent was massive and divided into different rooms by heavy canvas flaps, meaning there was enough distance between Wren and Julian that his conversations were reduced to droning questions and terse, muffled responses.

But as long as she heard that rumbling, she knew Julian was alive.

And that was enough to keep her sharp and ready.

She was currently slumped on the dirt, head hanging and manacled wrists heavy before her.

To the guard who sporadically peered in at her through the flap, she looked tired, defeated.

The first one? Yes. The second?

Never.

Wren Graven wasn't defeated. She was *digging*. Magically.

Searching for bones deep in the soil. She'd managed to find *something*, and though her power was weaker without her ring and other bone amplifiers like her weapons, she was managing to wiggle it toward the surface. It wouldn't be as useful as a sword or even bonedust, but she could sense it was broken, which meant sharp edges.

If she were clever like Leo, she might have been able to use it to pick the manacle locks. Since she wasn't, she'd probably just use it to threaten the guard's life instead.

They all had their strengths.

Besides, only fools would bring a bonesmith to a graveyard and not keep a closer watch.

They deserved what was coming for them.

And then, right on cue, the horn calls.

She heard terse words deeper inside the tent, and then shadows moved across the canvas. Two Red Guardsmen slipped past her tent flap and disappeared into the night, including the captain.

They seemed worried, and Wren couldn't blame them. She knew exactly the sort of thing that attacked people out here in the Breachlands, and she had seen how weak the bonesmith fortifications were around this place.

With those two gone . . . how many soldiers did that leave *inside* the tent?

Wren didn't fancy being found here by roving undead, bound and unarmed, but she didn't want to be here if the Red Guard captain returned either.

She pulled on the bone shard with more urgency. The guard outside the room had completely forgotten her, his head bent toward another soldier, their voices anxious. Shouts could be heard beyond, in addition to the distinctive sound of metal against metal. . . .

But the undead didn't wield weapons.

Finally the bone broke free of the soil, flying into Wren's hands just as one of the guards spoke. "Hey, what do you think you're—"

Wren's head snapped up, but the guards weren't looking at her.

There was a clank, another shout, and two loud *thumps.*

Then Julian poked his head into her room, his manacles dangling from a single wrist, bent and misshapen.

"Are you coming?"

Wren leapt to her feet, Julian sparing a single raised brow for the bone shard clutched in her hand before turning his attention to her restraints. He had clearly used his iron hand to pry the metal off his other wrist, but for Wren, he simply took hold of the chain that connected the two cuffs and squeezed. The links screeched in protest, but Wren found her attention shifting away from the task and to Julian himself.

Last time she'd seen him use his iron hand, she'd been wholly fixated on the magic. The power. The crushed metal lock.

This time she watched *him*.

While the effort seemed relatively minimal—there were no curses or grunts of exertion—it was plain to see it required intense concentration. Sweat dotted his brow, his lips were pressed tightly together, and his gaze never wavered.

Wren marveled at the control, at the infinitesimal movements required to make the hand *behave* like a hand when it appeared to be mostly metal. She wondered how much was muscle memory and how much was active, focused use of magic.

It must be exhausting. Then again, it was iron, and he was an ironsmith, which made it an amplifier. Its existence fed his magic, even as it drained it in turn. A self-sustaining loop.

Finally the link on the manacle cracked, the metal unable to bear any more pressure. Now Wren wore two metal bracelets as opposed to Julian's single shackle, but it would have to do.

"Thank you," Wren said, and he seemed taken aback at the sincerity.

"It's nothing," he said gruffly, but Wren knew that wasn't true.

Outside the tent, the camp was in chaos.

The Red Guard and Iron Citadel soldiers were running to and fro, their figures illuminated in shades of crimson and gold from the fire or else cast into nothing but inky silhouettes because of it. Some hastily redonned armor, while others launched arrows haphazardly from behind grave markers, and all the while the Red Guard captain issued orders and tried to get their forces to put up a proper defense.

Their attackers were mounted and tearing through the tumult with swords flashing, cutting off the regent's men from the paddock that held their own horses and would make this a more even fight.

One such rider passed by the fire, and Wren spotted the familiar Breachfort uniforms. Which meant there was at least one bonesmith somewhere in the mix . . .

Julian was taking in the scene as well. She turned to him. "We need to find Leo."

He nodded, his gaze scanning the crowds until it landed on the wagon parked on the outskirts of their camp. "Our weapons first."

Wren wanted to argue, but they were likely to *need* their weapons to spring Leo from whoever held him, not to mention that they had no idea where he was. They needed to start somewhere.

Darting through the shadows outside the glow of the fire, Wren and Julian ducked behind tents and dodged running soldiers. Luckily, they were less distinctive without their armor, so they were not immediately identifiable as prisoners in the chaos—or so Wren thought.

One of the Red Guard came out of nowhere and grabbed Wren by her hair, dragging her to the ground. She cried out in surprise, and Julian whirled around. He bared his teeth at Wren's attacker and decked the guard with his iron hand, dropping the man in a single, brutal punch.

Wren stared up at him in awe, her mind flashing back to the first time she'd met Julian, battling him in front of the Wall. She realized now how easily he could have dispatched her if he'd wanted to.

Despite that tingle of fear, when Julian extended the same hand to help her to her feet, she took it without question.

The wagon was almost within reach when Leo pelted at them out of nowhere, coming from the direction of the temple. He was running hard, manacled hands held aloft, while one of the Citadel soldiers was hot on his heels.

Leo collided with Wren, who practically caught him, while Julian stepped between them and the pursuer.

The soldier skidded to a halt, reaching for the blade at his belt, though he hesitated. His attention landed on Julian's unshackled wrists before flying up to his face, which was dark and scowling and half a foot higher than his own.

"Are we going to have a problem, Jake?" Julian said calmly, his tone at odds with the chaos all around them. Wren was surprised that he knew the boy by name, but of course he did. He probably knew most of the soldiers who'd captured them. Up until a few days ago, they'd been on the same side.

The soldier released the hilt of his sword, raising his empty hands. "I was just trying to protect him," he argued, gesturing at Leo. "We were inside the temple—perfectly safe—and he comes running out into the middle of a battlefield!"

Leo, who was still leaning on Wren as he gasped and clutched at an apparent stitch in his side, straightened. "Define *safe*, Jakob. You realize I'm a prisoner held against my will, right?"

"Your life wasn't in danger. Now it is."

"If that's all you're concerned with, we can take it from here," Julian said, moving as if he intended to turn his back on the soldier.

Jakob's eyes bulged slightly, his brows twin arcs bowing under the pressure of his frowning forehead. "Julian, I—I don't know what's happening. Lord Francis, he said—"

"What did he say?" Julian hissed, whirling around so quickly Wren barely saw him move. One second he was about to walk away, and the next he was right in Jakob's face. "That *I* kidnapped the prince?

That I was a traitor? You were *there.* You know what happened. But what you don't know is that Captain Royce was sent to kill me. He failed. And the prince I kidnapped? He's on my side now. So who do you think is telling the truth? *Me,* or him?"

Wren had never seen Julian look so fierce, so menacing. And after that stone-cold punch he'd just thrown? He was terrifying.

She was into it, but they didn't have time for this. Once both these parties realized the prize they were fighting over had escaped, they'd be in trouble.

Jakob deflated somewhat, though his jaw jutted out. "I can't just *let* you all walk out of here."

"*Let* me?" Julian asked dangerously.

Again, *into it,* but it was high time they got their possessions and made a run for it.

Wren was about to say as much when all the hairs on the back of her neck stood up.

She turned, knowing what she would see before she saw it.

A revenant.

Materializing from the blackness beyond the broken and battered bone palisade was a walking undead.

It looked alarmingly fresh, its clothes and body nearly perfectly intact, so that Wren could barely spot any ghostlight, and the telltale signs of gray pallor or blood were invisible in the darkness.

It was almost enough to make her second-guess herself, except that she could sense the wrongness. Besides, it wasn't dressed in a Breachfort uniform, Red Guard enamel, or the armor of the Iron Citadel soldiers. And the way it moved . . . lumbering and oblivious to soaring arrows and thundering hoofbeats.

Wren's stomach dropped. The bonesmith temple's palisade was

too damaged, which meant it wouldn't keep the undead out. This fight was about to get a whole lot worse.

Before she could open her mouth to raise the alarm, before she could do more than stare, one of the Red Guard across the camp had taken notice.

He was an archer, and seeing this new target, he nocked an arrow and loosed, hitting the undead in the shoulder.

The corpse didn't drop.

Instead, it turned its neck toward the source of the attack with a revolting, wet-sounding crack that Wren could *feel*, even though she knew it was too far for her to hear.

Suddenly, the archer understood. This was no Breachfort rider or opportunistic bandit.

He dropped his bow and ran. "*Revenants!*"

SEVEN

Wren whirled, reaching for blades she did not have.

The bone shard she'd unearthed inside the tent would be of little use, though she clutched it all the same, and while there were dozens more bones in the vicinity, there were none that she could get a proper magical grip of.

Not without her ring. With her ring, she could raise whole skeletons from the ground. She could take hold of the bones of the living *and* command the souls of the undead.

"My weapons," Wren said. No sooner had the shout gone up than several more undead materialized behind the first. They were in a more familiar state of decay, flesh rotten and bones exposed. *"Now."*

For once, Julian did not argue with her.

Without giving Jakob a second thought, they tore off toward the wagon.

All around them, the forces who'd been locked in battle with one another turned to this new, far more dangerous foe. Steel slashed and arrows landed true, but these were no ordinary adversaries. Every hack and slice revealed searing flashes of ghostlight, bathing the campsite in its sickly glow, but nothing stopped them. Nothing hurt them.

But *Wren* could.

She relished the thought. She was sick of running and hiding.

She was itching for a fight.

The wagon was within reach, and that's when Jakob decided to step in front of them, blade drawn and gripped with both hands—though they were shaking.

"I can't. This position, this is my *life*, my family's livelihood," he choked out. He looked around wildly, gaze darting from Iron Citadel soldiers and Red Guard warriors to Breachfort riders and, finally, to the revenants descending upon them all with slow, brutal eventuality. He wavered, swallowing thickly before returning his attention to them. "If I let you go," he began, shaking his head slightly. "If I'm *seen* . . ."

Hoofbeats sounded, and Wren turned just in time to see a mounted rider from the Breachfort approach, bow raised. Her mind stuttered to a halt, until she remembered that these soldiers had been sent to *collect* her, not kill her.

The arrow whizzed right by her head, giving her a breathless second to fear for Leo and Julian, but when she turned, it was to see the prince make a sudden wrenching motion at the air. Jakob lurched forward, falling to his knees, while the arrow *thwacked* into the wagon in the exact place his head had just been.

The Breachfort rider lowered his bow and reached for a sword instead. "I found th—"

Wren lunged, taking up the bone shard like a dagger and stabbing the rider in the leg. His shout was abruptly cut off, giving Julian a chance to tear him from his saddle and descend with his iron fist once more.

Leo, meanwhile, was helping Jakob to his feet. Jakob was rubbing at his neck, where a tarnished chain glinted. Was it gold? Is that how Leo had saved him? Jakob had dropped his sword when he'd fallen, but he didn't seem bothered with picking it up again.

"You say your family is relying on you," Leo said, considering the soldier closely. "I wonder, what do they get if you're dead?"

His silence was answer enough.

Seeing that Jakob was cowed, Julian leapt into the back of the wagon, Wren following close behind. Her heartbeat was erratic inside her chest until she unearthed her belongings and her fingers closed around her ring. She slipped it on, feeling a welcome surge of magic. Next came her armor and her blades, while Julian slid on his plate with practiced precision before moving on to his helmet, weapons, and finally, his good luck bracelet from Becca. Leo had joined them as well, hastily donning his personal items and hauling out the rest of their supplies. Once the three of them were armed, armored, and ready to go, they leapt from the wagon and faced the battlefield.

"Get back inside the temple," Wren said to Jakob, taking pity on the boy, who still appeared shaken. Whether it was from his near death, the swarming undead, or the fact that he was risking his position by letting them go, she couldn't be sure, but she didn't need him suddenly changing his mind and complicating things. "Bring as many with you as you can. The protections there will be the strongest."

They tore off into the night. With her blades drawn, Wren felt confident running at speed, slashing at any undead who veered too close. The urge to command them was there, an itch at the back of her throat, but she feared wasting the magic that remained inside the amplifier. They were about to journey into the Haunted Territory. She'd need all the power she could get.

Skirting the edges of the battlefield, they ran due north, hoping to disappear into the darkness without a trace.

The way was clear—until it wasn't.

A cloud of something rose before Wren, putting her in mind of the Breach again. She was running too fast to stop herself, but when she contacted the obstruction, she realized instantly what it was.

Bonedust?

She coughed and swiped her hand through the air, dispersing the cloud and blinking into the night for the source.

Inara Fell was striding toward them. She looked pissed.

"What the fuck?" Wren gasped, wiping at her face while Julian and Leo choked and spluttered.

"What the fuck yourself!" Inara said crossly. She looked more disheveled than Wren had ever seen her, the eye black on her face smeared into the blood that ran from a cut across her cheek, bits of dirt and grass lodged in her dark braids, and her pale bone armor dinged and scuffed. "What have you gotten yourself into, Graven? I help you free this one"—she jerked a thumb at Julian—"and now your damned father has the entire fort chasing after you? He's got me and half a dozen valkyrs protecting entire patrols of guards *in the Breachlands*. I always thought you were crazy, but the fact that you've willingly done this, *twice*, proves it! We were trailed by ghosts almost as soon as we crossed the palisade. It took every bit of ammunition I had to keep them at bay, and then we crossed fucking *bandits* yesterday. Sonya decided to just *run off*, and now this shit?" She gestured angrily at the fiery battlefield, dotted with ghostlight. The new corpses were piling up, either shot down by enemy fire or succumbing to deathrot. Inara took a deep, steadying breath. "This is *not* what I trained for. So tell me why I'm doing it."

Wren struggled to find the words. She'd never heard Inara swear so much or appear so rattled, and it was unsettling. "I don't know where to begin, Inara, and frankly, we don't have the time."

Inara took a decisive step closer to Wren, putting them face-to-face. "I have been misguiding these Breachfort soldiers for two days. Slowing them down, giving them false information. In short, I've been protecting you, and the only reason we're here now is because I knew you'd be safer with us than with this regent's Red Guard. So tell me why."

"I didn't ask you to do that," Wren snapped, though she was quite pleased.

Inara opened her mouth to retort when her gaze caught on something over Wren's shoulder. "*There* you are!" she said in annoyance, stepping around Wren toward a figure approaching them in the dark.

Wren couldn't see their face, but the telltale sweep of the reapyr's robes told her it must be Sonya.

Only, Sonya was not right. Her walk was off, her movements stilted, and when the wind caught the fabric of her robe, it billowed, revealing an arrow protruding from her chest.

There was no way she could be upright with a wound like that, and with a sinking feeling in her stomach, Wren knew what she'd find if she pulled that arrow free. Not blood, but a burst of ghostlight.

"*Inara,*" Wren said sharply, reaching for the valkyr, but Inara shook her off.

"Sonya, where have you been? I've been searching—"

She paused.

Something—probably a tent—had fallen into the campfire behind them, resulting in a huge flare of golden light. In the resulting glow, Sonya's face became visible. The colorless flesh. The dead, unblinking eyes . . . with a hint of sickly green ghostlight shining through.

While Inara had paused midstep, Sonya continued to approach. And in her hand, dangling by her side, was her gleaming metal scythe . . . dripping in blood.

"What are you doing?" Inara said, though Wren could tell from her tone that she didn't actually expect an answer. Inara must know what Sonya was, but it seemed her mind had not quite accepted it. She raised her favored weapon, her skull-tipped flail, but didn't strike.

For the first time in Wren's memory, Inara Fell had frozen.

Wren leapt forward, yanking Inara back and putting herself between the valkyr and the undead reapyr. She sheathed her swords and raised her hand between them, the amplifier ring on her finger. "Stop!"

There was a second when Wren feared it would not work, that the magic was gone and maybe she'd never even had it at all.

But it was only a second.

Her voice had sounded with that same familiar resonance. And she'd felt the pull within her, the pulse of magic.

Sonya staggered to a halt, mere feet away, and remained motionless.

Wren glanced at Inara, who had stumbled to the ground behind her, and saw her pale eyes widen in complete and utter shock. As far as she knew, the undead did not heed the commands of bonesmiths . . . but of course, Wren was no ordinary bonesmith.

Expelling a breath, she reached down to help Inara to her feet, but Julian and Leo had beaten her to it.

She turned back to the revenant. To *Sonya.*

Wren swallowed the lump in her throat. She'd never really liked Sonya—the girl *had* betrayed her during the Bonewood Trial—but this was not a fate she would wish on anyone. Worst of all, they couldn't help her. Not now, in the midst of a battle. Not when her corpse was so fresh and her anchor bone so well protected. The sad truth was, the only person here who could have freed Sonya was Sonya herself, and she was already gone.

"Go," Wren choked out. "Back—" She hesitated, struggling with the command. "Back where you came from."

Hopefully that would take her away from these living people, away from *them*, which was the best she could manage at the moment.

The revenant lumbered away, disappearing into the night.

Wren faced Inara, panting slightly from exertion and something like dread, but deeper. Sadder.

"That's why he wants you," Inara muttered, mostly to herself. "But that means . . ." She wavered. "What does that mean?"

"I'm a g-ghostsmith," Wren managed to spit out, hating the taste of the word. She had always hated it, but she hated it more speaking it aloud to Inara. Wren had never known anyone who loved being a bonesmith as much as she did . . . except for Inara. Now she awaited the girl's judgment.

Inara frowned, then her brows shot up. "Your mother?"

Wren nodded, glad Inara was quick on the uptake and couldn't help being smarter than everyone around her. "Odile knew. She told my father. He didn't like it. Or rather, didn't like the idea of Svetlana finding out. He wants to use me, to use this magic. . . ."

Inara's gaze was fixed on the empty darkness, but Wren knew she was staring at the place where Sonya had been. "I had no idea they were so powerful. Ghostsmiths."

Wren stared at her ring. "This is only the beginning. There's a well of magic in the heart of the Breach. I've been there. I've seen it. It's what makes the revenants rise, what causes the undead here to be so powerful. When you have access to that much magic, the things you can do are . . ."

"Inhuman," Julian supplied softly.

"Yes," Wren said. "The well is how Locke defeated the House of Iron during the Uprising. It's how he slaughtered our forces too, including himself."

Inara's expression, which had been as distant as her gaze, grew sharp as she met Wren's eyes.

"We're going to destroy it. Before my father can use it. Before other, even worse people can use it. Sonya will be the least of what they bring forth. Already they're building an army in the heart of the Breach, the Iron Regent and the Corpse Queen. Revenants in suits of armor."

Inara swallowed, but their conversation was interrupted by renewed commotion from the campsite. It seemed that both parties were abandoning the fight entirely in favor of retreat, the undead an unstoppable force, but the loss of their captives had finally been noted by the Red Guard. Angry shouts pierced the night, while horses neighed and hooves stomped.

Inara's resolve, tough as bone at the best of times, hardened into iron. "Tell me what to do."

"What you've *been* doing. Buy us time. Whatever Vance tries to do . . . make sure he *doesn't*. We've got enough to deal with over here without him interfering."

Inara nodded, her attention shifting to the battle. Her shoulders squared, and she lifted her flail. "Got it. Now go."

Just like that, she darted back into the fray. She dodged a few haphazard strikes from Red Guard soldiers before making for the nearest riderless horse.

Wren held her breath until Inara was mounted and clear from the carnage, putting the battlefield behind her.

"Uh, Wren?" came Leo's voice from behind her, taut and uncertain. Then there was the sound of sword against scabbard—Julian unsheathing his weapon.

Wren turned, redrawing her blades.

A lone figure stood before them, maybe ten paces away, emerging from the darkness beyond their camp.

A living figure.

Not just a living figure but a *familiar* one, wearing a ram's skull mask, curled horns protruding from his head and turning his outline into something from nightmares, while ghost-green eyes glowed from behind the dark bone veneer.

It was the ghostsmith she and Julian had seen that day in the ruins.

It was her brother.

EIGHT

The sight of him caused panic to flutter against Wren's breast.

He looked much as he had the last time she'd seen him, but now she noticed additional details she'd failed to register before. Like their mother, he wore bones around his wrists and neck, strung together on twine or carved into rounds. His clothes were poor, ripped and stained and a mix of fabric including leathers, furs, and wool, as if scrounged from corpses. He held a tall staff in his hand, an animal skull at its top, and a cloak trailed from his shoulders.

Wren wasn't prepared for this. Not yet. She'd known she'd have to face him again, and soon, but she'd thought it would happen somewhere in the Breach. She'd thought she'd have more time to figure out what she wanted to say and how she felt.

But she suspected that in two days or twenty, she still wouldn't know how to feel.

A part of her feared him—that skull mask didn't help things—but another part burned with curiosity. Who *was* he? He'd certainly *looked* like her the last time she saw him with his face uncovered. They had the same pale hair and ivory skin, delicate nose and stern brows . . . but what was his *personality* like? Was he stubborn and brazen, like Wren? Or would he be her opposite, calm and controlled?

When Wren had first heard the truth of him and her mother, she'd had the sense that her family had been split cleanly down the middle: mother and son on one side, father and daughter on the other. There was a literal Wall between them, not to mention time and space and magic, too.

But perhaps the divide could be different. After all, Wren was actively working against her father at this very moment, and she didn't yet know where her brother's loyalties lay.

It was time to find out.

Before she could think twice, Wren leveled her sword at him. "What are you doing here?" she demanded. There was no point beating around the bush.

He raised his hands, his amplifier ring—the twin to hers—a flash of white in the darkness, then opened his mouth. Before he could answer, Wren pressed the tip of the blade against his throat. "Careful," she breathed, fearing ghosts and revenants just out of sight. "I can command them too, and I'll chop off your hand before I see you use that ring against me."

He hesitated, then nodded as much as he dared with the sword so close. Wren lowered the blade enough for him to be able to speak.

"I—" he began, but she flicked the sword impatiently at his forehead, and he understood, pushing the mask off his face. "I came for you."

His voice was as low as she remembered, with a distinctive rasp, though it didn't scrape at her ears as it had when she'd heard him use it to command the undead.

"Why?"

He flinched slightly at Wren's aggressive tone, at every sound that emanated from the battlefield behind her. The clashing metal and cries of pain, the stomping boots and snorting, shrieking horses. The undead, silent but relentless, forcing men to cower in fear or run recklessly in retreat only to drop dead, soundless forever more.

"I was sent to retrieve you."

"By *her*," Wren said. It wasn't a question.

"Y-yes, by her." There was a timidness in him that Wren didn't recall before. A fragility. He recoiled at another loud sound from the campsite, as if unused to so much noise.

She supposed when compared to the living, the undead were much quieter company . . . even the ones that could talk.

"Do you know who I am?" She almost said *what* I am, but the two were essentially one and the same.

"You're Wren Graven," he said at once, the words tinged with something almost like awe. "My sister."

So he knew. Had he always known? Whatever. It wasn't important now. "Why were you sent for me?"

"I was sent to meet with the regent's men. I was to lead them and you to her."

"Why? What does she want with me?"

"You're her daughter." Wren blinked. Surely that wasn't the whole answer.

"And us?" Julian asked, indicating himself and Leo.

His green eyes flickered. "The prince was to be escorted somewhere for safekeeping. I do not know where."

"And me?" Julian pressed.

"You were to be given over to the regent. . . ." He hesitated. "Or rather, your body was."

"With your help?" Wren asked furiously. "If they'd killed him here, he'd have risen as a revenant long before he'd make it to the regent." She thought of Sonya with a pang. She'd been missing barely a day, and in that time she'd managed to be killed by an arrow *and* rise again. The magic in this land was far more potent than any of them understood, and they were still miles from the well. "Only *you* could stop his ghost from slaughtering them all."

Julian wore a fierce expression that told Wren if he *had* been killed, he'd have eagerly exacted his brutal revenge afterward.

Her brother, on the other hand, shrugged indifferently. "That would be their problem, not mine."

"So if you were meant to meet them here," Leo said, "why are you skulking in the shadows? Were these revenants your doing?"

His lip curled. "These revenants are not mine. And I wasn't *skulking*," he said, color appearing high on his cheekbones in the same place Wren tended to flush. "I heard the battle, and I . . . I do not care for fighting."

"You don't care for fighting. Meanwhile, I saw you making revenants armored in iron that are designed to do exactly that."

The color that had filled his cheeks quickly drained away. "You know who I serve. I had no choice."

"Because she's called herself a queen?" Wren scoffed.

He shook his head, his expression bleak. "Because she calls herself my mother."

"That doesn't mean you have to *obey* her," she argued, but even as the words left her mouth, she felt like a fraud. Up until recently, she had followed every command her father had ever made, heeded his every whim and desire.

"You're right," he said, licking his lips. "That's why I want to help you."

"You *what*?"

He swallowed. "Is it true, what you said to that bonesmith?"

"That . . . to Inara?" Wren glanced questioningly at Julian and Leo, but they looked as surprised as she felt. She turned an assessing gaze on her brother. "Yes, that's right. That well of magic—we've come to destroy it. To stop what you and your so-called queen are doing. Still want to help us?"

"Yes," he said, nodding eagerly.

"You do," Wren said flatly. "A minute ago, you were here on your mother's orders, and a few days ago, you were building her iron revenants. And now, out of nowhere, you want to turn your back on her?"

"*Our* mother," he clarified softly, before continuing in a louder voice. "And yes. I didn't know what you'd come here for—maybe you planned worse things than her. But if you want to stop this, and if you want that well destroyed, then we want the same thing. They . . . I . . . I *hate* them," he spat.

"Hate who?" Julian asked, confused.

"The *iron revenants*, as you call them. The human undead. They are vicious and violent. They follow me everywhere, cling to me like cobwebs, and I am forever commanding them to stay, to go . . . to kill. But if the well were destroyed, I would no longer be burdened with such power." His eyes glittered with hope. "I would be free."

The words tumbled out of him, sincere and unpracticed, but Wren still had trouble believing them. He was a *ghostsmith*. It would be like Julian ranting about how much he hated iron or Leo, gold.

It would be like Wren *hating* bones.

It didn't make sense.

And yet . . . iron and gold didn't walk. Didn't speak or attack. Even bones only managed to cause Wren trouble in the Breachlands, and that was because a ghost was attached.

When no one immediately shut him down, he seemed heartened. He straightened his posture and lifted his chin. "You need me. I know a way there. To the well. A secret way underground. You won't be troubled by the Red Guard, the Breachfort patrols . . . those bonesmiths sent by your father."

"*Our* father," Wren clarified absently. They had to get moving; the noise behind them was diminishing, and the sky was lightening to the east. They needed to disappear before the sun rose. "And what of our mother? Will *she* trouble us?"

"She will not know we are there."

Wren expelled a breath of frustration but lowered her sword slightly. "How can we possibly trust you?"

"I'm not sure we've got any other choice," Leo said reasonably. "He—I don't even know your name," he said, speaking directly to Wren's brother.

A stab of guilt pierced her gut. She didn't know his name either.

"Hawke," he rasped. "My name is Hawke."

"Hawke and Wren, isn't that charming," Leo said, and Wren glowered at him. She thought of their matching rings, each featuring both a songbird and a bird of prey. A wren and a hawk.

"Yes, it's like a fairy tale," Wren snapped. "Can we focus, please? He could lead us into a trap. He could take us *right* to her, just like he came here to do in the first place."

"I was also supposed to bring in the Red Guard," Hawke pointed out. "By leaving them behind, by leaving them to this"—he gestured at the ghostly battlefield—"I have already gone against my orders."

"And instead you crouched here in the bushes and *hid*," Wren said. "That doesn't inspire much confidence."

"I can do it," Hawke said quietly, as if convincing himself as much as them. "Please. You're my sister. I want to help you."

Wren was speechless, but luckily, Julian was not. "Even if it means betraying your mother?" he asked. "It is one thing to defy orders and quite another to openly work against her."

Hawke's lips compressed, and anger flashed in his eyes. "Does it count as betrayal if they are the ones who betrayed you first?"

"No," Julian said, lips pulling back into a vicious smile. "Then it's called revenge."

NINE

Inara traveled alone across the Breachlands, toward the Border Wall and its fort.

Toward safety.

She thought she saw riders behind her once or twice, but whether they were friend or foe, Breachfort guard or bandit—alive or undead—she couldn't be sure, so she kicked her heels and sped up, pushing her stolen horse to its limits and leaving them behind.

The worst was riding at night.

Inara had spent years fighting in the shadows, actively seeking out the horrors most would flee from, so fearing the dark was an entirely new experience for her.

But fear it she did.

A lifetime of training had not prepared Inara for what she had seen these past days, and even that had been the barest taste of what the Breachlands had in store, if the rumors were true. To actually *see* walking revenants after hearing tell of them for years . . . Well, the stories, books, and lessons did not do them justice.

She was on high alert, every thrust of rock or swaying tree becoming a hunched corpse or a skulking undead, waiting to pounce.

And each and every imagined nightmare wore Sonya's face.

That was a failure she wouldn't soon forget, but she couldn't dwell on it now.

Now was for survival, and what came after would require her full and considerable intellectual capabilities.

She arrived at the Breachfort gates before the sun, having ridden hard for nearly twenty-four hours straight.

Her body ached from the saddle but also from the tension tightening her shoulders and her own stubborn insistence on keeping her flail at the ready.

As she drew near, a shout echoed from somewhere above, but as the gates swung wide, the faces that greeted her were confused. They kept looking behind her, as if expecting additional riders to materialize out of thin air.

Her grim expression seemed to answer their unasked questions. Inara's patrol had been expected back yesterday, so surely with her solitary arrival, they could piece things together.

"Lord-Smith Vance requested an immediate report as soon as any surv—any*one* from the patrol returned," one of the guards said, stumbling over the words.

"Where is he?" Inara asked, dropping stiffly to the ground and handing the reins to the hostler.

"In Smith Odile's study."

† † † †

Inara descended the stairs to the basement temple and knocked on the door, voices rumbling on the other side.

Standing in the hall waiting after being ordered there felt distinctly like getting in trouble—and Inara didn't *get* in trouble. She was never called to private offices at late hours. Never rushed along dark corridors, a sense of doom growing with every footstep.

Well, except for the one time. The night before the Bonewood Trial.

She'd been summoned to Lord-Smith Vance Graven's door late that night, and here she was, summoned to his door again.

Like a lapdog. Or a lackey. Both things Inara had been accused of—mostly by Wren—and both things untrue. Especially now. She wasn't here to be bullied into another one of Vance's schemes.

She was here to stop him.

Or try to, anyway.

Typical of Wren to give her an impossible task like it was no big deal.

Whatever Vance tries to do . . . make sure he doesn't.

Might as well ask her to stop the moon from rising or the winter snows from falling.

Not unlike his daughter, Vance Graven did what he wanted, when he wanted, and now that he was at the Breachfort without his disapproving mother looking over his shoulder, Inara would be hard-pressed to find anyone or anything that could stand in his way.

Stupidly confident and thoughtlessly daring, just like his daughter. But as it turned out Wren was, Inara hated to admit, *special.* She could control those foul revenants, and if she did what she said she'd do—and, annoyingly, she usually did—then she'd put a stop to tier fives for good. That was something worth fighting for. The House of Bone existed to bring balance and order to the realms of living and undead, and this well of magic had thrown that harmony into disarray. The scales *had* to be righted.

Wren might be fearless and stubborn, but Inara was clever and possessed a dogged determination of her own.

She pressed her ear against the door. Though the words were muffled, she detected Commander Duncan's voice in the room beyond, and judging by the volume and tone of his speech, he wasn't happy.

She couldn't blame him.

Lord-Smith Vance had taken a stranglehold of the Breachfort ever since his arrival, overriding the commander's orders and clearing the barracks, sending out patrols and pairs of bonesmiths in an attempt to catch his daughter and the prisoners she'd taken with her. He'd also set up shop inside the fort's bonesmith temple, rather unceremoniously commandeering the dead reapyr's office and her position as head of the Breachfort bonesmiths.

It was all so . . . rash, so messy.

Inara saw where Wren got it from, the urge to act first and think second. To charge in blind. To throw everything at every problem, making bigger problems along the way. But what Vance was doing was a special kind of chaos, the sort that not even Wren Graven herself, queen of chaos, could have managed.

The man *was* capable of subterfuge—the Bonewood Trial was proof of that—but it was clear that when Vance's back was against the wall, all that plotting and planning went out the window. He thrived when things were going his way but flailed when things started to fall apart.

As such, he was the last sort of person you wanted in charge, and yet here he was, wielding power as he saw fit.

But not for much longer. Not if Inara could help it.

Leaning back, she raised her fist and knocked again. *Harder* this time.

Heavy footsteps approached. The door swung wide, revealing Lord-Smith Vance's slightly harassed face, his curling hair askew, as if fingers had run through it several times.

"Smith Inara," he said, shock wiping the irritation from his face. He took her by the shoulder and pulled her into the room. "As you can see, Commander Duncan, I have urgent matters to take care of. We can continue this discussion later."

The commander in question stood with arms crossed over his barrel chest, glowering. Vance's ability to evade was a skill he'd honed over years of being a frivolous heir and no-good father, and here he was doing it again. Inara had seen Vance deflect Wren time and time again, not to mention whatever other duties he deemed below his effort or interest.

But he would not deflect *her*.

"Continue it we will, Lord-Smith Vance," the commander said gravely. "King Augustus was very disturbed to hear tell that you allowed his son to be kidnapped *again*."

"That is why I told you to wait," Vance gritted out. "I can get him back. He's with *her*, and I know how to deal with her."

"Get him back, can you?" the commander asked, his dark gaze fixed on Inara. "How many rode out with you, Smith?"

Inara darted a look at Vance, but there was no lying—the details could be checked easily enough. "Twenty Breachfort guards and two bonesmiths."

"Twenty-two rode out, and only one returned," the commander said, turning to Vance. "You can't *get him back*. You can't even get our own soldiers back."

"I will get what matters."

The commander bristled. "You may not value the lives of my garrison, but I do. And as the king's *son* is in danger, I thought it best he was kept informed. He'd intended for his envoy to deal with whatever terms the Breachsiders decided to send, but with recent developments, his eldest son and heir is coming instead. You will have to answer to him."

"I can handle a spoiled heir," Vance shot back.

The commander's lips quirked in the corner. "I'll bet you can." He turned to go, then paused in the doorway. "Oh, one more thing. A letter arrived from Brighton. Your mother's due to arrive soon."

All smugness left Vance's face. "When?"

The commander's smirk turned into a full-blown smile. "Day after next." He walked from the room. "Chin up, Lord-Smith," he called from the hallway. "I'm sure you can handle her, too."

Vance watched the man go, his face flushed. "Smith Inara," he said gruffly, retaking his seat. "Report. What happened out there? Where is she?"

Inara told the truth . . . mostly. She explained how they'd tracked Wren and the others to Southbridge, but the Red Guard had beaten them to it. After encounters with roving bandits and walking undead, they'd set upon the enemy forces with the hopes of recapturing Wren and the others. They'd been unsuccessful.

"We might have managed it if not for the revenants. Nearly a dozen descended upon the camp, drawn to all the people clustered together. We were outnumbered, surrounded, and in the confusion . . ." She swallowed, a chill slipping down her spine at the memory of Sonya's undead face—at the way Wren had commanded her and how revenant Sonya had *heeded* that command. "I got away, but only just. I didn't see any other survivors."

She didn't know what she'd expected—a *show* of remorse, at least—but Vance bared his teeth in frustration, the gesture so like Wren that Inara had to look away.

He stood again and started to pace the office. "So they remain in the regent's custody?"

This was where the lying began. She had mulled it over, and convincing Vance that Wren was out of reach and in the hands of his enemy was surely the best strategy to slow his pursuit and keep him out of her way. "Yes, my lord. I suspect they are halfway to the Iron Citadel by now."

This way, even if he decided to chase her down, he'd be following the wrong trail and riding in the wrong direction. By the time he realized she wasn't there, it would be too late.

She hoped.

Footsteps echoed outside the door, and a bedraggled Breachfort guard stepped through the still-open door.

"My lord," the man said uncertainly, bobbing his head. He was dirty and travel-worn, with a bloody gash on his forearm that he currently used a wad of fabric to cover, but he was still familiar. Another member of Inara's patrolling party. He must have been the rider she'd thought she'd seen behind her. "They told me to report at once."

"Yes, yes," Vance said eagerly. "Come in, soldier. Smith Inara was just explaining about the undead attack, but perhaps you have new information? Where did you last see the targets?"

Inara held her breath.

"I didn't see them at all," the man began, and Inara pushed the air out slowly through her lips, until: "At first. It was nighttime, and with those walking corpses all around, I wasn't sure what was up and what was down."

Vance nodded impatiently, and Inara clenched her fists in newfound dread.

"But then, just as I took my wound, I saw them. They were well beyond the fighting, slipping away into the darkness. Four of them. The prince, the ironsmith, your daughter . . . and another. Couldn't see much beyond a skull mask with horns. I thought he was one of ours, a bonesmith"—he darted a look at Inara—"but then they disappeared."

"What direction?" Vance asked urgently. "Where did they go?"

"North," the man said. "Into the Haunted Territory."

While Vance's eyes gleamed and he drilled the man for any other useful details, Inara fought to keep her composure. Wren had set her a simple, if impossible, task, and Inara had failed at it.

Inara did not like failure.

Vance dismissed the man to seek medical care, retaking his seat.

Inara waited.

"We will have to go after her. In force."

"*Into* the Haunted Territory?" Inara asked, scrambling for something to say that might change his mind. Some objection she could raise. There were dozens, but Vance was not a man easily dissuaded. He and his daughter had that in common. Inara flashed back to the night before the Bonewood Trial, when all her perfectly reasonable and logical protestations went in one ear and out the other.

Then she was a mere novitiate, but even now, she was a very recently graduated valkyr, without rank or position or experience. The Fells were an important family within the House of Bone, but not important enough. Inara was not likely to have her opinions heard or her voice matter.

"We don't have enough soldiers," he said, shaking his head as he glanced down at his desk. The words gave Inara a glimmer of hope, but he was only shuffling papers until he found some sort of schedule or duty roster. "Not at the moment. I have two other patrols posted Breachside that have yet to return. That's two score soldiers; unless they came up against the same problems as *your* party, they should be back soon. Combined with the remaining garrison, that should give us a force equal to the one I marched into the Haunted Territory with during the Iron Uprising."

Inara gaped at him. The famously too-small force that was brutally killed—apparently by his own brother? So he would not only order them into dangerous, deadly territory en masse, offering up dozens of soldiers to the slaughter, but he would empty the Breachfort of its protections to do so?

"In the meantime, we will make preparations. I summoned additional bonesmiths from Brighton and a few smaller postings who should be arriving sometime later today. Get some rest, Smith Inara. We'll need all the help we can get if we're to journey into the Breach by this time tomorrow."

This time tomorrow. A full day before his mother's expected arrival.

Inara departed the bonesmith temple, but she didn't seek rest.

She *did* return to her room, though, fastidiously ignoring Sonya's bed with its few scattered possessions as she hastily undressed. She polished her armor, changed into clean leathers, and reapplied her eye black with a careful, practiced hand. She strapped on her weapons and strode for the stables.

The hostler looked surprised to see her back so soon. It was still not yet dawn, but she didn't have time to waste. Leaving the poor creature she'd arrived on to his rest, she requested a fresh horse and mounted up.

As with the hostler, the guards posted to the gate frowned at her. Inara lifted her chin and counted on the one thing she was certain she could: Vance Graven's ego.

As soon as he'd walked into the Breachfort, he'd made a point of taking control and establishing his superiority over Commander Duncan. How had he done that? By constantly reminding everyone of his rank as heir to the House of Bone.

Now the Breachfort garrison were following *his* orders.

His overreaching had thrown their internal order of command into disarray, and now these Breachfort soldiers didn't know who outranked whom. As far as they were concerned, any order from any bonesmith came from the *head* bonesmith. Or at least, that's what she was about to try to convince them of.

"Open the gate," she said, with all the lazy disdain she could muster, though her heart pounded in her chest.

"Why?"

She turned her attention to the guard who questioned her. "Lord-Smith Vance Graven's orders, that's why."

They opened the gate.

The sun was rising as she rode to the edge of the palisade and waited. Vance's plans hinged on two patrols returning to the fort.

Inara would simply have to make sure they never did.

TEN

Wren didn't like it. She didn't like it one bit—and she'd made it known. She'd frowned; she'd glowered; she'd crossed her arms and glared.

Putting themselves at the mercy of her brother felt like the last thing they should do, but despite her misgivings, she'd agreed. It wasn't just up to her, after all, and she was trying to do better in that regard.

We were supposed to be a team. We were in it together.

She hadn't just betrayed Julian's trust when she'd tied him up in that mill house. She'd robbed him of his choice in the matter. Leo, too, had been the victim of everyone else's schemes for far too long.

So she'd asked them what *they* wanted, and they'd reacted predictably.

Leo had been amiable as he admitted that it was likely the best course, while Julian had stared at her for a long time before saying, "You're *asking*?"

"Fuck off," she'd said, annoyed. She was *trying* to be gracious. An elegant, thoughtful leader. Instead, she just wanted to punch him square on his pretty, angular, ruggedly handsome jaw.

He'd actually smirked a little, though Wren didn't feel like she was in on the joke. It felt more like he was smiling at her expense.

Regardless, he had concurred with Leo, and so they'd hefted their bags and told her brother to lead on.

They'd walked for a while through the lightening dark, Hawke's bones rattling and cape billowing, until they arrived at the mouth of an ink-black fissure in the rising ground. It had felt distinctly like walking into the gaping maw of death itself, but what remained for them above ground was no safer.

Turning his attention to his staff, Hawke had flicked the animal skull at its tip, and ghostlight blossomed from within. There was a spirit tethered to the bone—trapped, like the iron revenants. Wren could make out the dark spike protruding from its forehead in the flickering green glow.

"Come along," he'd said, before stepping into the blackness.

They had been traveling for hours now, the ghostlight just barely penetrating the overwhelming gloom. There was a faint dripping sound and something that might have been the wind howling through distant channels of narrow stone, but otherwise, the world was close and tight, their footsteps crunching and breath panting loud in Wren's ears.

But not loud enough to drown the sense that she was going against her every instinct. Her brain shouted at her to turn back, to run, to put distance between herself and this boy—this *family*. Family had caused her nothing but pain, both recently and, if she looked back, throughout her entire life. The last thing she needed was to put her trust in someone who shared her tainted blood.

And yet . . .

If she wanted to destroy this well, if she wanted to outsmart her father and defeat her mother, if she wanted to stop the regent's plans for war . . . she needed help. In getting there and in tearing it all down, and her brother might just have the answers they needed.

So she wasn't *trusting* him, really. Not yet. He'd have to earn that from her. For now she was simply taking what he'd offered. But she would keep her guard up. Always.

Eventually the ground leveled out, and Wren's boot landed on what was clearly *polished* stone. Whether by hand or the passage of feet over time, she couldn't be sure, but she looked up to see Hawke come to a stop several steps ahead.

A soft tapping sound rang out again, the resonance familiar, and then another skull flickered to life. But this one was mounted on the rough-hewn wall to the right.

It was *human* . . . and it wasn't the only one.

The sound of Hawke's finger tapping the bone seemed to stretch and grow, echoing, along with a quiet word he whispered over and over into the dark.

"Wake."

One after another they blossomed into life, skulls in different sizes and states of erosion, fused with the natural stone and set at eye level like sconces lining a castle corridor.

On and on they went, illuminating a long, low passage that eventually bent out of sight.

"What is this?" Leo asked, sounding as stunned as Wren felt. They were still days from the Breach and the ghostsmith ruins within.

"The throughway," Hawke answered. As he turned around to face them, the ghostlight cast his flesh in sallow shades of sickly green, making him look wholly inhuman. "There are tunnels like this all over the Adamantine foothills. Makes for safe travel for the mancers and their thralls."

"The . . . what?" Julian asked uneasily.

"He means the ghostsmiths," Wren said, a bad taste in her mouth. "*Necro*mancers and their thralls—the undead."

"That's right," Hawke said, eyeing the nearest skull sconce with mild distaste. "The undead don't like the daylight, and we've always had to hide."

"That's because you were exiled," Wren said irritably. The ghostsmiths weren't *victims*. They'd done horrific things, including graverobbing, and the rest of the smiths had banished them. "As punishment for what you'd done. What you clearly continued to do long after."

Though Wren said the words with accusation, this wasn't just Hawke's history. It was *hers*, too, no matter how much she wanted to deny it.

But that's what this was all about. In rejecting her father's ambitions and her mother's schemes, she was rejecting this magic and this heritage. She was rejecting a part of herself she did not want to claim.

And by destroying the well, she was not only rejecting its power but erasing its legacy—denying it the opportunity to continue to take root in the present.

If she succeeded, she could wipe it all away. Then she could go back to being Wren Graven once more.

Bonesmith. Best damn valkyr of her generation.

Neglected daughter of the heir to the House of Bone.

It didn't sound as sweet as it once had.

Instead she'd be a *new* Wren Graven. One not beholden to her father's approval or exiled by her house.

She'd choose her own path.

Up ahead, Hawke lifted his hand, speaking to his amplifier ring. A burst of ghostlight erupted from the bone, coalescing into a ghost-bird that perched on his outstretched arm. A hawk.

The idea that it was *perching* at all fairly broke Wren's brain. It was a ghost—they didn't walk or stand or sit; they hovered. But as it shuffled its feet and shook out its great wings, the entire thing was horribly beautiful.

Wren had the sudden urge to run. It was too bizarre, the magic too strange, but at the same time . . . she couldn't look away.

Another whispered word from Hawke, and the ghost-bird took to the air, soaring down the passage and out of sight.

Ghosts don't fly. That fact had been drilled into her most of her life, but that was because she'd only ever learned about human ghosts. She'd seen bats in the Bonewood and knew in theory that a creature that could fly in life could also fly in death. But animal ghosts were usually so weak, their undead lives so short, that she never paid the concept much mind. Now she was seeing it before her, and it was unsettling.

"That bird, that *ghost*, where did you send it?" Wren asked.

"My familiar?" Hawke asked. Wren had never heard of such a thing. A ghost familiar? Was that like a pet? "I sent Talon ahead. To scout."

He'd *named* it? Definitely like a pet. Sending it ahead to scout seemed reasonable enough, even if she hadn't wholly dismissed her suspicion of him, but whatever skepticism she might have had was momentarily waylaid by the idea that the ghost could travel such a distance. That it could *scout* at all. What remained of its body was on Hawke's finger. It shouldn't have been able to travel more than a few feet from him.

It was extremely difficult to mark the passage of time in the dark, but several more hours passed before Hawke finally brought their party to a stop.

The tunnel had opened enough to make their footsteps echo high above, the ghostlight sconces illuminating what appeared to be a crossroad, the glowing skulls splintering off into three other directions.

And there, perched on a stalagmite, was their ghost-bird scout.

Apparently Wren was staring, because when the spirit took to the air and landed on Hawke's arm once more, he turned to her and asked, "Do you want to pet him? You're a ghostsmith, so you'll be immune to deathrot."

"What—*no*," Wren said, aghast. Yet she continued to stare all the same.

Hawke nodded, expression thoughtful as he stroked the top of the ghost-bird's head tenderly. He seemed completely at ease compared to his other interactions with the undead.

It was good to know that deathrot wouldn't affect her, but that didn't mean she wanted to touch the thing . . . though she found herself wondering what it felt like. Was it icy-cold mist, as she assumed all ghosts were? Or was there texture to be found? Stiff quills under silken feathers? But no—this was a ghost. A spirit. Feathers belonged to the living world, to this creature's *corpse*.

"How?" Wren asked. "The tether . . . How do they leave their bones so far behind? I thought the point of those spikes was to prevent that. I thought that's why you put them in the iron revenants."

"The linchpin," Hawke corrected. "It binds them to their corpse, yes. But it's all in the glyphs. The commands they imbue. Familiars are granted a longer tether, if the ghostsmith wishes it. The iron revenants, and these sconces, are not."

"Do they make them with humans?" Leo asked carefully. "Familiars?"

"Not familiars, no."

"No, instead humans are turned into sconces to light our path," said Julian, nodding his chin at their watchful light sources.

"And soldiers clad in suits of iron to wage war," Wren added. Their eyes met, and for a second things felt as they had in the Breach—when Wren and Julian had finally let their guards down. When they were on the same side.

Julian looked away first, shattering the moment.

Their guards were firmly back in place and stronger than ever, with high walls and deep ditches. Probably moats, too.

Hawke meanwhile was frowning, his gaze darting from his familiar to the ghostlight sconces and back again. "Is it so different from hitching oxen to a plow?"

"*Yes,*" Wren said. "We're talking about people, not animals."

"Servants, then. I've seen them being ordered about. Workers toiling in the mines."

"They do those tasks for *payment*."

"Even oxen get food and shelter for their trouble," added Leo.

"Exactly," Wren said. "What does a ghost get for lighting your way? What does a revenant get for wielding your sword? Nothing. What they get is denied peace."

"But they get to live forever."

"This"—she jabbed a finger at the nearest sconce—"is not living. And existing to serve others is not life."

Hawke considered her. "House of Ghost teachings would disagree with you on that. The aim of all ghostsmiths is to serve our house in life and in death."

"So these are dead ghostsmiths?" Leo asked uncomfortably, glancing around.

"Low-ranking ones, yes. Those of a higher caste served in more dignified ways, some even acting as teachers and advisers."

The undead advising the living? It was madness. "And the iron revenants?" Wren demanded.

"No. They needed to be well-preserved. That was more important than their lineage. The ghostsmiths would use any dead in certain instances, but we preferred our own. To serve in death was the highest honor a ghostsmith could achieve."

Wren wanted to shake him. To shout at him, but this was what he'd been taught. And he didn't understand that to be undead was to be in pain. If Ravenna or anyone else in the ruling Nekros line knew that fact, they weren't likely to share it. The subservience of their people relied on this faulty belief.

After several moments of uncomfortable silence, Hawke muttered under his breath, and Talon disappeared, swirling into shapeless mist before being sucked back inside the amplifier ring.

"We'll rest here," he said, drawing their attention to a structure built into the stone that Wren hadn't noticed until then. The entrance was flanked by pillars, carved similarly to those she had seen in the Breach, with skeletal figures in repeating patterns wrapping around the stone. There were more ghostlight sconces inside, which Hawke awakened, revealing a small square chamber with a hearth against the far wall. There was no furniture or any evidence of recent habitation, but there was an adjoining room where she glimpsed piles of firewood, stacks of blankets, and other odds and ends.

"Who uses this?" Julian asked, peering through the items with interest. Wren suspected he was thinking of the bandit supply caches they had looted above ground.

"Me," Hawke said, putting his staff aside and making himself comfortable. He pushed his skull mask off his head entirely, where it hung upside down around the back of his neck, and kicked off his boots—a strange choice given it was cold enough for Wren to see her breath and a fire had not yet been started. He dug through the foodstuffs, finding a jar of what appeared to be pickled herring and using his dirty fingers to fish out a piece. "There are way stations like this all along the throughway, but I'm the one who stocks them. I'm the only person who needs them, really. Mother doesn't need—" He stopped himself, glancing up at Wren, as if worried about how much mention of their mother she could handle. "She doesn't bother with them. As far as I can tell, it's just me and the wolves."

"Excuse me, *wolves*?" Leo asked, darting a look around the darkened tunnel.

Hawke shrugged, attention on his dinner. "*Something's* getting into the food, anyway."

"Forget the way stations, forget the food," Wren said, dropping her bag. "How long until we get to the well?"

Hawke swallowed his mouthful. "Two days. Maybe three."

"You know what it's made of—how it works?"

"Yes, I think so."

"Then tell me," she ordered. "Everything."

ELEVEN

"I'll start the fire," Julian said, gathering logs from the next room and getting to work. Wren knew she should help make camp, but she was too impatient. She waved her brother on.

He'd barely opened his mouth when a distant rumbling sound echoed from deep within one of the passages, and the ground beneath their feet started to shake. Wren whipped around, alarmed, but the tremors had already stopped, and silence reigned once more.

"What was that?" Leo asked, looking up from where he'd been rifling through the blankets—Wren assumed for something soft enough for a prince to sleep on.

"The well," Hawke said, hands spread in resignation. "It's not stable."

"Is the *tunnel*?" Leo pressed, somewhat shrilly.

"Stable enough," Hawke said, putting aside his jar. "Sometimes there are cave-ins, but it would be much louder if that were the case."

"How comforting," Leo said, returning his attention to the blankets. "Will that threat plague us for the rest of this journey?"

"More or less," Hawke said.

"So this throughway leads directly to the well?" Wren asked.

"Not this exact tunnel, no," Hawke said, staring at his feet. "But yes, we can take the throughway to the well. There are dozens of passages, and most feed directly into the necropolis."

"The necropolis," Wren said, stealing one of Leo's rejected blankets and throwing it onto the ground to sit on. "Is that where we saw you before? Julian and I?"

"That was Hollow Hall, the palace at the heart of the city—named after the House of Bone's seat," he added, referencing Marrow Hall in the Bonelands. "Behind it is the Keeper's Cathedral, another important monument. Much has been lost to the quakes, but those two structures remain. The well, however, is beneath them both. If we want to get there undetected, we'll have to avoid both the temple and the palace to reach it. Luckily, I know a way."

Now that Leo had found a suitable blanket, he settled himself down and withdrew his golden lockpicks again, angling his hands toward the glow of Julian's steadily growing fire as he started to work on his manacles. Wren inched closer, hoping he would handle hers next.

"And then what?" Julian asked, back turned to them as he stoked the flames. "Can we actually destroy this thing? Or is it some half-assed idea she's cooked up?"

Well, that was unnecessarily aggressive.

Though valid.

She looked at her brother, who continued to stare at the ground rather than at any of them. "I don't know. I don't think anybody has ever tried."

Julian snorted. "Of course not. That thing turns any average smith into a god, wielding powers that are supposed to be impossible."

Wren could only assume that the "average" part was aimed at her. Another jab. She pinched her lips together to stop from lashing out, though the effort clearly showed on her face, if the sidelong look Leo gave her was any indication.

"Crushing a field of bodies into dust and shattering a bone inside a living arm," Julian muttered. "Who wouldn't want that?"

Wren's anger surged, made hotter with shame. "That's why we're destroying it," she snapped. "Because some of us *don't* want that."

Julian cast her a look over his shoulder, mouth open as if to retort—but it seemed he thought better of it, returning his attention to the fire.

Wren stared at his back, his silence only making her angrier. But before she could say something she'd surely regret, Julian spoke into the flames.

"Why not?" he asked softly. "I've only known you to be ambitious. Why don't you want the power? Think of the respect you'd command, the *hero* you could be."

Wren couldn't believe her ears. "That's exactly what Locke Graven was thinking, and look how that turned out!"

"You're not him."

"No, I'm worse."

He turned, frowning, but it was Leo who spoke. "You don't know that."

Julian, meanwhile, shot her an assessing look. "What are you so afraid of?"

Afraid? Wren spluttered, trying to find an answer. "Iron revenants tearing down the Border Wall, for a start!"

"And?"

"*And?* Undead roaming free, swallowing up the Dominions. Being the *reason* it all goes to shit—"

"But you're not the reason."

Wren held up her hand with the ring. "But I *could* be! If I'm afraid of anything, it's myself."

It wasn't just Julian staring at her now, but Leo and Hawke too.

Wren shot to her feet. "Look what Locke did, and he was a *good* person. Honorable and self-sacrificing and . . . and I'm not. He wanted to be a hero, to save the world. All I've ever wanted was to save myself."

"That's not true," said Leo, his voice gentle. "What about me?"

"I think Julian was right there," Wren said, laughing humorlessly. "I only wanted to rescue you because it helped me. That's where it started. That's what motivated me. I'm selfish, reckless, and don't think things through." She raised her brows at Julian, daring him to contradict what he had already stated—several times. "Is that the kind of person you think should have limitless power?"

He shook his head. "No one should."

"Exactly," Wren said, gathering herself and her scattered emotions. Her heart was racing, her palms clammy with sweat. "So we'll destroy it."

She thumped back onto her blanket, wrapping her arms around her knees.

When Leo reached for her hand, she flinched, only to realize he was actually trying to take hold of her manacle so he could unlock it.

"Oh, thanks," Wren muttered.

Leo winked as he bent over the lock with his golden picks. "Can you tell us what it's made of, this well? How it works?" he asked Hawke. Wren felt Julian's eyes on her but refused to look up to meet them.

"It's a well like any other," Hawke said. "Except instead of drawing up water, it's drawing up magic. It pools deep underground. What most smiths access is what leaches into the soil and our respective materials. Iron ore, nuggets of gold"—he nodded at both Julian and Leo in turn before his gaze landed on Wren—"or bones. But like water, if you want more, you have to go directly to the source. And that's what the ancient ghostsmiths did. They dug deeper and deeper until they found it: raw magic, great big veins of it. Then they built a well to trap the power and draw it up to the surface."

"Raw magic," Wren repeated, recalling when Hawke had created that iron revenant. The way he had glowed with power.

"The part of it you've seen was actually a gathering pool, a basin that fills with magic from the well below. There are several others in the city."

"And they're leaking," Wren said, recalling the cracks surrounding the pool in the throne room. "Is that what's causing the quakes?"

Hawke nodded. "Magic is not meant to be contained in such a way. It isn't slow and steady like water. It is active. Violent. Like lava."

"So you basically drilled into a volcano?" Julian demanded. "And it's only a matter of time before it erupts?"

"It already has, hasn't it?" asked Leo. "The Breach. The overmining."

"Oh, it wasn't the mining," Hawke said matter-of-factly.

Julian latched on to the words. "It wasn't?" He'd already suspected as much when he'd passed through the mine and seen evidence of strange digging patterns.

"It was Ravenna."

Wren's mouth fell open. "Wait, what?" Wren mentally rifled through everything she'd overheard from Odile but didn't recall any mention of her mother actually *causing* the Breach.

"Well, not *just* her. Her and our grandparents. They'd been trying to find the old ruins for years. When the ironsmiths finally got close enough, Ravenna and her parents snuck into their mine. They . . . *convinced* a stonesmith to divert a tunnel, and there it was. But the sudden exposure of all that magic resulted in the Breach, and it collapsed on them. Killing everyone but our mother. She still hasn't found their bodies, but she got what she wanted in the end. What they all wanted."

"Death?" asked Leo, sounding more than mildly confused.

"Power," Hawke clarified. "The same power that built all this." He waved his hand to indicate the throughway and what lay beyond it: the lost ghostsmith kingdom. He leaned back, straightening his legs as he continued to speak. "Any smith who touches it will find their magic increased, and new powers will surface. No, that's not right." He frowned. "Not *new* powers, but latent ones—like your ghostsmith abilities," he said, nodding at Wren. "And for me, maybe bonesmith ones. Some limitations, like distance and the law of ratios . . . they are different. Expanded. In some cases, they no longer exist. You, for instance," he said, turning to Leo. "Gold is one of the softest metals. Malleable, whereas iron is not."

"That's right," said Leo. "I can soften and mold it with my bare hands"—he raised one of his lockpicks and bent it in the middle, as if it were made of straw, only to run his fingers over it in a practiced swipe, straightening it once more—"or my tongue." He waggled his brows at Julian, who rolled his eyes, but it was clear he was fighting back a smile. Wren was inordinately jealous.

Hawke looked between them, trying to understand the joke, then seemed to give up with a shrug. "Yes, well, I suspect if *you* were to draw from the well, you could even liquefy it. Perhaps pull it directly from the earth."

Wren's second manacle clicked loose, and Leo let out a low whistle. "Maybe Daddy would finally pay attention to me."

Wren snorted, rubbing gratefully at her bare skin, while Leo gestured for Julian's still-shackled wrist.

He held it out but wore an expression of distaste. "Don't say Daddy."

Wren shook her head. Again, Hawke watched the scene with something like confused fascination. She wondered if he'd interacted much with people who weren't his mother.

Normal people.

Although, did Leopold Valorian, the Gold Prince and spare's spare; Julian Knight, the almost-assassinated heir apparent to a fallen house; and Wren "ghostsmith" Graven, failed valkyr, exiled bonesmith, and daughter of a betrayer or a murderer (or both), *really* count as normal?

"Iron, on the other hand . . . well, it has unique properties of its own," Hawke continued.

"Such as?" Julian asked.

"Well, iron can be magnetized, can it not?"

Julian nodded. "There are naturally occurring magnets—an iron oxide called magnetite—that can be used to add a magnetic charge to regular iron."

"I suspect the well's magic would provide all the charge you'd need."

Julian blinked. "So you could turn *any* iron into a magnet? Just with this magic and your hands?"

Hawke shrugged. "I don't see why not."

"Imagine you magnetized your hand," Leo said. "You'd never drop your sword."

"I never drop my sword anyway," Julian said defensively, though they all knew that to be untrue. The dent he'd had to repair on his helmet—courtesy of Leo—had been proof of that. "Most of the time," he added under his breath.

Wren turned her attention back to Hawke. "Does it do anything else on its own besides raise the dead? Does it, I don't know . . . change those *without* magic? Could it give them smith abilities?"

Hawke considered. "I don't think so. It's been leaking into the ground for years now, and I've not heard mention of any newly made smiths in the area."

"Would you have?" Wren asked dubiously, watching as the lock clicked on Julian's wrist, the final manacle dropping to the ground with a clatter and a murmured word of thanks. "Do you have much interaction with the rest of the Breachlands?"

Hawke's expression shuttered, and she got the feeling that she'd hit on a touchy subject, though it hadn't been her intention. "I keep up on the gossip." She waited for him to elaborate, and he shrugged self-consciously. "I eavesdrop. Or have *them* do it for me."

Wren didn't know if he meant regular undead and walking revenants or his familiar, but either way, the idea was fascinating. And disturbing.

"Did you know we were here?" she asked abruptly. He cocked his head at her. "When Julian and I first entered the Haunted Territory, there were revenants in the Norwood telling us to go. Did they report to you? Did you order them to keep us out?"

Hawke looked away. "I ordered them to keep *everyone* out. We've enough corpses already, we don't need any more, so I use some of the revenants to protect the perimeter."

"Protect?" Julian practically squawked. "They attacked us."

"That's because I attacked *them*, remember?" Wren reminded him, pointing a finger at her chest. "Reckless."

He gave her a look that was somehow both satisfied at being right *then* and annoyed at being wrong *now*.

"Their obedience is not absolute," Hawke said. "Especially as they stray too far from my presence. As a vessel, I can only wield so much magic, and they are not bound to me the way familiars are—through amplifiers and constant contact. Still, better one dead and the rest turned back in fear than the whole party taken down, no?" He looked between them anxiously, as if genuinely unsure.

"Grim, but I suppose the math does add up," said Leo.

"So, did you order them to protect the perimeter on the Corpse Queen's orders?" Wren asked. "Or your own?"

"Those orders were mine. She would not care either way. She does not concern herself with such matters—she's focused on her own ambitions. When it comes to the living and the undead, she is . . . ruthless."

Despite the growing warmth of the fire, a chill ran its finger down Wren's spine. She realized that the true challenge here would likely not be the destruction of the well but, rather, the defeat of the Corpse Queen.

"Where is she now? Your mo—the queen?" asked Julian, glancing at Wren as if unsure how to address the woman. His guess was as good as hers. Wren felt no connection to her, despite the blood that bound them. Perhaps it was better that way. It would make the prospect of coming face-to-face with her, of fighting against her, easier. "And where are the iron revenants? We'll have to get past them both if we're to have any shot at this."

Despite the coldness between them, Wren felt a flush of warm relief that he still seemed on board with her plan, however "half-assed."

That he was still willing to try.

"Ravenna is in the palace, awaiting my return. If we are careful, we can slip by her undetected. By the time she realizes something is amiss, we'll already be in position. As for the iron revenants, they are in the Keeper's Cathedral. They cannot be mobilized in strength without me. There are . . . too many."

"*How* many?" Wren whispered.

Hawke shuffled his feet. "I am unsure of the exact number."

"We don't blame you," Leo said gently. "For whatever it is she made you do."

Wren glanced at Leo appreciatively. He always knew what to say.

Hawke expelled a breath and looked up. "Many. A hundred at least."

Wren had feared as much, but hearing the number said aloud caused a sense of bleak purpose to settle over the group.

"Even if we get past Ravenna *and* the iron revenants, even if we make it safely to the well . . . we still don't know how to destroy this thing," said Julian, bringing the conversation back to the task at hand.

"I think I do," Hawke replied evenly.

Wren stared at him. "How?"

"Well," Hawke began, shifting forward slightly. "In order to create the well, ancient ghostsmiths had to find a material that attracted and absorbed magic."

Leo straightened, as if he'd caught on to something Wren had yet to piece together.

"One they had mastery over," Hawke continued, and now Wren understood.

"Hang on; you're telling me the well is made of *undead*?"

"No," Julian said at once.

"Once they'd delved deep enough into the earth to find the magic, they needed a way to draw it up. What better way than with undead, the source and focus of their own unique magic?"

"I expect any smith material would work, in theory," Leo said thoughtfully. "If it'd been ironsmiths or goldsmiths, they could have built a well of solid iron or gold to achieve the same effect."

"But we're talking about undead," Wren argued. "*Ghosts.* How could a structure be made of something incorporeal?"

"Can you think of no way to make them corporeal?" Hawke asked quietly.

"Revenants," Julian said.

Wren looked to Hawke for confirmation. "So are they bound to their bones, then? Like the iron revenants? With those linchpins?"

Hawke inclined his head. "It's the best way to keep the well strong. The ghost is what keeps undead bones intact over centuries. If they were to leave their bones behind, they would rot faster, and the well would leak even more than it already is."

"You said you know how to destroy it," Leo said slowly, as if trying to puzzle it out as he spoke.

"It's obvious, isn't it?" Hawke said. "Destroy the bones and you destroy the well."

All three of them turned to stare at Wren. "Destroy the bones? That won't free the ghosts. . . . It'll just give them nowhere to go."

"It will weaken them," Hawke said. "And if you destroy the bones thoroughly enough, they will be little more than vapor, unable to draw in more magic."

Wren lurched to her feet. She felt everyone's eyes on her, Julian's most of all. They had *just* been talking about this. She did not want to be another Locke Graven, trying to save the world and leaving lives shattered in her wake.

"How many undead are we talking here?" asked Leo.

"Hundreds."

Wren felt sick. "No, there's . . . No. There has to be another way."

"Sacrifice hundreds of souls to save thousands? To save the Dominions?" asked Hawke. "Seems a worthy price to me."

Wren squeezed her eyes shut. *Was* it a worthy price? Had it been, even then? Locke had stopped a war, after all. Surely *more* would have perished had he not done what he'd done. Civilians. Innocents.

But eternal damnation . . . That was a terrible cost indeed.

"The iron revenants—what will become of them if the well is destroyed?" Wren asked.

"The well's magic was already used to make them, but it must be used *again* to send them marching. I can command one or two at a time, but to send all of them at once, especially over such a distance? The well is a necessity. If it's destroyed, that power will not be available. They'll essentially be stuck here."

It would still be a monumental task to eliminate them, but at least they wouldn't be unleashed upon the Dominions. Wren's heart soared at the thought of destroying both the well *and* immobilizing the iron revenants in the same fell swoop, but then she remembered what she'd have to do to make that happen. . . .

"Are you *sure* about this?" Julian asked Hawke, tearing his gaze from Wren. "How can you know this will work?"

"I can't," Hawke said. "It's just a guess. But I know what it's made of. And I understand magic. It will work. It *has* to."

"This is a terrible idea," Julian said. "We could walk all the way there, and he could be *wrong*. We can't risk our lives based on a hunch."

Though he was, in some ways, saying exactly what Wren was thinking, she also knew that they likely wouldn't get another chance at this. They had to try. And however limited Hawke's knowledge was, it still far outstripped their own.

"Have you got a better idea?" she said. "We asked how to destroy it, and he told us."

"So you're okay with this?" Julian asked, brows raised.

"No, I—I don't know, but at least it's *something*."

"We left the Breachfort being hunted by both sides and with no idea how to destroy the well," Leo said reasonably. "At least we're on the right path."

"Exactly," Wren said. "We've got a plan and a guide, and we found a route that will keep us out of sight of both your uncle and my father. I think we're doing pretty well so far."

"I think you've got low standards," Julian scoffed.

Wren smiled. Cocked her head. "I kissed you, didn't I? I guess you're right."

TWELVE

Things were decidedly *tense* as they prepared to bed down for the night.

Wren stared at the back of Julian's head, which he had treated her to the second those words came out of her mouth.

I kissed you, didn't I? I guess you're right.

Wren sighed.

It had been immature.

And Julian had every right to be angry at her, forever, for what she'd done.

But that didn't mean she had to be happy about it. That she had to suffer it with grace and dignity.

No. She'd suffer as she'd always suffered, with a scowl and a bad attitude.

But for now, with the fire burning low and rest their goal, she suffered in silence.

Sleep descended with the weight of a heavy blanket, leaving Wren utterly disoriented when she was awoken sometime later by a flash of ghostlight. She blinked in confusion, reminding herself of where she was and who she was with, before squinting into the distance at a low, prowling shape.

A ghost?

But no . . . this figure wasn't as bright or as clearly defined. Its edges flickered and blurred, distorted by the rotting corpse that encased it. A revenant, then.

Wren lurched upright. "Hawke?" she whispered, but he was gone—nowhere to be found in the pressing darkness. He'd told them he would keep watch, and he *was* the best one to help if trouble came. But trouble was here . . . and he was not.

Luckily, Wren was. She could command the undead, even if the ability was distasteful to her, and she was a bonesmith. They could certainly do worse.

"Julian," she muttered, shoving his armored shoulder. He'd chosen to sleep in full plate—everything but his helmet—despite how uncomfortable it must be. In fairness, Wren still wore her armor, too, but at least hers would actually serve a purpose down here. His was surely just for mental comfort, though she supposed it came in handy right now, making him ready at a moment's notice. "Leo," she added, kicking him—mostly because he was out of reach and partly, perhaps, to get him back for their time sleeping together in the cellar. "Get up!"

Julian responded first, alert as always and quick to leap to his feet. Leo stumbled after him. "What is it?"

Wren wasn't quite sure yet. Her senses were tingling, but the smoldering fire did little to illuminate their quarry, and all the ghost-light sconces had gone out.

"Wake," Wren muttered. The nearest sconce flickered but remained dormant. She focused, twisting her ring, and put all her intention into it. "Wake!"

The sconces blazed to life all around, flaring bright enough for Julian and Leo to cry out, but eyes streaming, Wren forced herself to stare at the undead as it approached.

It was hunched, crawling . . . No, it was four-legged, an *animal* revenant. The concept had never even occurred to her, since animal spirits rarely remained long in the world. But they were in the Breach-lands. That rule no longer applied.

As it moved into the ghostlight, she saw a bloody gray pelt and wide, gaping jaws.

What had Hawke said about *wolves*?

A low, rumbling growl echoed in Wren's ears. Animal undead were *usually* peaceful, but not always. Even they could be worked up into a frenzy or lash out at the living.

Before she could warn the others, who wouldn't have heard the growl, another louder, deeper rumble echoed down the passage, one she felt through her feet and that Julian and Leo definitely heard.

"Was that—" Leo asked, whirling on the spot.

"The tunnel," Julian said gravely, shoving his helmet back on. The sound seemed to come from directly ahead of them, the same as the revenant. "This creature is likely fleeing it."

"Yeah, right toward us," Wren said.

"Perfect," said Leo. "Where is your brother?"

"I don't know. Get behind me," Wren ordered, withdrawing her blades. She stepped out into the middle of the crossroad, hoping to head the revenant off. It approached from the northern tunnel, while they had arrived from the south. The other two passages were dark, the sconces there still unlit.

A *snick* and a rattle told Wren that Julian had released his whip sword, and she trusted him to protect Leo as she took on the revenant wolf.

"Stop," Wren said, loud and clear. She felt the familiar vibration in her vocal cords, the low timbre that ghostsmith magic drew out of her.

The wolf was close enough now that Wren could see its hairless tail, bony and sharp, the trailing bits of fur and flesh that dragged behind it. The revenant paused, and relief swept through her—but too soon.

The creature growled again, lower and more threatening, and its spirit flared larger, mimicking the way a living wolf's hair would stand on end, its hackles raised.

"Stop," Wren said again, voice shaking slightly. "STOP!"

It didn't heed her words. It continued to stalk her. Retreating slowly, Wren glanced down at the ring on her hand. Had the magic run out? But she'd just activated the sconces without much difficulty. What had changed?

She stared into the wolf's empty eye sockets, ghostlight shining through. Then its rotted muscles bunched, its bones creaking as it prepared to pounce.

"No!" she shouted, but it didn't matter.

It lunged, jaws gaping wide, and Wren froze, waiting for the moment it would latch on to her skin. Distantly, she found herself hoping her brother was right when he said she was immune to deathrot. She also found herself wondering if she would survive that threat only to have those razor-sharp teeth rip her throat out instead.

Before she could meet her fate, there was another blaze of ghostlight. Wren feared more revenants, but instead a smaller ghostly figure—another animal?—whipped past, running straight at the wolf. Its sudden appearance caused the wolf to rear back in confusion, buying time for Hawke to step in front of Wren, putting himself between her and the onrushing danger.

As the two undead animals circled each other, one ghost and one revenant, Wren's brother turned to her and the others. He wore his skull mask again, his eyes glinting ghostly green in the darkness.

"Make for the eastern passage. Quick. I'll hold it off."

Wren's brain was stuttering over what had happened. Was that another ghost familiar? And why didn't Hawke just command the wolf to back down like the other revenants?

"Wren," came Julian's voice, close by her ear. "Come on."

She gave her head a shake and lifted her swords, following Julian and Leo as they ran toward the eastern passage.

Wren couldn't bring herself to speak, afraid the magic she so loathed had failed her entirely, so she flicked the nearest sconce instead. It worked, awakening the ghost within as surely as her voice, and a measure of relief swept through her as she moved down the passage, bringing them to life one at a time.

While Leo led the way, Julian remained next to Wren, guiding her with a touch on her shoulder while she walked backward, guarding their retreat.

The passage continued on, shadowy, damp, and silent—until it wasn't.

The ground trembled underfoot once more, closer than before, and a burst of white light oozed from a crack that opened in the wall next to them.

It dissipated like steam as soon as it hit the air, telling Wren what it was at once: magic. Raw magic, *here*, days from the Breach.

"The well," she said, distant groans and creaks warning them that this was not the last of the tremors.

Sheathing one of her blades, she reached a hand toward the rivulets of magic but fell short of actually touching it. "There must be veins of magic throughout the Breachlands."

"That's why revenants rise up all around, not just in the Breach," Julian said, coming to stand next to her. "The land itself is oversaturated."

Leo remained several paces away from them, apparently uninterested in the magical revelation. "Fascinating as that is, I don't fancy being here when that wolf catches up *or* when this tunnel caves—"

Before he could finish the sentence, the ground shook again, so powerfully that Wren stumbled, staggering into the wall of the passage near the magical leak. A fresh crack rippled through the stone beneath her palm with an accompanying clap and boom, like thunder.

Wren yanked her hand away, the stone continuing to splinter, the crack climbing up the wall and to the ceiling.

The sound grew along with the damage, until the racket was nearly earsplitting and seemed to come from everywhere at once.

Leo shouted something, but the noise drowned him out, while Julian was looking left and right, trying to track the destruction.

Then there was a final, rumbling crunch from above, and a massive piece of stone started to shake loose.

All Wren could do was stare, stupefied, as death rushed down to meet her.

But Julian met it first.

With his left hand—his iron hand—extended, he leapt into harm's way, stopping the block's descent with an echoing clang as he stood over Wren. She'd flinched and ducked down, and now stared, awestruck, at the sight of him holding the ceiling up to protect her from being crushed.

The stone had crashed into him with so much force, and the iron of his hand was so strong, that the surface of the rock crumbled around his fingers, fractures spidering out like cobwebs.

His arm shook, his eyes wide as his body started to tremble. The stone above them swayed, a cascade of pebbles and dust raining down on them, but he held his position.

For now.

"Go," he gasped out, blinking down at her. Wren hesitated—how could she leave him like this?—but then did as told, because she couldn't help him, either. She scrambled out from underneath him just as the weight brought him down, hard, onto one ironclad knee.

The impact *thunk*ed loudly, and Julian expelled a heavy breath, raising his other arm in an attempt to lighten the load—but it wasn't reinforced with iron. It was flesh and blood and would not hold.

Wren collided with Leo, who had run forward, and now the pair of them watched helplessly as Julian struggled to keep his hold.

His gaze darted around, as if seeking escape, before landing squarely on Wren's. There was resignation there, his brows angled and his mouth tense.

But there was something else she couldn't place. Anger? Regret?

Longing?

Whatever it was, the unspoken sentiment hit Wren like an arrow to the heart. What was she *doing,* standing here and watching while he risked his life for her?

While he died for her?

That was not how this worked between them. They fought *together,* they battled and brawled *side by side.* And when death came knocking, they faced it head-on.

Wren took a step forward, but Leo held her arm. She attempted to shake him off, but before she could lose him, there was another echoing groan.

An infinitesimal pause of silence, and then—a deluge.

The ceiling split open, releasing an avalanche of rocks, burying Julian within.

THIRTEEN

There was a cacophony of sound.

There was sudden, suffocating darkness.

And there was pain.

Julian crouched, tucking in on himself and doing the only thing he could do: wait.

He wondered if, after all that had happened, this was how he'd die. That he could survive a childhood surrounded by undead, an assassination attempt by a murderous uncle, and traveling into the actual Breach, only to succumb to a rockslide.

Only to be buried alive.

His breath started to thin, air wheezing into his lungs in short, sharp gasps.

He wondered if this was how his mother had felt before the end. She'd died when a tunnel collapsed on her while trying to evacuate a mine after the Breach.

Buried, just like Julian.

His chest tightened further at the thought.

Had she been afraid? Or contented, knowing she'd died doing the right thing?

Did she have regrets?

Surely she had. She'd left a son and a husband behind.

Julian had no such ties, and yet . . . he had regrets of his own. He had a sister, after all. And his murderous uncle was still regent of the Iron Citadel.

But instead of dwelling on those far more pressing concerns, he found himself thinking of black lips and fierce, bone-colored eyes. Of pale skin, warm spring water, and clinging white mist . . .

Minutes or hours passed, he couldn't be sure, but eventually he became aware of the silence. The deafening sounds of falling rocks had stopped, and he dared to open his eyes.

He expected pure blackness—but instead there was a grayish light before him, illuminating his foot on the ground, his other knee next to it. His hands were above his head, and he shifted them carefully, causing a wash of rubble to rain down on him.

He surveyed his body, seeking life-ending damage . . . but he found none. His armor—scratched and dinged but otherwise intact—had done its job, and strangely enough, the large hunk of stone that he'd been holding above his head had actually been his salvation. It had taken the worst of the impact, sliding sideways off Julian's hands to slam hard into the ground, creating a kind of sloping roof above him. Protecting him.

What surrounded him was smaller debris, pebbles and shale and the odd larger stone.

Beams of light shone through, showing him that he wasn't as buried as he'd thought.

Showing him the way out.

Gathering his strength and expelling a breath, Julian stood, heaving with his thighs to send the massive block falling to the side and the last dregs of the rockslide cascading off his shoulders.

He emerged, standing above the pile like a climber atop a mountain.

"Julian!" Wren shrieked, and he looked around to see her and Leopold digging through the mess, their hands filthy and their faces smeared with dirt. And was that . . . ? Were there tears on Wren's cheeks?

She clambered over the rocks, heedless of shifting scree and uneven footing, until she collided with him, her hands on his face, on his chest, seeking blood and wounds that weren't there.

"I'm all right," he heard himself saying, unable to tear his gaze away from her expression—so panic-stricken, so stripped bare. So honest. "I'm all right."

Finally, the words penetrated. She blinked up at him, her hands going still. Then, abruptly, she let go.

Julian clenched his jaw, trying to remember why hating her was so important. Why it had been thoughts of her—and not his anger—that had kept him company at the end.

"So it's true what they say about ironsmiths," Leopold said, extending a hand to help first Wren and then Julian down.

"What do they say?"

"You're hard to kill."

Julian huffed out a breath and shook his head. Leopold looked pleased to have wrought even that much of a reaction out of him. The three of them gathered their breath for a moment, coughing in the haze of dust that floated in the air. Julian spotted his sword, which he'd dropped in order to catch the falling ceiling. He lifted it now, checking it quickly for damage, while Wren also collected her abandoned blade from the ground.

The sudden clatter of rocks sent him whirling around, seeking the source of the next deluge, only to find Hawke climbing over the pile of stones. His mask was dangling off the back of his neck again, his pale hair standing on end and his forehead shining with sweat.

"The wolf?" Wren asked. Julian lifted his sword, body poised for action, and Wren did the same.

"Distracted, for now," Hawke wheezed, as if he'd run here.

"Now what?" Julian asked, peering around. The collapsed tunnel had trapped them, and it was clearly unsafe to turn back with a revenant wolf on the loose.

Hawke was examining the cave-in blocking their path—or rather, the ceiling above the cave-in.

Julian copied him, and his jaw dropped.

There was an opening to the stars. The rockfall had clouded the passage with enough dust to mask both the sight and the scent, but Julian seized the newfound opportunity, leaping onto the nearest stone.

"It's narrow," he said, though the sliver of sky that was visible from the ground was actually wider than it appeared. "But we should fit."

When he glanced down, it was to see both Hawke and Wren's heads snap back the way they had come, in the direction of the intersecting tunnels, as if they'd heard something. Julian imagined a ghostly wolf's howl and fought off a chill of revulsion.

As Leopold started to move, Wren flung out an arresting hand. "We need to get to the well."

"We will," Hawke said.

"It's not safe for us out there," Wren continued, glancing at Julian, her tone bordering on frantic. "We can't risk being seen. You said you'd take us to the well. You promised, and—"

"You won't be seen," Hawke insisted. "Not by those searching for you." Climbing up next to Julian, he peered out of the opening above. There wasn't much to see but the night sky and distant peaks. "We're going to come out into the southern tip of the Horseshoe Valley. It's west of the road, hemmed in by the Adamantine foothills. No Breachfort patrols or Red Guard riders will cross our path."

Julian's stomach dropped. "Horseshoe Valley?"

Hawke hesitated, darting a guilty look his way. "That's right."

Wren and Leopold stared up at them, uncomprehending. But also unmoving.

"Look, it's either this," Hawke said, speaking directly to his sister, "or we face down an angry revenant wolf in tight quarters. *We* might be fine. But them?" He jerked his chin at Julian and Leopold.

That's what did it.

"Fine," Wren snapped. She sheathed her blade and shoved Leopold forward after Hawke, who had already pulled himself through the opening with Julian's help.

Heart hammering in his chest and the imagined scrabble of claws echoing in his ears, Julian reached a gloved hand for Wren.

She looked at it. "You first," she insisted, and Julian scowled.

"You need my help to get up."

"If that wolf—"

"*Wren*," he said, his tone brooking no argument.

She took his hand.

† † † †

Julian scrambled out of the crack in the ground a little more sloppily than he wished, though the others didn't seem to notice. Despite his insistence that Wren go before him, he *was* afraid the wolf would grab hold of his dangling foot and drag him down, but he made it to the surface unscathed. Standing, he took in a vast sea of stars glittering in the bruised purple sky of predawn.

Hawke was leading the way ahead, climbing a steep slope that rose to their left, presumably to get some kind of vantage point. Once Julian joined them, he, Leopold, and Wren followed.

When Julian crested the rise, the air left his chest.

There it was.

Nestled in the heart of Horseshoe Valley, a massive lake enveloped the landscape, reflecting the stars and concealing what truly lay beneath.

"Scenic," Leopold said absently. Julian held his tongue, waiting . . . "Hang on," the prince continued, brows lowering as he squinted into the distance. "Is that—are those buildings poking out of the water?"

"Welcome to Laketown." Julian sighed, taking in the scene with a heavy sense of dread.

"Laketown?" Leopold repeated, coming to stand next to him. "Sounds familiar."

"It should," Julian said, unable to keep the edge from his voice. It had once been a bustling center and the heart of the Ironlands. "It was our largest city."

"The Laketown Flood," Leopold said, realization dawning. "The Breach did this."

"It was one of the first catastrophes," Julian said, throat tight. "Everyone's attention was on the mines: getting people out, stabilizing structures, salvaging what tools and materials they could. No one was looking farther south. You remember the aqueducts at Caston?"

He turned that question to Wren, who nodded. "We had a complex system of dams to harness the water for mills and other machinery, but also to make mines in places like Caston possible, since they would have been submerged otherwise. The largest dam—just south of the Norwood—burst. The rush of water flooded the man-made lake next to the city, drowning it in a day. Some people got out, but most . . . There must be thousands of dead down there."

Julian had never been here, but he'd heard tell of it.

In truth, he'd never *wanted* to see it. Another reminder of the House of Iron's inability to protect their people.

While the lake was huge and stretched from the base of steep mountain peaks on each side, its surface was not unbroken, as Leopold had noticed. Buildings poked through the water like tombstones in a cemetery, marking the final resting place of those poor souls trapped below. There was a faint hint of ghostlight, difficult to discern in the lightening sky, but it was there, flickering beneath the water or glowing from darkened windows.

"So it's a literal fucking ghost town?" Wren asked with her usual tact, rounding angrily on her brother. "And you want to take us there?"

"Around it," he clarified. "There's a way back into the throughway on the other side. Besides, it's water. Most of the undead there are trapped beneath the surface."

Most.

"I'd rather take my chances with the revenant wolf," Wren muttered. "How much will this slow us down?" she asked, still not convinced. Her stubbornness knew no bounds. "If we have to circle an *entire* lake—"

"Oh no, not the whole lake," Hawke said easily, as if this solved everything.

"Half a lake, then," Wren said with exasperation. "We need to get back inside as quickly as possible."

"Then let's stop dawdling," Julian cut in. "We can't go back the way we came. We have to move forward."

He met Wren's eyes, and something unspoken passed between them. A secondary meaning to the words.

They had to move forward.

Julian was trying. He was *trying*, but the weight of the past sat heavy on his shoulders, the burden substantial enough to pin him in place as thoroughly as that rockslide.

And it wasn't just her.

It was this place—the Breachlands in general and Laketown in particular. There were reminders of his family's failures everywhere.

They hadn't caused the Breach, as originally believed, but they *had* allowed Ravenna and her ghostsmith faction to fester right under their noses, and when the ghostsmiths had gotten what they'd wanted, the House of Iron had been powerless to stop it.

His mother had tried to fix things, after the Breach. She had tried to save people, but she had lost her life instead. His father, meanwhile, had lost himself long before he'd died, and now Julian had allowed his scheming uncle to step into his father's place and rule these lands unchallenged. Julian had thought he'd needed the help, needed someone to show him the way. But what had Francis actually shown Julian? How to use fear to gain subservience? Because, looking back, Julian realized with a pang that he'd never loved or even respected the man, not really. He'd been afraid of him.

Julian *had* to make these things right. Otherwise, his whole family would be remembered as failures, the ones who'd doomed their house and these lands.

History was told by the victors, and Julian had already seen this in action through the lies told west of the Wall about the Breach and the Uprising. He could only imagine the story his uncle would spin if his plans came to fruition. He'd already started by postering the Breachlands and branding Julian as a traitor and a kidnapper.

If Julian died without fixing this, without making things right . . .

No.

He *would* succeed where his parents had failed. He had to.

Besides, he had allies that his parents hadn't had. He glanced at Wren, fierce and dangerous; at Hawke, their ghostsmith guide; *and* he had Prince Leopold Valorian on his side. Not the most useful in a fight, but his word would hold weight when all this was through.

Of course, to make full use of the people before him, Julian had to *trust* them.

He had to trust Wren.

But he *had* trusted her. And look what had happened.

She had betrayed him, just as his uncle had.

But . . . Wren had apologized. His uncle never had, not for what he'd done to Julian's father and certainly not for what he'd done to Julian himself. What he continued to do.

Thinking back on the moment in the throughway when the tunnel had started to collapse, Julian hadn't hesitated. Hadn't thought of betrayal or resentment.

Hadn't even considered his anger, his frustration, or his lack of trust. He'd acted to save her, even at risk to himself.

Perhaps his body had already started to do what his mind refused to acknowledge.

I have to forgive her.

If only to move forward. If only to *finish* this. To ensure what had happened in Laketown never happened again.

"Ready?" Wren asked, drawing Julian back to the present. Hawke had started to pick a way down to the rocky shore, Leopold just behind him.

Julian looked at her. "Yes."

FOURTEEN

For Wren, it wasn't just the sight of Laketown.

It was the *feel.*

She could sense them there, under the water. Countless bones and their earthbound ghosts, trapped in a way that was wholly different from the battlefield she'd stumbled across with Julian. At least those undead were beyond consciousness, their existence little more than the impression their shattered bones left in Wren's mind—dust on the wind.

Of course, that had also been before she had awakened her other abilities. Her ghostsmith abilities. Now her senses were deeper and more dynamic. She felt not just bones but *ghosts.*

And the ghosts of these undead . . . they were aware of their circumstances and railed against them. They pushed hard against their shackles. Yearning . . . reaching.

In fact, she could almost *hear* them. Murmurs and pleas. Moans and wordless, shapeless laments.

Wren twisted the ring on her finger, toying with the idea of removing it, wanting to free herself from their haunting cries. But while that might dim her ghostsmith senses, it wouldn't obscure them entirely.

She'd heard the undead without it before, after all.

Thinking about her magic caused a new question to surface in her mind.

"How come that revenant wolf didn't obey me?" Wren asked her brother, sidling up to him as he picked a way across the sloping ground toward the lake's edge. Leo was slipping on the uneven ground, and when Julian withdrew his staff to use as a walking stick, Leo insisted on holding his arm, like an elderly relative needing an escort. Or a courting couple out on a walk in the countryside.

"Huh?" Hawke asked, using his own staff to test the ground underfoot.

"The revenant wolf. I tried to command it to stop, but it didn't obey me. And you—you didn't even try."

"Why would I? It wouldn't listen."

"Wouldn't . . . ?" Wren trailed off. "You mean because it's an animal?"

Hawke glanced up at her, smiling slightly. "Would you expect a *living* wolf to obey your commands?"

"No—but—the magic," Wren spluttered. "I thought it was a form of compulsion."

He paused, tugging off his mask and wiping sweat from his brow. His hair was wilder even than hers, icy-blond strands sticking up at all angles. "It is," he conceded. "But the undead can still resist if they want. That's why some are harder to control than others."

"So you're saying you *couldn't* control that wolf?" Wren asked.

He shrugged. "I could have, if I'd pushed harder. Squeezed the will out of it." His lip curled a bit at that. "But it would have been difficult, time consuming, and unnecessary."

"Unnecessary? It could have killed us!"

"We had it well in hand," Hawke said, presumably referring to that four-legged ghost he'd employed to keep the wolf at bay.

Wren frowned. She had seen Hawke command undead humans, seemingly without a second thought, yet he appeared squeamish at the idea of commanding a ravenous wolf in order to save all their lives.

"Why are your familiars so obedient?"

"Because they are *familiars*—we have a physical and mental bond, thanks to the amplifier, which makes them more inclined to listen to me than some random spirit. I also trained them, like you would any living pet."

As they spoke, one of the familiars in question burst from the ground before them, cutting through the wall of the tunnel they'd just left below. Wren reared back, reaching for a handful of knucklebones—her bonesmith instincts kicking in—as the spirit circled Hawke several times before coming to a stop before him.

Now that Wren could see it clearly, she could pick out the tufted tail and pointed ears. A fox.

Hawke knelt, murmuring and reaching out a hand. The ghost-fox brushed up against it, like a dog or cat, before disappearing in a wisp. The skull atop his staff started to glow, marking it as the creature's anchor bone.

"Animals are trained with food and positive reinforcement," Wren said, releasing her bandolier. "How can you *train* the undead? They don't eat, so how do you reward them?"

Hawke stood. "What do ghosts want most of all? Why do they linger here, following the living? Why do they seek us out?"

Wren blanked for a moment before remembering years of lessons. "They want life. To be close to it, to—"

He held out his hand. "To touch it."

Wren frowned, considering that. She fought her natural distaste, trying to make herself listen and understand. If she'd known there was no chance the wolf would obey her, she could have gotten herself, Leo, and Julian to safety more quickly.

She might not want her ghostsmith magic, but she'd surely need it again before all this was through.

Hawke gave her an assessing look. "Don't worry. You'll figure it out. I know this is all pretty new to you."

"Pretty new?" Wren repeated faintly. "I spent the first seventeen years of my life being a bonesmith, only to have this long-lost magic thrust upon me."

"It was always there," Hawke said. "Lying dormant, like your familiar. Once you entered the Haunted Territory, the well brought those powers to the surface."

Wren barely heard the rest of what Hawke said. "My familiar . . . ," she repeated, staring down at her ring. "So I have a *ghost* trapped inside this thing?" She held out her hand, fingers splayed as if she didn't want to touch the object any more than she already had to, given she was wearing it. She had suspected as much when Julian had explained about amplifiers, but she hadn't given it much thought since. Not even when Hawke summoned his own familiar.

Hawke frowned at Wren's distaste. "It won't hurt you. It's meant to be your companion. A gift. It's . . ." He seemed to struggle for the word before he landed on it. "Tradition."

Ghostsmith tradition.

"There's no need to be afraid," he added. "It will obey you. It's bound to you."

"I'm not afraid," Wren snapped, clenching her hand into a fist. "But how is it bound to me? Through the ring?"

"That's right. Our mother made it while she was pregnant and marked it as yours with the appropriate glyphs."

"But . . . why?" Julian asked. "Why make a familiar when you could just make a simple amplifier?"

"It was once common for ghostsmith tutors to use familiars to teach magic," Hawke explained. "Training them to heed your will and obey complex orders is good practice for more challenging spirits, like humans or wild animals. Creating them is also an important lesson." His demeanor changed slightly, his face growing somber. "Catching the living animal, killing it, then carving the bone . . . all important skills for a ghostsmith. At least, according to our mother. She made—she *taught* me how." He cleared his throat. "After, their haunted bones act as amplifiers, yes, and some ghostsmiths leave it that way, never summoning them once they are bound."

"Not you, though," Leo prompted.

"I never summon the ram," Hawke said, indicating his skull mask. "I didn't make this amplifier; it's quite old, and I never felt a connection to it in that way. But as for the others?" He shrugged. "One was made for me, and the other I made myself, so it felt different. Besides, I like the companionship."

"But I thought you hated the undead," Wren said, trying to puzzle it out.

"I hate undead *humans*. Undead animals are entirely different.

Even that revenant wolf was not as violent as most undead humans. It was just defending its territory."

His obvious affection for animals explained a lot, and Wren understood to a certain degree. Human undead emanated cold hatred and a crackling, relentless brutality. Animal undead were by comparison usually docile and relatively harmless.

"Besides, they make great lookouts and distractions. Even messengers."

Wren lifted her hand again. If it was something children could master, it was something *she* could master. And no matter how much she disliked it, she needed all the tools at her disposal. "What do I do? Do I need to be wearing the ring to summon my familiar?"

Smiling slightly, Hawke shook his head and slid the bone ring off her finger. "Proximity helps, but you don't need to be touching it at all. It's similar to waking the sconces, really," he said. "You *can* touch them, but you can also ask them to wake with a verbal command. You know what a wren looks like?"

Of course it would be a wren, just as Talon was a hawk. She nodded, sweat breaking out across the back of her neck, though she wasn't sure why. Maybe she *was* afraid after all.

"Picture a wren in your mind, and call to it."

"Out loud?" Wren asked, somewhat shrilly. She still wasn't used to it, the idea of *talking* to the undead.

"That would probably be easiest, though eventually you'll be able to summon it with a thought."

She blew out a breath and let her eyes flutter closed. She pictured the small songbird she'd seen in the forests outside Marrow Hall—not the Bonewood, of course, but natural forests, with real trees and *living* wildlife.

She imagined its stout, round body and pointy beak. She heard its twittering birdsong.

"Come to me," she whispered, and opened her eyes.

Hawke held her amplifier ring on his open palm. And as the four of them looked on, a burst of ghostlight erupted from the bone, materializing into a tiny little bird, its ephemeral wings flapping as it hovered before her.

Wren startled, fought the urge to rear back. To fight.

"Good," said Hawke, sounding truly pleased. "*Good.* Now tell it—"

"Go," Wren said abruptly, completely overwhelmed. Despite her whirling emotions, her voice was steady, her command firm.

Just as quickly as it had come, the ghost-bird disappeared in a wisp.

Relief washed through her, followed quickly by shame—at her fear, at her overreaction.

At her *desire*.

She'd wanted to touch her familiar. To watch it swoop and soar through the sky.

To test her theory about how ghostly feathers felt.

Hawke looked the most surprised, though both Julian and Leo also seemed startled by her reaction.

Her brother handed her the ring. "Well, there you have it. With practice, you'll get even stronger."

"Great," Wren muttered, sliding the ring back onto her finger.

Hawke turned away from her, making for the lake's edge, the rest of them following. The sun had risen, the partially submerged ruins glowing brightly on one side and casting long, dark shadows on the other.

"We'll cross here," Hawke said. "We just need to find a path through."

"Looks like we're not the first ones," said Leo, pointing at a swaying rope bridge visible between two buildings, glinting with dew in the morning light. "Unless that was you?" He turned to Hawke, who shook his head.

Wren squinted, seeing bridges spanning many of the visible rooftops and crumbling towers, some made of rope, others of beams of wood, and even what appeared to be a ladder on its side. There were paths all over Laketown's ruins, which would surely allow them to cut their travel time in half.

Attention focused on the water, Hawke summoned Talon. Now that Wren knew to look for it, she saw the way he touched the ghost as he spoke, lacing his commands with magic as well as life.

She also saw how the spirit reacted, rippling in pleasure and glowing brighter. Hawke murmured quietly, but soon the ghost-bird was off, soaring high in the air before circling back around to hover near the shore.

Leading the way.

"But—the water," Wren said. "How can it cross the water?" Flying or not, she'd always been taught that water acted as a barrier against undead.

"It's all about distance. At a certain point, the effect of the water ceases to be a factor. Think of underground lakes and rivers, or even man-made bridges." Wren recalled seeing both at play in the Haunted Territory. "As long as Talon flies high enough, the water doesn't trouble him."

Wren sighed, wondering grimly how her life had come to this, letting a *ghost* lead her to safety—never mind a *pet* ghost named Talon—but after Hawke leapt onto the nearest rooftop, she knew she had no choice but to follow.

The four of them made it across the first few buildings without incident, the pathways they encountered in good condition. Wren's mind worked away on that as she edged across. These catwalks were recent or well-maintained, which meant they were in use. But by who?

As she reached the opposite side, her gaze raked the nearest buildings. Their windows were absent of both flame and ghostlight, which was some measure of relief, even if they felt like empty eye sockets watching them.

Talon continued to float above, his presence likely scaring away any *living* birds that might want to fly here—except, what was that? In the distance, another flying figure steadily approached. This one was darker, certainly no ghost, yet something about its movements made the hairs on the back of Wren's neck stand up. And the closer it got, the more certain she became that it was not a living thing.

A flash of ghostlight from its pinprick eyes, and she knew.

A revenant bird. A crow or a raven, by the look of its black plumage.

If its corpse was in decent enough shape, Wren supposed the same magical mechanics that allowed a dead human to walk could allow a dead bird to fly.

But it was unsettling all the same.

"What is—" she began, but Hawke had seen it too.

"Get down," he said sharply, and high above, Talon disappeared in a wisp.

Luckily for them, they were currently on a rooftop with a bell tower at its center, allowing the four of them to crouch behind it as the revenant bird soared above Laketown in wide, sweeping arcs.

"What is it?" Wren hissed. "What's the matter?"

"Nothing," Hawke said, eyes tracking the creature through the sky. "Nothing, but I don't want to draw its attention. I can't control it, and a revenant that flies is hard to evade."

As if walking revenants weren't bad enough, there were flying ones too?

They needed to get back inside the throughway.

Hawke, it seemed, felt the same way. As soon as the bird turned its beak north, disappearing over the distant peaks, he darted from the tower and made for the next bridge without delay.

They were moving faster now, the sun rising in the sky and casting their every movement into bright, *visible* light. There was no hiding out here.

Unfortunately, after several hours of steady progress, they reached their first true obstacle: a tattered rope bridge.

Julian was twice as heavy as the rest of them with his ironsmith plate, and as soon as his foot landed on the rope, the entire thing creaked ominously.

Leo was already across, with Hawke on the far side and Wren waiting behind him. She cursed; they should have seen this coming and tried a different route.

Julian shook his head in irritation, likely thinking the same. He continued on carefully, the bridge wobbling with every step, but it held.

Until he reached the middle.

The entire thing bowed under his weight, bringing Julian dangerously close to the water and forcing him to crouch in order to steady himself.

"Hold it!" Hawke cried, but Julian had already frozen in place.

After he remained motionless for several tense seconds, the bridge eventually ceased swaying. Julian looked both ways, then started to straighten, when the rope beneath his left foot snapped. His leg fell through, the rest of his body falling after it. He landed flat on his stomach against the ropes, his left foot splashing into the lake below.

"*Shit*," Wren hissed, taking an impotent step forward. The impact of his boot in the water echoed around them, bouncing off the buildings in a watery chorus.

There was a heartbeat of silence, and then the water stirred again—though Julian's boot no longer touched it.

Bubbles rose to the surface, just a few at first, but then the water began to gurgle and churn, ripples emanating from the source of the disturbance and slapping against the nearest buildings, including the one Wren stood on.

Light began to shimmer from deep within. Ghostlight, illuminating the watery boulevards and crumbling archways below. The light grew brighter as dozens of undead flickered into existence, rising to the surface among a mass of dark, waterlogged objects, including plants, beams of wood . . . and bones.

"Move," Wren said, her voice strangled. "*Move!*"

Before Julian could do more than scramble forward, attempting to drag his body along the partially frayed rope, a skeletal hand burst from the frothing water below.

Wren flung a handful of knucklebones across the expanse between them. They ricocheted off the outstretched hand, causing it to flinch just long enough for Julian to lift his leg out of its reach, but a second later the hand was back again, and it wasn't alone.

Dozens more burst from the lake, and they were coming for Julian.

Wren didn't think; she reacted.

She ran to the roof's edge and jumped.

FIFTEEN

Wren hit the water with a shock and a splash. It was *freezing*, and filled with undead, and why had she thought this was a good idea?

When she exploded up to the surface, it was to hear Julian yelling at her, something along the lines of "*What the hell are you doing?*"

Wren didn't bother to answer. What she was doing was rather obvious, she thought, and she didn't have the air to waste.

The boiling mass of undead had turned at the commotion and was starting to head Wren's way. That was good.

Also bad.

"Get off the bridge!" Wren gasped, struggling to keep her head above water with her armor and weapons weighing her down.

"What? I can't—" Julian argued.

"*Get off!*" Wren barked. If he could throw himself under a rock-slide for her, she could put herself between him and the undead. She was a ghostsmith, after all. Immune to their touch.

She was not, however, immune to drowning.

She was so preoccupied with yelling at Julian that she'd forgotten she had more than deathrot to worry about. Something gripped her ankle from the depths and pulled her back under.

The breath arrested in Wren's lungs. She kicked and spun—or tried to—the terrifying darkness behind her eyelids forcing her to wrench her eyes open. But sight was much, much worse.

She thought back to her fall into the spring inside the Breach . . . except this time, all her nightmares were coming true.

Corpses were suspended in the water all around her, reaching and dragging her down, their dead-fish eyes glowing green, their hair and clothing swirling and tangling like underwater weeds.

Their faces were expressionless, but their ghosts . . . they pulsed with feelings of anger, hunger, and desperation beyond what Wren had ever experienced before.

One of them still held her ankle, and another had her wrist. She struggled, but the water slowed her movements, made it difficult to gain leverage, and her chest ached with the need to *breathe.*

And the silence . . . the heavy, oppressive, seething silence was worst of all.

Help me, she thought desperately, and something burst from the shadows below—a streak of ghostlight that was there and then gone—up toward the surface.

Panic, wild and insistent, seized Wren's chest.

She lashed out, trying to wrench her arm free of the skeletal grasp, her bone armor useless against the revenant.

Her foot connected with one body, her knee another, but when her other hand swiped viciously at an undead crowding in, her bare skin passed through a particularly cold patch of water.

She whirled, coming face-to-face with a ghost. Its shape was difficult to discern in the current, the waves shifting and distorting it, but she noted wide, sad eyes and a gaping mouth.

Before she could do more than wonder if that ghostly touch would kill her, visions exploded before her waking eyes.

Was she dying, her life flashing before her? No, these memories—these people and places—were not hers.

She saw cobblestone streets and running children. She saw market stalls and horse-drawn carts lumbering down twisting lanes.

She saw the ground shake, the walls tremble, and a rising tide of cries and shouts.

She saw waves careening down wide boulevards, crashing through buildings and swallowing everything and everyone whole.

The weight of the visions bore down on her, and she stopped struggling, stopped swimming, her body still as it sank lower, lower . . . into the darkness.

A distant splash, a ripple in the water, and then strong hands clamped under Wren's arms, pulling her upward.

The touch wrenched her away from the undead, and she blinked, coming back to herself.

It was her brother.

Hawke's pale hair streaked behind him as he kicked his legs, hauling Wren's lifeless form back to the surface.

She tried to help, but she had been too long without air. Her limbs were like lead. Her chest spasmed, her lungs protested . . . and she sucked in a mouthful of foul lake water.

They were nearer the surface, the sunlight sparkling above and illuminating three figures bent over the water in a glimmering apparition—or maybe Wren was finally losing consciousness.

Just when it seemed they were about to break the surface, their ascent came to an abrupt halt. Revenants had followed them, coming back for what Hawke had attempted to claim, but now they wanted them both.

Hawke kicked and struggled, but then something pierced the water, zipping past Wren to embed in the chest of the nearest revenant. A crossbow bolt?

Another object whizzed past, leaving a trail of bubbles and landing in the shoulder of another undead—the one that currently held her brother.

Suddenly free, he swam hard, reaching for Wren, but though her eyes were open, the darkness was closing in. . . .

The next thing Wren knew, someone was pounding their fist on her chest, hard.

She lurched upright and spewed a fountain of water partially onto the ground and partially onto Prince-Smith Leopold Valorian.

"Sorry," Wren croaked, collapsing onto her back.

"Nonsense," said Leo, waving aside her apology. His face floated above her, wearing his usual winning smile—though it looked strained. "I never liked these boots anyway."

Wren tried to laugh, but her chest was on fire, and she coughed instead. Blinking through streaming eyes, she spotted her brother just behind Leo, sodden and dripping, while nearer at hand was Julian.

His expression was graver than Wren had ever seen it, and to her surprise, his gloved hand clutched her clammy one. She looked down, and when she did, he released her, twisting himself away and getting abruptly to his feet. He showed her his back, concealing whatever emotion had flickered across his face. His clenched fists and rigidly stiff shoulders were all she had to go on.

How long had she been down there, under the water?

How long had she been lying here, unconscious?

Speaking of unconscious, Wren sought the person who'd brought her forcefully back to wakefulness with fists against her ribs . . . and found a corpse?

She flinched, shaking away the dregs of fear that clung to her mind to take in what she actually saw.

What appeared to be a corpse was actually a living person covered in bone from head to toe, including a human skull mask that obscured their face. The bones were "raw" or untreated, not shaped and honed like Wren's into armor by a talented fabricator. A crossbow lay on the ground next to them, and Wren recalled projectiles piercing the water and taking out the revenants. Peering into the stranger's quiver, she spotted bolts tipped with sharpened bone, though the rest of the shaft shone dull black, like iron. Wren realized they were designed not for distance but for *power*. Instead of fletching, there were hooked prongs at the end. It was an ingenious bit of weaponry; the bone would pierce the ghost, the prongs would catch on the body, and the iron was heavy enough to weigh the corpse down, carrying the revenant into the depths and possibly pinning it somewhere below.

They also carried a bone sword, though like their "armor," it was rough and more closely resembled the femur it had once been rather than the sword it had become, as if crafted by a valkyr on the fly.

Excitement surged inside her. Surely this *was* a valkyr? Even as the idea took hold—who else could fight these creatures with such calm?—Wren spotted a flash of steel. Was that a scythe on their belt?

"Come, bonesmith," the stranger said from behind their skull mask, their voice rough but feminine. "We must tend your flesh. The rot—"

Wren looked down at herself, soaked from being submerged with revenants, then at her hand, which had specifically touched a ghost. That thought brought a barrage of confusing memories, but she pushed those thoughts aside as she examined her skin. Her limbs tingled as blood slowly warmed her nearly frozen body, but the flesh she could see was pink, not black, and feeling was returning.

She was immune, just as her brother had said she would be.

The bonesmith paused, staring at Wren, pale eyes only just visible behind the shadowy holes of the mask.

"Perhaps not," she said. Wren didn't know if she was referring to the threat of deathrot or the designation of bonesmith, for her attention had now landed on Wren's *other* hand, which wore the ghostsmith ring.

"Thank you," Wren said, struggling to get to her feet. "For saving me. Saving us."

Anger, sudden and surprising, reared up inside her.

She rounded on her brother. "What were you thinking?" His expression twisted into confusion. "The water," she said, flailing at his sodden state. "You just *jumped in* after me?"

He appeared as if he hadn't given it much thought. "Yes."

"You could have gotten yourself killed."

"So could you," he said, calm in the face of her fury. "Do you know how deep you were? The only reason I could find you was thanks to your familiar."

"My . . ." Wren trailed off, another detail resurfacing in her mind. She stared down at her ring. Her familiar was nowhere to be seen, which meant the ghost-bird must have already returned to its anchor bone even without her command.

"*Still*," Wren argued, "it was stupid and reckless and—"

"I think what you *mean* to say is thank you?" Leo said, censure in his voice, though it lacked true edge. Julian, meanwhile, coughed slightly at the tirade Wren was unleashing, no doubt thinking something along the lines of "if that's not the pot calling the kettle black" and various other ironic idioms.

Wren swallowed, trying to get a grip on herself. She had nearly died, and she was not handling it terribly well. Her body ached, her brain was fuzzy, and something had *happened* down there, something she couldn't explain. And so she needed someone to be angry at, because the alternative was to be angry at herself, and that wasn't nearly as satisfying.

"It's just, we need him, and—"

"We need you, too," Julian said quietly, and that shut Wren right up. She stared at Julian for several breathless seconds before turning to her brother.

Thank you, Leo mouthed encouragingly.

"Thank you," Wren said automatically. "But next time, just . . . be more careful."

Hawke frowned uncertainly, then nodded. Julian rolled his eyes, while Leo put his arm around Wren, draping his jacket over her shoulders like a cloak. "Rein it in there, big sister," he added in an undertone. "Rein it in."

Wren was annoyed at him for bailing her brother out—and smiling all the while—but her irritation faltered when his words actually penetrated her mind. Big sister. She supposed she was, in a way, as she'd been born first, even if it was on the same day.

Strange. She had known that Hawke's existence gave her a brother, but she hadn't yet acclimated to the idea that *she* was a *sister*.

And an elder sister. Surely she should be saving his life and not the other way around? Her eyes met Hawke's over Leo's shoulder, apology in her mind, though she didn't speak a word.

He nodded slightly, as if she didn't have to.

Needing to focus on something else, she returned her attention to the bonesmith. "My name is Wren Graven of House Bone. This is Julian, Leo, and Hawke."

"Graven . . . ," the bonesmith repeated, and Wren supposed that the name would be familiar to any bonesmith in the Dominions. Then again, the Breachlands weren't technically in the Dominions anymore. "Lady-Smith Svetlana's granddaughter, I presume?"

Wren nodded.

"Call me Mercy," she said gruffly, pushing the mask off her face. It was a strange name, but certainly not the strangest thing about her. She appeared in her late twenties or early thirties, which would have made her a child when the Breach swallowed Laketown. Her hair was ink black, long and braided down her back, and her smooth, olive skin was marred by a deep scar, running from the middle of her cheek and hooking down, across her jawline and into the scarf she wore around her neck. "Deathrot aside, you two need dry clothes and a warm hearth," she said matter-of-factly. "I have both. You'll come with me."

SIXTEEN

The offer of dry clothes and a warm hearth was highly appealing, but they needed to *get there* first, and Wren's near-drowning had definitely cut into their daylight travel time. Now they'd be lucky to make it across the city before nightfall.

As Wren and Hawke were already shivering from the cold, they had to improvise, stripping off the worst of their sodden clothes and borrowing from the others. Wren wore Leo's jacket over Julian's undershirt, while Hawke looked absolutely ridiculous with a blanket wrapped around his waist and his cloak—which he'd removed before diving in after her—over his bare chest.

Wren couldn't help the smile that tugged at her lips, though she surely looked just as absurd, forgoing pants entirely and engulfed in Julian's oversize shirt, which she kept surreptitiously sniffing as she went, inhaling his familiar, half-forgotten scent. The fabric still held the vestiges of whatever soap had once been used to launder it, coupled with the oddly comforting smell of iron.

Together they zigged and zagged across the rooftops, making for Mercy's home on the far shore.

"You're a bonesmith, aren't you?" Wren asked as they arrived on the latest rooftop. In order to cross, they had to journey inward to the heart of the sunken city, passing over recognizable structures like stables, granaries, and warehouses. Wren's question was an unnecessary one—Mercy's bone-white eyes told all—but she wasn't sure if the woman was a valkyr or a reapyr. "I didn't think there were any bonesmiths east of the Wall. Not anymore."

"No bonesmiths," Mercy said, casting a sidelong look at Julian. "No ironsmiths, either." Then her gaze landed on Hawke, his green eyes bright in the rays of sun striping across the rooftop. "And you . . . Well, you're not meant to exist at all, are you?" Wren scrabbled for an explanation for them both, but Mercy held up a hand. "Relax. You're not the first ghostsmiths to cross my path."

Wait . . . Did that mean Mercy knew Ravenna?

Before Wren could ask, the woman's attention shifted to Leo.

Her gaze raked him up and down. He was dressed rather unimpressively compared to when Wren had first met him, but there was more to Leo than his clothing. There was his bearing, his manner of speech, and the way his fine breeding and royal upbringing fairly oozed from his skin.

Not to mention his fat golden rings and matching eyes.

"And a goldsmith of all things—an *important* one too, I'd wager," Mercy said. When none of them replied, she chuckled darkly. "It makes no difference to me. Rest assured, I will help you, whatever your titles or bloodlines. I know these bridges better than anyone, on account of the fact that I made them. But we'd best not dawdle; you don't want to be wandering these hills when the stars come out."

They passed an ironsmith temple next, identifiable thanks to its black iron steeple, the structure untouched by rust or rot despite the water lapping at its beams. They also passed a bonesmith temple.

"I've had to do some looting, over the years," Mercy lamented, indicating the absence of the usual skull and crossbones above its doorway, as well as some of the extraneous adornments that made bonesmith temples stand out like no others.

Over the years . . .

"Were you here when it happened?" Julian asked quietly as they crossed the temple's roof. "The flood?"

He'd been quiet ever since Wren's near drowning, and she couldn't figure out if he was bottling up his anger at her, waiting to unleash it, or if it was being here, in this place, that had so unsettled him. Perhaps both.

Mercy glanced over her shoulder at him. "I was here," she admitted. "Training not thirty feet below us. I was a new novitiate, barely out of my practice blade, but as I have no family, I'd been living at the temple since I was born."

Sometimes that happened. Orphans turned up, smith-born and hoping for a chance at a better life. If they had talent, most temples would take them in or sponsor their training at Marrow Hall.

"Despite what the stories claim, we had some time to flee—or at least, those of us in the center of the city did. The main boulevards were elevated, built on a rise because there was a lake here before the Breach, and the streets were prone to flooding. Those on the northern shores were swallowed up before they knew what'd hit them, and those in the south were knee-deep before we'd gotten so much as a drop. Of course, we had to pass *through* the southern outskirts to get to safety. It was anarchy. It all happened in half a day, maybe less.

Most survivors headed to the coastal towns, seeking refuge, but the bonesmiths were about to be conscripted for war."

"Did you fight?" Wren asked, before realizing her mistake. "No, you couldn't have—you were too young."

Mercy snorted, though Wren sensed the contempt wasn't directed at her. "Sometimes you don't have a choice. The flood killed so many and disturbed those who were already resting. And the revenants . . . they were rising here, too, in shocking numbers. Whatever's in that Breach, whatever dark magic calls them, I think it came here, too. It's in the water. It's in the *ground.* The revenants were everywhere, and we had to fight our way out. I reaped my first ghost at eleven."

Wren gaped. Most bonesmiths hadn't even seen a ghost at that age. Their education was primarily classroom-based until they were thirteen, revolving around textbooks and dead bones.

"So you're a reapyr?"

They'd come to the next bridge, and Mercy paused with a boot on its edge. "Not sure what I am now, truth be told. I was trained to be a reapyr in the beginning, but I learned to fight like everyone else. And not just the undead. Bandits would prey on the refugees. There was an ambush, and the others, they thought I was done for"—she indicated the scar along her face and neck—"so . . . they left me behind. They headed west. I'm sure many of them marched right back into the Breach, into the war, but . . . I never saw them again. I traveled with some of the displaced Laketowners for a while after, giving them what protection I could as a makeshift valkyr, but duty called me back." She waved a hand around the sunken city.

"Duty?" Hawke asked, his tone bright and curious. "To a drowned city? Or to the bonesmiths who left you behind?"

Wren shot him a quelling look, not wanting to offend Mercy, but she didn't seem bothered.

"My duty is to the dead, boy. We all of us will wind up ghosts one day, and I can only hope that there will be a bonesmith nearby to set me free. To show me mercy."

So it was more than an unusual name, then. It was a mission.

"Mercy?" Hawke repeated, frowning. "But they're savage killers, the undead. Surely the mercy you're showing is to the living?"

His tone wasn't judgmental; Wren suspected he truly didn't understand.

"There's certainly some truth in that," Mercy conceded. "The living deserve their peace as well. But do you know *why* the undead are savage killers? Do you know why they torment us so?" Hawke shook his head. "They are in agony. Relentless, never-ending misery every moment they are forced to exist here as they are. Not alive. Not dead. *That* is why they deserve mercy, and that is why I give it to them."

Hawke lowered his head, taking that in, before angling his attention to the sky. He had not summoned Talon since they'd spotted that revenant bird, but Wren suspected he was thinking of him. Sure, the familiar acted like any living bird, and yet . . . it didn't fly but rather floated in an uncanny impersonation. It never ate, never slept, never hunted or built a nest. It existed to do Hawke's bidding and nothing else.

Mercy followed his gaze, and while there was currently nothing there, she'd likely seen Talon above the town before she'd come to their rescue. "The animal undead may not be as violent. And yes, under your magical hand, they might even behave quite docilely. But make no mistake, young *ghostsmith*—that is not life."

Her words echoed Wren's statement about the sconces inside the throughway, and though he'd heard it before, Hawke still struggled to accept it.

"But . . . it's the next best thing, right? They get to exist forever, to be *near* life. Isn't that what all undead want?"

Mercy turned a pitying look on him. "Who told you that?"

"Starling."

"Who?" Wren asked, startled. She'd been expecting him to say Ravenna.

"My wet nurse. Mother wasn't able to feed me, so she found a replacement. Another ghostsmith woman."

"Another . . . ," Wren repeated, shocked. "There are others living here in the Breachlands?"

According to Odile's story, Ravenna had claimed to be the last remaining ghostsmith. Perhaps Wren had been foolish to take her word as truth, or maybe the details had gotten garbled in the retelling. Ravenna was probably the last of her line—the last Nekros—until Wren and Hawke had arrived, and maybe that was all that was important to her.

Hawke nodded, though he looked sad. "Not many." Mercy looked unsurprised at this information, answering Wren's earlier question of what other ghostsmiths had apparently crossed her path. "They're mostly nomadic, traveling the edges of the Breachlands, avoiding the heavily civilized areas for fear of persecution. The undead don't bother them, so they can cross the Haunted Territory without issue, but it's all ruins and not an easy place to live. Mother and her parents used to stay with them, until, well . . . they had disagreements about what it meant to be a ghostsmith. About how they should lead their lives."

He avoided Wren's eyes, and she assumed he meant their mother's pursuit of the lost ghostsmith necropolis and the power within. Considering their civilization had already been buried once, Wren wouldn't be surprised if most who survived saw the place as cursed and avoided it. Clearly, Ravenna and her family felt differently, and thanks to them, there'd been a second cataclysm: the Breach.

"But despite their past conflicts, they agreed to take me in," Hawke continued. "Starling had a son, but he died in his infancy, so she fed and raised me until I was twelve. Then one night Mother came for me. She told me it would be fine, that I could see them again whenever I wanted. She lied."

Suddenly, her brother's willingness to betray their mother made a little more sense. In his head—and likely his heart—Starling was his true mother, and Ravenna was the woman who'd stolen him from her.

"Is this the betrayal you mentioned?"

"She *swore* I'd see them again," he said angrily. "But when I asked, she forbade it. When they tried to see me, she refused them—violently. I haven't seen Starling, or any of them, since."

Wren considered that. It seemed unnecessarily cruel, but Ravenna surely had her reasons, and isolating someone was an easy way to keep them under your thumb.

"Well, your Starling may well be speaking the truth of what she was taught, but the undead don't want to be *near* life—they want to be *alive*. There is a difference. And if they can't have that, they would rather be nothing at all."

"How can you possibly know that?" Hawke asked.

"Once you've freed a spirit, once you've seen their relief . . . you'd never fathom doing what you do ever again, I promise you."

Hawke looked troubled. He stared down at his ring, turning it idly on his finger.

They crossed the rest of Laketown without incident, though Wren could sense some of the undead beneath the water, tracking their progress. Her mind returned to what had happened when she was down there among them.

She had seen their memories. Flashes of the destruction of the town, the drowned soul's last moments alive . . .

How was that even possible? Mercy mentioned seeing a spirit's relief, but Wren had seen and heard far more than relief. She had experienced vivid visions. And they had come after touching a ghost. Surely this was the realm of ghostsmith magic.

She darted a glance at the back of her brother's head. Had he seen the same things? Was this normal for a ghostsmith? Or normal for a ghostsmith in the Breachlands, where raw magic leaked from the well and saturated everything?

"Are you all right?" Julian asked, sidling up to her. The question was so surprising, it completely derailed Wren's train of thought.

"Am I . . . ?" she repeated dumbly. He wasn't looking at her—his eyes were ahead as they clambered over a steepled rooftop—which made it difficult to read his intent. "I'm fine."

"I know you want to do the right thing, but it's not worth dying for."

Wren stopped as she reached the roof's apex, forcing him to do the same. "Says the person who threw themselves under a fucking rockslide."

"I was fine—I *am* fine."

"So. Am. I," Wren said.

"You're the most stubborn person I've ever met."

"I know what you're doing. You're trying to catch me out, to prove that this plan is stupid and reckless, just like me, and—"

"What I'm *trying* to do is show you that I care. About *you*. That's it."

He left her there, skidding down the opposite side of the roof with more balance and grace than should be allowed, really, forcing Wren to stagger and stumble after him.

The far shore was as rocky and barren as the one they had left behind, yet as they drew nearer, Wren spotted signs of civilization tucked into the cracks and crevices of the land. There was a small dwelling built of wood that was likely salvaged from Laketown, a fenced-in area, plus a tiered garden with flashes of green visible, even at a distance. A windmill, an assortment of buckets and tools, and what looked like a cistern meant to catch rainwater.

"Did you make yourself a moat?" asked Leo. He was pointing at the cistern, and sure enough, Wren noted a spout feeding water into a trench that circled the entire compound. It resembled the man-made defenses at Caston, though the waterway was narrow enough for a living person to simply step over. Still, it would do well to keep anything undead from crossing. If only the Border Wall hadn't been such a long stretch of land, they'd likely have tried to do the same.

"Bones are well enough, but nothing beats water for keeping the walking undead at bay."

Despite that statement, she certainly hadn't skimped out on the more standard protections. There were bones everywhere: attached to the fence, the roof, and circling the gardens. There was a skull and crossbones mounted over the door, and outside the fence and beyond the moat were other strange objects either made of bone or reinforced with it. Some of them looked suspiciously like boxes or . . .

"Are those . . . ?" Wren began, as they mounted the slope toward Mercy's house.

"Cages?" asked Julian uneasily.

"Traps," Hawke clarified, indicating ropes and pulleys, systems built to lure and capture. And with so much bone, Wren had a good idea what they were meant to catch. What had Mercy said? That they didn't want to be wandering these hills when the stars came out?

"I spend most of my time fishing," Mercy said, breath puffing as they climbed the steep rise. "Undead," she clarified. "That's why I built those bridges. For crossing, yes, but they also allow me to move around the entire city. I can reap two or three souls on a good day, but they won't trouble me once I make it to these shores. Land-dwellers, on the other hand . . . then I have to become a hunter. Hence the traps."

The snares put Wren in mind of the cells beneath the Wall at the Breachfort.

"If these are traps," she asked, as Mercy opened the gate. "What do you use as bait?"

The woman looked over her shoulder and smiled. "Myself, of course. My living here is like a beacon, and with the four of you added to the mix . . . our lives will burn as bright as an inferno. We'll see what we can catch tonight—but whatever you do, do not stray beyond the fence."

SEVENTEEN

With the sun setting and their stomachs grumbling, Leo was relieved when Mercy quickly took the dinner preparations in hand, assigning them each tasks with surprising acuity for a person who apparently lived and worked entirely alone.

Wren was sent inside with her sodden clothes, ordered to get warm and dry and stoke the fire hot enough to cook on.

Julian was sent to the garden with a bucket and shovel to dig up potatoes, while Leo, who was "clearly more suited to delicate work," according to Mercy, was assigned the task of picking herbs and runner beans.

After one look at Hawke, who seemed utterly unfazed by the cold, Mercy brought him with her as she went out to the coop where she housed chickens.

Perhaps she didn't fully trust him and wanted to keep him in her line of sight.

Or perhaps she wanted to show him what *living* animals were like, so he could understand the difference.

As Wren stomped into the house and Hawke followed Mercy toward the gentle sounds of clucking and shuffling wings, Leo took up his basket.

"Ready?" he said to Julian, whose attention was fixed on Wren as she disappeared into the cottage.

"Yes, of course," Julian said at once, realizing that Leo had caught him staring. He turned on his heel and marched around the back of the house, toward the garden next to the fence.

Together they knelt in the dirt, Julian using his small shovel to dig through the soil for his quarry, while Leo plucked beans from crawling vines.

"I'm glad I've finally got you alone," Leo said, and Julian raised his brows expectantly, as if waiting for the punch line on some kind of flirtatious joke. "Oh, not like that." Leo laughed, though it felt a bit forced. He cleared his throat. "I wanted to say I'm sorry—for the incident at the mill house," he clarified. "Wren wasn't the only person to leave you behind that day. I know you've directed most of your anger at her, but I was involved as well."

"It was *her* idea," Julian said, tossing aside his shovel and digging through the dirt with his hands.

"Yes, but I agreed to it all the same." Julian shot him a dark look, and suddenly Leo wondered why, exactly, he was convincing this person of his guilt. This dangerous, angry person who had kidnapped him for ransom, even if he'd since changed his mind.

Julian said nothing, and Leo was not very good with silence.

"She's trying, can't you see?" he burst out. "Think of all she's been through. This is her *father* who has betrayed her, to say nothing of her mother, and her hitherto unknown *twin brother* made the bloody iron revenants! And still she's here, fighting. She made a mistake, yes, but she has owned it and is trying to do better."

Julian scowled, continuing to dig. Then: "She was the one who said we should team up in the first place! And then she just . . ." He stopped himself.

"Constantly striving for approval you're never likely to get . . . it wears on a person." Julian cast him a sidelong look, understanding that Leo spoke from experience. "It makes them desperate. Desperate enough to do something they regret."

Julian considered that for a time, returning his hands to the soil. "I might find it easier to forgive," he said at last, "if she hadn't made me into the very thing my uncle has always accused me of being. A fool."

"Just because he said it doesn't make it so," Leo said sagely. "And if *you* are a fool, Julian Knight, then *I* am truly beyond redemption."

The corner of Julian's mouth lifted before his expression turned thoughtful. "Redemption?"

"Well, you're not the only person who's been labeled in a way they do not appreciate. But while your criticism comes from a solitary figure—who, incidentally, has much to gain by belittling you and undermining your confidence—mine comes from an entire kingdom. Useless. Irresponsible. A spare's spare and no more. It's true that aspects of my reputation have occasionally been self-inflicted, but I suppose that when I started this journey, I had hoped it was not beyond salvation."

"You wish to prove yourself," Julian guessed, and Leo nodded. "To your family?"

"Fuck *them*," Leo scoffed, with more sincerity than he felt, but the words earned him what he'd been seeking. Julian smirked, and Leo saw in his eyes that the sentiment had made him think of Wren, the happiness on his face dimming somewhat.

It was a strange sort of pining—half yearning, half hating oneself for the yearning. Unfortunately, Leo knew such feelings intimately and had nursed more doomed infatuations than he'd care to count.

"No," Leo continued. He wanted to be more than the spare's spare, the frivolous, handsome, *useless* prince, but not for his king-father or his princely brothers, his distant mother or his precocious sister. "I think I'd rather like to prove it to myself."

Julian wore an expression Leo couldn't place. He was tempted to call it respect but thought perhaps it was closer to surprised approval.

Thinking of doomed infatuations, Leo cleared his throat. "Incidentally, I know you think that your uncle has some hold over the Breachlands—"

"I think Arthur's behavior proves that."

"Arthur's behavior proves that the poor and the craven can be bought. That is nothing new." Julian inclined his head, conceding the point. "If you'll recall, the voices *against* what Arthur did were far louder than those that were for it."

"The Red Guard," Julian spat. "And the Iron Citadel soldiers."

"Well, about that . . . I don't think they are as loyal as you might fear. The Citadel soldiers, anyway. Like Jakob. He was clearly conflicted, but in the end, he did help us."

Julian sighed. "He's a good sort. Tries hard. Follows orders. Which I suppose I can hardly hold against him."

"He was kind to me, during the first kidnapping and the second."

Julian snorted. "Well, you're Leopold Valorian. A prince. And a good-looking one, too."

"I think you're good-looking too, Julian," Leo said graciously, his tone placating. Julian rolled his eyes. "And please, call me Leo. But what I meant to insinuate wasn't that the poor boy was sweet on me"—though Leo certainly wasn't opposed to the idea—"but rather, that he might be sympathetic to your cause. He and the other Citadel soldiers are only following orders, as you said. And from what I've seen and heard, they hold no particular love for the regent. Not like—"

"The Red Guard," Julian cut in. "They were handpicked by my uncle. My father never employed a personal guard, but Francis carefully chose his retinue. The more brutal and cutthroat, the better."

"Well, as I said, I don't believe you're as alone as you think you are. In the Breachlands or in the wider Dominions."

"The wider Dominions?" he repeated skeptically.

"If we survive all this, you don't think I'll forget about you when I get home, do you?"

Julian shook his head, smiling slightly. "In that case, Leo, apology accepted."

Leo grinned in delight, before casting a glance back toward the house. "Perhaps you can find it in you to accept another apology? If the events of today are any indication, things will only be more treacherous from here on out. So if you have something you need to say, you should say it."

EIGHTEEN

Wren was wrapped in a blanket and staring moodily into the fire when Julian arrived inside the house with two objects in hand: a basket filled with potatoes and a bucket filled with rainwater from the cistern.

She leapt to her bare feet, all her clothing spread out before the hearth, which was just now starting to grow hot enough to banish the chill in her bones.

Julian, meanwhile, was fully dressed. This was, oddly enough, a familiar dynamic between them.

Also familiar was the way Julian's gaze averted when he saw Wren wore a blanket and nothing else.

"Leo is helping your brother and Mercy with the chickens," he said by way of explanation.

"Oh, right. Good," Wren said, the awkwardness pressing in on her. They hadn't been alone together since she had betrayed him. Not even the image of the Gold Prince crouched inside a shit-spattered, feather-covered chicken coop could distract her.

Julian cleared his throat and plunked the bucket of water onto the ground beside the small wooden table with a slosh, then the potatoes next to it, apparently preparing to wash them for dinner.

They had been on the run for days, chased by enemies and surrounded by undead, and it was as unsettling to consider peeling and slicing potatoes as it had been to return to the Breachfort after all she had seen in the Breach. The quiet, the calm, the mundanity of it all grated against Wren's nerves. She was a person of action who preferred to be in motion, always striving for the next goal—or running from the fallout of the last one—and the *stillness* of the night unfolding before her was almost more than she could bear.

Stillness would give her time to think, and that was the last thing she needed. There were too many subjects she was avoiding, not least of which was a certain ironsmith standing opposite her.

The house, while containing only a single room, had a massive fireplace large enough to cook in, a square kitchen table, plus a bed tucked into the far corner under the window.

After taking in the space, Julian seemed to decide he'd not have a better time to remove his armor, stacking his helmet and heavy plate near the door. Wren was reminded, suddenly, of their night at the mill house—the first time around. She didn't like thinking about the second.

The first time they'd been on guard and wary of each other, but things had also been much simpler. Now, thanks in no small part to their second visit, things were . . . complicated.

As he rolled out his shoulders and combed his gloved hands through his hair, something fell to the ground.

Wren's heart stopped.

It was the handkerchief he had given her outside Caston to

remove her bonesmith makeup. It still bore her inky black lip stain across the gleaming white fabric and must have fallen from a pocket in his shirt.

"I . . . ," Julian began, swallowing audibly. "I didn't realize I still had that." He hesitated, then bent to pick it up. After darting a look at Wren, he tucked the stained handkerchief back into his pocket.

Wren's heart thumped back to life as he took a seat in the nearest chair and lifted a dirty potato.

The wood creaked, the water splashed, and Wren clenched her hands into fists.

While stillness was bad, silence was infinitely worse.

So, as was typical for her, Wren chose to shatter it.

"Let me do that," she said, more gruffly than was necessary, snatching the dirty potato and dropping into the seat next to him. It felt important, suddenly, that she do something nice. Something to prove that she was worthy of such a keepsake.

Julian watched as she scrubbed vigorously, then wiped the potato on the corner of her blanket, placing it neatly on the table before reaching for another.

Withdrawing one of his knives, Julian deftly peeled the potatoes Wren gave him.

The air was heavy with all they had and hadn't said, and Wren couldn't take her eyes off the blade he had chosen.

He was using Ironheart.

She didn't know what irritated her more: that he had taken back his gift, or that she'd deserved it. She wanted him to trust her, to believe in her, but why should he?

And *why* was he still wearing his *fucking* gloves, as if Wren didn't know what lay beneath?

"I don't know why you bother," she said, returning her attention to the water, scrubbing furiously at a particularly dirty tuber.

"With what?" Julian asked, still focused on his work, the peel coming away in a single, careful coil.

"With those gloves," she said. Julian stilled, and Wren knew she was treading dangerous ground here. She sat back, softening her tone. "It's not like I don't know what's underneath them."

Julian started peeling his potato again, though the movements were less smooth than before. "Maybe I don't want to remind you."

"Maybe you don't want to remind *yourself*," she countered.

He opened his mouth, then closed it. "Maybe."

"You have nothing to be ashamed of," she blurted.

"You don't know what it's like, to hate a part of yours—" He halted and lifted his gaze to hers.

"Don't I?" Wren said, lips pursed bitterly.

Julian considered that, then bent his head over his work again. Wren did the same.

"It's different," he said at last. "You didn't have a choice in the matter, but I . . ." He trailed off, and Wren found herself holding her breath, waiting. "I did."

He put down the potato he'd been working on, only half-peeled, and stared at his hands.

After what felt like an eternity, Wren mustered the courage to whisper, "What kind of choice?"

"There was an accident. When I was training. A rack of weapons fell onto my hand and crushed the bones. They could either amputate or try something . . . experimental. I was fourteen."

"Wow, that's *some* choice," Wren said sarcastically.

"It's not the choice that haunts me, really," he said, opening and closing his hand. "I mean, besides the fact that it's ugly and exhausting and aches every damn day of my life. It's the reason I made it that bothers me." He sighed. "My uncle said it was all about strength. 'Imagine it, my boy—an amplifier in your very skin! Think of the *power*.' Meanwhile, every time I look at it, all I see is my own weakness. My desire to please him, whatever the cost."

"Sounds familiar." She hesitated, then: "I'd have done the same thing, even without the injury," she said. "*Eagerly*, and without question, if he'd have asked it of me." She meant her father, and from a glimpse out of the corner of her eye, she saw that Julian knew that. "If it had given me a chance to be stronger or better. If it would have held his attention for more than a day or two . . ."

"That might have been true then, but not now," Julian said. "When you told your father about that ring and explained the well's magic, when you showed him what you could do with it . . ." Wren recalled breaking the guard's arm with a *crack*, a shudder crawling down her spine. "You certainly had his attention then, but you never wavered. Never turned back."

He was right. Wren hadn't looked at it that way before. But she'd inadvertently been tested . . . and she'd passed. A wave of immense relief washed over her, so powerful she had to close her eyes for a moment. When she opened them, Julian was watching her.

She cleared her throat. "I guess I know who I am now, and I don't mean my parentage or magical bloodline. His approval isn't something I need anymore."

She wanted to tell Julian that he was part of the reason. That traveling the Breachlands with him had given her confidence—true confidence, not the arrogance she'd paraded around in its place—in herself and her abilities. In who she truly was, without the Graven name and the respect and judgment that came with it. He hadn't known her identity or her past, her status as her father's wartime mistake and the shame of their house.

He had known only *her* . . . and had seemed to like her anyway.

All she'd wanted when she was exiled to the Breachfort was to return home and be deemed a worthy valkyr, but those days with Julian had been the best of her life. If *that* was what her future held, even with the fear and danger, she'd choose it over a life with her father's hollow, fickle approval a thousand times over.

"And it's not ugly, by the way. Not to me." Then, because she couldn't bear the intensity of his gaze, she added, "Not like *this*." She twisted the ring on her finger, though of course she referenced more than the ring. She referenced the magic it represented.

"Ghostsmith magic saved your life in the water today. It probably saved mine, too, since you jumped in to distract them from me." His voice held a ripple of checked anger at her, for risking herself for him. "It also saved our lives in the Breach," he added, his tone more even. "So I'm not sure I can wholly condemn it. It's not always ugly. . . . It's capable of darkness, like all magic is. But it's also capable of light."

"Such as?" Wren asked.

He shrugged, avoiding her eye. "Your familiar was quite beautiful."

Wren shook her head in silent refusal, even as her heart lightened at the idea that her very existence didn't completely repulse him.

"But there is so much darkness. The throughway sconces, the iron revenants . . . that battlefield from the Uprising."

"The iron revenants were the work of both ghostsmiths *and* ironsmiths. And the battlefield from the Uprising was technically bonesmith magic—however altered by the well," he added quickly. "See? The magic itself isn't bad or wrong. It's the user."

"Right, and you saw what I did to that guard in the dungeon," Wren practically choked out. "That was *me*. I shattered his arm. I *wanted* to do it. I'd do it again."

"You didn't want to. I saw your face," Julian said forcefully. "You wanted to stop him, to protect us. You didn't want to do . . . *that*. I know it."

"I'm sort of struggling with the fact that you're *defending* me right now," she admitted, smiling slightly.

He huffed a laugh, though the humor quickly died. "I've been working through a lot of things lately—my uncle's villainous turn, for a start—and I definitely took some of it out on you. I'm sorry for that, and . . . I accept your apology."

Wren blinked. "You do?"

"You are a lot of things, Wren Graven. Bold. Brash. Rec—"

"Don't," Wren cut in, but with no real heat.

His eyes crinkled in the corners. "But you're also daring. *Fearless*, or so it seems. Today, when I saw you go under, when those corpses were pulling you down and we couldn't see you anymore . . ." He swallowed, shaking his head as if to dispel the image. "What you did, it wasn't reckless or selfish. It was brave. And you did it for me."

Wren's mouth was suddenly very dry. "You caught that rockfall for me."

Julian tried to shrug nonchalantly, but his shoulders were too tense. "Like I said before: We need you."

"Need?" Wren pressed, hoping he would understand. That he, too, would recall a certain conversation inside the Breach, when Wren had asked Julian why he had come back for her. She could almost smell the damp spring and feel the pattering rain.

Julian lifted his head, leveling her with his darkest, most inescapable gaze. "Want, then."

Wren had inadvertently slid forward on her chair. The blanket had gotten rucked up, her bare thighs were exposed, her knees pressing against his. The contact caused goose bumps to ripple through her body, despite the heat of the hearth.

"And," he said, his voice slightly ragged, "what you did at the mill house . . . if I thought it would protect you, if I thought it was the *right thing*, well, I hope I'd have had the courage to do the same."

He wasn't just forgiving her for a betrayal; he was absolving her from a choice that had haunted her sleeping and waking thoughts. He was telling her he understood her decision, her determination . . . and maybe even respected it.

Wren's lips parted—and Julian's gaze latched on to the movement. A pulse of desire beat through her, and she was half a heartbeat away from climbing into his lap when the door to the house slammed open.

Leo stood on the threshold, basket of beans in hand. Wren leapt backward, though they'd hardly been touching, and Julian did the same, chair legs screeching.

Leo's brow quirked before he tossed the basket onto the floor. "Sorry to interrupt, but there's something I think the two of you ought to see."

Still wrapped in only a blanket—but carrying one of her swords—Wren followed Leo to the edge of Mercy's land, Julian just behind them. Mercy and Hawke were standing together next to one of her traps. . . .

And it wasn't empty.

As she neared, Wren felt the alarm bells in her mind, sensing the presence of the undead. She expected to see something human, but the sight of a revenant wolf brought her up short.

"Is it—"

"The same one?" Hawke interjected, eyes bright as he prowled around the cage. "Don't think so. These hills are full of them."

"Them," Mercy agreed. "And revenant deer, revenant dogs . . . I've even seen revenant cats. I knew you lot would be good for something. Wouldn't be surprised if the rest of these traps filled up before the night was through." She turned to Hawke. "Go on, then. Talk to it. Settle it if you can."

"It's wild," Hawke said, but he crouched before the trap all the same. Mercy, meanwhile, took up his earlier movement, circling the cage, watching the wolf closely, as if looking for something. . . .

The anchor bone, Wren realized. She was trying to find the anchor bone on a *revenant*. Talk about brave.

As Hawke knelt before the cage, murmuring softly, the ghost within the rotting corpse coalesced, withdrawing from the wolf's extremities until it had bunched in the skull, eyes glowing painfully bright.

The others squinted, and even Wren's eye black—reapplied after the lake—wasn't enough to stop her from blinking rapidly. Hawke, however, appeared unaffected.

"It's all right," he was saying, calming the wolf, which up until that point had been snarling and snapping as it tried to lunge at the cage's bone bars before recoiling in anger. Wren suspected it was very close to leaving its body behind—which was surely what Mercy hoped for—its attention fixed on Hawke.

When the ghost continued to quiver in place, uncertain, Hawke reached his hand between the bars. Wren's instincts had her taking hold of his forearm as if to yank it back before she remembered he was immune. Her touch caused him to flinch, as if he were unused to physical contact.

It took him a second to recover before he returned his focus to the undead, and Wren did the same.

She watched with eerie fascination as the ghost trembled from within its skull, unable to get past the bone bars but still capable of clamping its teeth onto Hawke's pale wrist and snapping the bones . . . but it didn't.

Instead, after several more coaxing words from Hawke, the ghost started to move.

"Yes, that's it," Hawke said, delight on his face. For the first time, Wren saw her brother wielding ghostsmith magic in a way that didn't make her feel sick. He wasn't ordering or commanding, he was *connecting*, the behavior as human, as natural, as breathing.

Not dark but light, like Julian had said.

The ghost quivered, then oozed from the skull, making contact with Hawke's fingertips before crawling over his hand, weaving between his knuckles like a glowing green cloud brought down to earth.

Everyone watched, stunned into silence, until an echoing *crack* cut through the moment. Wren knew that sound intrinsically, spotting Mercy's scythe buried deep into the wolf's spine, one of the vertebrae fractured down the middle.

Something like heartbreak flickered across Hawke's features, and it occurred to Wren how very lonely his life must have been, ever since he'd been taken from Starling and the other nomad ghostsmiths. How his animal familiars were probably the only connections he'd been able to have since then. And the very idea that they were in pain, that they were prisoners, didn't sit well with him because it meant that one of the small joys he'd found in his life had come at a terrible cost.

Pity bloomed in Wren's chest at her brother's slumped shoulders and sloping brows, but abruptly the sadness in Hawke's expression changed. He startled, almost, his attention focused on the ghost still clinging to his fingertips. He watched, green eyes blazing, as the spirit softened and separated, turning into wisps.

Wren found herself staring too, confused—until she felt something. A flash of emotion. A frisson of tension. And then, just as quickly, a soul-deep relief. An unspooling. A release as peaceful as floating in a warm bath, as essential as those blissful moments when sleep comes upon you and the rest of the world fades away.

Wanting to know more, to see if what had happened in the lake was a fluke or her own imagination, Wren reached through the bars and clasped her brother's hand.

"Wren!" Julian cried out, but his voice was already fading away.

As the spirit swirled around them both, Wren saw images flash before her mind, along with smells and sounds that flooded her senses: cool water on her tongue, dewy grass under her feet, and the scent of prey in her nostrils. The world at night, black and white and clearer than should have been possible in the light of the sickle moon. The wind in her fur, her muscles propelling her forward with exhilarating speed—then pain, sudden and fierce . . . and after that? Nothing.

When she came back to herself, the ghost was gone, and her cheeks were wet with tears. Julian's hand was on her upper arm, as if he'd been shaking her.

She looked at her brother, and their eyes met, a question passing between them.

He had felt the pain and the release, she was sure of that. But had he seen and experienced all that she had?

Wren turned to Mercy, who had been looking between them, something knowing in her features. "Do you feel it too? The emotion?"

"I don't feel it the way you do," she said, nodding at Wren's tears, which Wren hastily swiped away. "But I sense the release of pressure. The lack of tension. The relief."

As Mercy turned her attention to opening the cage and removing the body with Julian's help, Wren sidled over to her brother.

"I need to talk to you. Now."

NINETEEN

Unfortunately, Wren and Hawke had to help the others deal with the reaped revenant's body first.

Mercy had a cemetery she had built for herself behind the house, and after carrying the corpse to the back of her property, their group started digging.

Traditional bonesmith burials usually involved interring a *fresh* body—spirit still attached—in a bone-lined graveyard. Then, after the flesh had rotted away, a reapyr could free the ghost and claim the anchor bone.

In this case, the wolf's spirit had already been dealt with, but it was still an important part of the ritual to give what remained of the living flesh back to the earth. Once that was done, Mercy could dig it up again and claim the anchor bone for weapons or talismans and use the others to fill out her defenses or build more traps.

It was all part of the never-ending cycle of life and death in the Dominions.

Afterward, Wren had hoped she and her brother could sneak away, but darkness was falling, and it was time to clean up and prepare dinner.

Wren redressed in her dried clothes and shoveled her food down, not even appreciating the first warm meal she'd had in days, her mind still racing. Hawke had yet to put his clothes back on, looking as bizarre as ever in his blanket and cloak as he caught Wren's eye and wandered out the door while everyone finished eating, his own plate mostly untouched.

"Go on," Leo said under his breath, being more perceptive than most. Nodding toward the door, he took up Wren's plate to help with the cleaning while Mercy went digging in a cupboard for extra blankets, piling them into Julian's waiting arms so they could make pallets on the floor.

Outside, full dark had fallen, but Hawke was easy to see.

He was seated atop a large boulder just outside the bone fence, illuminated by the light of his familiars. But for the first time since she'd seen them, they brought no joy to his face. The night was quiet, save for the gentle lapping of the lake against the shore, so the crunch of Wren's boot steps alerted him to her approach.

"What's its name?" she asked, nodding at the ghost-fox.

"His name is Tail," he said. Talon and Tail. Not the most inspired monikers, but Hawke had surely been a boy when he'd named them. "I know what you're going to ask," he said without looking her way.

"Do you?" Wren said, coming to stand beside him.

"You want to know if I felt it. When that ghost was reaped."

"I *know* you felt it," Wren said. "It was written all over your face."

He sighed heavily, reaching toward Tail as the ghost-fox pressed his nose to the ground in a ghostly mimicry of a sniff, but letting his hand drop before he made contact. "All these years, and I only ever touched them while tethered. Human undead are all the same, foul and hateful, but animals . . . I didn't know they were in pain. Not until I felt the absence of it."

Wren understood. She'd never touched a ghost before, but she'd seen many reapings. Like Mercy, she'd sensed the relief the undead felt to have their tethers cut, even if they fought it at first. It manifested itself in the very air, as if their undead presence disrupted the world around it—an invisible bubble that became apparent only when it popped.

"So you felt its emotion—the wolf," Wren said, trying to choose her words carefully.

"I suppose so," Hawke said, considering. "I certainly felt its relief, its . . . gratitude, maybe?"

Wren nodded. "Did you feel anything else? *See* anything?"

He frowned, turning to face her at last. "See?"

Wren blew out a breath. "When I touched the wolf's ghost, I saw things . . . *through* its eyes. Its last moments alive, I think. And its death. Or the pain of it."

Hawke listened with great intensity, his unnatural green eyes gleaming in the moonlight.

"And," Wren added, "it happened in the lake, too. When I was under. I saw the flood happening. I saw that person's death. Is that . . . ? Have you ever seen anything like that?" she asked, because Hawke still hadn't spoken.

"You have Vision," he said, sounding impressed.

"I have what?"

"Vision. It's a very rare ghostsmith skill."

"You mean you don't have it?" Wren asked, her heart sinking. Bad enough she was a ghostsmith at all, but now she had to be an unusual one?

Hawke shook his head.

"But how could *I* have an ability *you* don't, when I was barely a ghostsmith a couple of weeks ago? Shouldn't you be stronger than me?"

He quirked her a small grin. "I'm definitely stronger," he said, and Wren saw a whisper of her own self-assuredness shining through. "But Vision isn't about strength. It also tends to be recessive and usually skips a generation."

"What does it do? What does it *mean*?"

"Vision allows you to see a ghost's memories. Usually their last memories, before death, but if you practiced . . . you could see their entire lives. That's why ghostsmiths never reaped the undead. They are a font of knowledge for those who are able to seek it."

Wren swallowed. "Does Ravenna have it?"

Hawke's shoulders slumped, his excitement dimming. He glanced away. "Yes. That's how she was able to find the well. Interrogate enough undead and one of them will have the answers you seek."

Wren forced herself to consider it objectively. Here was another horrifying layer to this magic, another new ability to master . . . but a potentially extremely useful one.

"Can you teach me?" she asked. "How to use it?"

"It's just like commanding the undead. Except, in this case, you're not commanding them to act. You're commanding them to share something with you."

Wren made a noise of disgust in her throat, but now was not the time to chicken out.

"Okay. Fine. Let's . . . let's try it. I'll use . . ." She waved a hand at Hawke's familiars, before her attention fell on her ring.

"It might be easier to start there," Hawke said, apparently agreeing with her unspoken line of thought. "With your own familiar."

This time, since Wren was actually wearing her ring, when she thought about summoning the creature, it started to coalesce before she'd fully formed the request. "Come," was all she said before the bird was hovering before her.

"That's it," Hawke said encouragingly. "Well done."

It was stupid, but those simple words of praise brought a flush of pleasure to Wren's cheeks. It wasn't that she'd never been praised before; she had, by instructors and fellow classmates, however reluctantly. Wren's arrogance didn't often endear her to either party; nor did it make her a likely candidate for compliments.

But something about hearing it from a family member made the words land differently. Recognition from her father had always been sparing to the point where Wren was nearly starved for his approval, and her grandmother had never once said a kind thing about her—certainly not to her face.

"Now, this time, tell your familiar what you want to see. Request a memory."

"But how will it understand such a complex command? I haven't trained it."

"It's your familiar; you are connected. Show it in your mind. Focus on the meaning behind the command. And make sure you're touching the ghost when you do it. Go on."

She hesitated; rather than randomly poking her hand through her familiar's spirit, she held it out, palm up, for the ghost-bird to land on.

And it did. Even without a command, it seemed to understand her will, as Hawke said it would.

Wren's hand shook as she stared at the tiny songbird, sitting comfortably in her palm, a spot of icy cold against her skin. Her mind still rebelled at the sight, shouting about deathrot, but she was clearly not at risk. She recalled the time when she was younger and she'd had a brush with a ghost, spending the night in bed shivering. Of course, her ghostsmith powers hadn't been awakened yet, so perhaps her immunity hadn't either. Or perhaps her latent magic had saved her, and the icy chill had been her own imagination.

Her familiar shuffled its wings, gazing up at her with a calm focus she swore she'd never seen in a living bird . . . or a ghost.

"All right," Wren said. The bird cocked its head, listening. Wren blew out a shaky breath.

When she'd first used this ability, it had been purely by accident, the memories coming at her in a barrage and without conscious choice. The same thing had happened with the revenant wolf. Maybe it had been Wren's panicked mind that had gone searching for them. Or maybe it had been the undead's own troubled state. But now she was touching this ghost, and nothing was happening.

"Show me your life," Wren said, though she sensed the command was too vague. Picturing the words in her mind, she tried again. "Show me your favorite place."

On cue, images burst to life before Wren's waking eyes, bright and vivid and blocking out the rest of the world. This time she soared through the sky, dipping and diving, utterly free. There was a grove of trees, their swaying boughs hanging low as they brushed the earth. . . .

"Wren," came Hawke's voice from very far away. Then there was pressure on her shoulders, and she blinked away the visions to see his pale face before her.

She shook off the last dregs and glanced around. She still held her familiar in her hand, still stood next to the bone fence, but everything looked different somehow.

"She loved to fly," Wren found herself saying. "Especially in the willow tree grove. Do you know of one?"

Hawke shook his head, and for some reason that made Wren sad. How long had this poor bird been dead? And where had she come from?

Because the bird *was* a she. Wren knew that now, though she couldn't say how she knew.

"Your familiar, she—"

"Willow," Wren interjected. Hawke stared at her, but Wren refused to meet his gaze. Surely it was easier to name her familiar than to keep calling it "her familiar," especially when Hawke had at least two of his own. It was just confusing.

It didn't mean anything.

"Willow," Hawke corrected himself. "She had a good grip on you."

"A grip on me?" Wren asked uncertainly. The ghost-bird was as docile as ever in her palm.

"With her memories. Your eyes had closed and your body was starting to go lax. . . . If I hadn't pulled you out, you might have lost consciousness."

"Oh," Wren said, new fear blossoming in her chest. She recalled drifting into darkness in the lake before Hawke had jumped in to save her. And with the revenant wolf, Julian had touched her arm, bringing her back to herself. "How do I make sure I can pull myself out?"

"Try to keep one foot here, with yourself. Maybe touching something, like the fence, or . . ."

"Give me your hand," she said, before she could overthink it.

He did, his palm cool. This time, when Wren dove into Willow's memories, Hawke's hand acted like an anchor, ensuring she didn't go too far adrift. She still felt Willow's life—the wind through her feathers—but she maintained a connection to herself and her own body.

When she drew back from the memories on her own, Hawke grinned.

Wren couldn't help the smug smile that tugged at her lips. She was a born show-off and loved to excel at anything. Apparently even this.

"You said you use them as messengers. How?"

Her enthusiasm was feeding into Hawke's as well. He shifted on the rock, leaning forward eagerly. "It's simple, really. You just come up with a code they can replicate. For Tail, I use taps." He knelt before Tail, extending his hand, into which the ghost-fox rested one glowing green paw. "For scouting, one tap means 'all is well.' Two taps signal a friend approaching. Three taps mean a foe. But you can utilize as many commands as you can come up with. They learn quickly, thanks to the bond." He stood, waving his hand and sending Talon soaring up into the sky. "With birds, they can give a verbal report."

The ghost-hawk's glowing form stood out starkly against the darkness, making the stars dull by comparison. Even the moon couldn't compete, in brightness or in beauty, with the spirit swooping in graceful arcs, trailing scraps of ghostlight in its wake.

"It doesn't bother you? The glare?" Wren asked, indicating her eye black.

Hawke shrugged. "Used to it, I guess."

Wren glanced down at her own familiar, whom she still held in her palm. She wondered if the ghost itched to take to the sky, to relive the feeling of flight, however unsatisfactory it must be to the real thing.

She wondered if she could feel joy, as she had in life. As Wren had felt in her memories. Or if it was only and always pain.

While some ghosts had the good fortune of dying from natural causes, their undead existence a less tormented one, familiars were sought out and killed *on purpose*. Strange to think how docile they were when their deaths were so violent, so cold-blooded and premeditated. Wren supposed that was the power of the ghostsmiths . . . to turn the world's deadliest and most dangerous foes into mindless servants.

Wren might have gotten caught up in the moment, but the truth remained: these ghosts did not want to be here. They wanted to be free, not tethered to a ghostsmith, no matter how close, how comfortable, how *familiar.*

They were servants. They were slaves.

"We'll have to let them go, you know," Wren said softly. "Not now. Now, we need them. But eventually. We'll have to let them go."

Hawke nodded, and just like that, their bubble of contentment, of joy in their magic, burst, and melancholy settled over them both.

Above, Talon was coming back their way, and a piercing shriek echoed through the night—though only Wren and Hawke could hear it.

One cry for the all-clear. Hawke smiled sadly, holding out his arm for Talon to land.

But then the ghost-bird emitted a second cry. Friend? Wren glanced at the house—was someone coming outside? Hawke frowned, just as a third call rent the night.

Foe?

But this last cry was tentative, quieter than the others. Uncertain. Like he didn't know what he'd seen.

Talon landed on Hawke's arm, bringing a gust of otherworldly air with him, enough to cause Willow to shuffle anxiously on Wren's palm.

"Go," Wren said quietly, and the ghost-bird disappeared. "What is it? What has he seen?"

Raising his fist to eye level, Hawke stared at his familiar as he shook out his wings and dipped his head repeatedly.

"I don't know," Hawke said at last, still frowning, though now he shifted his attention wide, over the hillside.

"Could he show me?" Wren asked, thinking to use her Vision.

Hawke shook his head. "They can share *living* memories only."

"Maybe he saw revenants," Wren said uncertainly. They were all around, the Laketown valley surrounded by a ring of high peaks that were dotted with distant pockets of ghostlight, demarcating dozens of ghosts and revenants prowling these hills, to say nothing of the faint glow emanating from the lake.

"Maybe," Hawke said, though he didn't sound convinced. He dismissed his familiars soon after, and they made their way back inside.

The others were spread out on the floor of the tiny cottage, the firelight a warm, welcoming contrast to the chill night beyond its wooden walls and bone fence.

But even with a warm blanket and all Mercy's protections, Wren struggled to sleep, haunted by willow trees and wings that would never fly again.

TWENTY

Inara stood in the Breachfort courtyard in the light of the nearest brazier with the rest of the welcoming party.

Lord-Smith Vance was to her left, next to Commander Duncan and his steward, and on the steps below them were a handful of other officials and administrators, plus servants and a patrol's worth of guards who were not on duty.

It was late, and the wind was bitter as it whipped against the Border Wall, stoking the fires that lined the courtyard and causing the flag atop the approaching wagon to ripple and snap.

When at last she caught sight of the skull and crossbones insignia, Inara's heart leapt.

Help had arrived.

For her, anyway.

It had been a trying couple of days. Inara owed Wren an apology for thinking her a slacker all these years—she'd had no idea that being a nuisance was such hard work.

Or maybe it was that Gravens possessed an astounding level of impossible self-belief, so that no barrier, no obstruction, could truly get in the way of their hard heads.

She had thought stopping the return of the two Breachside patrols would be enough to waylay Vance. Without those forty-odd soldiers, their numbers were far too small to mount an attack on the Haunted Territory. Inara didn't fool herself into thinking he cared about casualties, but he certainly cared about himself. There was no way he'd travel east if it made *him* vulnerable.

So she had done it. She had taken a horse to the edge of the palisade and waited hours for their arrival. When the scouts reached her, she hastened to send them off again, telling them to ride for Silver Gate and to remain there until further notice. If they thought to question their orders, they didn't, because Inara was a bonesmith.

They took her word as Vance's word. Again.

When the first day passed into night and still the patrols had not come back, Inara congratulated herself on a scheme well executed . . . until Vance summoned her to Odile's room once more.

She thought she'd been found out, but instead Vance announced that they'd be heading out first thing the following morning—with or without the additional soldiers. The extra bonesmiths he had summoned would more than make up for their lack of mere "undead fodder," as he'd called the Breachfort garrison, but Inara knew from very recent experience that double, triple the amount of soldiers—*and* bonesmiths—would not be enough.

Whatever Vance tries to do . . . make sure he doesn't.

Inara had felt like it was the night before a test and she'd forgotten to study. There was no time to plan, to prepare, to *strategize*. But even if there had been, there were no legitimate means of stopping him.

Which meant she'd just have to turn to some illegitimate ones.

She would play cheap and dirty, just like him. Lie, cheat, and cut corners.

She'd looked to Wren for inspiration.

Wren had attempted to avoid dozens of tests, assignments, and duties over the years, using tactics that ranged from *mildly* poisoning a professor to unleashing a ghost inside the catacombs.

Inara *did* consider poison, but she didn't have the necessary materials and didn't trust the silversmith healer not to talk if she was caught poking around their supplies. And, inconveniently, the Breachfort didn't have any ghosts.

But there'd been another time several years back when Wren, Inara, and the rest of the valkyr novitiates had been ordered to ride to Severton to help dig a dozen graves at the local cemetery. Wren had succeeded in avoiding the task not by targeting the teacher who had given the order but by targeting their mode of transportation.

So, like Wren before her, Inara had set fire to the stables.

More specifically, to the tack room.

You could still smell the smoke, the scent of charred wood and melted leather permeating the courtyard.

To Inara it smelled like victory.

It had been a near thing, though. Since the horses were fine, simply saddleless, Vance had been *this close* to suggesting some soldiers ride bareback before, finally, mercifully, the news had arrived.

Lady-Smith Svetlana Graven would be there within the hour.

When Inara looked over at him now, it was clear Vance could not be *less* pleased to see the House of Bone flag, while next to him, Commander Duncan appeared smug.

Vance might outrank *him*, but he did not outrank his mother.

The carriage rolled to a stop at the base of the stairs, and like a dutiful son, Vance waved off the nearest servant and hastened down the steps to open his mother's door himself.

The woman exited the conveyance, her gaze raking over her son before rising up to the commander and the rest of the welcoming party.

Inara couldn't help but grin. She had done what she could, but it was time for the professionals, and no one could mess things up like a Graven.

The commander descended the stairs, greeting Svetlana warmly. "I'm glad to know the fort will be in good hands while I am gone." He turned a meaningful look at Vance before continuing. "I leave before dawn to meet the prince's retinue and escort them here personally, and I hated the idea of leaving my post . . . unattended."

"Indeed," Svetlana said, her cold eyes flicking toward her son. Stepping aside, the commander waved for the servants to unload her bags. "Show me to my chambers," she said to her son by way of greeting.

Vance darted a look at the servants milling about. "They're just being prep—"

"I'll have yours, then. I am weary and in need of rest."

"Yes, Mother. Of course."

He offered his arm—which she ignored—before jerking his chin at Inara, indicating that she should follow.

It wasn't that Inara was in his confidence or important enough to walk with the noble Gravens; it was more that he liked to have subordinates around. People to walk behind him, bow to him, and heed his wishes.

The walk to Vance's rooms was utterly silent, save for their echoing footsteps and the distant sounds of trunks and bags being carried up the stairs and down the hall behind them.

They reached the door. "See me in one hour," Svetlana said, neatly dismissing him *and* depriving him of the opportunity to gather any of his own possessions. He bowed his head curtly, jaw clenched, but before he could go—"Oh, and, Vance? Bring my dinner with you."

After Vance stormed off, ignoring Inara entirely, she lingered in the hallway as servants came and went from his rooms.

She had an hour to get into position.

Not only had Wren shown her how to be an irritant, a saboteur, and an overall pain in the ass, but she'd also shown her how to get in and out of Vance's chamber *without* using the door.

If Svetlana was about to tear out Vance's plans by the root, Inara wanted a front-row seat.

As a discussion broke out over whether all of Svetlana's trunks should be brought *here* or if they should only bring her necessities and continue preparing her original chamber, Inara slipped into the empty room next door.

It was small and unremarkable, containing a few pieces of furniture draped in fabric, but Inara strode past it all to the balcony. She swung the doors wide, peering across the gap to the matching balcony that led to Vance's rooms.

Light spilled out from the glass panes, but it was muted, indicating that the curtains were drawn.

She climbed over the railing and leapt the distance, *barely* making the jump and cursing Wren for making this look easier than it was.

She caught her breath, listening hard, but the sounds within remained undisturbed.

Climbing the balustrade and crouching in the darkness, she

peered through a gap in the curtains and pressed her ear to the glass. When a particularly large trunk was dropped into the center of the room, she turned the handle on the door and opened it the barest of cracks.

The voices within crystallized, every scuff and mutter as clear as a bell, and no one had noticed the door shifting behind its curtain. If she angled her head just right, she could even see into the room beyond.

Servants moved back and forth, bags were unpacked, and trunks shifted.

Finally, Svetlana waved them off and took a seat at the table before the balcony, head angled toward the door. Waiting.

He was late.

Inara couldn't be certain, but she'd bet Nightstalker all over again that Vance had *chosen* to be late in an attempt to regain some measure of control. It was a juvenile tactic, but Vance was a juvenile man.

More time passed, *just* enough to be noticed but not enough to cause true ire, when a knock sounded.

The door swung open without waiting for a response, and in strode Vance.

He had deposited the requested dinner tray into the hands of one of the guards who had been posted outside the door, then gestured for the man to carry the food in himself. The guard looked at Lady-Smith Svetlana uncertainly, and it was clear to Inara that the man had insisted on the knock—and Vance had quickly overridden him.

Svetlana waved her dinner into the room. As soon as the tray was in place, she dismissed the guard. "Leave us."

As she took up her cutlery and began to eat, Vance hovered before her, hands clasped behind his back. She'd not invited him to sit, and Inara suspected that was very much on purpose. She seemed in no rush to speak to him, either, methodically slicing her meat and drinking her wine as if he weren't there at all.

Vance cleared his throat. "Is there something you needed, Mother? You have come at a busy time; I am in the midst of preparations. I'll be leading a contingent of bonesmiths and Breachfort soldiers into the Breachlands. We're going to get her back—get all of them back. We're going to win."

"*You're* leading the soldiers, are you?" Svetlana asked, as if he were a precocious toddler announcing a war campaign. "On whose authority?"

"My own," he bit out.

"You forget that any and all authority you possess is by *my* leave, and I have not approved this mission, nor will I."

Inara grinned, a weight lifting from her shoulders. Svetlana was putting a stop to this in typical, brutal fashion, and there was nothing Vance could do about it.

"You have summoned bonesmith reinforcements?" Svetlana continued. "Good. We will keep them here. We will prove to the prince that we are a strong and capable house and that we have the situation in hand, that we are *competent*, even if the truth is that you've made nothing but a mess of it since you arrived—not to mention what you've done to land us here in the first place."

Vance's lips pressed together as he forced a breath out of his nostrils. "What I've *done* is to make us relevant again. Already we have a proper royal visit—not some third son on an inspection—and if you would only let me *continue* my operations, I'd have the entire Dominions falling on their knees before the week was out."

Svetlana shook her head, smirking slightly. "All smoke and no fire.

You want a *show* of power instead of true power. The House of Bone is ingrained in this land as surely as magic itself. We are a part of its fabric, its foundation. Our place was never in question."

"Wasn't it? Isn't that what you threw in my face every chance you got?"

"Someone had to remind you of your foolishness lest you repeat your mistakes—and clearly, even my constant reprimands did not work because here you are again, dallying east of the Wall."

"It is too late to put the alka back in the bottle," he said, voice rising, though he quickly tamped it back down. "Those undead soldiers . . . We cannot stop them. But *she* can. So either you let me go and take that power for ourselves, or we step aside and watch as the Dominions are torn apart."

"Isn't that what you wanted?" Svetlana asked, putting her cutlery down with a clatter.

"You know it isn't!" he shot back. "Not truly. I only ever intended to give the regent enough rope to hang himself, that's all. Let him kidnap princes and make lofty demands—I thought we'd get a second Uprising, not *this*. I knew nothing of these so-called iron revenants. So I pivoted, seeking to use the very power they have turned against us. I had everything under control before you turned up."

Svetlana barked a cruel laugh. "Am I wrong, or had you not lost your leverage, your salvation, *and* your daughter well before I arrived?"

"Do not laugh at me," Vance said, his voice trembling with suppressed rage.

Svetlana's eyes flashed, her good humor gone. "Do not *threaten* me," she said, getting to her feet. "Do not forget that it is by *my* intervention, *my* support, and *my* name that you are not downstairs in a cell next to Lord Galen."

Vance's eyes grew extra bright. "I have given my account. Why on earth anyone would take *his* word over mine is—"

"I have heard your *account*," Svetlana said with venom. "And I have read the transcript of his. It's safe to say the two do not add up. Strange that Odile sent me a letter right before she was killed. It's almost as if she saw this coming. Stranger *still* that her letter names *you* as a conspirator and not Galen. So watch your tone with me, Vance, or I'll submit that letter as evidence in the upcoming trial."

Vance's head dropped to his chest. When he lifted it, his expression was wiped clean of emotion.

"This letter, you mean?" he asked lightly. Withdrawing his hands from behind his back, he held a piece of paper before Svetlana. For the first time, the woman looked unsettled. She glanced around her room, but whatever trunk or bag he'd taken it from, it clearly wasn't here. "Odile told me the letter did not contain anything incriminating. Nothing about Ravenna, my deal with the regent, or Wren." He sighed. "She lied."

He strode over to the nearest candle and, before Svetlana could open her mouth, set the letter on fire, holding it as the flames curled across the paper.

"You can destroy that letter, but the truth will not die with Odile. Galen is alive and well."

"It's funny; Odile knew I was involved, but Galen did not. He knew he was speaking to the House of Bone, though. Who else could deliver Wren Graven to the Breachfort? Actually, technically, *I* didn't deliver her at all. You did."

Svetlana's face paled; coupled with her bonesmith eyes and silvering hair, she appeared utterly leeched of color.

"And as you've just pointed out, I do nothing without *your leave*,"

Vance said, smiling vindictively as the noose tightened around her neck. "What do you think I'll say if you try to use this against me, hm?" He adopted an innocent tone. "I did all of this on *your* orders, after all. I am but your humble servant. Your heir. Your devoted son." He smiled bitterly. "If I go down, Mother, I'm taking you down with me."

Still Svetlana didn't speak, though her hands clenched into fists at her sides.

"So, what will it be? Will you destroy us both, or will you get the hell out of my way?"

Another moment of silence, and then Svetlana dropped, unspeaking, into her chair.

Inara's heart plummeted into her stomach as Vance smiled, dipped into a mocking bow, and strode from the room, leaving his mother—and Inara's best chance at stopping him—behind.

Inara leapt the gap and hid in the adjoining chamber until morning.

She slipped into the bustling hall to hear news that the "confused" patrol members that had *mistakenly* been sent to Silver Gate had finally returned, which meant Vance had everything he wanted in order to march east. They even brought extra saddles with them to replace the damaged ones from the fire.

This was a complete and utter disaster.

Inara was now faced with a choice. She could back down like Lady-Smith Svetlana had. She could do what she had always done and choose self-preservation. Walk the line. Heed the orders. Be a good and loyal bonesmith.

Or she could do what she knew was right . . . even if it was as stupid and dangerous as she had ever accused Wren of being.

She'd been following the Graven example for the past few days. . . . What was a few more?

Besides, Inara had come up short, and she hated to see a job left undone.

She rode out with Vance's forces as the gate rose and the early-morning sun spilled into the courtyard, flashing off steel and bone. As they turned north on the Old Road that ran alongside the Wall, preparing to take a mountain pass that Vance had used during the Uprising, Inara allowed herself to drift to the back of the column.

Vance believed he could get into the heart of the Haunted Territory—the Breach itself—in two days.

Inara could do it in one.

Wren was there, and she needed to be warned. Her father was on his way, and however hard her task had been beforehand, it was about to get a whole lot worse.

TWENTY-ONE

Wren awoke in the predawn darkness, Mercy next to her.

"Something draws near."

A glance at the window showed Wren nothing but the familiar, eerie Laketown landscape.

"Revenants?" Wren croaked, still half-asleep.

Mercy shook her head. "Riders."

Riders? Is that what Talon had seen the night before? She and Hawke hadn't bothered to alert Mercy of his familiar's seemingly confused warning, but perhaps that had been a mistake.

Wren joined her next to the window. "Do we know who they are? Travelers, or . . . ?"

"They wear the regent's colors." Those words came from Hawke, who Wren had failed to notice was already awake behind her.

Sure enough, when Mercy pointed into the distance, Wren spotted a flash of red between the trees.

"Red Guard," Wren said, glancing over her shoulder at Julian. Both he and Leo had awoken as well and were sitting up from their beds on the floor. "But this place is so haunted. How can they risk traveling here?"

"There are protections along the path that leads to the road," Mercy said with a shrug. "In case I've need to travel—or travelers have need to see me. Most don't know about the safe passage, but this is not the first time the Red Guard have come calling."

"Why?" Wren asked warily.

Mercy shrugged. "Information, mostly. Which I offer in exchange for supplies."

"They can't find us here," Wren said.

Mercy frowned at Wren before turning her attention to Julian. As an ironsmith, the regent and the Red Guard were meant to be his allies.

"There's a price on my head," Julian confessed, though he spoke as if the words tasted foul in his mouth.

"There are *interested parties* looking for all three of us," Leo clarified, gesturing to Wren as well.

"And you?" Mercy asked Hawke. "They say there's a queen who prowls these lands. I've heard she has a loyal servant who does her bidding, to say nothing of what else she plans down in the deep."

"It's not what you think," Wren said hastily. "We're working against her. We need to get to the Breach. That dark magic—that power you think is in the water—we're going to destroy it."

Mercy cocked her head, taking in their ragtag crew in an assessing sort of way. Eventually she nodded. "There's a chance they don't know you're here and are simply making a quick stop-in. Stay inside, and I'll try to divert them."

"We can't risk being trapped," Wren said. She wouldn't gamble with their lives. With Julian's life. "If they surround the house, we're finished."

"What is your route?" Mercy asked, turning to Hawke. "What path do you intend to take?"

"The throughway. There's an entrance around the bend—"

"Impossible," Mercy said. "That entrance stands between us and them, and these riders will beat you to it. You either wait here while I try to send them off, or you find another route."

"There is no other route," Hawke argued, but even as he said it, his expression flickered, as if he'd remembered something.

"There is," Mercy said.

"But it's no good," Hawke said, already shaking his head. "It'll take us days off course."

"Shit," Wren said. She could actually hear the approaching horses now. "We could fight our way out of here. I'm sure with the help of a few undead, we could kill enough of them to—"

"No," Hawke said forcefully before composing himself. "No, I . . . We'll have to take the detour."

"But—" Wren began, though Julian was quick to cut her off.

"There's still a chance they don't know we're here," he said. "We're better off keeping it that way. We'll take the other tunnel. A day or two is better than not arriving at all."

Wren wanted to argue, but a glance at Leo told her she was outnumbered.

Hawke took up his staff and slid his skull mask over his face. "We'll need to do some climbing."

"Climbing? Where is it?" Wren asked, still peering out the front window. Hawke strode to the smaller window at the back, pointing to a spot a good twenty feet above them, nestled into the cliff and surrounded by sloping hills and shale.

Leo and Julian, who were shouldering bags and grabbing weapons, hurried forward to see for themselves.

"Wait until I have their attention, then slip out the window," Mercy said, moving toward the door. "If things go south, well . . . I'll slow them down if I can."

"You shouldn't risk it," said Julian, as he sheathed his sword and placed his helmet on his head. "They won't hesitate to harm you."

"Nor I them," Mercy said matter-of-factly, hefting her crossbow. "I think a few warning shots ought to tell them I mean business."

"Mercy," Wren said before the woman could go. "Thank you. For everything."

"Good luck to you," Mercy said brusquely. "If your task is true, it is a worthy one and will change this world for the better. Now get moving. And, bonesmith?" Wren looked up from her preparations, checking her bandolier and securing her swords. "There are more undead in these hills than you can count—or command, I'd wager. So . . . ready your blade."

Wren nodded, and then Mercy was out the door.

She called a greeting, hailing the Red Guard as they approached the front of the house and drawing their attention so that Wren and the others could sneak out the window at the back of the house.

The four of them crouched in the shadows, listening as Mercy conversed easily with the newcomers. Despite her chipper tone, Wren knew her loaded crossbow would say what the woman herself did not: that she was dangerous.

Wren itched to start climbing, to get away before the regent's men realized they'd even been here, but as soon as they ascended higher than Mercy's house, they'd be exposed.

As they waited in silence, the tone of the words being exchanged on the other side of the house changed slightly. They became blunter and more aggressive. Mercy cried out in anger, and the door to her house slammed open. Red Guard were likely searching inside, and it wouldn't take long for them to see the extra sleeping beds.

"Time to go," Wren said.

Hawke slid his staff into a holder on his back to free his hands and took a moment to crane his neck to choose a likely path.

It wasn't entirely sheer. In fact, there were sloping sections and shelves of stone large enough for feet to walk across, but Wren was more concerned with how exposed it was. If the Red Guard had any archers with them . . .

"There," Julian murmured, tracing a path they could follow all the way to the top.

They started to climb, moving quickly as the voices below grew louder.

Apparently they had found the bedding and were now demanding answers from Mercy.

Wren and the others hadn't yet been spotted, but all that changed when Leo's foot slipped and a cascade of stones went clattering down the hillside.

Wren's head whipped around, and sure enough, a dozen Red Guard turned their way.

Before they could react, however, Mercy fired her crossbow—not at anyone or anything in particular, but it worked all the same. In response to the bolts whizzing past, the Red Guard ducked and scattered, buying Wren and the others a few precious moments.

But not nearly enough of them.

They hurried upward, heedless of the drop, of eyes upon them, and even when arrows ricocheted off the nearby stone, they continued to climb, because what else could they do?

At one point Hawke turned his masked face down at Wren. "I don't—"

But before he could even finish his sentence, another arrow soared their way, and this one landed true, right in Hawke's shoulder.

He cried out, losing his grip and falling backward.

He fell past Leo, past Wren—who could only stare in horror—and right into Julian's outstretched hand, his other gripping the cliff-side with the help of his vambrace blade, which he had inserted into the stone.

Using the weapon for leverage, he'd leaned out dangerously far to catch Hawke, and now, with an almighty heave, Julian dragged the pair of them back toward the rock face, pressing Hawke between himself and the wall.

While Julian caught his breath, Hawke hunched over his wounded arm, which was bleeding freely from the arrow shaft embedded in the flesh.

"Get him up," Wren ordered, lifting her ring to her mouth and whispering in a trembling voice. "Help me."

Willow appeared, and Wren stared at the Red Guard, particularly the archer who had wounded her brother and was currently in the process of nocking another arrow.

"Stop him," Wren said, and her familiar dove down at once toward their attackers.

Those who saw the undead coming ducked into the house or jumped from their saddles in an attempt to get out of the ghost's path, but Willow made a beeline for the archer.

He cried out and swiped fruitlessly at the air, but it was no good. She flew right through his chest, bursting out the other side as the man's arms went instantly slack, dropping both bow and arrow as he slumped forward in his saddle.

Worse than dead.

Wren watched it happen, hating the surge of pleasure in her chest, the surge of vindictive delight at taking out the person who had tried to take out her brother, but in tandem with that satisfaction was a visceral fear that tightened her stomach and turned her bowels to water.

Julian, meanwhile, withdrew his whip sword and released it, tossing it in a wide arc through the sky until he found a hold above and secured it.

Between himself, Leo, and the makeshift rope, they helped Hawke climb to the next ridge.

Willow, meanwhile, had circled back around, and with Mercy still nearby, Wren hastened to get a hold of her familiar.

"Back to me!" she shouted. The ghost-bird hesitated, attracted as they all were to the living, but eventually she looped around, causing more distraction and distress, before returning to Wren's outstretched hand.

Willow disappeared into the ring, and Wren turned her attention to scaling the last of the cliff, making for the tunnel entrance above.

The others had crested the top, dragging Hawke to lay against a cluster of stones to survey the damage. Hawke shoved his bone mask off his face with his good hand, revealing his expression for the first time. He was grimacing in pain, his skin paler than the mask and drenched with sweat.

They were currently out of view and out of range from the Red

Guard below, but that didn't mean the soldiers wouldn't decide to start climbing.

Hawke was panting, his teeth clenched, while Julian hastily sheathed his sword and crouched to examine the wound.

"It didn't puncture the bone, and it passed straight through. You got lucky, believe it or not."

Hawke's response was to whimper feebly.

"We need to get inside the tunnel," Wren said urgently, peering over the edge. Already several of the Red Guard were gathering below and preparing to ascend.

"He needs to be treated," Julian said.

"The tunnel," Hawke croaked.

With a look to Leo, Julian and the prince knelt beside Hawke and lifted him gingerly, then half walked, half dragged him into the darkness of the tunnel entrance.

Wren brought up the rear, walking backward with swords raised.

By the time the first Red Guard mounted the rise, Wren's group was deep in the passage. The Red Guard paused, silhouetted in the open mouth of the cave—but didn't pursue.

Wren wouldn't take any chances. Reaching backward, she withdrew Hawke's staff from the holder on his back, glancing first at his pained face and then at the skull on its tip.

This was Hawke's familiar, and it wasn't meant to obey anyone but him.

But they were twins, weren't they? They shared the same blood and bones. The same magic.

Wren flicked the skull. "Come, Hawke needs you."

A second later, it burst into life.

Turning, she jammed the staff into the ground, where it glowed an eerie green visible from outside. She thought of the command she had given Willow.

It had been terrible.

And effective.

"If they follow us," Wren whispered, staring as a second Red Guard joined the first, both of them looking her way. "Stop them."

TWENTY-TWO

They rounded a corner, and Leo and Julian staggered to a halt, leaving Hawke leaning against the wall as they caught their breath.

Unlike the other throughway passages, there were no skull sconces that Wren could detect. No way of lighting their path, except . . .

Willow appeared without Wren's needing to speak, hovering above them like a flickering lantern. Talon appeared as well, bursting to life from the ring on Hawke's hand, but rather than hovering above as Willow did, he perched on Hawke's good shoulder.

Hawke slid to the ground, his pallor worse than before—though that could be from the ghostlight. At least Wren could better see him now.

His eyes were closed, his lids fluttering fitfully, and Wren thought the ghost-bird might have been summoned accidentally by Hawke's pain.

Julian, who had crouched next to him, leapt back in alarm. Wren opened her mouth to chide her brother for being careless—or to order the ghost away herself—but the way it brushed its beak against her brother's face caused her to falter. It was comforting him, yes, but it was also *strengthening* him through his magic. He was a ghostsmith, after all.

She took up Julian's place next to her brother. "Tell me what to do."

Julian looked between Wren and Hawke, as if seeing something he hadn't seen there before. "We need to cut off the head of the arrow."

He held out a knife, and Wren reached without looking closely—but her fingers, they felt the familiar handle at once.

She looked down. Julian had given her Ironheart.

She met his gaze, uncertain. His expression was surprisingly soft for a moment before he nodded his chin at Hawke.

It was a subtle nudge, but Wren received it like a slap to the face. Her brother was in pain.

Whirling around and careful not to disturb Talon, whose presence had calmed her brother's frantic breathing and anguished moaning, Wren reached around her brother's back to find the arrowhead poking out the other side.

"This is going to hurt," she warned. He opened his eyes long enough to steel himself and nod, then closed them again. Wren felt his complete trust in her. It made her throat tighten.

Bending over, she sawed carefully at the wooden shaft, doing her best not to bump and jostle it.

Luckily, ironsmith metal was the sharpest there was, and Julian kept all his weapons in good condition. The blade passed through easily, with a clean cut and no splintering on the wood.

"Good," Julian said gently. Wren expelled a shaky breath, knowing the task was not yet done and determined to do it well. "Now we need to slide the arrow shaft out. Slowly. Leo, get something to stem the flow."

"Will he . . . ? Will he bleed out?" Wren asked quietly, not wanting Hawke to hear her.

But he did.

"Just get me patched up enough to move," he gritted out, eyes open once more. "The well will heal me."

"The well . . . ?" Wren repeated, trailing off. "It can heal you? Are you sure?"

Hawke nodded, expression strained. "It has before."

"What? How? When?"

"Later," Julian cut in. Right. Of course. She kept losing focus. "Take the arrow shaft," he prompted, redirecting Wren to the task at hand.

"And I can close it up afterward," Leo said, causing both Wren and Julian to turn to him in surprise. He shrugged self-consciously. "I'm good with needle and thread. Gold isn't as effective as silver, but it will do in a pinch."

"Whoever said you were useless was clearly an idiot," Julian said bluntly.

For the first time in his life, Leo was speechless.

"Ready?" Wren asked Hawke, placing one hand on his arm to keep it still and taking hold of the wooden shaft with the other.

"Yes," Hawke whispered.

"Three, two—"

She pulled. The sensation of the wood fibers sliding against skin and muscle was enough to turn Wren's stomach, to say nothing of the pain it must have caused her brother.

He cried out as the arrow tore free, Talon flaring brightly in response, and Wren suspected his presence was the only thing keeping her brother conscious.

As soon as the arrow was out, there was a spurt of blood, and Leo leapt in with a wad of fabric, applying pressure to the wound. Wren did the same on the other side.

Minutes passed; Hawke's labored breathing slowed once more, as did the pulse of his blood.

"I'd prefer to clean it first," Leo said when Julian took over the task of applying pressure, and Leo created a needle and thread, this time using one of his necklaces, the fine gold chain thinning and thinning under Leo's hands.

"Water will have to do," Julian said. "Hopefully the well will handle the rest."

"It will," Hawke rasped.

When it came time to actually stitch, the wound rinsed with water and patted dry, Wren held Hawke's other hand in a tight grip, while Julian offered the padded leather handle from one of his daggers for Hawke to bite onto.

Wren thought of Ironheart, which she'd left on the ground, extremely aware of the fact that Julian had not yet reclaimed it.

Hawke bore the stab and pull of the needle and thread with far more dignity than Wren would have, though he'd called Tail to his side in the process. Wren just hoped the Red Guard wouldn't take the ghost's absence as an opportunity to enter the cave.

When the stitches were done, the thread knotted and the wound covered with the cut corner of a blanket, Leo fashioned a sling with the remaining fabric, and Julian disposed of the bloody rags.

Wren, meanwhile, went back to retrieve Hawke's staff, relieved to see the passage empty and the mouth of the cave abandoned. Apparently the Red Guard soldiers who had made the climb had decided to abandon the chase.

When she returned, Hawke took it gratefully, using it to get to his feet and to keep him steady. Tail returned to his anchor bone, his glowing skull lighting the way, and Talon rode on Hawke's good shoulder.

Julian and Leo were packed up and ready to go, and Ironheart was no longer on the ground. Julian must have taken it back. Wren was about to feel bad about that when—

"You dropped this," said Julian. He held the dagger in his gloved hands.

"Oh, I . . ." Wren trailed off, uncertain. "I guess I was finished with it and I . . . I didn't know what you wanted."

She didn't mean to imply the greater question, but she supposed it was unavoidable.

"Are you?" Julian asked carefully. "Finished?"

Again, it felt like they were having an entirely different conversation beneath the mundane one. "No," Wren said softly. "No, I'm not."

Julian nodded, something like relief flickering across his features before he wiped them blank once more. "Then you should keep it for now. In case."

"Right," Wren said, lifting the weapon from his hands. *For now* was better than not at all.

As soon as she'd unburdened him, he cleared his throat and sidled up to Hawke and Leo.

As Wren joined them, she saw Leo wiping his fingers against the tunnel wall. She frowned . . . and the expression only deepened when she saw a smear of golddust left behind. It was nearly invisible, until Talon ruffled his feathers or Willow bobbed in the air, the metallic powder catching the ghostlight.

Julian saw it too and quirked a brow at him.

"If we need help getting out of here," Leo said quietly, flipping closed what was evidently a hidden compartment atop one of his rings, where the powdered gold was stored. Leave it to the Gold Prince to have cosmetics on him, even here in the Breachlands.

As he spoke, Leo nodded at the back of Hawke's head, which was bent over his arm as he fidgeted with his sling, distracted.

What he meant was: in case Hawke lost consciousness—or worse—and they wound up totally lost. "I've been doing it since we started this little underground adventure."

"Clever," Wren conceded.

Julian also looked impressed. "As I said, whoever discounted you was either stupid or jealous."

"Probably both," Wren said, and Leo beamed.

They set out again, and though Hawke was in less pain now that the arrow was removed, he was still grimacing with every step. Wren sought a means to distract him.

"So the well . . . it's healed you before?"

"I was ghost-born," he said wearily, darting a glance at her. "Have you heard of it?" She shook her head. "I was born close to death."

Wren recalled Odile's tale of her birth, how the second child, the son, was not expected to live long. Even Ravenna had been on the brink, and it had been a shock for Odile to discover years later that they had both survived. Amid all the other surprises Wren had overheard, she'd never given the *how* of it much thought.

"Among ghostsmiths, it's considered a blessing. Those that survive, anyway. I wasn't just close to death—I was dying. We both were."

"Me?" Wren asked, confused. That wasn't what Odile had said.

"No. *Her.* Our mother. But she took me to one of the well's gathering pools. She'd ridden a horse for two days right after giving birth to twins, bleeding out in the saddle, in order to save me."

A stab of guilt wormed its way into Wren's chest. Was she wrong for wanting to destroy this thing? But no. The well was man-made. It pulled raw magic up from where it belonged deep in the earth and gave humans huge amounts of unchecked power. The ghostsmiths were stealing magic for themselves, for their own gain, with no thought to the repercussions. Not only was the land unstable, with raw magic leaking all over the place, but it was *taking* magic from the source that the rest of the Dominions drew upon. If woodsmiths and watersmiths had disappeared from their lands, maybe this well was why. Smith magic was becoming less and less potent, supposedly because of the dilution of the bloodlines, but perhaps it had more to do with magic being diverted and redirected. Siphoned off and delivered to a lucky few and not to everyone. If that was the case, how long until Marrow Hall was magicless, and bonesmiths, too, a thing of the past?

And how much longer would the Dominions survive if that were to happen?

"It sounds like it saved *both* of you," Wren clarified.

She had to admit that Ravenna had been brave to make that journey on her own. And maybe a little bit reckless, like Wren herself, though she loathed using the same adjective for both of them. But Ravenna had saved *herself* as well as Hawke, hadn't she? She hadn't done it for him alone. It hadn't been altruistic or sacrificial. It had been survival.

Wren needed Hawke to understand that.

It was like Vance. Everything he had done to supposedly protect

Wren had also been to protect himself. He had murdered Odile's messenger and buried the truth of the well and of Wren's origins—for Wren, he'd claimed, but clearly he'd also benefited from those decisions.

It was difficult to spot, and Wren had certainly taken too long to see it herself, but this was not the true love of a parent. And seeing the way Ravenna used Hawke to achieve her own ambitions, she recognized the same behavior.

"She gave me my life," he said simply, as if that were all that mattered.

"And has *used* you ever since," Wren argued.

Hawke made no response, and when Wren opened her mouth to prod some more, she felt a gentle touch on her arm. She expected Leo and was surprised to find Julian next to her instead.

"He needs to conserve his strength," he said quietly. She slowed her pace to walk with him, letting Hawke continue on alone. "Arguing with you requires all of one's faculties."

He smirked, and Wren's heart skipped a beat, her hand coming to rest on Ironheart.

They continued on in the darkness, the lack of ghostlight sconces making the tunnels even more oppressive than before. Wren would have thought the absence of the undead could only make her feel safer, but it seemed the endless black, the unknown, was worse. The passage was roughly hewn and irregular, forcing them to duck or climb or shimmy sideways, not to mention the cracks and crevices and evidence of past cave-ins. The occasional tremors and rumbling echoes didn't help, either.

There was a sense of foreboding, of danger, around every corner.

Suddenly Leo's voice rang out, his tone sharp. "What is that?"

A dark shape loomed ahead in the tunnel, lying across their path.

With a trembling hand, Hawke lifted his staff, the ghostlight flaring more brightly as it crawled across the ground, slowly highlighting rough stone, bits of gravel . . . and a hand, covered in blood.

Wren's stomach dropped. "It's a body."

TWENTY-THREE

All of them froze in place at the sight, including Hawke, the body only just visible at the edge of the pool of ghostlight.

"Willow," Wren whispered, and the ghost fluttered toward the figure, adding more illumination. The ghost was braver than her to venture so close, but of course, she had nothing to fear.

Willow's fluttering, flickering glow finished the image Wren's mind was already trying to piece together: a body covered in blood from vicious slashes that had torn through fabric and flesh, leaving the person—a woman—nearly unrecognizable.

The blood was fresh: a bright, alarming red, but it no longer flowed.

The person was dead, but recently. How long until she rose to wander this passage, fury and hatred in her heart?

Hawke made a choking sound and then dove toward the woman, reaching for that pale, lifeless hand and dropping his staff in the process. It clattered to the ground, ghostlight bouncing, casting the scene in jarring flashes of light and dark.

"Hawke!" Wren said, following him, though whether the woman was a corpse or a revenant, he was in no immediate danger. "Stay back," she ordered Leo and Julian before crouching next to her brother.

He was just staring at the corpse, almost blankly, but with a kind of intensity that pushed Wren to do something. Anything.

Stomach clenched tight, she reached her fingertips toward the woman's neck, where a trio of slashes cut from her jawline down to her collarbone. She found the place where a pulse would beat, pressing her fingers against the flesh. It was too cold to be alive, but she waited all the same for a heartbeat she knew would never come.

"Maybe we can get her to the well?" Leo asked uncertainly.

Wren sighed. "You can't heal the dead."

Her brother didn't react, just remained poised there, still clasping the woman's hand. Wren reached for his arm, intending to pry him away, when she noticed something. There was a bracelet made of bone on the woman's limp wrist.

"She's a ghostsmith," Wren said, mostly to herself, turning her attention back to the rest of the body. The clothes were nondescript and her features difficult to identify, but a second bone bracelet sat on her other wrist, along with a bone ring on her finger. While bonesmiths wore bone armor and carried bone weapons, only ghostsmiths wore bone jewelry.

"Starling," said Hawke hoarsely, and Wren whipped around to stare at him.

"This is your wet nurse? The woman who raised you?"

"For a time," Hawke said, almost automatically, but his blank, expressionless face had started to crack. His lips trembled, and moisture had started to gather on his lower eyelids.

"What was she doing here alone?" Wren demanded.

Hawke squeezed his eyes shut, causing tears to trace tracks down his cheeks, and abruptly stood.

Julian edged forward then, frowning down at the body. Wren watched his eyes trace the wounds, wondering, as she was, who or what could have done this to her.

"Maybe she wasn't alone," Leo said. "Maybe the others were forced to leave her behind when whatever did this—"

"Revenant wolves, I expect," came Hawke's voice. He had retreated to the far side of the passage, his back against the cold stone wall, and had taken up his fallen staff. He looked like he'd collected himself, though a certain fragility remained in his rigidness—as if rather than bend, he was likely to break.

"Wolves—are you sure?" asked Julian skeptically. The wounds were certainly animalistic, but there was no evidence of the sort of ripping and tearing typical of claws and teeth.

"You heard Mercy. These hills are filled with revenants," he said, his face averted from Starling's body. "She . . ." He swallowed. "She should have known better."

"Sometimes people make dangerous choices out of desperation," Wren said. "Look at us."

"But these cuts . . . ," Julian said, shaking his head. "They're too clean for a wolf, alive or undead. And the attack pattern—a wolf would go for the throat, not hack and slash like this."

He spoke gently, not wanting to upset Hawke, but Wren didn't think her brother was even listening. He remained standing, gaze distant and jaw set.

"I could find out, you know," Wren said.

Julian and Leo frowned at her, while Hawke's eyes widened. He'd definitely heard that.

"Find out? How?" Leo asked.

Wren glanced up at Willow, who continued to float above them, providing light for them to see by. "I have Vision, apparently; it's a rare ghostsmith ability. I can see the memories of the dead. When I was in the lake, I saw their deaths. I saw the flood. I was able to see Willow's—my familiar's—memories as well." If Leo or Julian had a reaction to the fact that Wren had named her familiar, they didn't show it.

"No," Hawke said, sharply enough to make them all startle. "It's too dangerous. The fresh dead are too strong, and her ghost hasn't even formed yet. Besides, the wolf could be back any moment, and those Red Guard could be reporting to the regent and Ravenna as we speak. We have a head start, and we need to use it."

Right. Their mission. Their goal here.

"Here, let me . . . ," said Leo gently, reaching for Hawke's arm. Hawke looked confused until he realized his sling had come undone, the fabric hanging loosely from his neck.

Julian helped as well, leaving Wren alone with the body.

Hawke was right, there *was* no sign of the ghost, and yet . . . she could feel it if she tried. Her senses could already tell that this was a rotting corpse with the ghost attached and not a living person.

To her surprise, Willow fluttered down and landed on the woman's shoulder, right where it met her neck. Where the deepest slash existed.

The death wound.

With the others still preoccupied, Wren extended her magic the way she would to sense for bones—except this time, she sought a ghost.

It was there, clinging to the body but loosening by the second, and if Wren tugged, just a little, like pulling on a loose thread . . .

Careful not to completely lose herself to her magic, she extended her other hand toward the wound, toward the faintest shimmer of ghost-green glow, and the instant it touched her skin, it had her.

Her vision whited out, the wash of nothingness materializing into the brightest sunlight. There were flashes of color, laughter, and a pale-haired boy running in tall grass—Hawke? There were more images, too many to keep track of, the scenes flickering in and out of her mind before she could fully grasp them. But she knew she'd gone back too far, so she tried to bring the whirlwind to a halt, dragging herself closer to the present, to the moment of death. . . .

Inky blackness descended over her eyes.

Wren blinked, suddenly blind and fearing she was about to pass out, until the sounds filled her ears. Running footsteps slapping against stone, sharp breaths forming stitches in her sides, and a bone-deep sense of betrayal.

She stumbled, tripping on an unseen obstruction and hitting the ground hard. She gasped, and kicked out, and pleaded for mercy. And right before the first, searing slice, a wash of something floral hit her senses, jarring and unexpected in the dank passage. Then it was pain, pain, pain, the death slow and agonizing with every scraping slash—

Wren yanked herself from the vision, ashamed to admit it was the pain she was fleeing, the sensation visceral and terrifying.

The others hadn't noticed. While Leo still adjusted Hawke's sling, Julian was digging inside one of their packs. As he turned, he held up one of their remaining blankets.

After a second of confusion, Wren understood. While Hawke looked on, she covered the body, giving what dignity they could before they moved on. Before Starling's ghost detached entirely or decided to rise and bring her body with it.

Wren didn't fully understand what she'd seen, because of course there hadn't been much to actually see in the darkness. But her breaths still came fast as if *she'd* been the one running for her life, and she couldn't dispel the cloying floral scent from her nostrils or the sensation of a blade tearing through flesh.

Whatever had attacked Starling, it had not been a wolf.

"Wait," Hawke said as Wren was about to pull the blanket over the woman's face. Using his good hand, he reached under his shirt and withdrew a necklace of woven thread with a wishbone on the end. He tugged, and the rope snapped. "She made this for me," he said solemnly, before tucking it into her lifeless hand. Wren frowned, presuming it was sentiment that drove him, until he added, "It can help with the transition. If the undead has something from their life to cling to, a positive reminder of who they were, it can make their spirit less violent."

Well, wouldn't *that* have been nice to know? Wren imagined how many lives might have been saved, how many reapings less dangerous, if the undead had simply been buried with some token from their lives. Again, she was forced to reckon with the fact that not all ghostsmith lore was evil and that, perhaps, the bonesmiths had made a mistake in severing their ties all those centuries ago.

As their journey wore on, Hawke grew quieter and more subdued. He'd been wounded physically and emotionally, and Wren feared he might not have what it took to finish what they'd started.

When they reached a fork in the road, he stood at the junction for a long time, almost as if he'd forgotten the way, before finally taking the passage to the right. While the tunnel to the left had sloped downward into darkness, the one to the right continued straight.

"Do you know when we'll arrive?" Wren asked.

Hawke positively jumped in his skin when she spoke, as if he'd been lost in thought.

"Oh, uh, probably within a day or so."

Wren frowned. "You said this tunnel was a detour. That it would cost us days."

"That's what I thought," he said. "If we'd gone left at the fork, it would have. This passage was supposed to have collapsed, but it seems intact so far. If it stays that way, we'll be in good shape."

As they continued on, Wren tried to mentally prepare herself for what was to come, but instead, her mind kept flashing back to Starling's memories. She hadn't seen a wolf, but she hadn't seen anything at all, had she? Already, the sensations were slipping from her mind, making her question what she'd been certain of mere hours before. Wren feared *something* dangerous within these tunnels. . . . Could it have been one of the other ghostsmiths? Was Hawke not telling her the full story of the nomads?

They stopped when night had likely fallen outside the throughway, making camp next to an underground river, the gentle rush a soothing sound as they got what sleep they could. When they set out again hours later, the way was still clear—no tunnel collapse in sight—which according to Hawke's estimation meant they'd be arriving soon.

Though the passage of time was difficult to mark, the tunnel itself was changing, shifting gradually into something that more closely resembled the rest of the throughway they'd seen so far. The ground was smoother, the walls more uniform, and when they turned a corner, it was to discover they had arrived at the base of a set of stairs, twisting and climbing slowly up and out of view.

Hawke mounted the steps. Wren wasn't sure he should be ascending on his own, but he seemed hale enough, his staff taking on the brunt of his weight. Still, he stopped at the top and muttered to Talon, who leapt from his shoulder and disappeared down the passage.

"He's scouting ahead," Hawke said by way of explanation, lowering himself to sit on the topmost step. He used the staff both to help him sit and to lean his forehead against while he waited. "You should rest again while you can. We'll be there soon."

As they made themselves comfortable, Willow explored the open space, her light allowing Wren to pick out additional details like a half-finished carving, empty niches, abandoned chisels, and even a bench.

"Strange," Julian said, taking it all in himself. "The undead did this. But it all looks so normal. So . . . *human.*"

Willow looped around the open space playfully, taking advantage of the chance to spread her ghostly wings, and Wren couldn't help but smile.

"I never thought I'd see the day," Leo said jovially.

"What do you mean?"

"Wren Graven, fearsome bonesmith valkyr—"

"*Failed* valkyr," Wren interjected.

"—smiling at a ghost, of all things."

The comment was playful, but Wren felt judgment in it. Not from Leo, but from herself. Truly, what was she doing? Had she forgotten all she'd learned? Willow might *seem* happy, if such a thing were even possible for the undead, but she was not. She was a prisoner. She was suffering. She was the product of dark magic and even darker rituals, and Wren was about to put a stop to it.

At the cost of more suffering, she reminded herself. If Hawke was right, she would have to shatter the bones of the undead that made up the well. She'd be no better than her uncle before her—worse, even, because she knew and understood what she was doing. Had seen the results firsthand. But they had to stop the iron revenants. They had to stop Ravenna. This was the only way.

Still, her mood plummeted.

"This food won't distribute *itself*, Your Highness," Julian said. Wren had the strangest feeling he was trying to bail her out. Indeed, while Leo made his apologies and helped dig through what remained of the food in their bags, Julian caught her eye before looking away.

Wren returned her attention to her familiar. "Go," she whispered, and the ghost-bird disappeared in a wisp, leaving the room darker in her absence.

"It's not the worst thing in the world, you know," Julian said quietly, coming up to Wren and handing her the last of the jerky they'd pilfered from the Breachfort.

"What isn't?"

"*Liking* it. Enjoying your magic."

A couple of weeks ago, Wren would have agreed with him. But back then she'd been a mere bonesmith. Now she was something else.

"That's easy for you to say," she said with a sigh.

"You think so?" Julian asked, staring down at his gloved hand.

"This is different. Your hand is still *your* hand, which means whatever you do with it will be good and just because that's who *you* are. But this magic . . . Yes, there might be interesting elements to their lore—knowledge that could serve the Dominions." She thought of the wishbone necklace and the way familiar items could ease the passing of the dead, how her Vision could solve crimes and potentially help reapyrs find missing remains. "But commanding and controlling the undead . . . It's *wrong*, right down to its core."

Color had appeared high on Julian's pale cheeks as she spoke, and Wren realized she'd complimented him rather shamelessly. But it was true, so she didn't take it back.

He cleared his throat. "Maybe, but I imagine your reapings would go a lot more smoothly with a ghostsmith in tow, soothing the ghost rather than battling it."

It was dangerously close to Wren's own thoughts. "Easy there, ironsmith," she said, trying to make light of the subject. To stop herself from a somewhat unnerving line of thought. "You'd put me out of a job." Strange that the idea didn't threaten her as it once would have. Her identity had been so tied up in being a valkyr that the thought of doing anything else was incomprehensible to her. Her reaction to being sent to the Breachfort was proof of that. But she'd been through so much since then and didn't know if she even *could* go back to being a regular valkyr. In truth, she had a hard time seeing the undead as her enemy now, when it was so much more complicated than that.

Maybe she *was* meant for more, as Julian had said to her when she'd betrayed him.

Maybe her whole house was.

He raised his hands in surrender. "I'll leave that to the House of Bone, then."

"You'd best," Wren said, appreciating that they could talk this way to each other again, but the thoughts lingered long after their conversation had ended.

"It's time," said Hawke. All three of them looked up to see him standing atop the stairs, Talon back on his shoulder.

As they climbed the steps and entered the wide tunnel, Wren knew they were close. She could *feel* it. The swell of magic.

She became aware of the ring on her finger, the almost indiscernible vibration of magic within it. And her senses, both bonesmith and budding ghostsmith, were on high alert. It was an awareness that made the hairs on the back of her neck stand up and the muscles in her stomach tighten with anticipation.

The ground leveled out underfoot, and Wren assumed they must be entering the building that contained the well. They would soon see what lay beneath Hollow Hall, the idea as intriguing as it was unsettling.

The passage reached a carved archway that led into a vast corridor, and rather than ghostlight sconces, a row of skull and bone chandeliers hung high above, leading toward another carved archway and the mouth of a massive chamber. She wondered if Hawke had awakened them or if they always remained lit in endless servitude.

As they passed under the second archway, more chandeliers glowed above, the eerie green light glinting off every surface: the glittering carved pillars, the smooth stone floor . . . and row upon row of iron suits of armor.

Row upon row.

Wren's breath caught, the world seeming to bottom out beneath her.

There were definitely more than a hundred, as Hawke had claimed.

Much more.

At least two hundred of them stood before her, and these were not empty suits. They did appear dormant, however, immobile, but their bodies, their ghosts, were already trapped within. Her magic was alive with the sudden influx of *bones bones bones*. And there, with them, were *ghosts ghosts ghosts*.

But why had Hawke led them here? They were meant to pass below the city, below the place where the iron revenants waited.

She rounded on her brother, opening her mouth to question him, but the words died on her lips. Whatever faith she'd held in him shattered at the sight of his head dipped low, his gaze refusing to meet hers.

Guilt. That was what she saw there. She didn't know when he'd decided to betray them—maybe it had been his plan all along—but it didn't matter. He had.

Wren wanted to rip her ring off and throw it at him. She wanted to take him by the shoulders and shake that look off his face.

But the worst, it seemed, was yet to come.

They remained at the entrance of the chamber, their progress halted by the room's haunting occupants. It was not Hollow Hall, the palace she and Julian had seen their last time here. That had featured some sort of throne room, long and empty and surrounded by a gallery. A place for speeches and balls and official audiences.

This must be the Keeper's Cathedral that Hawke had mentioned. The ceiling was impossibly high, even the ghostlight chandeliers not fully penetrating its dark heights, while the walls featured scenes from ghostsmith lore, ancient necromancers carved in stone, their ghostly thralls depicted in subservient swirls or attached to their moldering bones, knees bent and heads bowed.

The iron revenants were collected in the center of the room atop a massive platform, while a raised walkway bisected the space and connected four doorways. Below these walkways was something of a moat, either an intentional water feature or flooding from the nearby spring. At the end of each walkway was one of the doors that led into the room.

As Wren squinted into the darkness of the door opposite, hoping for a way out, a metal grate came sliding down over the entrance.

She whirled around to stare at the door they'd entered through.

She, Hawke, and Julian were several feet inside the room, standing on the raised walkway, but Leo remained just under the arch. His eyes met hers, just as more metallic shrieking echoed around them, announcing three more descending grates.

"Run," Wren breathed, before reaching out and shoving Leo hard in the chest. He staggered backward, falling into the passage behind him just as the grate came thundering down, landing on the ground with a resounding clang.

TWENTY-FOUR

Wren stared at Leo on the other side of the bars, relief washing through her. He got to his feet, face striped with shadow and ghost-light.

"Stop him," came a familiar voice. Standing in the doorway she'd just been looking through was Lord-Smith Francis, regent of the Iron Citadel.

Wren's brain backtracked, trying to figure out how he had beaten them here. . . . Then she recalled the Red Guard descending upon them at Mercy's, almost as if they'd *known* they were there. And then they'd chased Wren and the others into the very tunnel that led them here.

Had that been the plan all along? Not to find them, but to redirect them? And Starling's body . . . Suddenly, all the circumstances that had landed them here felt not coincidental but deliberate.

And if that were the case . . . how much had Hawke known?

Julian glowered at his uncle, drawing his whip sword. Footsteps echoed from all around, Citadel soldiers and members of the Red Guard moving through the chamber and heading their way.

"Hurry," Wren said to Leo, racing to the grate. She tossed him one of her smaller bone blades—it was all that would fit between the bars—and drew her swords. "Go to the fort. Tell them. *Warn* them."

Behind her, a dozen or so soldiers poured from around the ranks of iron revenants, making for the narrow walkway that led to the door Wren and Julian now defended.

Across the chamber, the regent extended his hand. Apparently the grates were iron, because the metal started to lift—until Julian slammed it back down. But despite not needing to touch the bars to keep it lowered, he was quickly distracted by the oncoming soldiers. Wren raised her swords but knew they'd soon be hacked to pieces by the Red Guard's iron blades.

She had to be smarter than that. Using them to deflect the first blow and duck the second, Wren reached for her bonedust instead. Clouds of it obscured their surroundings and made the soldiers stumble and cough, but when the air cleared, Wren and Julian were still outnumbered, and the regent was still attempting to lift the grate.

Knucklebones and throwing knives bought Wren a few more breathless seconds, but then a gauntleted fist landed against her stomach, and another cracked the side of her head.

"Wren!" Julian shouted, his whip lancing out and slicing her attacker, but he wasn't the only one to object.

"You said you wouldn't hurt her!" came Hawke's anguished voice. Wren had forgotten about him. Looking up from the ground, her gaze bleary, she spotted his pale face amid the red-enameled soldiers . . . and he wasn't alone.

Next to him was a woman in a long black veil and a crown of bone.

On her shoulder perched a black raven, its eyes glowing ghost-bright. Wren thought she knew how the Red Guard had found them in Laketown. . . . The revenant raven they'd seen in the sky that day had clearly been a spy or a scout. A servant of the Corpse Queen.

And Hawke had *known* it. That was why he'd been so uneasy. Why he'd tried to hide from it. But that meant . . . Had he still been on their side then? Or was he simply trying to keep Wren from asking too many questions?

Wren spit the blood from her mouth and got shakily to her feet. She and Julian were surrounded by soldiers now, the fighting finished.

She could feel her mother's eyes on her, though Wren couldn't actually see her face through the veil, only the faint green of ghostsmith irises.

Reaching into her belt, Wren withdrew a throwing knife and launched it, hard, at her mother's face.

Just to see what she'd do.

The blade flew end over end, and Ravenna didn't so much as flinch. Instead, the raven on her shoulder dove at the exact right moment, taking the blade to the chest.

The bird dropped to the ground, the bone piercing the ghost within.

Ravenna kicked it aside.

The sweep of her veil caused a surprising hint of scent to wash over Wren, not dusty stone or metallic tang but something softer. Something floral.

Something familiar.

Heavy boots on stone announced the arrival of the regent. He looked as grand and excessive in his enameled armor and spiked helmet as the last time Wren had seen him.

The Red Guard who had circled Julian stepped back, leaving the regent alone before his nephew.

"Try me," Julian said, rolling his shoulders and causing his whip sword to drag sparks across the ground.

The regent smiled—and went for Wren instead.

She was out of his reach, except suddenly she was in his grasp, tugged there by an invisible force at her midsection.

Then his hand was on her belt while the other wrenched her around. He withdrew Ironheart from the sheath at her waist and lifted it to his eyes with a smirk.

The regent shook his head. "Sentimental. Like your father."

Julian extended his hand, and Wren thought he might have been reaching for the dagger. It should have come to him; not only did the knife belong to Julian and his mother before him, giving him a more powerful bond to the weapon, but he also had an iron hand. His power should outstrip his uncle's, and yet the dagger didn't move.

The regent grinned wider before leveling the knife at Wren's throat. Julian dropped his hand at once.

"Seize him, and make sure his hands are tied *behind* his back."

The Red Guard approached warily, and when it was clear Julian didn't intend to fight, they snatched away his weapons and removed his helmet before binding his wrists not with manacles but with heavy rope.

Wren thought of his vambrace blade, but it appeared that, like Julian's hand, his uncle knew of the concealed weapon, telling one of his soldiers to remove it.

They forced Julian to his knees, and once they were done with him, the regent removed the dagger from Wren's throat and allowed his men to disarm her as well. They didn't bother to tie her up, just held her arms behind her back as she was pushed onto her knees next to Julian.

The grate behind them lifted, but much to Wren's relief, Leo was nowhere in sight.

"Follow him," the regent commanded.

While the Red Guard remained with the regent, some of the Citadel soldiers hurried forward to heed the order.

Jakob was among them, making for the darkened tunnel. He and the others paused only long enough to light several torches before they disappeared from view.

Wren swallowed, the taste of blood heavy on her tongue. Leo was badly outnumbered, but he'd had a head start, and he'd been through those passages already. With any luck, he'd be able to outrun them or find someplace to hide at the very least.

And then it was just a matter of traversing the endless throughway without a ghostsmith or a bonesmith for protection before finding his way across the wild and mostly uninhabited Breachlands to the fort.

Had she just sent the prince to his death?

Anger, sudden and hot, sluiced through her, and she needed someone to unleash it on.

She stared up at her brother. "I should have fucking known," she spat. She thought of Leo, alone in the dark. She thought of Julian, bound on his knees before the uncle who had tried to kill him. She thought of Hawke, saving her life only to betray her now. "This whole thing was a setup, wasn't it? The undead attack, the Laketown detour. Starling's murder."

Hawke flinched visibly at that, his eyes wide and pleading, his chin lifting, pulling to the side—only to stop midmotion. She could have sworn he was about to shake his head until he caught sight of his mother.

Starling's murderer.

After all, Wren knew exactly where she had smelled that floral scent before: in Starling's final memories.

Hawke's chin dipped to his chest, and he said nothing.

Wren's lungs heaved with suppressed confusion and frustration. She laughed harshly, straining against the hands that held her, but it was no use. "I guess now I know you really are my family. You betrayed me without a second thought. You lied to me. You—"

"He sprang a trap, and you rushed recklessly into it," Ravenna said in that raw, grating voice Wren remembered. "Just like your father before you."

That word. That fucking word. Wren might be reckless, and thoughtless, and maybe even selfish, too, but this woman—this *stranger*—didn't know her at all and had no right to pretend otherwise. "*Which* father?" Wren asked, smiling up at her.

"Oh, it doesn't really matter, does it?" she said, amusement in her voice. "You Gravens are all the same. Plenty of brawn. No brain." Her head turned toward the fallen raven as if it were proof.

Next to her, Hawke twitched, and Wren wondered how often Ravenna did that—insult Hawke right to his face and expect him not to notice. Or to take it even if he did. He was as much a Graven as Wren was, even if she was the bonesmith.

"And here I was thinking both my *parents* are the same. Selfish pieces of shit who use their children to achieve their own ambitions."

"Do not compare our ambitions," Ravenna said, voice laced with anger for the first time. "The House of Bone has sought to use and control what it does not understand for centuries. To charge in without a care for the consequences like a child in search of a sweet. Meanwhile, the House of Ghost is patient like dripping water, slowly wearing away at obstacles. Playing the long game. We could not be more different—which is perhaps why our union did not last."

"I'd hardly call what you and my father had a *union*," Wren said sarcastically.

"I speak of a much older coupling," Ravenna said. "We were once one and the same, you know."

Wren glanced to Hawke—to the regent and the surrounding soldiers, all watching this exchange. To Julian. "What are you talking about?"

"Ghostsmiths. Bonesmiths."

"I know we used to hunt the undead together," Wren said, but the crowned head with its obscuring veil shook from side to side.

"We were more than *partners*. There was no House of Bone or House of Ghost. There was only the House of the Dead."

Wren reeled from the thought, even if it was simply an expansion of her own, unwanted heritage. She thought of the glyphs on the ring that looked so familiar, of the vast Marrow Hall catacombs and the sprawling cemeteries, some of which were a millennium old. Surely there was much buried there that Wren was unaware of. Much that those in the House of Bone did not want her—or anyone—to know.

"We were an immensely powerful house. The *only* house that mattered, long before the Valorians invaded and other smiths attempted to gain a stranglehold on these lands. We would have ruled the island, if not for the schism between two siblings. The first, who you no doubt know as the Gravedigger, and the second: the Gravekeeper."

The Keeper's Cathedral.

She'd never thought to ask about the name. She'd never thought to care.

"Together, they had a monopoly on death, and business was good. They unified the bonesmiths and ghostsmiths, and *together* they built Marrow Hall. They could have had everything until the Gravedigger lost his nerve. He felt threatened by his powerful brother, whose magical ability was rivaled only by his intellectual prowess. The Gravekeeper was bright. Curious. Daring. And for that, he was banished. Those who shared his abilities were banished with him. But as you can see, they continued to thrive on their own. They built, they grew, and they challenged the very laws of the world. *This* world. Made safe by us and our ancestors. And therefore, ours to claim."

"Ours?" Wren repeated. "You and my brother."

"And you. We are a family, after all, and you have my blood. My magic."

"I don't want it," Wren said.

The queen bent before her, their faces mere inches apart. "Too bad." Despite the already grave situation, fresh alarm bells sounded in Wren's mind. "We *will* claim what is ours, and you will help us do it."

As she drew back and angled her head, Wren followed the movement. Behind her ranged the iron revenant army . . . the dangerous but currently *immobile* revenant army. They needed the well's magic to be activated, needed the surge of extra power to be able to march. And they no doubt needed a ghostsmith to capture it and imbue the commands.

Could it be so simple?

"Wait—you want *me* to help *you*? With *that*?" Wren choked out a laugh. "Fuck no."

While her mother remained motionless before her, Wren looked to Hawke for some indication of how her refusal had been taken. He didn't appear angry, or surprised, or worried. He looked resigned. Defeated.

The alarm bells rang in her mind once more.

"You misunderstand me," Ravenna said. "I'm not asking. You *will* help us—with or without your consent."

TWENTY-FIVE

"What? You can't *make* me—" Wren spluttered, but at a nod from the queen, she was dragged across the narrow bridge toward the center of the room. Behind her, she heard Julian struggle and then a blunt sound of impact that she suspected was a fist to the face. Wren tried to look back, but ranks of Red Guard and the regent himself blocked her view. All of them were coming with her, it seemed. To keep her in line . . . or to watch what happened next?

"What do you know about amplifiers?" Ravenna asked once they'd all come to a halt.

In the center of the ranks of iron revenants was an open space. The ground was carved with deep rectangular grooves that emanated from a gathering pool in the center of the chamber. This one was larger than what Wren remembered from the throne room—at least ten feet square—but shallower, too. She could actually see the bottom, with ghostsmith runes carved into the stone, visible through the swirling magic.

Some of the glyphs matched Wren's ring. She fiddled with it on her finger, though her arms were held fast.

Ravenna saw the movement. "That's right. Like your ring, amplifiers are made of the material in which the smith has command. In this case, a haunted bone with the ghost still attached. But what if that bone—what if that ghost—were more than a mere animal? Familiarity is the cornerstone of magic, so imagine an amplifier made of bone and ghost that were *connected* to the smith? Irrevocably tied to them by *more* than magic. By blood. After all, there is nothing more familiar than family."

Wren had learned much about ghostsmiths over the past few days, and she'd begun to see something beyond only evil in what her brother did. But the majority of it was wrong—terribly, horribly wrong—and yet she could understand how, being raised the way he was, he might not see it that way. There was a level of innocent ignorance about it. And when Wren looked back at her own ignorance—toward the ironsmiths, the undead in general and revenants specifically, she could perhaps forgive her brother some of his wayward notions.

But Ravenna was neither innocent nor ignorant. She knew what she did, understood it deeply . . . and what she suggested now was no different.

Wren was exactly what she spoke of: a sack of bones with a ghost still attached. She had seen the way the well magic worked, the way it had filled her brother up, reaching from the tips of his toes through his various amplifiers and all the way to the horned skull mask he'd worn on his head. But how much more powerful, more potent, would he be if he could fill up and then draw upon a secondary source—one that was just as large as he was? Just as magical?

They didn't need Wren to be a ghostsmith.

No, they needed her to be a ghostsmith *amplifier*.

Wren would help her brother wake these iron revenants and send them off to war whether she liked it or not and be complicit in all they did just the same.

She was his ideal amplifier, made of the same blood and bone, *born* for this, and lured here in order to fulfill this purpose.

And she had let it happen. She had walked here of her own free will and handed them the very thing they needed to complete their plans: herself.

Wren struggled harder now, panic rising in her chest like a tide that threatened to drown her.

While she'd been distracted, Hawke had come up behind her. Suddenly a rusted steel shackle clamped on to her wrist, and when Wren turned, she saw it connected to a chain he held in his hand.

Wren stared at him, dared him to meet her gaze, but he refused.

"Fucking coward," she said. "At least have the decency to look me in the eye after you stab me in the back."

He lifted his chin, his vivid green eyes sad—and a little defiant. The expression on his face was familiar.

It was hers.

"So you'd prefer it if I stabbed you in the front?"

Wren cocked her head. "No. But I'd respect it."

He gritted his teeth and turned his attention to the chain he held in his good hand. "I didn't have a choice," he said softly.

"You did," Wren insisted, turning away from Ravenna to speak to him. "You *do.*"

He shook his head. "You don't understand. She's our mother, and I owe her my life. This is *her* will . . . and I will see it done. Whatever the cost."

"Me," Wren said, fear creeping into her voice despite her efforts to squash it. "It will cost you me."

He frowned. "It won't *kill* you."

That was less than reassuring. "That's not what I meant. You go through with this, and you'll no longer have a sister."

He blinked, darted a glance at their mother, then shook his head. "You mean that metaphorically. She means it literally."

"She—what—" Wren said as he yanked the chain on her wrist, pulling her toward the gathering pool. She resisted on instinct, and with his wounded shoulder Hawke wasn't strong enough to control her, but the Red Guards on either side shoved her whenever she lagged.

She looked back at Julian. His dark eyes were wide and tortured as he struggled fruitlessly against his bonds. But there was nothing he could do.

They were too outnumbered.

Still, her footsteps faltered, stumbling toward him even though she knew she'd never get there. But then the regent stepped into her field of vision and put a gauntleted hand on his nephew's shoulder.

The simple gesture worked better than any blade, the threat just as plain.

She wanted to shout, to curse, to *beg*—but every word, every action, was ammunition to be used against her. Proof of how much she cared.

She turned away and blew out her cheeks. Hopefully that meant he would be safe. If he was their leverage, they wouldn't dispose of it.

Not yet.

Not until the job was done.

Hawke entered the pool first, moving stiffly, with Wren trailing behind him. He'd left his mask and staff behind—apparently unnecessary when he had a human amplifier in Wren and they were actually submerging themselves in the well's magic.

Her boots swirled through the mist, and she expected a splash, but the magic crackled against her body with a resonating hum, like a vibration. Still, it had weight to it, a pressure not unlike water the deeper they got. A resistance that made her movements slow and somewhat labored.

Until suddenly that steady pulse of magic, that heaviness against her limbs, took on a different note. Started to come not from the world around her but from *within*.

She was absorbing it, the magic filling her up with heady, raw power.

There was a loud clank; Hawke had taken the other end of the chain and latched it to a loop embedded into the floor of the gathering pool. Proving this kind of thing had been done before. She tried to pull against it, but her efforts were sluggish, the motion blurring before her eyes, and the metal was too strong.

Her limbs glowed as they moved in front of her face, the bones visible as they shone through her skin. She was a beacon, a vessel, an overflowing cup.

Higher the magic crawled, the brightness turning everything around her into a glowing haze as it filled her body to the top of her head.

Hawke took her hand. The touch sent shock waves through her, a crackling, almost painful connection as magic pulsed between them. Through them.

She tried to fight it, to pull back, but her muscles were leaden, and they were connected as powerfully as magnets—as if the magic itself had fused them together. They had started out this way, together in the womb, and here they were again.

As one.

Their eyes met, and Wren knew he felt it too. Knew that if there had ever been any doubt about their relation, about their ties to each other, they were now gone. She had never felt closer to someone.

She'd also never felt farther away as he turned his back to her, taking her hand and placing it on his wounded shoulder, freeing his own hands to do what he needed to do.

His bones glowed beneath her fingertips, every rib visible, so bright now that Wren's eyes streamed. And his shoulder . . . Though she couldn't see muscle and sinew, she swore she could feel the moment his arrow wound healed itself, the flesh stitching itself together around Leo's improvised golden thread. Hawke's posture straightened, and the pain he'd been feeling—an echo of it present in Wren's body—dissipated.

She reeled, pulling herself back from the minutiae before she drowned in it, and watched what came next.

Bending over the edge of the pool, Hawke placed both palms flat on the ground.

Suddenly Wren was no longer an overflowing cup. She was a conduit. A channel. A dam filled to the brink and ready to burst, and he was the release valve.

Magic poured from him, drawn up from the well, from Wren, and filling the dozens of lines that were carved into the floor with brilliant light. The magic flowed steadily until it hit the feet of the nearest revenant. The suit of armor lit up, glowing from within just as it had done in the throne room the first time Wren had seen Hawke do this . . . but he didn't stop at one.

He hadn't been lying when he'd said he was stronger than her. It was evident in his control. This power had killed Locke, yet Hawke wielded it with intense focus and skill, reaching hundreds of undead without physical touch. Wren, meanwhile, struggled to remain conscious amid the onslaught.

The stream reached another revenant, and another, each of them flickering into existence like stars in the sky.

Once the magic reached the top of their helmets, the revenants would come alive, their rigid postures unlocking as they turned their heads and shifted their shoulders, testing out their new and better bodies.

All while Wren remained motionless, powerless, a spectator—even as the magic surged through her, bringing them to life.

Hours passed. Her muscles twitched, and her eyes rolled.

Time faded away, the darkness pulling her under. The world lost its shape, time lost its importance, and the difference between life and death lost all meaning.

But then, ringing out from somewhere in the shadows of her mind, came Hawke's booming voice, drenched in power.

"Your army is ready, my queen."

TWENTY-SIX

Julian's knees ached against the cold stone floor and his shoulders throbbed, his arms wrenched backward to allow his wrists to be bound. He'd been twisting his hands, both in an attempt to keep blood flowing and with the hopes of loosening his binds, but he'd made virtually no progress in either regard.

But all of that was happening in the back of his mind, in the distant recesses that remained in tune with his body and his surroundings. The rest of him, his true attention, was focused squarely on Wren.

Hawke had finished his task. He had spoken the words and cut off the magical supply, and now Wren lay slumped against the bottom of the gathering pool, her eyes twitching behind their lids, her body still aglow with all that raw magic, though the pulsing nature of it had subsided.

Hawke also continued to emanate that strange, magical light, but as he left the pool, it abated.

He came to stand next to his mother, a silent servant. A ghost of a person.

Julian wanted to hate him for what he'd done, but the sight of him there, round-shouldered and eyes downcast . . . He'd never seen someone look so defeated.

A sword's edge may grow dull, but it is still a sword.

That was something his uncle used to say. It meant that you couldn't change the nature of what something—or someone—was made for. Hawke was his mother's son, and this world was all he'd ever known. He'd been raised for this, and so no, Julian's anger didn't burn for him, not really.

It burned for someone else.

The regent had seemingly forgotten Julian was there, so enraptured by the sight of his undead soldiers that he'd actually taken an unconscious step toward the nearest one. Like a moth to the undead flame.

How could Julian have missed it? All those years, his uncle had been passionate about the survival of their house and reclaiming what they'd lost. About *any means necessary*. Julian had thought his obsession with the undead was born from hatred for those who had stolen their lands and ravaged their people. But it had been something else.

It had been admiration.

His uncle didn't see right or wrong. He saw strength and weakness. And in his mind, the undead were the epitome of strong. Combine their strength with the House of Iron's strength, and you had something *stronger*.

And that was all the rationalization he'd needed to do *this*. To unleash these abominations on the world.

Julian had to stop this before the House of Iron had the blood of the entirety of the Dominions on its hands. But Wren was out cold, Leo was running for his life, and Julian was bound on his knees . . . watching it unfold.

The Corpse Queen stepped forward, something in her gloved hand. It was a long iron rod topped with the bones of a human hand, clenched into a fist.

She raised it, and the hand began to glow a bright, ghostly green, as if it were haunted.

Though the queen's face was concealed by her black shroud, Julian sensed her attention on the iron revenants as she raised the scepter aloft, shoulders squared and feet braced.

He expected to see some great show of magic, and sure enough, the fist grew brighter and brighter, just as Wren and Hawke had when they'd drawn upon the well.

But the glow Julian saw was not the bright white of raw magic. Instead, it was that sickly, ghostly green. Furthermore, the glow didn't appear to be coming from the hand at all but from the queen, the light crawling up her arm from within the folds of her veil and gown, where it coalesced inside the skeletal fist.

Before Julian could begin to try to understand what was happening, the ball of illumination at the tip of the scepter exploded, fracturing into hundreds of scraps of ghost-green light. They hovered in the air, frozen in space and time, before fluttering down to earth like snowflakes.

Julian flinched, fearing they might land on him, but they moved purposefully toward the iron revenants. One by one they descended atop their iron helms, absorbed by the undead, who flashed green before returning to normal.

Looking back at the queen, Julian was surprised to see Hawke holding her elbow, bracing her, as if she needed help standing upright. She did appear a bit unsteady, the arm that held the scepter trembling ever so slightly, but she shoved Hawke aside before Julian's uncle noticed.

"Army of undead," the Corpse Queen said, her voice ringing out. The iron revenants snapped to attention, no less than two hundred soldiers lifting their gauntleted hands in unison to offer a haunting, synchronized salute.

His uncle flinched terribly, and Julian grinned, enjoying the simple sight of this arrogant man brought back down to earth, even just momentarily.

It appeared that the ritual, the magic, was complete. Wren and Hawke had filled these soldiers with enough power to make them able to lift their armor and march, and the queen was now issuing commands. But those floating green lights that had landed on their helmets nagged at him. He'd seen raw magic several times, and it always glowed *white*, not ghost-green, even when a ghostsmith used it. What he had seen was ghostlight, and ghostlight belonged to the undead.

The queen turned to his uncle. "This scepter is called the Hand of the Queen. Whosoever wields it controls the queen's army."

She held it out to the regent.

He took it eagerly, hefting the rod in his hand, though a certain wariness remained as he examined the skeletal fist at its tip.

"It is not haunted," the queen said, amusement coloring her voice. "But *they* certainly are." She gestured to the iron revenants.

"And their loyalty is to this scepter . . . not to you?" the regent said, a shrewd edge to the words.

She inclined her head. The regent nodded, thoughtful, then turned to the nearest iron revenant.

"Soldier," he barked, and the iron revenant's helmet turned his way. "Attack the Corpse Queen. Bring me her head."

Julian froze, utterly shocked, but the revenant obeyed the command, its iron-booted feet echoing as it stomped toward Ravenna. Hawke tensed, looking between his mother and the revenant, but the queen remained perfectly still, right up until the soldier's gauntleted hands extended toward her throat. . . .

"Stop!" the regent said, mere seconds before the undead made contact. Its hands froze midair, inches from the queen's neck. "Back in formation." The revenant turned on its heel, stomping back into position.

"Satisfied?" the queen asked, apparently unperturbed by the attempt on her life.

"Very satisfied," the regent said, smiling wolfishly. He turned to the room at large, raising his voice. "Army of undead. It is time to march. Make for the Breachfort with all haste. Tear it down. Leave no survivors."

TWENTY-SEVEN

Apparently, using a living human as an amplifier had its drawbacks.

At least for the amplifier.

Wren had been in and out of consciousness throughout the process, and when she next came to, the chamber had emptied.

Well, not entirely.

She'd been lying on the steps of the magical pool, sprawled on the hard stone, and now forced herself to sit up, to look around. Her brother stood a few feet away, speaking to their mother in a low voice. He looked the way Wren felt—wrung out, his pale skin verging upon sallow. His head was bowed again, though Wren saw that more as a show of subservience to their mother than a sign of exhaustion.

Wren felt dazed and disoriented, but even as consciousness returned, the overwhelming surge of the well's magic did not. She remained inside the gathering pool, but the magic seemed to swirl around her rather than within her. She wriggled her fingers, and a few wisps penetrated her skin, but no more. Perhaps her body had simply taken all it could. Perhaps she needed time to recover.

As she lifted her head, her attention latched on to a pair of dark eyes across the chamber.

Julian. He remained under guard, bound and on his knees, hair askew and mouth tight. A look of intense relief washed over his features when he saw she was awake, and Wren was overwhelmed by how dear he was to her. At the proof that she was, in fact, dear to him too.

How long had she been out for? What had she missed? How far had the army marched?

Voices drew her attention to the other remaining occupants inside the cathedral.

". . . and they will continue to obey me, even at a distance?" That was the regent. He held something strange in his hand, a short black staff with a skeletal hand on the end.

"As I've told you," Ravenna rasped. "You hold the scepter, you control the army."

Wren considered that. An *object* that could control the undead? Had she and Hawke powered that up too, somehow? Or was there some other ghostsmith magic at work here that she didn't understand?

"We have done our part," Ravenna continued. "Now it is time you do yours."

"Oh, I'll do my part," he said with relish.

"Enjoy your conquest and your crown."

"And you're sure you do not want the same?" the regent asked. He made it sound like idle chatter, but surely he wondered why Ravenna would *hand over* control of an unkillable army when she could keep it for herself. "I cannot help but feel like I am getting the better end of the deal."

"Ease your conscience, Iron Regent. I've no interest in playing politics. You stay out of my way and off *my* lands, and I'll stay out of yours. As we discussed."

He dipped his head. "As we discussed. Aside from the mines, the Breach will be yours." He turned away from her, his attention shifting to the rest of the chamber. "But first . . . some unfinished business."

While the majority of the Red Guard were standing at the ready near one of the four entrances to the cathedral, a handful of them remained ranged around Julian. The regent approached.

Wren moved toward them unconsciously, and her manacle clanked.

Hawke and Ravenna looked her way, while the regent smiled, noting how Wren and Julian were staring at each other.

"Ah yes, she has served her purpose well. And so have you," the regent said, speaking to Julian. "Thank you for leading them both exactly where I needed them to go. The prince may have gotten away, but he will be back in my possession soon enough."

"You won't catch him," Wren said, desperate for the words to be true. "He'll get to the fort before you. He'll warn them, and—"

"Don't be so sure," the regent said calmly. He hefted the scepter, eyeing it as he spoke. "My undead army moves swiftly, and it is a long way to travel by foot. Especially for a spoiled prince. My Citadel soldiers will have him before long, if they don't have him already."

Julian's lip curled. "He can be very persuasive, Uncle. You might find the loyalty of your Citadel soldiers is not as ironclad as you think."

"You'd like to believe that, wouldn't you, son? That they'd all turn tail and flock to you instead?" He chuckled, sliding the scepter into his belt before indicating Julian's position on his knees, his hands bound. "You are an inspiring sight to be sure, Julian Knight, but I think perhaps *you* are the one who's been worked over by a smooth-talking royal. Rest assured, my servants are loyal to me because they are loyal to *power*."

"They are loyal to the House of Iron," Julian said fiercely. "And if they knew the truth, they'd never serve you."

"It's a good thing for me that they don't, then, isn't it?"

Reaching again for his belt, this time he withdrew a dagger.

Ironheart.

Wren's breath caught. "No!" she cried out, scrambling to her feet—but the shackle yanked her back down again. Panic flared inside her breast.

"Uncle," Julian said, also trying to stand. After a moment of struggle, he appeared to relax—only to surge upward, catching the guards who held his arms by surprise. They stumbled, but a blow to the back of Julian's head from a third guard temporarily stunned him, making him easy to subdue once more.

"Consider this a life lesson," the regent said, strolling casually toward his nephew, attention focused on the blade in his hands. "If you want something done right, you have to do it yourself."

"Stop!" Wren screamed, yanking her arm until the joints in her wrist protested and her skin was scraped raw. "Don't you dare touch him!"

The regent cast an amused look over his shoulder at Wren, then turned his words to Ravenna. "Muzzle your dog."

"Shut your mouth!" Julian snapped, a vein bulging in his neck as he strained against his captors with renewed vigor. "You're the animal here."

"Julian, my boy, you are too softhearted. Like your father. If I have one regret, it's that I didn't squash that out of you while I had the chance. Though I suppose that would have made things more difficult, in the end. . . ."

Wren was barely listening. A red mist had come over her, blurring her vision worse than the magic had while she helped her brother awaken the army of undead. With conscious effort she reached for that same power that pooled at her feet, forcefully absorbing it in a burst.

The magic swirled within her as she moved. With brutal efficiency, she wrenched her hand *through* the manacle, using her heightened bonesmith magic to willfully shatter her own bones in the process. The pain was extraordinary, temporarily robbing her of breath, but it didn't matter.

She was free.

Surging from the pool, she flung her hands out—one broken, one intact—and took magical hold of Julian's captors. With a brutal twist, their bones shattered. Their eyes bled. She tossed them roughly aside.

Then she turned to the regent.

He looked surprised—the arrogant smirk was gone from his face—but when she tried to break the arm that held the knife, she came up against something that was neither alive nor dead.

She stumbled, confused, until his grin returned. He yanked off his glove, revealing a hand made of iron . . . just like Julian's.

Wren growled. Perhaps that iron would save his hand . . . but did it extend all the way to his skull?

Bearing her teeth, she reached out once more—but before she could take hold, something knocked her over from behind. She hit the ground, throbbing shock waves reverberating through her broken hand, the pain made worse when a boot stomped on it soon after.

She gasped, looking up into the veiled face of her mother. With Wren's hand immobilized, the queen reached down and wrenched the amplifier ring off her broken finger.

The surplus magic left her in a rush, the agony of her broken bones slamming through her body tenfold. She actually gagged from the waves of pain, but it was nothing compared to what was happening inside her heart.

Though Wren had killed two of them, ten more Red Guard had rushed in to take their place.

Julian had seized the opportunity she had given him, straining against the ropes that bound his arms with so much force that the threads had begun to fray, the bonds viciously torn apart.

Determined to fight by his side, Wren scrambled to free herself. Though her self-inflicted wound was brutal and distracting, her magic drew her attention to a knife in the queen's boot. She reached with her good hand and withdrew the haunted bone blade.

With a vicious slash, she scraped the blade across the exposed flesh of her mother's leg, just visible over the top of her boot and the hem of her long black skirts.

The cut was quick and deep, opening the flesh in a long laceration . . . that didn't bleed. Wren recoiled, her brain struggling to understand what her eyes were seeing.

And the flesh . . . it was not the pale shade of Wren and Hawke, but something colder and grayer . . . something bloodless.

Again Ravenna's veiled head tilted in Wren's direction. This time it wasn't just her eyes that flashed a sickly, *ghostly* green.

It was her entire gaunt, sunken, skull-like face.

A cry of pain ripped Wren's attention back to Julian's fight. Though he'd managed to free his hands and land a few blows, he had been overpowered. Lip bleeding and hair askew, he was once again forced to his knees.

"Say goodbye to the heir of the Iron Citadel," the regent said to the room at large, before stepping up behind his nephew and dragging Ironheart—Julian's mother's blade—across his throat in a single swift motion.

A gasp of shock slipped out of Wren's mouth as a spurt of blood sprayed in an arc across the ground. Julian's eyes were wide and wild, his hands frantically scrabbling at the wound in his neck as his guards released him. He flopped to the ground, his armor clanking, but he was not still.

He continued to fight, slow and sluggish, attempting to pull himself forward.

Toward Wren.

Toward the *gathering pool*. Toward the well's magic.

It had healed Hawke, just as he'd said it would.

Maybe now it could heal Julian, too.

The queen had abandoned Wren, believing her powerless without her amplifier. Wren dragged herself toward Julian as he dragged himself toward her. Their eyes locked, fixed on each other as Wren's hand throbbed and Julian's face lost all color, a trail of blood smearing the ground.

They were two handspans apart.

One.

"Put an end to this," came Ravenna's cold, cruel voice.

Then someone appeared in Wren's peripheral vision. She looked up. Hawke stood there, a hard, desperate expression on his face.

Then he turned to Julian. He closed his eyes, clenched his fists, and lifted his foot.

He planted the bottom of his boot on Julian's side, then kicked out, pushing Julian over the edge of the platform and into the watery moat below with a splash.

Out of Wren's reach . . . forever.

Nothing followed but silence. The darkness that had been crowding into Wren's mind finally took hold, and she knew no more.

TWENTY-EIGHT

Leo crouched in his hiding place . . . waiting.

He'd known from the start he wouldn't be able to outrun his pursuers. He'd barely made it out of the hall of ghostlight chandeliers and stumbled down the stairs before the grate lifted and the regent's men began their chase.

They'd have caught him in moments, so Leo had done the only thing he could do and stopped running. There was no shame in hiding—and even if there were, there was wisdom in it too.

But first he'd had to find his golden trail.

It was the key to getting out of the throughway alive.

When they'd traveled these tunnels earlier, Hawke had noted a passage that ran east to west, leading from Laketown to the Serpentine. Leo had made a point of marking the intersection in case they needed a quick way back toward the Breachfort.

And he needed it now more than ever.

When at last the torchlight behind him reflected a golden cross smeared onto the stone, Leo had screeched to a halt.

Feeling around in the shadows, he'd found a rock and hurled it down the passage to the left, leading back the way they had originally come. While the stone clattered and rolled, hopefully leading the soldiers in the wrong direction, Leo had darted right.

The tunnels were jagged and uneven, with many a nook and cranny, and Leo eventually settled on a kind of shelf that he had to climb on top of, but the angle would protect him from the torchlight below and give him a good view.

If he was still and silent, he might just be able to wait them out.

However, he'd been hiding for mere moments when voices sounded from the main passage.

"Did you hear that?" one of them said. "There—that way." Footsteps receded, heading in the direction of Leo's thrown rock.

His heart leapt, only for another voice to chime in. "While they check that out, you two follow the main passage. We'll try heading west."

Leo blew out a slow stream of air, eyes briefly fluttering closed. He supposed it had been too much to ask that they'd *all* pursue the sounds coming from the opposite passage. Now, even if they missed his hiding place, Leo might have to wait for hours until they turned back. He needed to get to the fort, and all three avenues were lost to him.

As his pursuers drew nearer, the torch lit the first of the regent's men. It was a Citadel soldier, his gaze keen as it raked every inch of the passage, his sword gleaming in the firelight.

"Hurry up. We'll never catch him if you keep this pace," said the second man. While his face remained in shadow, his voice was familiar.

"He's a prince—a coward. Like as not, he'll stop and hide."

Leo's mouth fell open in indignation. He wasn't hiding because he was a coward. He was hiding because *strategy*.

Though that strategy was currently failing him, so what did that say about his intelligence? Perhaps it was better to cop to being afraid than to admit he wasn't as smart as he thought he was.

As his pursuers drew nearer, the ledge beneath Leo's foot started to loosen and crumble. He held his breath as several pebbles cascaded to the ground, louder than an earthquake in the silence.

The light lifted, and Leo was caught.

The nearer guard dropped the torch and reached for Leo, dragging him to the ground. Leo tried to wield his bone knife, but instead he dropped it as he collapsed on the passage floor next to the still-burning torch. When he looked up, it was to find a sword leveled at his face.

The man smirked triumphantly, opening his mouth—to shout his victory, Leo assumed, or summon his comrades—but he never got the chance.

There was a dull *thump*, and the man's eyes rolled to the back of his head. He dropped, and standing behind him was Jakob, the butt of his sword raised.

Leo gaped.

"On your feet, Your Highness," he said, smirking slightly as he reached his other hand down to take Leo's.

Leo stood in a daze, looking from the prone man on the ground and back up into Jakob's face. "I . . . What are you doing?" he asked, rather dumbly. "Your family, you said—"

Jakob sheathed his sword. Shrugged. "I know, but you were right. My family gets nothing if I die, and besides, I owe you my life. You saved me from that arrow during the fight along the Coastal Road. It seemed only right that I return the favor."

Leo shook his head, still stunned. "He'll report you," he said, nodding at the unconscious guard.

"We were ambushed," Jakob said breezily. "You fled and I pursued, but eventually I lost you in the tunnels." His nonchalance dissipated. "Now come on. We need to move. Do you know a way out of here?"

Leo opened his mouth. Closed it. "Yes. This passage leads west, out toward the Serpentine."

"Where are you heading? To the Breachfort?"

Leo hesitated but saw no point in lying. Where else would he be going? "Yes."

"Let's go," Jakob said, picking up the fallen torch and the bone blade. He stared down at it, then held it out to Leo. "Are you coming or not?"

As it turned out, he was.

"You keep it," Leo said. "You'll be better with it than I am."

It was a more companionable journey than Leo could have hoped, and Jakob's steady presence was *almost* enough to make him forget the distant shouts and footsteps that eventually echoed back to them, not to mention the odd tremor and burst of magic through cracks and seams in the stone.

They didn't cross any undead—animal or otherwise—and Leo tried to take heart from it, even if it likely meant that the lot of them were in the Breach, with Wren and Julian.

"They're going to die, aren't they?" he eventually asked after they'd put enough distance between themselves and the junction point that Leo felt confident they would not be heard if they spoke at a normal volume. "I'm on the fence about Wren—I think they need her, somehow—but Julian . . . The regent is going to kill him."

Jakob's expression was grim in the torchlight. "I suspect he'll try. But Julian, he's strong. Fierce. He won't . . ." He swallowed, glancing at Leo. "He won't make it easy."

"Neither of them will," Leo said, proud and devastated in equal measure. "Do you know what they plan to do with Wren?" Surely it had something to do with the iron revenants. Otherwise, those soldiers would have marched already.

Jakob shook his head. "I have no idea. Our orders didn't extend beyond the handoff at the bonesmith temple."

Leo went over everything that had happened since then, how they'd wound up walking into this trap. Perhaps somewhere along the way Hawke had gotten cold feet and changed his mind about turning his back on his mother. Or perhaps he'd always intended to betray them—but Leo doubted it. When he thought of Hawke's behavior over the previous days, something had definitely shifted after Laketown, specifically after he'd discovered his dead wet nurse. That would be enough to rattle anyone. Plus, he'd been shot with an arrow first. He'd been shaken, and people who were dealing with a traumatic experience didn't often make the best choices.

"At least *you* got away," Jakob said, as if trying to be encouraging.

"Only thanks to a smarter, faster friend." Despair threatened to rise up, and he quickly squashed it. That same smart, fast friend would survive what was to come. He had to believe that.

And he had to believe Julian would, too.

"Or, rather," Leo said, casting a sidelong look at Jakob. "*Two* friends. Is that what you are, Jakob? A friend?"

"I wouldn't presume to count a prince among my friends, but . . . I'd like to."

Leo snorted, a decidedly *unprincely* sound. "More like you had a score to settle. I saved your life, now you've saved mine. You're off the hook. There's no need to—"

"You're not safe. Not yet. And until you are, I'm staying with you."

Leo frowned, refusing to find the words noble and comforting. "When last we spoke, you still served the regent. Reluctantly, perhaps, but faithfully."

"Not faithfully. Not with my heart," Jakob said, with so much earnestness that Leo tried to resist teasing him—and failed.

"Why? Because your regent is commanding an army of undead to stomp out civilization, or because you realized I'm cute and you didn't want me dead after all?"

Jakob spluttered, but then he caught Leo's expression and barked out something like a laugh. He ran a hand through his hair. "It was Julian, actually."

"Should have known you'd break my heart," Leo said with a dramatic sigh.

"No, not—" Jakob shook his head with exasperation. Then a tiny smile quirked his lips. "I mean, he *is* handsome. . . ."

Leo recognized he was being teased in turn and rolled his eyes, though he was also grinning.

Jakob's humor faded. "When I saw those posters . . . I had always idolized Julian. He and I grew up together, served side by side on various missions." He frowned. "The regent was lying, and I knew then that I no longer believed in our cause. But when I saw those soldiers in the Breach? To serve on the same side as those iron-clad monsters when they could be set loose at any moment—when families like mine could suffer from it? All I ever wanted was for us Breachsiders to get a fair chance. To get help *defeating* the undead so we could live without fear. The fact that the regent has *allied* with them . . . It doesn't sit right with me."

"That we can agree on."

"I don't think it sits right with most of them, to be honest. The soldiers. But we're trained to follow orders, and that's easier than carving your own path. Better to be an invisible part of the whole than a visible, solitary dissenter."

Leo cocked his head, surprised. "Nicely put, soldier."

Jakob looked away, clearing his throat in embarrassment.

"That's very brave," Leo added with more sincerity. "You know, I've always been a fan of the 'carving your own path' approach myself."

"Yeah?" Jakob asked. "Why? So you can stand out? You don't seem like you'd need help with that."

Leo scoffed, though he was secretly pleased. "I do it because it's more fun."

Hours passed, but Leo insisted they keep moving. He drilled Jakob for everything he knew about the iron revenants, but it was unfortunately precious little.

"They're planning to march tomorrow, I think." That confirmed Leo's theory that they needed Wren in order to make the undead soldiers march. "They can move quickly, despite their size and weight. It's . . . unnerving. They've even got the materials required to build a bridge so they can cross the Serpentine. You may have a head start, but if you continue on foot, they'll likely reach the fort before you do."

Leo's mind snagged on the bridge concept—and the proof that they couldn't cross water without some sort of aid—and he unconsciously picked up the pace.

He thought they were nearing the end of the tunnel; the quality of the light had started to change, giving Leo hope.

He was just thinking how lucky they'd gotten by *not* encountering any revenants when the end of the passage became visible up ahead . . .

. . . and something skeletal, rotten, and unmistakably dead blocked their path. It was silhouetted in the doorway, its body glowing with eerie green light.

Jakob pushed Leo behind him and raised his sword in one hand and Wren's bone knife in the other, but he'd not been trained for this. He had no idea how to fight something that couldn't die.

"Maybe if we turn around," Leo began, "we can—"

Before he could finish his sentence, a bone sword burst from the revenant's rib cage. The undead trembled, its spirit exploding in a puff of smoke before the body dropped to the ground, revealing an armor-clad bonesmith standing behind it.

Not just any bonesmith, but a familiar one: Inara.

She was dirt-spattered and panting, but her movements were precise as she pressed a boot against the corpse and yanked her blade free.

That's when she saw Jakob.

She lifted her weapon, but Leo rushed forward into the light of the world outside. It was nighttime, but the sky was alive with stars, and dawn tinted the distant horizon.

"Prince Leopold?" she asked, squinting at him. Then her gaze flicked back to Jakob, who wore the familiar clothing of Breachside soldiers loyal to the House of Iron. To the regent.

"This is Jakob," Leo hastened to add. "He helped me escape. Jakob, this is Inara, a bonesmith valkyr."

The two sized each other up for a moment, and then Jakob lowered his weapons. "She'll come in handy," he said.

"Handier than you," Inara said coolly, sheathing her sword. The words were delivered in a calm, unruffled tone, though they managed to make Jakob scowl. She turned to Leo. "Where's Wren? I need to speak to her immediately."

"You can't," Leo said. He saw that Inara had a horse outside the passage and hurried toward it. "She was captured. She's in the Breach under heavy guard. I think they're using her to activate the iron revenant army, and they're doing it tonight. Jakob says they could be marching by daybreak."

"Marching where?" Inara asked, though her expression said she already knew.

"The Breachfort. We have to warn them. They need to prepare for battle."

He moved to mount the horse—they could talk on the way—but Inara grabbed his arm. Her pale white eyes, so stark against her dark skin and bonesmith eye black, were wide. "There's no one to warn. Vance, he's just emptied the entire fort. Every guard, bonesmith, and sentry is marching into the Breach."

"Maybe they'll cross paths . . . ?" Jakob said uncertainly.

Inara shook her head. "Doubtful. He's taking them north via the Old Road along the Wall before cutting through some pass at the base of the Adamantines."

"And the Breachfort is a straight shot east from the Breach, so it's very unlikely they'll meet," Leo said. "They've got the means to cross the river—materials to build a hasty bridge. Will that work? Can undead cross water in such a way?"

She considered. "If there is enough distance between themselves and the flow . . . I suspect that yes, they can."

Leo swallowed. "We need to call for help. Send word to my father—"

"Actually," Inara cut in, something like hope flickering in her gaze for the first time. "Your brother was on his way when I left. Surely he travels with soldiers?"

"He'll have a few squads with him at least. Maybe fifty? It won't be enough."

"It'll have to be," said Inara. She mounted up and held out her hand, intending to pull him up behind her.

He hesitated, looking over at Jakob.

"Go ahead," Jakob said. "I'll keep them off your tail."

"Right," Leo said. "Right." He had to go. There wasn't time for this. "I . . . Thank you."

"You're welcome. Here," he said, sheathing his sword and holding out the bone knife.

Leo shook his head. "You keep it. She's got enough weapons for the both of us," he said, jerking his thumb over his shoulder at Inara.

Jakob drew the blade back. Nodded.

Then, since everything was falling apart and their chances of survival seemed to dwindle by the second, Leo took hold of the front of Jakob's jacket and planted a kiss on his mouth. Pulling away, he winked and hurried back to Inara.

She greeted him with rolled eyes and a hand up. "No need to be jealous," Leo murmured. "There's plenty of me to go around."

"Too much," Inara shot back, and Leo grinned.

He turned to see Jakob's cheeks flush bright pink in the gray light. Trying to fight a smile, he bowed his head. "Farewell, Your Highness."

TWENTY-NINE

Wren jerked awake, her body drenched in blood.

No, not blood. Sweat.

And tears.

She rolled to the side just in time to vomit over the edge of the hard stone bed. Her stomach was empty, the bile hitting the ground with a splatter. She coughed. And wept.

And gritted her teeth.

She forced herself to sit up, her head spinning. Her amplifier ring was gone, along with her bone armor, and her weapons had been taken as soon as they'd been captured. But as she searched herself for some means of protection, some way to save herself from this waking nightmare, she noticed something else was amiss.

Her hand . . . She had broken it, had crunched each individual bone in order to free herself of that shackle and get to Julian.

Before . . . before . . .

A sob escaped her lips, a physical reaction that was outside her control. Her heart ached like an open wound in her chest, but her mind refused to accept what had happened. Every time she tried to think about it, to picture it, her brain slammed the door shut on the memories. All that remained was cold sweat and a throat so tight she could barely breathe.

Forcing the air in through her nostrils, she stared at her hand. It helped ground her, bring her back to herself. To this moment.

Despite what she had done, her bones were intact. The flesh was smooth and unmarred, the muscles aching and tight but otherwise entirely healed.

This was the work of the well. Of pure, powerful magic.

Julian had dragged himself with the very last scraps of his strength, of his life, in pursuit of this magic, but he had come up short.

Instead, Wren had been granted the healing that should have been his.

No, that wasn't right. She shook her head; the truth was there, but her brain tried to hide it to save her from the horror. But she knew he hadn't come up short. No, he'd been *denied* this magic. Forcefully.

Wren lurched to her feet, the world spinning until she staggered against a set of metal bars. She was in some sort of cell, the world lit from beyond her small room with familiar ghostly light.

Sconces were mounted on the walls at regular intervals, and at her movement, footsteps scraped against stone.

A figure appeared before her.

A pale figure with Wren's nose and a monster's eyes.

She threw herself against the bars, her hands savagely swiping the air bare inches from her brother's face. He didn't flinch, didn't react at all.

He just stood there, stripped of much of his usual ghostsmith accoutrements—no staff, no skull mask, no sweeping cape. Just ragged clothes to match his ragged appearance. He looked impossibly sad, defeated in a way that made his eyes duller, his skin paler, and his edges indistinct. Or maybe that was Wren's exhaustion and fatigue making itself known.

Her hands fumbled to grip the bars—not in an attempt to tear them loose but in order to stay upright.

"Tell me," she croaked, closing her eyes to gather her strength before fixing them on him once more. "Tell me why."

His face twisted in pain or discomfort. "Wren, I—"

"Tell me *why!*" she shouted.

"I—I had to," he said. "She'd have killed you if I didn't."

"Liar," Wren spat. "She needed me. To awaken the iron revenants. To fill them with magic. They couldn't carry all that metal without the well's power."

"Yes," Hawke said tremulously. "And if I hadn't helped her, she'd still have used you—but after, she'd have tossed you into a coffin, not a cell."

"If you hadn't helped her, we'd have made it to the well. And Julian—" *No,* her brain said. *Too raw. Too recent.* "Unless all of that was a lie." She laughed bitterly. "There was never a chance, was there?"

"No, that's not true," he said, voice anguished. "I didn't lie about any of that. I wanted to do it. I wanted to help you."

"Why?"

He seemed surprised by the question. "Because you're my sister," he said, as if it were obvious. "All I've ever wanted was to meet you." Wren gaped at him. "I know you just learned about me, but I've always known about you." He actually smiled a little. "Starling let it slip once. I don't think Ravenna would have told me otherwise. At least, not then. Most of my childhood games revolved around the two of us."

Wren flashed back to the memories she'd seen through Starling's ghost. Now that she took the time to focus, she could pick out individual details from the rush of colors and sound: Hawke creating a drawing of two pale-haired children holding hands; Hawke swimming in a river and splashing someone who wasn't there; and finally, Hawke going to bed at night, pretending to tuck someone in next to him.

"People thought I had an imaginary friend, but you were real," he said fiercely. "You just weren't with me. But you *existed,* and that's what mattered to me. You were this—this shining beacon of hope. So whenever I felt alone, when I was forced to leave Starling and the rest of the nomads behind, when my familiars weren't enough, I reminded myself that I wasn't alone. Not really. I had you."

Wren swallowed around a sudden lump in her throat. "Oh yeah?" she said, her voice wobbly. "Then what changed?"

The faint melancholy smile that lit his face evaporated, and he glanced away. "She knew. Ravenna. She knew I'd turned against her. I don't know when it started, but . . . she'd been following us."

"That revenant raven," Wren said, recalling the creature on Ravenna's shoulder and its resemblance to the bird they'd seen flying over Laketown. "And Talon's warning."

"He wasn't sure what he'd seen," Hawke said softly. "I think it was actually Ravenna herself. But was she a friend or foe?" He shook his head. "Even still, I thought we could outrun her," he said desperately. "I thought, by the time she figured out where we were going, it'd be too late. But then those Red Guard came, forcing us into the tunnel that led directly here, and . . ."

Wren recalled the fork in the road, the path not taken.

"If you were really on my side then, why didn't you tell me she was watching us? And forcing me to charge up those revenants—you *knew* that was why she wanted me, but you pretended it was just because I'm her daughter. Why did you lie?"

He hugged his arms around his chest. "I was afraid you'd decide to go back."

Wren pulled a skeptical expression. "Do I really seem like the type to give up so easily?"

"Well, no. But we hardly knew each other then, and—"

"We hardly know each other now."

"Yes." He sighed. "But I believed in you, and I guess I didn't think you believed in me. If I'd told you straight off what Ravenna really wanted with you, if I'd shared that she had been following us, that she didn't trust me, I thought you might turn your suspicions on to me instead. That you might . . ." He shrugged. "Turn against me."

Wren's chin hit her chest. While their first meeting had been brief and disconcerting, when they had next spoken, Wren had greeted him with a sword. She'd also threatened him.

I'll chop off your hand before I see you use that ring against me.

She supposed she couldn't blame him for thinking she'd turn her back on him. She'd not wanted to be on his side at all.

"You say you believe in me, but it doesn't change anything, does it? You're serving her now. Otherwise, you'd be getting me out from behind these bars and not talking to me through them."

"I have to. If I don't . . ."

"She'll do to me what she did to Starling."

It wasn't difficult to piece together. Hawke had been on their side right up until the Red Guard chased them into that tunnel. And what had they found? Hawke's nursemaid brutally murdered by Ravenna. Suddenly, the tunnel wasn't a detour that would take them days to traverse because he'd changed their destination, leading them not to the well but to the city itself.

"Starling's body was a warning," Hawke said. "No, it was more than a warning. More than a threat. It was a *promise*."

"So you sacrificed the *Dominions* for me?" Wren asked incredulously. Angrily. He should have known that she wouldn't want that. He should have known that she didn't need him to protect her. "You sacrificed *Julian*?"

Hawke's eyes were wide and pleading, but Wren had had enough. At the thought of Julian, the memories tried once again to resurface in her mind—and this time they succeeded. The flesh of his throat parting for the knife. The blood oozing onto the floor. His dark eyes, always so sharp, so *present*, gone hazy and distant. His hand reaching for hers . . .

Suddenly Wren's breaths came hard and fast, as if she'd run a mile, and black dots speckled her vision. She slid down onto the cold stone floor.

Hawke watched her anxiously. "I brought you something to drink," he said, as if just remembering. He disappeared from view before returning with a tray. "And something to eat."

Next to her was a small, square-shaped door in the cell. He crouched, opening it and sliding the food inside.

Wren turned, stared down at it, then reached for the tray. She lifted it only long enough to fling the lot of it into her brother's face. The plate and cup clattered against the bars, splashing him with water and bits of food.

"Fuck you," she whispered.

Then, basking in her shallow victory, Wren lost consciousness once more.

† † † †

When Wren next became aware of herself, she was alone. Her back ached from passing out against the wall, and when she shifted, her hand brushed up against a fresh tray of food. Or maybe fresh was the wrong word. It had surely been sitting there for hours, unless that mysterious brownish slop had always been ice cold.

Even with the lingering pain and her hunger, Wren's head was starting to clear from the magical overuse. How much time had passed? Enough for a second and, there behind it, a *third* tray to be delivered, *and* for the mess of the first to be cleared away.

She dragged the least-congealed-looking of the food forward and forced herself to eat. She needed to regain her strength. As she choked the meal down, she rifled through what she remembered of her conversation with her brother, skipping over the most painful bits, until she landed on one indisputable truth: she was alive. In a cell, not a coffin, as Hawke had put it.

That meant Ravenna must still need her for something . . . right? Unless she'd simply kept her word to keep Hawke happy, but for some reason Wren doubted that.

What Ravenna had been like before, Wren would probably never know, but the Corpse Queen did not seem the type to concern herself with pleasing anyone.

No matter her plans, Wren wasn't going to sit here and wait for something to happen. She had to *make* something happen.

Hours had passed, which meant the iron revenant army was hours closer to its goal: the Breachfort. Whether Leo had arrived in time to warn them or not, Wren knew they couldn't hold the Border Wall forever. Even if the entirety of the Dominions army turned up, their foe was undead. It couldn't be killed. Perhaps with specialized tools and a strategy, they could be stopped or penned in, but the Dominions simply weren't prepared for that. And how many would die in the interim?

They had to be stopped, but how? Her mind flashed back to that strange scepter she'd seen the regent holding. Could that be the key? But he and the scepter, like the undead army, were surely miles away by now. . . .

She shook her head and focused. She'd figure it all out eventually, but first she needed out of this cell.

She was alone, without friends or allies . . . but that didn't mean she was powerless.

She *was* weakened, though. Despite sitting in that gathering pool for hours, her magic was utterly depleted. She'd done too much, and now her body was trying to recover.

Her ability to sense the ghostlight sconces, still lit, was virtually nonexistent, and even her armor and weapons, tucked into an alcove down the hall, were barely detectable to her. That was the most startling part. It was one thing to feel her ghostsmith magic grow distant—she had felt that before, when the extra power in her amplifier ring was used up—but to have her bonesmith abilities diminish? It was like plugging her ears or covering her eyes. The sense was not *gone* but so badly obscured that she only realized how much she relied on it now that she *couldn't.*

Of course, even if she'd been able to summon her armor or blades, what could she do with them? Bone wasn't like gold; she couldn't fashion lockpicks like Leo, and it wasn't strong like iron, able to make things bend and break.

And as for her *other* magic, well . . .

Wren sat up. She stretched her senses and . . . *Yes,* her ring was down here, too, tucked away with the rest of her belongings. She couldn't draw the amplifier to her, but perhaps she could summon something else.

She'd done it before, hadn't she?

Getting to her feet, Wren pushed her head against the bars in an attempt to peer down the hall. She couldn't *see* it, but she knew it was there.

"Willow?" Wren whispered, though she immediately started to doubt herself. "Are you there? Can you hear me?" Her words echoed in the empty hall. She closed her eyes, took a deep breath, and tried again. Not just with her words but with her mind. "*Willow.* Come to me."

She felt it then—the low vibration in her throat, the magic lacing the words. There was a burst of ghostlight, and then Willow was there, floating down the hall and through the bars to Wren's cell. She extended her hand without a second thought, feeling the coldness from the ghost pool in her palm.

The joy she felt at her success, at the sight of her familiar, quickly dimmed. Now what? What could a *spirit* do? Wren slumped onto the ledge that acted as a bed, the ghost-bird coming with her.

She sighed, the gust of air causing Willow's shape to swirl and rematerialize.

At least she wasn't alone.

But then her mind chose that moment to make her think of Julian.

Her head told her he was a goner. But her heart . . . her heart. It *raged.* At the regent, at Hawke and Ravenna . . . but at herself most of all. They had thrown away what little time they'd had, being stubborn and foolish and judgmental, when they *should* have been taking advantage of every second they had together. If she could go back, she'd tell him she thought he was fierce and brave and strong, too, but it was his goodness she admired most. All those people at Southbridge, they'd rioted for him not because he was heir to a fallen house but because of who he was on the inside. Always doing what was best for his people, like his mother before him.

He'd deserved better. Better than that duplicitous uncle in place of his parents. Better than assassination attempts and wanted posters. Better than Wren Graven, selfish and reckless and betraying.

Better than a sliced throat, a life cut short, his body washed away into the darkness.

Where would it come to rest? And when would he rise again?

And how could she go on, not knowing for certain?

Suddenly, Wren flashed back to a conversation she'd had with Julian after she'd fallen into the Breach. She'd asked him why he'd come back for her, searching in the most haunted place in the world, when she was surely a goner.

But you weren't, were you? he'd said. *I had to know.*

Footsteps sounded from somewhere down the hall, soft but growing louder.

"Willow," Wren whispered. "Find Julian. Can you do that? The ironsmith, the . . ." She trailed off, picturing him in her mind instead. "He's my friend. Look for him, and if you find him, and he's *alive* . . . one chirp."

The footsteps were drawing closer, so she added the rest in a rush. "You help him first, though. Lead him to the surface, and then come tell me. If you *can't* find him, two chirps. And if you find him, and he doesn't live . . ." Wren could barely bring herself to say it. "If he doesn't live, three chirps."

Wren knew she was asking too much. But she was out of time.

"Go," she said, and Willow lifted from her palm and flew straight into the wall, vanishing just as Wren's visitor appeared between the bars.

It was Hawke again.

He didn't have a tray of food, which told Wren either he'd come to talk . . . or to release her.

"Has Mother sent you?" Wren asked with false brightness. "What, are there more undead monsters that need making?"

He didn't answer. Instead he glanced down the passage behind him, as if he were expecting someone.

"Speaking of mothers and monsters," she said, continuing the conversation while she could, before her other visitor—surely Ravenna—arrived. "I thought ghostsmiths had power *over* the undead. The ability to control ghosts and revenants and familiars, too."

"Yes . . . ," Hawke said, frowning in obvious confusion.

"Then tell me," Wren said, leaning back against the stone wall and crossing her arms over her chest. "Why are you serving one?"

His gaze flickered. "What do you mean?"

"You know exactly what I mean," Wren said angrily, lurching upright and pointing at him. "I cut her, and she didn't bleed. I pulled the knife from her boot and sliced her an inch deep, and there wasn't a cry of pain or a drop of blood. I've never seen her face. And why wouldn't *she* help you animate the iron revenants instead of using me? She's a ghostsmith, after all, and you share blood—the same as us. But she can't wield ghostsmith magic, can she? Because our mother is *dead*."

Hawke swallowed and glanced away.

"You told me the well saved your lives," Wren persisted, but even as she said it, she realized that wasn't quite true. He'd said the well saved *his* life and that he owed his mother a debt because of it, but he'd never mentioned *Ravenna's* life.

Hawke shook his head, anguish on his features, a lifelong burden bending his shoulders.

"She was too late, wasn't she?" Wren muttered, trying to piece it all together. "But how—"

"By the time she got here," he began, lowering his voice and taking a step closer to the bars, "she was in rough shape. But I was rougher. Pale. Starving. She hadn't been able to feed me on the journey. Her milk hadn't come in. It'd been hours since I'd made a sound. So when she finally stumbled from her horse, she put *me* into the pool first. It must have been *seconds*, a few labored heartbeats, before she followed me . . . but it was the difference between a life saved—mine—and a life lost. Hers."

"She's a revenant," Wren whispered, knowing it was true but still struggling to believe it. The fact that Ravenna was dead certainly explained her cold cruelty as well as Hawke's hatred for human undead. After all, he'd been living under the thumb of one for years.

Hawke shook his head fervently. "She is more than that. Her body died, but her ghost, it rose almost instantly, thanks to the well. Her connection to her remains is strong, and her mind . . . She remembers everything. I think that is the key. The longer they are dead, the more their memory—their connection to their living self—deteriorates, and so with it, their strength. What they call her, according to ghost-lore, is a lich."

Wren had never heard the term, but it sent a shudder through her all the same. "A lich," she repeated. "Some sort of especially strong revenant."

"Yes," Hawke breathed, his gaze distant. "Their existence is considered unnatural. *Wrong.* They cannot be commanded, you see, and so they upset the natural order. The undead are meant to *serve,* to exist beneath the living ghostsmiths, not be superior to them. She is capable of things that defy the laws of magic—certainly the laws of the undead. Her control over her ghost . . ."

"I've never *seen* her ghost," Wren said. Unless you counted her eyes, but Wren had sliced open her flesh and seen no hint of ghost glow.

"Nor will you, unless she wishes you to. She can conceal it, shift and reshape it . . . even *split* it."

Split it? But why? To what purpose? A thousand more questions flitted through Wren's mind, but before she could voice even a single one, more footsteps echoed down the passage.

Only, it wasn't her mother who appeared in the flickering ghostlight.

It was her father.

"Hello, little bird."

THIRTY

Wren gaped.

What was he *doing* here? How had he *gotten* here?

And why was he not in a cell beside her?

Had his insane idea to offer Ravenna marriage actually worked? She glanced at Hawke, but his expression revealed nothing.

Vance strode forward, a key jingling in his hand.

"I will give you two a moment," Hawke said tersely, edging awkwardly around Vance.

"Thanks, son," he said, affecting a false gravitas. The words sounded so forced, so insincere, that Wren wanted to gag on them. Lucky her father's head was turned, or he might have seen her eyes roll.

Her brother saw them, though, before he disappeared down the passage.

Wren remained immobile as the lock clicked and the door swung wide.

Her gaze darted to her weapons, then back to her father, but before she could think what to do, he'd seized her in a hug.

Her muscles twitched and trembled—with exhaustion, with the urge to push him off, and with the weak, shameful desire to hug him back.

He withdrew before she'd given in to the urge, and with his hands on her shoulders, he took her in. "I hear you've been through it these last days." He tipped up her chin to examine her face, but Wren pulled away.

They stood on the threshold of the cell, and when she walked past him, he let her. She reached for her weapons, and again, he let it happen. She armed herself as quickly as she could, thinking fast. But as she scooped up item after item—breastplate and bandolier, swords and throwing knives—she failed to locate her ring. She slid her hand along the shelf and peered down at the shadows by her feet.

It wasn't here. But she'd *sensed it*. She was sure of it. While her bone weapons and armor would help amplify her bonesmith abilities, without her ring, her ghostsmith powers would remain faint and difficult to grasp. Perhaps she could absorb some residual well magic through the stones, like she had when she'd first entered the Breach, but she knew it wouldn't be enough. Not for anything significant.

She pushed the thought aside. Her father was a complication she *really* didn't need right now, but she was out of her cell for the first time in at least a day, maybe more.

"Tell me what's happening. How did you get here, and why are you letting me out of my cell?"

He folded his arms across his chest and leaned against the wall as she strapped blades and fastened buckles. He wore typical bonesmith leathers but had forgone the bone armor and weapons. He looked as he often did, like a bonesmith off duty.

"After you evaded my attempts to recapture you," he said, almost smiling, as if it were an inside joke between them, "I was forced to form an alternative plan. Nothing was going my way for a while—the stables even caught fire," he chattered, and Wren felt a spark of appreciation for what had surely been Inara's handiwork. "Then your grandmother arrived, and you know how she and I disagree. But I was able to talk her around."

Talk her around? Svetlana Graven was not the type of woman to be *convinced*. There was something else happening here that Vance wasn't telling her.

"Now she finally sees the big picture."

"The big picture," Wren repeated flatly.

He sidled up next to her, glancing down the passage where Hawke had gone before he spoke. "This place. This *power*. It will be ours before the night is through. With Mother no longer in my way, I am able to do what I please with the resources at my disposal. That is how I got here. I emptied the Breachfort and rode here in force."

Wren's ears were ringing. He'd *emptied* the Breachfort? The iron revenants were marching there right now, possibly arriving at any moment, and the place had been stripped of its defenders? All so her father could play with forces he didn't understand?

"Even with a party nearly a hundred strong, we barely survived several undead encounters. But finally, by the time we crossed into the Haunted Territory, she sent them. Armored revenants. Two of them. They came for me and escorted me here. I think Ravenna knew that if I was coming to see her, I'd have something worthwhile to say. I had to leave my forces behind, of course, but I told them to remain Breachside."

Wren squeezed her eyes shut. Her father was so prideful, so

arrogant, that he'd followed Ravenna blindly—utterly defenseless—assuming that *he* was the one with power here, in the Haunted Territory. In the very *heart* of the Breach.

"Do you know what you've done?" she asked, cutting him off before he could spew more nonsense, her eyes still closed. When she opened them, he looked surprised. She'd never have dared interrupt him when she was younger, and if she had, his disappointed look would be enough to quell her, but no longer. "The iron revenant army has already left." Wren glanced at the ghostlight sconces, wary, suddenly, of being overheard. Were they capable of spying the way familiars were? And where had Hawke gone? "They used me, they *forced* me to activate them, to send them marching. And you've emptied the Breachfort! They'll stroll through that gate like it's nothing. We have to get out of here."

"We'll handle it, Wren," he said easily—unconcernedly. "In due time. Best to let the Dominions know just how much they need us before we rush in and save their hides. That's what I tried to tell Locke all those years ago, but he wouldn't hear of it."

"How?" Wren hissed as she slid her last weapon into place and straightened. "*How* will we 'handle it'?"

He smiled with deep self-satisfaction. "She needs me. Ravenna. She wants an alliance between our houses, and I am the only person who can give her that. But once the ritual is complete, once that crown is upon my head, I will have full access to the necropolis, the well of magic, everything."

"Ritual . . . crown . . . You're going to *marry* her?"

"Don't look so shocked. There is power in such ceremonies, Wren. There is *magic* in the binding of two people, of two houses. And even if there wasn't, *she* believes there is. The ghostsmiths were zealots, to be sure, and she is no different. Once we are wed, all this will be mine."

Wren speared her fingers through her hair and gripped, hard. "Have you lost your fucking mind?" she asked faintly, before dropping her hands. "She is *dead*. Do you hear me? Dead! They call her a lich. Something like a revenant, but smarter. Stronger. You won't be able to just take what you want and do what you please." She thought of what Ravenna had done to Starling in order to stop Hawke. "She won't allow it."

"Is that fear in your voice, Wren Graven? Since when do you back down from the undead?"

Wren glared at him, her cheeks heating. "I am not backing down! *You're* the one marrying her," she added, somewhat petulantly. Her father always knew exactly how to shame her, but suddenly Wren saw the comment for what it was. A deflection. A diversionary tactic. She crossed her arms, frowning at him. "Hang on—you knew? How?"

He shrugged, looking almost sheepish. "I didn't, but Odile certainly had her suspicions. I found some rather convincing notes and research after I took over her office. She'd even written to Marrow Hall years ago, requesting some old volumes from the archives. The picture she'd pieced together suggested that Ravenna was no longer a mere ghostsmith. That she was something . . . else. I wasn't certain until I came here, though. But when I saw her, well . . . She was a true beauty when she was alive, the kind of girl men fought over." He cleared his throat. "Ceremonial garb or not, she only wears that veil because she has to. Why else would she conceal one of her greatest weapons?"

"She has other weapons now," Wren said darkly.

"Yes. Limitless corpses and an overflowing well of magic."

"And the fact that she's undead and cannot be killed."

"Why do you think I'm so certain I can defeat her?" he asked, hitching a confident smile onto his face. "We're bonesmiths, Wren. This is what we do. And I will *do it*. I'll marry her in this backwoods necromantic ceremony, I'll give her the 'union of ghost and bone' that she so longs for, and I'll promise to help her resurrect the House of the Dead—whatever it takes to prove that I'm on her side. Then she'll give me access to the well, and I'll destroy her and her undead army. I'll be the hero of this story, not Locke. I'll do it better than he ever did," he finished fervently, his eyes alight with the vision he saw of himself triumphant over the literal ghosts of his past.

The sight unsettled Wren. Was this how she had always looked and sounded when she'd talked about regaining her place in the House of Bone? Of earning her father's respect? Desperate and unhinged? Foolish?

"Dad," Wren said awkwardly, putting her hand on his arm. "You don't have to do this."

She struggled to find the words. While she was angry with him, the truth was, she pitied him too. After all this time, he still hadn't let it go. Again, Wren thought of her own circumstances. If she had failed to rescue Leo, if she'd been left to rot at the Breachfort for twenty years . . . would she have turned out the same?

"You don't have to surpass or defeat Locke. He's dead," she continued. "He's already defeated. You don't have to prove anything to anyone."

Please, she thought desperately. Because beyond pity, she also felt panic. She did not have time for this. She did not need to worry about destroying the well *and* stopping her father from getting himself killed.

He blinked at her, then shook off her touch. "This isn't about him," he said. "Not really. It's not about the past. It's about the *future*. Whatever was, whatever might have been, it doesn't matter."

Wren tried to parse that out. Did he know that Wren had overheard about Locke possibly being her father? Did it matter, when he clearly wanted to bury it, along with everything else?

"That is why I must do this. I must secure this power for the House of Bone."

His certainty was intoxicating, to himself most of all. It was a potent blend of eagerness and arrogance, of talent and luck and perseverance. A person like that saw failure as mere setback and constantly took risks. When it worked out, they appeared as if they'd known all along that it would. If it didn't, they blamed others and twisted the facts, moving inexorably toward their next goals, not stopping long enough to linger, to let people question.

Wren recognized it because it was in her, too. And because she knew these traits intimately, she also knew that that kind of confidence was not an inner power but an outer shield. A means to deflect reality and plow through obstacles heedless of the risk until only one of you was left standing.

But there was no plowing through this.

"You can't *claim* it," she gritted out. "The magic, it's leaking everywhere—it's in the ground and the water." That thought made something stir in the back of her mind, but she pushed it aside. "It sends shock waves through the earth, causing tunnels to collapse and whole cities to be destroyed. It's dangerous and unstable. It *killed* Locke, along with hundreds of others. You cannot trap raw magic in such a way. The well must be destroyed. I think I might be able to do it. If I can get to it, I can—"

"Everything I've worked for my entire life is on the brink of being secured, and you want to destroy it?" he asked incredulously. "Trust me. I'm doing what's best for us."

For me was what he meant. It was what he *always* meant.

And she had stopped trusting him the moment she'd discovered just how far he was willing to go to get what he wanted and how willingly he had betrayed her along the way.

Wren opened her mouth to argue, to point out one of a dozen flaws in his plan, his logic, and his general life choices, but she knew he'd never listen.

Besides, he had taken her out of her cell and allowed her to arm herself. If she played along, if she pretended to give him the benefit of the doubt . . . perhaps she could use him as a distraction at the very least. Get close enough to the gathering pool to recharge her magic so she could fight her way out, then go in search of the well. If what Hawke had told her was true, if it was made of haunted bone, she would destroy it—*before* her father could get his foolish hands on it.

"I . . . okay," Wren said, nodding in submission.

To his credit, her father had enough knowledge of his daughter to look suspicious at her hasty acquiescence but not enough presence of mind to question his own ability to see his plan through.

His frown cleared and he smiled just as Hawke returned at the end of the passage.

He was fully decked out in his ghostsmith gear again, his skull mask atop his head, cape on his shoulders, and staff in hand. His gaze flicked in her direction before settling back on Vance.

"We're ready."

THIRTY-ONE

Julian washed up on the shore, his limbs heavy and his hair dripping in his eyes as he pulled himself toward dry land. There were rocks and slippery bits of carved stone underneath his palms, and all was darkness.

He drew in a deep, shuddering gasp, the burst of air cold against his searing throat.

Remembering, his hand flew up, but rather than finding torn flesh and blood, he found a scar that felt weeks old—tender but fully closed.

He shivered at the memory of the blade dragging through his skin, at the cruel look in his uncle's eyes. Even after everything, some part of him hadn't thought the man capable of it. Contriving a devious plan and giving a calculated order? Yes. But actually wielding the knife? And doing so without so much as a hesitation? A flash of emotion or regret?

Had there ever been a true moment between them? Or had every flash of anger or smile of pleasure been a means to make Julian more susceptible to manipulation? The whole thing was like some sick play, some farce, and while Julian had tried and pushed and acted with sincerity, his uncle had been like a suit of iron: hard, unyielding . . . and empty.

Something glowed in his peripheral vision, and Julian whirled around to see a ghost.

A familiar ghost. A bird.

He reared back, fear and confusion lancing through him, along with more painful memories.

Hawke had betrayed them. Julian had been dragging himself to Wren, to the gathering pool—clinging desperately to life—and Hawke had kicked him into the water, disposing of him like garbage. Was this ghost here to finish the job?

But then Julian blinked. He *had* seen this ghost before, but it did not belong to Hawke.

This was Wren's familiar, Willow.

Julian briefly closed his eyes, trying to gather his wits about him while his heart thundered in his chest.

He looked at the ghost-bird again. She was perched on a rock, and next to her was one of those magical leaks, dripping from a crack in the stone.

The raw magic flowed directly into the water that rushed by him in a gentle but steady current, like a river that ran from the iron revenant chamber to here and then beyond.

Julian frowned. Had Hawke *known* he would be swept away here, to this spot where magic overflowed and filled the water?

Francis had dealt him a mortal wound; Julian had been there, on the edge. The brink.

And this magic had brought him back. Hawke had said it was

possible—that it had healed him when he was a baby, and Julian had *seen* it heal him after he took that arrow wound.

Did that mean Hawke had kicked him into this water on purpose? That he'd intended to actually *help* Julian? That perhaps, despite his betrayal, his allegiance was still split?

Surely the fact that Julian was alive was proof of *something* . . . inner conflict at the very least. Possibly a change of heart?

Maybe Wren wouldn't be alone after all.

He stared at the bird again, who stared back at him.

Expelling a breath, Julian lifted a hand to his hair—and froze. His hand, it was *glowing*, just like Wren and Hawke had been when they'd stood in the gathering pool and animated those iron revenants.

Apparently, the well magic had done more than save his life. He'd been floating in it for who knew how long, and now he was saturated with it. With consciousness and mental clarity steadily returning, he was aware of it in a way he hadn't been before.

He could feel it inside him, *surrounding* him. He stared down at his armor. It should have sunk to the bottom of the water, bringing Julian with it. But instead, it had filled with magic that kept him alive, kept him afloat, and now . . . ?

Given him access to power he could never have imagined.

Was *this* what Locke Graven had felt when he'd tried to end the Uprising? What Wren had felt her first time in contact with the well's power? He knew now that he'd not given her enough credit for walking away from it—for wanting to destroy it in the first place. Instead he had scoffed at the lure of this magic, at the godlike abilities it bestowed, without really understanding at all.

This wasn't just power—it was potential, the ability to do anything. Or at least, that's how it felt.

The glow was slowly subsiding, perhaps just the residual effect of being in contact with the magic so recently, but the extra power remained.

Tentatively, he reached out with his iron hand and extended his senses.

Instantly he felt iron in the stone before him. Veins of it running deep in the foundations of this place. They sprawled everywhere, some near and some impossibly far, making a mockery of his usual range.

Julian inhaled deeply, the power swirling within him and begging for release.

He latched on to the nearest piece, suspended in the wall opposite, and *pulled.*

It burst from the rock in an explosion of pebbles and debris, the hunk of iron slamming into his palm.

It was heavy, yet not. Julian's muscles were bolstered as surely as his magic was, his armor like a second, better skin. An exoskeleton. Staring down at the raw iron, he clenched his hand, cracking the ore as if it were made of chalk.

When he opened his palm, the hunk of iron had been reduced to scattered, coin-size pieces. Thinking of Wren's knucklebones, Julian narrowed his focus and tossed the iron into the air—and kept it there, suspended before him. Then he moved it, in a slow circle at first, then faster. All of them zipping and whirling around his head in a dizzying orbit.

He isolated a single piece. Locating a target across the chamber, he sent it flying through the air as fast as he could.

The iron pierced the stone pillar, leaving a perfect hole sliced clean through, and then came zooming back to him.

Julian grinned savagely.

His uncle had taken all his weapons, but Julian had just created some of his own.

What else was he capable of? Gold might be liquefiable, but iron was not a malleable metal.

It was, however, a magnetizable one.

Hawke had said the magic could act as a charge, the same way an existing magnet could charge regular iron.

So, if Julian was full of magic, he should be able to funnel that magic into a charge and—

He'd been staring at his iron hand as he worked through his idea, the shards of metal still swirling around his head, but before he could even finish his thought, all of them had dropped from the air and fastened on to his hand.

He tried to pull them off, but they were stuck fast, and as he lowered his arm in awe, he allowed it to get a little too close to his breastplate. His hand slammed against it with a thud hard enough to knock the air from Julian's lungs.

He gasped, laughing a bit hysterically, and tried to concentrate. He had turned his hand into a magnet. . . . Surely he could remove that charge?

It took a few minutes, but once he started visualizing the power within him and drawing it back from his hand, it released from his breastplate, and the iron shards fell to the ground.

When he reached for them again—wary of his intent and how much magical force he put behind it—they obeyed his call *without* magnetization.

That was good. Very good.

Already the possibilities spread out before him.

Thinking of his uncle caused a fire to burn low in his belly, his anger deep, pure, and absolute.

He had betrayed Julian and his family for the last time.

But on the heels of that rage came a softer emotion. The look in Wren's eyes when she'd seen his throat cut. The way she had dragged *herself* to get to *him*, both of them desperate to get to each other.

If he had doubted her feelings for him up until now, he didn't any longer. He had wasted so much energy being angry with her. What if he *had* died, and he'd never gotten the chance to kiss her again? To tell her how he felt?

Where was she now? Was she all right? Julian was stronger than ever before. He could save her.

Or could he? Wren's foes were undead, their magic a world away from his. Iron shards and magnetization were useless weapons against ghosts and revenants. . . .

Unless they were clad in iron.

And there was that scepter. It apparently controlled the undead army, and it was currently in his uncle's scheming, lying, blood-stained iron hands.

Julian would *take it from him.*

Wren didn't need him to save her. What she needed was someone to *help her* finish the job. He'd stop his uncle and stop this army.

Still, Julian hesitated. A thousand terrible scenarios flashed before his eyes when he thought of where he'd left her—and with whom—but with effort he shoved them aside and focused on something different. He saw not vulnerability but opportunity. He saw Wren's fearlessness, her bravery, her daring. Bone blades flashing and pale eyes gleaming. *Ghost-green* eyes shining in the darkness.

She would do this.

She would save them all.

And she had sent her familiar here, hadn't she? Surely that meant she was unharmed.

His resolve solidified. He looked at the ghost-bird again.

"So," Julian said, speaking into the silence. He was no ghostsmith, but it was worth a shot. "How do I get out of here?"

The fact that he was asking a ghost *for directions* was truly a sign of how much his life had been upended ever since he'd locked eyes with a wild bonesmith girl in the middle of a kidnapping that was about to go horribly, spectacularly wrong.

The ghost-bird cocked its head, then fluttered toward the back of the chamber, its light illuminating the mouth of an ink-black passage.

Julian followed.

THIRTY-TWO

Wren, Vance, and Hawke emerged from the dungeons into a familiar space: the throne room from her first foray into the Breach. This was Hollow Hall, the ghostsmith palace.

Instead of entering from the front through the main doorway, as Wren had before, they walked into the long, cavernous chamber from the back, near the throne. There had been three chairs the last time Wren was here, but it appeared a fourth one had been recently added. Now there was the high seat in the middle, carved into the wall behind, and two chairs on the right of it and one on the left.

As before, the gathering pool glowed from the center of the room, sending dancing light across the pillars that lined the chamber and casting shadows on the gallery above. *Unlike* before, ghostlight torches and chandeliers had been lit, illuminating the thrones, and the space was filled with dozens of idle revenants, who provided their own flickering glow.

Spectators, Wren thought uneasily.

Vance looked around with interest, but not shock or surprise—he'd clearly been expecting this.

Ravenna stepped out of the darkness, and now that she knew to look for it, Wren *felt* her undead presence for the first time. That seemed a good sign; her magic had recovered somewhat, her body likely absorbing small amounts of it from the room itself. Still, she did not have the power she'd had when she'd been submerged in the pool or when she'd worn her amplifier ring.

She tried to extend her senses but couldn't detect anything beyond the circle of ghostlight, and that immediately put her on high alert. Who knew what other horrors were concealed in the shadows.

Frustration rose up. The gathering pool was *right there*. If she could touch it, she could regain her strength tenfold and get out of here. Get to the well and bring down that army.

But if she made her intentions known, if she gave herself away, she'd wind up back inside that cell.

Or worse.

Hawke knew why she had agreed to come here, surely, but perhaps he was confident he and his revenants could stop any attempts she might make. Perhaps she was no longer considered any sort of threat, with her ring gone and her friends gone too.

Taking a deep, steadying breath, she reeled herself in and refocused.

She had to get to the gathering pool so she could fight her way out of here, but she had to wait for the right opportunity.

"My lady," Vance said, bowing in a revolting parody of a courtly gentleman.

Ravenna inclined her head stiffly but did not return the bow nor the respectful pleasantries. Wren recalled that she did not like being called "lady" when she had styled herself a queen instead, but apparently her father didn't know that.

While she still wore her usual floor-length veil and bone crown, strands of dried flowers in shades of ivory and yellow had been sewn into the hem and twined between the prongs. In her gloved hand, she held three garlands twisted of the same pale flowers. Hawke retrieved them, laying one over his own head to rest around his neck before handing one each to Wren and Vance.

Vance smiled and clapped him on the shoulder in a pathetic attempt to appear fatherly, smiling in a way that caused old pain to echo in the pit of Wren's stomach, distant and only vaguely familiar to her. It whispered that she was not enough—that he'd have been happier with a different child.

She didn't care. His happiness was no longer her concern.

While Vance placed his garland on his neck happily, Wren glared at her brother as she did so, feeling like a child playing dress-up. Was she really about to stand witness to her father marrying a dead woman?

Did she have any choice in the matter?

As the garland settled about her shoulders, Wren caught a whiff of that same floral scent she'd detected on Ravenna before—both in the Keeper's Cathedral and in Starling's memories.

Now that they were appropriately trimmed, Wren and her father waited for what would come next. Who officiated ghostsmith weddings? Revenants? Or would Hawke do the honors?

As her father met Ravenna at the bottom of the dais where the thrones were perched, Wren stared at her feet. There were the cracks and crevices she had noticed on her first visit, though they weren't soaked in magic as they had been before. Not yet.

What she *hadn't* noticed before were the channels carved deliberately in the rock, like in the Keeper's Cathedral, leading from the pool across the floor and toward the thrones. She could almost see it now, necromantic kings and queens seated on high, decked out in dead flowers and haunted bones, absorbing magic through the ground. Keeping them healthy and strong and drenched in power.

And before her now stood a *new* king and queen: one of bone and one of ghost.

The sight caused anger to spike in Wren's veins.

Her father truly thought he could take what he wanted here, that he was a step ahead and cleverer than Ravenna. That he could outmaneuver her and, once the ceremony was complete, out-magic her.

That last bit might be true. Could a lich wield magic? Wren assumed that whatever power Ravenna had, it was no longer ghostsmith. Otherwise, she could have raised that army without Wren.

But the rest? This was Ravenna's domain, and these undead were *her* servants. How she controlled them was harder to discern. Perhaps it all came down to Hawke? Or perhaps undead revered more powerful undead. Regardless, even when her father joined her on those thrones, he was no ghostsmith. He could not command or control them. And he was not immune.

She'd tried to warn him, and he wouldn't hear it. Now all she could do was watch him make his bed and hope that when the time came to lie in it, he'd still be alive.

Ravenna turned to Hawke and nodded. Striding over to the gathering pool, he lowered his mask over his face and put his staff aside. He placed one hand inside the swirling mist and pressed the other to the ground outside it. As he had done in the iron revenant chamber,

Hawke absorbed magic into his body only to send it back out again, through the carved grooves in the ground.

Wren watched the progress with interest, but her father's attention was ravenous. It was clear he hungered for this power, longed to taste it himself, but the deep grooves of glowing light shot past him and Ravenna, toward the thrones and beyond. Wren looked down at her feet again, but it seemed her brother was being more deliberate than before, because even after activating the pool, the cracks in the stones remained unlit.

The wall behind the chairs—shadowy and indistinct—started to glow with light. Not the pure white light of magic but the sinister, sickly green of ghostlight.

What Wren had taken for vague additional carvings upon first sight soon materialized into a wall of bones. *Haunted* bones.

They reminded her of the throughway sconces at first, their eyes shining brightly and their mouths agape. But soon entire skeletons became discernible, mounted with their arms crossed over their chests. They looked like bodies prepared for a burial, though all that remained of their bodies was bones, every inch carved with symbols and glyphs.

"Elders," Hawke said, voice ringing out in the silence. "Heed me."

"*Son of Death*," they boomed in unison, their ghostlight flaring. All the hairs on Wren's body stood up. No wonder Hawke had needed extra well magic to activate them. These undead were not like the sconces, docile and waiting to obey a command. They emanated a powerful sentience, even if they were subservient too.

A hand landed on Wren's wrist, making her jump—but it was only her father, leaning toward her to whisper, "They were ghostsmiths, once. All vassals to the House of Ghost swore their *eternal* allegiance, in life and in death, but these ones trained for this position while they were alive, dedicating decades to the study of history and ghostlore." Was this one of the "more dignified" ways to serve that Hawke had mentioned before? "According to Odile's research, their duty is to ensure the House of Ghost holds fast to its traditions. They act as something like priests or councilmembers, presiding over important events and even advising on various issues."

"Advising? But ghosts don't—they're dead; they can't *learn* new information. . . ." She trailed off, thinking of familiars and how they acted as messengers and lookouts. How they scouted and gave warnings.

To Wren's surprise, it was Hawke who answered. "Most undead are capable of simple commands and mimicry, no more. But with time and magic, they can become something greater. And the Elders have been feeding on a steady diet of well magic for centuries."

"And now they serve the throne and whoever sits upon it," Vance finished. His eyes gleamed.

"Bear witness," Hawke said, averting his eyes to avoid the searing light, "to this union. This binding. This new beginning."

Binding . . . Something about that word caused a strange sense of foreboding to settle over Wren like a cloak. As if the situation wasn't already haunting enough.

The Elders spoke again. *"Your will is our command."* Their glow dimmed, settling into a steadier illumination that set the stage for what was to come.

"Repeat after me," said Ravenna, and then she began to recite a familiar chorus—the words of the House of Bone. Only . . . they were different. Altered. Perhaps these had once been the words of the House of the Dead, and when they split, each new house changed them to suit their purpose.

"Death is as certain as the dawn, and just as a new day will come, so too will the new dead rise. And we will be there. To find. To guide. *To rule.* So the living may thrive, and the dead may serve, for *death is not the end.*"

While all the changes were disturbing, like a jarring note in a familiar song, the last few words were particularly so. *Death is not the end.* Wren recalled Ravenna speaking them to the regent outside the inn in Caston. It wasn't that the words were surprising—the proof was all around them—but rather, it was the way they were spoken, more threat than promise.

Vance clearly noted the difference too, a slight frown drawing his brows together, but he said them all the same. The glow of the gathering pool was visible in his eyes, and Wren feared it blinded him more than any ghostlight.

She thought about trying to warn him again. He was a fool who had chased her here and had caused this mess in the first place. He was stubborn and overly ambitious, and she feared this day would be his doom.

But he was still her father, whether by blood or not.

"Dad," she began, but Vance had turned his back to her. Ravenna was reaching into the layers of fabric beneath her veil. She fiddled with something, her bone adornments clicking and clacking together before she removed one of them and withdrew it.

It was a sternum set on a long chain, the stubs of ribs sprawling from the center like a star. It had clearly been worn on her neck, and the fact that she wore bones that were not her own was all the proof Wren needed to know that a lich was powerful. She handed the sternum to Hawke, who then placed the chain around Vance's neck. Perhaps it was a way to seal the deal, like a ring in a Dominion's marriage ceremony.

Wren found herself wondering who the bone had belonged to and tensed as it rested in the center of her father's chest, perfectly overlapping his own sternum. If it was haunted, the spirit within was dormant, keeping her father safe—for now—though he appeared anxious to wear it all the same.

One wrong move, one word from Hawke or Ravenna, and he'd be dead.

With the necklace in place, Ravenna reached up to her crown. Wren thought she was about to remove it, but when her hands lifted the crown from her head, part of it remained—the two circlets cleverly overlapping each other.

Again, Hawke took the adornment from her hands and brought it to Vance, lowering the bone crown onto his head.

Expressions warred on Vance's face: fierce pride coupled with vague distaste. In all the ways he'd likely imagined himself crowned over the years, having it happen in a ruined necropolis with a corpse for a bride and a crowd of undead as the congregation was surely not one of them.

Still, he lifted his chin, his vanity winning out.

Ravenna led the way up the steps to the chairs. While she took the high-backed throne, Vance took the other, smaller seat to her right. Wren sensed his ego prickle at that, but surely it was a familiar sensation to him—always being second, next, not-quite-best.

Hawke sidled next to Wren in his obscuring ram's skull mask, intending to guide her toward the seat beside her father. He, presumably, would take the one to his mother's left.

Wren stared at her father. How long was this charade meant to carry on? The ceremony was complete, wasn't it? When was he going to *do* something?

She hesitated, fighting the urge to look toward the gathering pool again. Could she make a run for it? Dive in and then worry about the repercussions later? That was her usual move—and at least she'd have super-charged magic, however temporary.

"Wren," her father said, voice only slightly edged. He smiled encouragingly, nodding toward her seat. She glanced at Hawke, then at the droves of revenants milling about the space, essentially blocking her path.

She blew out a breath and walked the stairs. Only once she was seated in her chair did Hawke take his.

Before them, the undead congregation pushed nearer, nearer, drawn inescapably toward the living.

"Bow down," said Hawke, his voice echoing, proving his strength once again as he commanded so many at once. "Kneel before your Corpse Queen and her King, rulers of the House of the Dead."

And they did. Revenants bent their trembling knees with pops and cracks, lowering their rotted heads, and ghosts sank to the ground in rippling swirls, all surrendering themselves in subservience before this newmade necromantic family. An undead dynasty that could tear the world apart.

But *not* if Wren Graven had anything to say about it.

THIRTY-THREE

Leo recalled the last time he had made this journey. He had shared a horse with Wren, not Inara, and they had been fleeing the Haunted Territory and the regent's men, much like today.

Then, Leo had felt urgency of the sort that was slow burning. As long as there was nobody behind him, he was content.

But today? Impatience seared like fire in his veins. It didn't matter what was behind, not truly. What mattered was what lay ahead. As a new day dawned and the fort drew ever nearer, Leo worried they'd arrive to the sight of an iron revenant army breaking down the Wall, their armor flashing in the sun.

Luckily, Inara was not the sort to dawdle. She pushed the horse as hard as was humane, making their stops brief and conversation even briefer.

Unfortunately, the more nervous Leo was, the more his mouth started moving.

"Warm day, considering. I wonder if that matters? They hate

daylight, but of course those iron suits would prevent the worst of it. Though they'd also heat up in the sun. Is it the heat they dislike, or the brightness?"

There was a pause; then Inara turned in the saddle, surprised. "Was that a question for me, Your Highness?"

"Who else?"

Inara considered. "Thirty minutes ago, you said, 'Such a good girl. When we arrive, we'll get you a treat.' Was that *also* meant for me?"

Leo laughed. As Inara was not much of a conversationalist and his other companion was a *horse,* Leo had often chosen to talk to both and neither of them at the same time—with mixed results.

"Because I *am* a good girl and could certainly do with a treat."

"My apologies," Leo said, actually feeling a hint of embarrassment. "I'm afraid you've caught me on a bad day. I'm not quite my usual, charming self."

"Apology accepted," Inara said primly. "They hate the warmth *and* the light but don't seem affected by fire, so . . . it's hard to know how they will react. Bone protections, on the other hand, will likely be rendered useless thanks to their iron armor. If it cannot make contact with the ghost, it cannot harm it."

"Indeed," Leo said. "That's not to mention their fortified *strength.* You've seen how the usual revenants fall apart. That won't be an issue with these."

"No, I don't suppose it will. They will be nearly invulnerable."

Nearly, Leo thought, though he decided to stop talking after that.

When they arrived at the Breachfort that afternoon, there was no patrol riding out to meet them like last time. No welcome from the commander and Wren's father. The entire place looked disturbingly quiet and unoccupied.

At least the revenants had not yet arrived. But when they did? This place would be overrun like a piece of fruit by a swarm of ants.

Leo just hoped his brother was here and that he'd brought a sizable force with him.

Despite the fort looking empty, when Inara drew the horse up at the gate, the portcullis lifted, and they were allowed inside.

The commander flew into the courtyard, with Leo's brother, Crown Prince Laurent, right behind. He was dressed in steel armor, the gold filigree on the plate done by Leo himself, his light brown hair chin length, his white teeth flashing, and his eyes bright.

A mix of emotions washed over Leo.

Shame, for some reason. Embarrassment. He'd allowed himself to be kidnapped, which Laurent would never have done. He also looked a mess and smelled worse—another offense his brother would never commit.

Despite these feelings of inferiority, Leo hitched his usual smile in place and held his head high.

Inara dismounted first, and when Leo followed, Laurent was next to him. "Holy shit, you're here," he said, stunned, before he burst into a jovial laugh and drew Leo into a hug. "Seen better days, eh, little brother?"

"That is an understatement," Leo said, drawing back.

"At least I've *some* good news to send to Father," Laurent said, glancing over at the commander as if referencing a recent topic of conversation.

"Don't dip your nib yet," Leo warned, whatever lightness he'd felt at his brother's welcome quickly dissipating. He turned to the commander. "There's an army on the march. I suspect it will be here by nightfall."

"An army?" the commander repeated, frowning.

"An undead army," Inara chimed in.

"They are commanded by the Corpse Queen and armored by the regent of the Iron Citadel. They were made for one purpose: to tear down the Wall and unleash horror upon the Dominions."

They withdrew to Commander Duncan's chambers. Laurent insisted that Leo needed to eat, rest—*bathe*—but Leo stated plainly that there wasn't time for that.

The four of them bent over a map strewn across the table. Leo pointed out where the army was coming from and their most likely route and offered Jakob's intelligence on their fast speed and their hastily assembled bridge. They'd be able to cut through the dense forest that usually made that part of the Breachlands unsurpassable, and they'd likely started their march early this morning. As afternoon sunlight sliced through the room, everyone's eyes met. Nothing but silence could be heard outside the windows, but that peace would soon be shattered.

"Riders," the commander said. He looked to the door, where the steward awaited orders. "Send scouts. I want some kind of warning before they arrive. Tell them not to engage."

"Yes, sir," the steward said, turning on his heel.

There go a few more defenders, Leo thought grimly, but advance warning *would* be ideal.

"We also have to send word to Father," Laurent said. "If this *undead army* is real," he said, with a tone that suggested he hadn't yet fully conceded that point, "then we need more soldiers."

"It's too late for that," Leo said shortly. He knew the commander would have difficulty disagreeing with the Crown Prince, but Leo could do it freely and without reservation. "It would take days to muster a force large enough to defeat them, and more days for them to arrive."

"So what are you saying? You want us to stay here and die?" Laurent shot back.

"No," Leo said patiently. "I want us to stall them. Buy time."

"For what?"

Leo glanced at Inara. "For Wren."

"Who?"

Inara actually smiled a little. "Wren Graven, the self-appointed best valkyr of her generation."

"Graven—you mean Vance's daughter? He's just betrayed us, and now you expect his daughter to stop these iron revenants somehow? A lone bonesmith against an army?"

She wasn't just a bonesmith, but Leo thought it was best not to get into all that. "Yes," he said simply.

Laurent scoffed. "I'm sending out a request for aid."

"Do it," Leo said. "But we will have to defend the fort until they arrive. The iron revenants aren't here yet, and I think if we are smart about it, we could do any number of things to bolster our defenses."

"Bolster our defenses . . . You mean ride out beyond the Wall?" Despite Laurent's dismissive tone, Leo was pleased to hear the slight squeak behind his words, revealing his true fear. "This is what the fort was built for. We will not ride out."

"The fort was not built for undead like this," Leo shot back. "We have to enhance what defenses we have, then set some traps, maybe, to divide their forces and lure them away. Mounted riders would be able to keep their distance and remain safe, harrying—"

"Of the two of us, who has true combat experience?" Laurent said, cutting into Leo's speech.

"Yes, brother, you've chased down bandits and even went on a sea campaign. I'm telling you, this foe is unlike any other. And *of the two of us*, who has seen them in action before? Who has *faced* them before? Who has been beyond the Wall . . . twice?"

Laurent rolled his eyes. "I'd hardly call getting kidnapped 'seeing action,' Leo." He smiled condescendingly, and he looked so very like their father when he did that. He clapped a hand on Leo's shoulder. "There is a *reason* we build fortifications and towering walls. I won't sacrifice my soldiers in a battle you're telling me we can't win. We will send word to Father and await reinforcements. In the meantime, the fort will hold, and we will stay behind the Wall. End of discussion."

Leo bowed his head. "Yes, Your Highness."

After, when the riders had been sent and the fort's small garrison had been briefed, Leo sat alone in the dining hall. He was not at the high table, where his brother currently held court with his soldiers—which had amounted to fifty of his own and twenty left over from Leo's personal guard—but in a corner near the back.

He was trying to eat but mostly just staring at his food and waiting in tense silence for the alarm to sound.

Inara slid onto the bench opposite. "I didn't take you for the sort to be so easily dissuaded."

He frowned at her. "Who says I'm dissuaded?"

She quirked a brow, and he adjusted his mostly untouched plate of food to reveal a piece of paper covered in scrawled notes and rudimentary drawings.

"Tell me," she said, and his confidence wavered.

"I'm not sure the two of us can pull it off."

"What about three?"

Commander Duncan stood behind him. He glanced up at the high table before sliding onto the bench next to Leo. He certainly looked more beaten down than when Leo had first arrived at the Breachfort, but of course, a lot had happened since then—and Leo doubted he looked much better himself. But there was a certain *freedom* in that. Leo felt it, and he saw it on the commander's face. When everything else had already gone horribly, spectacularly wrong . . . what more was there to lose?

"When we were Breachside, we met this reapyr. She'd been living there since the Breach and had all manner of tricks at her disposal. I don't think she'd ever faced armored revenants, but surely some of her ideas could translate?"

"Such as?" prompted the commander.

"Water," said Leo. That's what it all came back to. Yes, they could try to bait traps or use riders to lure the iron revenants off course, but those things would require time and manpower they didn't currently have. But what they *did* have was access to the fort's resources. "They brought a bridge with them because they could not cross the Serpentine without it. That means we can utilize the same barrier here."

"But if they carried the bridge with them . . . might they not bring it here, to the Wall?" Inara asked.

"I doubt it," said Leo. He'd given it a great deal of thought, including racking his brain for everything he'd ever learned about portable bridges used in warfare. "There are no other rivers or bodies of water to cross from here to the capital. I suspect the time required to dismantle and carry with them is time they won't take." At least, he hoped. The others nodded with his reasoning, so he plowed on. "I assume you keep stores of fresh water?"

"At least fifty barrels, plus there's a cistern in the kitchen courtyard," the commander replied.

"The kitchen courtyard . . ." Leo looked around, trying to get his bearings.

"Adjacent to the main courtyard," Inara said. Leaning over Leo's rough doodle of the fort, she drew a line with her finger from the front gate and the main courtyard it led into, across the kitchens and the connected dining hall where they now sat, to an empty space on the other side. Leo quickly labeled it, then sat back.

He glanced up at his brother, but he was laughing and talking and doing his best to act as if they had everything well in hand.

It was the right thing to do, even if Leo didn't agree with some of his brother's other decisions. Showing confidence was important.

So yes, it *was* the right thing to do, but not the *only* thing.

"I've got an idea," he said, and the others bowed their heads to listen.

They slipped out of the dining hall unnoticed and got to work. While Leo and the commander focused their attention on the cistern, Inara rode out to "survey the perimeter" and check the bonesmith defenses, along with a pair of strapping stonesmith craftsmen who happened to be at the Breachfort seeing to other repairs.

Several hours later, Inara returned. "The perimeter is secured," she said.

"Perfect," Leo replied, continuing to fiddle with one of the cistern's pipes. "Now we just—"

"What's going on here?"

Laurent stood at the entrance to the courtyard, and he looked livid. Leo knew it wasn't because a handful of people had found a different—and more productive way—to pass the time. It was because Leo had gone ahead with his own ideas after Laurent had told him otherwise.

Commanded him otherwise.

Leo was questioning his authority, and he'd encouraged others to do the same.

"Laur, listen," Leo began, but his brother held up a hand to silence him.

"I told you this fort was built to withstand assault! I told you that *I* have more combat experience and that we don't need our soldiers risking their lives on foolish tricks and gimmicks. I thought you'd have outgrown this by now."

When his brother called Leo's tactics foolish, what he was really doing was calling *Leo* foolish. It wouldn't be the first time. "Outgrown what, exactly?"

"This desire to always do things your own way, usually to the detriment of yourself and those around you."

Leo sucked in a breath. "Are you trying to lay this mess at *my* feet? The man responsible, our dear cousin, is currently in a cell in this very fort."

Laurent rolled his eyes. "You know what I meant. You can never just listen, fall in line, and do what you're told. Like a th—"

He stopped himself. Leo smiled savagely. "Like a *third* son ought to? Just because I wasn't born to lead doesn't mean I don't have a brain, with ideas and knowledge that outstrips even your own, Crown Prince. Firstborn son."

Laurent's expression tightened, and he glanced around the courtyard at their small audience, which included several tributes and some of his own soldiers, who milled around the nearest door.

Laurent took a step forward. "Watch what you say to me, little brother, or I'll have you in a cell next to our *dear cousin* before the night is through."

Leo's mouth dropped open, and Laurent's gaze flickered with something like regret. It was an empty threat. Leo knew that, but it didn't make it any less shocking.

"Look," Laurent started, but then a sudden chorus of bells sounded from somewhere above.

Both brothers looked up in alarm before turning to the commander, who said, "That's the Wall sentries. Something's been sighted."

"What about the riders?" Laurent asked, but Leo thought he probably already knew.

They hadn't made it back.

Together, all of them made for the nearest staircase, which led up to the battlements.

They peered through the crenellations, craning their necks until something became visible to the east. The sun was setting behind them, casting the Wall's shadow onto the ground before them, but farther out and still bathed in daylight was the second wall, the palisade. It gleamed white, and there, growing larger with every moment, was a force of armored soldiers.

The iron revenants.

Sunlight flashed on their dark armor, and their heavy footsteps echoed across the barren plain.

They marched in perfect unison, every thump of their boots like a battle drum, ringing out in a terrible, haunting beat. The bell still tolled distantly, but Leo couldn't wrench his gaze away from the sight before them.

"Soldiers of the Dominions!" Laurent cried out, turning from the view to shout down into the courtyard and across the battlements. "Man your stations and prepare for battle!"

THIRTY-FOUR

"Is it done?" Vance asked, looking around the room. "Is the ceremony complete?"

"Almost," said Ravenna, her voice soft.

Wren frowned, extremely uneasy.

There was a sense of taut expectation settling over the room, and it grated against Wren's skin. Surely Ravenna wanted more than just a husband. More than a symbolic union of their houses. She wouldn't just *let him* take the well's power without there being something in it for herself. But what?

Wren clenched her hands into fists. Her patience was running out, and she was frankly sick of this grotesque display of ghostsmith magic. The undead remained bowed before them, ranged in a half circle, and the wall of Elders continued to glow brightly behind them, crackling against her senses.

While Vance stared expectantly at Ravenna, Wren watched Hawke.

He knew what was next. The heavy feeling in Wren's stomach was mirrored in his eyes.

With her focus fixed on him, it was a shock when something clamped down on her wrists.

Rusted manacles, locked into place by a revenant that had managed to sneak up behind her. Wren tried to fight free, but her reaction was too slow.

"Wait! Stop! Undo that!" she said, but the revenant did little more than twitch at her words, the barest of reactions that she may well have imagined. With her magic depleted and without her amplifier ring, she held no sway over them.

Meanwhile, next to her, Vance had *also* been manacled to his chair—though he suffered it with far less grace. First he recoiled from the revenant that had activated his restraints. Then he fought and struggled, eyes wide and hair askew. His crown was crooked on his head.

"What are you playing at? We had a *deal,* Ravenna! Whatever this is about, we can discuss it like adults. There's no need to—"

"Silence," she hissed, getting to her feet and descending the stairs to stand before the thrones. "Your constant drivel is intolerable."

His mouth snapped shut. "We had a deal," he said again, unable to stop himself.

"I *will* resurrect the House of the Dead, and I *will* have a Corpse King. . . . He simply will not be you."

What did *that* mean?

"And me?" Wren asked desperately, still straining. "Am I to be used again? A living amplifier to charge your puppet?"

She almost wished it were true. At least then they'd give her back her ring and access to the well's magic, and maybe this time she'd be able to fight.

Ravenna shook her head as the puppet in question, Hawke, joined her at the foot of the stairs.

"That project required breadth and scale," she said. "This one requires precision."

"Then why . . . ?" Wren began, but she stopped herself. She looked at her father. One reason they might lock her down was so that she could not react to what came next.

"Speaking of . . . ," Ravenna said, turning to Hawke. "I'll take it now."

Wren frowned. Take what? Then Hawke reached into his pocket and withdrew a ring made of bone.

Wren's ring.

Ravenna held out her hand, palm up, and Hawke placed it there.

"Has the familiar returned?" she asked, her head tilted down at the ring.

Wren's stomach dropped. They knew?

Hawke darted a look Wren's way. "Not yet."

"Where did she send it?"

"I can't be certain," Hawke said carefully. "To get help, maybe."

Wren stared at him. Was he lying, or did he truly not know? He could have easily overheard her in her cell, but if he had, why lie?

Ravenna made a dismissive noise in her throat. "No matter. I shall know soon enough."

Then, to Wren's dismay, she placed the ring on her own finger. Now, even if Wren could get to the gathering pool, she'd only be able to use as much magic as her body could hold, and she wouldn't be able to carry any surplus with her.

She hung her head, anger blossoming in her stomach.

When she looked up again, it was to see her brother staring at

Ravenna's hand, at the ring. Did he wish Ravenna had given it to him instead?

He twisted his own ring on his finger but said nothing. Did nothing.

Until.

Until Ravenna turned to him and said, "Prepare yourself."

Alarm flashed across his features, and he looked at Wren again. "Mother, I—I don't think . . . I don't want—"

"Are we going to have a problem?" Ravenna asked, cutting into his rambling with a voice devoid of emotion yet heavy with threat. "I'd hate to have to teach you another lesson, so close to the last."

Hawke dipped his head. Wren wanted to yell at him, tell him to grow a backbone and stand up for himself. That Ravenna wouldn't actually go through with her threats. But of course, she already had. And Wren was locked to her chair. Utterly defenseless.

He was right to fear their mother and her threats, and there was nothing Wren could do about it.

Hawke clenched his jaw before making for the gathering pool once more. Rather than dip his hand as before, Hawke traversed the pool from one end to the other, filling himself and his amplifiers with well magic, making his entire body glow.

"What's happening?" Vance said faintly, and Wren wondered if the question was for her, for Ravenna . . . or for anyone or anything listening.

Wren didn't answer because she didn't know. Her father was a bonesmith, and not one with latent ghostsmith magic. So what did they want from him?

"My tools," Hawke said as he emerged from the pool, and one of the nearby revenants ambled over with a tray. On it lay two items.

One she'd seen before, the small hammer he'd used to drive a linchpin into the skull of one of the iron revenants.

But the second item . . .

Wren's mouth went dry. It looked like a linchpin, but it was the largest one she'd ever seen. The one in her ring was barely as long as her pinkie fingernail, while the one she'd seen piercing the skull of the iron revenant was closer to the length of that finger, but this one? It was as long as her entire hand.

What did he intend to puncture with *that*?

Seeing Wren's gaze fixed on it, Ravenna spoke. "It's called a lifepin. It's not so different from a linchpin—it's still dead bone carved into a stake, then treated with acid and iron salt, which allows it to fuse more easily to a haunted bone. Once joined, the dead bone can no longer harm the ghost. They become one. Pins are often engraved with glyphs that, when embedded into the anchor bone, connect to complete a command."

Linchpins were made from bone? Wren couldn't believe she hadn't known that—hadn't sensed it. Then again, it would be difficult for her magic to know the difference between the linchpin bone and the bone it pierced, especially if they "became one," as Ravenna said.

"You look surprised," Ravenna commented, amusement in her voice. "We were once the same house if you'll recall. We know all your bonesmith tricks; we took them, studied them, and perfected them. The anchor bone's magic is good for more than just weapons. Pierce it with a linchpin and bind a ghost to its body, making a servant, a soldier—a magical amplifier. Much more powerful than a sword, wouldn't you agree?"

Wren's mind was reeling. Rather than cutting the ley line with steel, ghostsmiths used bone, essentially pinning the tether in place and trapping the ghost rather than freeing it.

But if Wren could use her amplified bonesmith magic to remove those linchpins *without* damaging the bone beneath, would that reap the spirits? Maybe she didn't need to shatter the well's undead and condemn hundreds of souls to the same fate as those on the Uprising battlefield in order to destroy it. Maybe she could destroy the well and *free* the undead instead?

"A *lifepin,* however, serves a unique purpose. It does not bind a ghost to its own undead bones; it binds a ghost to a living body."

Wren's heart stopped in her chest.

What ghost?

And what living body?

At a nod from Ravenna, Hawke took up hammer and pin and walked slowly toward the dais.

"It was a ritual saved only for the royal line. After the Gravekeeper died the first time, he was resurrected into a new body. Again and again, for centuries. The same for his queen. A ghost may exist after death, but only a Nekros may truly live forever."

Well, that explained a lot. Their society was built upon the lie of eternal life, but only their leaders truly experienced anything close to that. The rest gained eternal servitude, no more.

"Some say it was during a failed resurrection ceremony that the first cataclysm, the first rupture of the well, occurred, burying all this." She flicked her wrist at their surroundings, evidence of that initial catastrophe visible in the cracked floors and broken columns. The collapsed buildings and flooded chambers. "You see, the ghost will not attach to just *any* living body—not with permanence. The body will reject it."

Wren flashed back to what Julian had said when he'd first spoken to her about amplifiers being embedded within a body: how sometimes the implanted object was rejected. She had considered silver and gold—and, knowing what she did now about his hand, iron—but the idea of a *ghost* being embedded was truly horrifying.

"Over the years, the bloodline had become too diluted," Ravenna continued. "The new vessels were distant relations. The link wasn't strong enough. There must be a bond of blood. The closer the relation, the better the bond."

Hawke came to a stop in front of the vacant throne. Then he turned his attention not to Wren but to Vance.

Suddenly Wren thought she knew who the sternum must belong to.

"Hawke, don't!" Wren said, breathless. "Please don't!"

Hawke *did* stop, for a moment at least. He froze, pin and hammer in hand, his entire body glowing with magic.

"He's your father," Ravenna said pointedly, speaking directly to Hawke. "This is what he deserves."

Vance didn't yet understand—hadn't quite pieced it together. He struggled violently. "Son, please, I don't deserve this."

"I'm not your son," Hawke said, then placed the pin not on Vance's forehead, as he had done with the iron revenant, but directly over the sternum pendant.

The haunted sternum that held the ghost of Locke Graven.

Who apparently *was* Wren and Hawke's father, just as Odile had claimed.

That lifepin wouldn't simply pierce Locke's disembodied sternum. It would pass straight *through* the anchor bone and into Vance's chest beneath. Into *his* bones.

Binding the ghost to his *living* body. Resurrecting Locke.

Would he just ride Vance's body like ghosts usually rode their rotting corpses? And what would happen to Vance? To *his* spirit?

Hawke lifted the hammer. Vance squirmed and cried out, shouting threats and promises in equal measure.

Wren, meanwhile, had gone still as a statue, her entire being homing in on that pointed tip, Hawke's fingers alight with magic.

His green-eyed gaze darted her way.

"Don't," she pleaded.

He did.

There was a resounding crack, the impact of hammer against pin and pin against bone. The blow caused Vance to grunt and expel a breath of air, but it wasn't until the second strike that the lifepin landed home. Hand shaking, Hawke struck again, and this time Vance made a wet, gurgling sound, blood oozing from his chest and staining Hawke's hands.

Staggering away, Hawke made for the pool again, this time filling the channels with magic that went straight to Vance's chair. The magic touched his feet, then climbed upward, illuminating his body with brilliant light, shining all the more brightly from his chest. Was that because of the wound or the lifepin?

"Dad?" Wren whispered, because that's who he was to her, no matter what Ravenna said. After long, silent moments passed, the blood stopped dripping onto the floor. The wound had been healed. As the light dimmed, Vance's head, which had fallen forward onto his chest, lifted and turned her way.

Green eyes stared back at her.

Wren recoiled in horror.

His brow furrowed, his movements slow as recognition failed to dawn.

He looked away.

"I am . . . ," he said, but his voice, while familiar, sounded not at all like him. "I am."

Ravenna rushed forward. "Welcome back to the land of the living, Locke Graven."

THIRTY-FIVE

"Release him," Ravenna ordered. Hawke, who was hunched over next to the gathering pool, panting with exertion, wiped his bloody hands on his cloak and hurried forward to unlatch the restraints. He kept darting anxious glances at the man, perhaps hoping for acknowledgment or praise, but he received neither. Once freed, Vance—no, *Locke*—stood on shaky legs.

"You should rest, my love," said Ravenna, stepping forward to meet him.

Was *that* what this was? Love? It was said that in death, whatever hopes, dreams, and desires a person had were frozen in their ghost form, forever unchanging, because only things that *lived* could evolve and adapt.

However, Wren wasn't sure that was entirely true. The familiars were able to learn and change to serve their ghostsmith masters, and the Elders, while drawing upon a bank of knowledge created while they were alive, clearly absorbed new information, too. Even if it was all due to the well's unnatural influence, Ravenna had been in its presence for years. If any undead were capable of change, she should be.

But that didn't account for personality. Ravenna had been dead for seventeen years, and the love she'd felt for Locke remained, along with her ambitions for herself and her house. Was that because she was undead or simply because she was stubborn?

Vance-Locke flinched slightly at her proximity. Did he understand that she was undead, or was he just disoriented?

"The binding requires time to take hold," Ravenna explained. "He will be resisting you."

He. Vance. Did that mean he was still alive? Still in there, somewhere?

"Yes," Vance-Locke said, voice distracted. "Yes, he is here. Fighting me. As always." He turned to Ravenna. "Where are they? The children."

The children. He shouldn't know about them—he had died before they'd been born—but perhaps Ravenna had told him she was pregnant.

Or maybe she had told him since.

"This is your son, Hawke," she said, gripping Hawke by the shirt to drag him forward. She flapped her hand impatiently at his face, so Hawke hastily pushed the mask up onto his head, though he kept his gaze averted.

Vance-Locke had no reaction, his glowing green eyes staring right through him. "There were two, you said."

Ravenna hesitated. "The girl is of no concern to you. A bonesmith, and raised by Vance. She's not—"

"Let me see her."

Ravenna gestured over Vance-Locke's shoulder, where Wren was seated in the chair next to him.

He turned stiffly, clearly still struggling to master the use of his body, and leaned forward. Those glowing eyes raked her over from head to foot, and Wren wondered what was happening inside his mind. Was Vance there, looking with him? Or was Locke working through his own thoughts?

"It seems a waste," he said eventually. "And she is very young. Too young."

"Vessels always are. That's what makes their sacrifice worth it. Believe me, if I'd had another choice, you wouldn't be inside that festering middle-aged man."

Hawke stiffened, though Ravenna failed to notice.

"It is good to be middle-aged," Vance-Locke said. "It is good to live long enough to bear wrinkles and scars."

Ravenna made an impatient noise. "Unfortunately, I don't have that option. The blood-bond is too important, and I have no other family." Her head turned in Wren's direction. "She'll have to do."

Wren's insides turned cold. "Do for what?" she asked, though in the back of her mind, she already knew. "You want to take my body? When you've just married my father? The Dominions won't accept this union and you know it. It's repulsive!"

"The marriage would be in name only," Ravenna said dismissively. "For the purposes of ruling. The resurrected cannot bear children. It will be down to Hawke to continue our line."

Wren's mouth twisted with revulsion and outrage—as if that one bit of "good" news made the whole thing better?

For once her brother seemed as confused, as indignant, as she was. He glared at Ravenna, and she took him by the shoulders and pulled him aside.

His attention shifted to her gloved hands, and Wren realized she'd not seen the woman touch him until now. Did it unsettle him, or did he crave it?

It seemed to make him uncomfortable regardless, his face screwed up as her grip moved from his arms to his cheeks.

"I need you to be strong and to honor your duty. Your debt."

"No," Hawke said, shaking her off and coming to stand in front of Wren. He shook his head vehemently. "You told me if I delivered them here, if I did what you said, no harm would come to her. You *promised* me Wren would be okay. You swore it."

Wren's throat tightened. There was anguish in him, and though he'd told her before, the truth of his statement hadn't truly resonated until now. He *had* done it all for her.

"She's my sister," Hawke finished on a whisper. "She's my family."

"And what am I?" Ravenna demanded. "You spend a few days with her and forget where you come from? How you got here in the first place? What I *sacrificed* for you."

Her hands reached up, took hold of her veil, and ripped.

It tore away in shreds, revealing, at last, what lay beneath.

There were vestiges of her former looks, her former beauty. But only the barest glimpse. What remained was a complexion that was waxen and hollowed out, pallid and sickly looking. Her hair was wispy and white instead of pale blond, like Wren and her brother's. And her bones . . . they stood out starkly across her cheeks, chin, and neck, her low-cut gown exposing her pointed clavicles beneath a flimsy layer of skin. Below that? The flesh had rotted away entirely, revealing a glowing green chest cavity exposing each individual rib. Hawke said she had the ability to conceal her spirit, to dim its light; otherwise people would have seen it through the veil.

Ghostlight flickered from within her milky, opaque eyes, and more of the white and yellow flowers were weaved through her exposed bones, the dried strands crawling over her body like creeping vines—for the smell, Wren realized. To mask the scent of rotting flesh. But after witnessing Starling's gruesome memories and seeing Ravenna's corpse, the flowers served only to remind Wren of death and decay.

Her insides tightened in a deep, visceral response. Proximity to the well had allowed Ravenna's bones to remain strong, to keep her body poised, balanced, and upright, but her flesh was almost entirely gone. The fact that her lips and tongue could still form speech was a testament to its power, and to Ravenna's, as a lich. Somehow, her ghost was keeping it all together, mind and body, however damaged.

Hawke turned his head away, as if he, too, were alarmed by the sight. Wren found herself wondering if Hawke had ever seen her body exposed this way, and if he had, how much worse her body had deteriorated since. "I haven't forgotten. But surely there's another way."

"What way? They hunt us in the Dominions and besmirch our name—"

"We hunt *you*," Wren snarled. "Because you're a walking corpse, *Mother*. You're unnatural, and you don't belong here anymore. The fact that you would sacrifice the living for the dead is proof of that."

"You see?" Ravenna said, waving a hand at Wren. "They want us gone. They have no respect for our magic, our traditions, which are *just as old as theirs*. We will never be safe unless we take control, take power."

"And remake the House of the Dead," said Vance-Locke. He had been listening idly to their conversation, clenching and unclenching his hands, turning his head this way and that—familiarizing himself with his new body. "The most powerful house in the Dominions and *rightful* rulers of this land. Without us, there would be no Dominions at all."

"You said this was about protection," Hawke argued, looking between them.

"Don't be a fool," Ravenna said, frustration boiling over. "You know we cannot skulk in the shadows forever. And you know we'll never convince anyone we aren't a threat."

"But we *are* a threat—your actions with the iron revenant army only prove it," Hawke said.

"*Your* actions, you mean," Ravenna said, her voice deathly quiet. Hawke's lips trembled slightly. "Do not pretend innocence. Not now, when we are so close."

"I have only ever done what you've told me to do," Hawke said desperately. "I never wanted this."

"You never wanted to know your father?" Ravenna snapped. "Never wanted your mother to survive?"

Hawke's hand pressed against his chest—the place where Starling's wishbone necklace had once sat. Would he tell Ravenna the truth? That Starling had been more a mother to him than she ever had, and Ravenna had killed her?

"Not like this," Hawke eventually muttered, lowering his hand. He darted a glance at Wren. "Not like this."

"The price must be paid," said Vance-Locke. "For survival. For the good of our house, the Dominions must fall."

He spoke the words as if they'd been memorized, as if they weren't his at all, but rather, had been repeated and learned by heart.

"But you died *defending* the Dominions!" Wren argued. "To this day you're honored as a hero! Now you want to destroy them?"

She could guess how Locke's ghost had spent the last seventeen years . . . who he had been talking to and what they had told him about his life. Like the existence of his children, all of this had been carefully fed to him by Ravenna.

And as jarring as this situation was, Locke was a ghost like any other—clinging to life, even as day by day, year by year, he drifted farther and farther away from it.

There was a chance he didn't even remember who he was independent of what Ravenna had told him.

He frowned, confusion marring her father's brow. "I died . . . defending the Dominions?"

"You died defending me and the children I carried," Ravenna cut in. "You died defending our family and our way of life from those who would have taken it from us."

Wren tossed an incredulous look at Hawke—was this the narrative he believed as well? Honestly, even Wren couldn't be entirely sure of the truth.

But there was someone here who could be.

"Ask your brother!" Wren said, speaking to Vance-Locke. "You said he's still there, fighting you. Ask him what happened that day. He'll tell you the truth. He won't be able to hide it with you inside his mind." She hoped, anyway.

Apparently her suspicions about Vance were correct, because with a growl of frustration, Ravenna took up Hawke's staff from where it lay on the ground and knocked Vance-Locke upside the head.

He crumpled to the floor, causing Hawke to cry out and bend over him.

"He's fine," Ravenna said, lowering the staff. "I didn't break his skull. He's confused. I will talk him through everything . . . *after*."

"You're the reason he's confused," Wren argued, her best hope for a distraction or a delay in the proceedings now lying unconscious at her feet.

"I'm the reason he's not spitting angry and trying to kill the both of you," Ravenna said. "Now that he's resurrected, your talents won't work on him." She turned those last words to Hawke, though of course they applied to Wren as well. Did she know about Wren's Vision? Had Hawke told her? "The truth is, it took years to get him this docile. This . . . *malleable.* He was furious at first. In pain. As all undead are . . ." She paused, and Wren wondered if she was talking about herself. "I summoned him nightly. Soothed him. Told him stories of his life, his past, which was already slipping away from him."

"Told him *lies*, you mean," Wren cut in, unable to help herself. Ravenna hadn't just filled his head with falsehoods—she'd rewritten history, just as Vance had done, repeating lie after lie until they became all Locke knew. Now that he was resurrected . . . would he eventually remember who and what he had been? Or was that lost forever?

Or could Wren find it for him? Buried deep in his living memories? Maybe, if she got the chance, she could find the truth and dredge it up to the surface? But to do that, she'd have to touch his ghost, and it was currently bound to her father's body, completely protected.

"Truth is all about perspective. Locke's truth is different from my truth, and my truth is different from Vance's truth."

"That sounds like a convoluted way of saying yes."

Ravenna's expression twitched, and Wren imagined that on a face with more flesh, annoyance would have flashed across her features. As it was, she simply looked like every other revenant who'd crossed Wren's path: undead and inhuman.

"I will not claim a lie I did not speak."

"But you did lie," Hawke interjected, straightening from Vance-Locke's prone form. He walked forward, coming to stand next to Wren's chair again. He gripped the armrest. "You lied to *me*."

"But she won't be harmed, my dear," Ravenna said, her voice turning soft and cajoling. "Not really. She will be safe. And when the time comes, she will have a second life of her own, in a host of her choosing. That is her right as heir to my throne, the same as you. That is how all this was built." She gestured to the grand chamber above before lowering her hand toward the well below. "Centuries of knowledge kept and preserved through the very process we have undertaken today. It is hard, I know, to fully understand. You were not indoctrinated the way I was by my mother, and her mother before her. But trust me, this is the only way forward."

Wren struggled with a sense of fragile optimism that maybe her brother would refuse to perform the ritual, coupled with spine-tingling revulsion at what her mother suggested: that Wren might live trapped inside her own body for countless years until she was *allowed* to live again—if it could even be called that—subjecting some other person to the same fate?

"I will not give up my body or my mind. I will fight you," Wren said, straining against her bonds. "You will never know peace."

Ravenna's lips twisted into a smile. "Even the strong can be broken, in time and with patience. I have lived a half-life for nearly two decades, daughter. I have a great deal of patience." She turned to Hawke. "Now, come. Let's finish this. We will be a family again, and all this nastiness, all these years of fear and hiding will be behind us."

Hawke turned away from his mother to look at Wren. *Really* look at her. His green eyes roved her face, blinking furiously, and Wren sensed he was seeing but not seeing, waging an internal battle with himself.

"And if you refuse," Ravenna said, each word loosed like carefully placed arrows, meant to wound. "I will kill her here and now." Hawke's eyes widened, his head shaking as if to refute what she'd said. He looked over his shoulder at Ravenna, and she nodded. "I would prefer my own daughter, but I'll find another host . . . perhaps a child of your own in a few years' time." She smiled, her waxen flesh pulling back from her teeth in a truly haunting sight. "As I said, I am patient."

Hawke closed his eyes and sighed, all the tension unspooling from his body, and Wren felt it in her bones that she had lost the battle—lost him. He would make this choice for her. He would choose to "save her" rather than lose her the way he had lost Starling.

"Hawke, *no*—please, I'd rather die." It was true. Terrible and devastating but true. With Julian . . . and her father . . . it did not feel so hard to imagine. To succumb to.

"I'm sorry," he whispered, his eyes still shut.

Then he took her hand and squeezed. . . . But when he pulled away, he left a small, round item behind in the center of her closed fist.

His *ring*.

Hawke's eyes opened, and Wren met them with painful hope and uncertainty. He nodded, a fraction of an inch—a barely perceptible movement—but it rocketed through Wren like an earthquake.

When he stepped back, his hand slid under the armrest, and something metal clicked, the sound lost in the scuff of his boot against stone.

Her manacle was unlocked.

His amplifier ring was in her hand.

Wren clenched her fist, felt the magic surge through her.

The real fight was about to begin.

THIRTY-SIX

Julian stared at the back of his uncle's spike-helmeted head.

He was riding at the center of a squadron of Red Guard, while the iron revenants were nowhere in sight. Clearly Francis intended them to do the *actual* fighting. Then he would stroll through the wreckage afterward before riding for the capital.

They were traveling at a steady clip, but they weren't pushing the horses hard.

Still, they were *riding*, and they'd had a head start . . . so the fact that Julian had caught up to them was something close to miraculous.

But he'd had his own advantages.

First, Willow had led him through some kind of underground shortcut; the two had spent hours wandering in the dark, but when they'd finally emerged, it was atop a cliff overlooking a familiar landscape. They were north of the mill house ravine and west of the river, with a view of rocky ground, swaths of forest, and a party of riders heading south on the Old Road that ran alongside the Wall.

Then, it was just a matter of catching them—which was Julian's *second* advantage.

Horses were faster than humans on foot, but they were not faster than an ironsmith flooded with raw magic and wearing head-to-toe amplifiers—because that's what his armor had become. Vessels filled with power ready for the taking, and Julian had *taken* it.

His every movement was lighter because of it, the law of ratios obliterated, allowing him to leap from cliffs and climb steep inclines with the barest effort. But the magic did more than make his ability to move his armor easier. It allowed him to essentially *throw* his armor ahead of himself, which in turn carried his body with it.

That was how he'd been crossing the ground since he'd begun his pursuit. He flung one leg and then the other, his strides like giant leaps, his momentum catapulting him along the countryside at a speed that turned everything around him into a blur.

But his senses were *fixed* on the iron ahead of him, his uncle's armor shining like a beacon, calling him forward.

And now he was directly ahead of Julian, his party within hailing distance.

Julian decided on a different approach.

He leapt, at first *pulling* on his uncle's iron to draw himself forward and then *pushing* on it to soar over him, through the air above his head.

He landed on the ground in a crouch, the impact cracking the road beneath him and causing the charging horses to shriek and rear up, nearly unseating their riders.

His uncle was at the fore, and he was the first to react. Shock had robbed him temporarily of speech as Julian literally fell from the sky, but he soon recovered.

"Guards!" he shouted, speaking to the soldiers on either side of him. His gaze never left Julian's face—except once, to flick down to Julian's neck. "Seize hi—"

Before he could finish, Julian lifted his hands, his iron shards swirling in his open palms. He sent the projectiles left and right, the iron zipping past at an impossible speed as it sliced through armor and skin and bone. The guards cried out in confusion and pain, dropping weapons they attempted to draw, bloody wounds blossoming in legs and arms and the sides of heads. Julian didn't intend to murder them all, but he would gladly weaken them to take them out of the fight.

The regent surveyed Julian's attack with calm eyes. He'd taken his nephew's weapons—Julian could sense them strapped to his uncle's horse—but Julian had found a way around that.

He had *also* taken Julian's life . . . and Julian had found a way around that, too.

With his Red Guard roughed up and reeling, the regent dismounted. Julian spotted the scepter on his belt but knew it would be no easy task to take it.

His uncle withdrew his sword, the blade embellished with red enamel like all his armor, and when he squeezed the grip, spikes of iron sprang from within, creating something like a serrated blade on two sides—less a sword to slice and more a saw to hack and slash.

He stood before his nephew.

"Give me my sword," Julian said. "It's only fair."

The regent laughed. "Why on earth would I want things *fair*?"

And then he lunged.

Few people knew it, but Francis was a highly skilled ironsmith warrior. A sword who had trained Julian himself. The man preferred not to get his hands dirty, fancying himself a politician more than a soldier, but he would fight when necessary.

And he would fight *viciously*.

He brought his blade down in a wide arc, his movements even faster than Julian remembered them.

But Julian was faster now too.

He dodged the blow, rolling to the side and sending a handful of iron shards pelting toward his uncle. The projectiles pinged off his armor, the plate thicker and of better quality than his Red Guard's protections. His only vulnerability was his eyes, but he'd lowered his face plate to protect himself, making him virtually invulnerable.

Raw iron was strong, but it was nowhere near as strong as ironsmith-crafted metal. While his uncle swept the iron shards aside, Julian used the distraction to leap for the horse.

The jump was a good five feet, and when he landed, his uncle was watching him closely.

"You're looking very spry today, nephew," he commented idly. He had lowered his sword and now leaned on it one-handed, point-down, in the dirt—entirely at his ease.

"That's one way to put it," Julian said.

"What's the other way?"

Julian smiled humorlessly. "You're not the only one with secrets."

As he made to reach for his weapons, his uncle sent a throwing knife at him. He lifted his arm and deflected it with his vambrace. When the second knife came, he snatched it straight out of the air.

"Thanks," he said, using the blade to slice through a strap on the horse, freeing his helmet, sword, staff, and other weapons. He smacked the horse on its rump to send it out of the line of fire, then faced his uncle, putting his helmet in place.

His uncle seemed less surprised at Julian's lightning-fast movements and more angry. "It was the well, wasn't it? That raw magic. She said it only worked for ghostsmiths, but I should have known she'd keep the best of it for herself."

"She gave you the scepter," Julian said. "Why don't you try it out?"

Francis smiled tightly. "I don't need undead soldiers to defeat you, nephew, whatever magical enhancement you've undergone."

"Are you sure? Seems a pity to waste such an advantage," Julian pressed. Maybe he could goad his uncle into calling the revenant army back here to protect him. It would buy Wren and the Breachfort time at the very least, and he was pretty sure he could outrun the undead soldiers.

"I am all the advantage I need."

Julian shrugged. "If you say so."

Now it was *his* turn to attack. He brought his sword down again and again, allowing the anger to flow through him, fueling his already magically powered movements. Francis gave ground with every strike, and when Julian saw an opening, he released his sword into a whip. The blade segments wrapped around his uncle's sword arm, stopping him midswing.

With a growl, the regent clenched his hand into a fist, and like his sword, spikes burst from his armor all along his arm in an attempt to dislodge the whip. Several of the segments slid out of place, and Julian's grip loosened for a second before he pulled even more tightly with muscles and magic alike. The metal screeched and crunched until the iron plate started to crumple like cheap bitter steel. His uncle's grip slackened, and his sword dropped.

If he'd been an ordinary ironsmith, his arm underneath would be a ruin of broken bones and torn flesh.

But he wasn't.

Julian released his whip, forcing Francis to stagger backward. Panting, he pulled the ruined pieces of plate from his arm, revealing not just an iron hand but an iron limb that went all the way up to his shoulder.

Unlike Julian, who had bits of iron used to reinforce a damaged arm, it appeared as though his uncle had had the entire appendage removed. There was no sign of any skin or bone that he could see. The only difference between his arm and his armor was that his arm wasn't enameled in red, like the rest of his suit.

Though his iron limb had fared far better than any living one would have, Julian saw that the fragments of his broken armor had done damage, nearly severing the arm at the elbow and leaving other marks and gauges.

The regent stared down at it. "That shouldn't be possible. It's made of the highest-grade ironsmith metal."

"So am I," Julian said, retracting his whip into a blade once more. "Remember?"

Francis caught Julian's eye and grinned. "You didn't think I was going to let *you* have all the fun, did you? Why do you think I had them *test* the procedure on you in the first place?"

Fury coursed through Julian's body, but it wasn't hot rage like he was used to. This emotion was cold as ice. "Test?" he repeated flatly. "I suppose the *accident* that ruined my natural hand was no accident then, either?"

His uncle held his arms wide in a placating gesture. "It all worked out, didn't it? You gained strength you sorely needed, and I had the guinea pig I required. Still, it took years of practice before I could manipulate it properly. You think a single hand is difficult, try a full limb."

"I didn't want strength," Julian said bitterly. "I just wanted your approval."

"Which is why you can't defeat me. You let your emotions and sentimentalities weaken you. Fill you with fear. And your own power? You feared that most of all."

"I guess you don't know me as well as you think, Uncle. I don't want or need your approval anymore. And as for my power?" He raised his iron hand, calling Francis's blade to his open palm. Seeing this, his uncle did the same—and the blade answered *Julian,* not him.

It should never have been possible. But the well's magic made it so.

Staring his uncle hard in the face, he crushed the weapon in his hand and tossed the ruined blade aside. "I am flooded with raw magic. You can't defeat me. I fear nothing."

"Oh no?" the regent asked, brows raised as he clenched and unclenched the fist on his damaged arm. He nodded down at Julian's wrist, where the iron bracelet from Becca lay. "I'd have given the throne to Rebecca, you know. Her and that Gold Prince. I'd have been content to rule from the shadows. But since you see fit to try to deny me that . . . perhaps I will deny her as well. If I take the throne for myself with a Valorian bride—I believe the prince has a little sister?—then I don't actually need her at all."

"She's your niece. Your sister's child," Julian said through clenched teeth.

"She's *disposable,* the same as you and your father."

Julian charged.

He crossed the distance between them in a single bound, his sword swinging down hard. The emotions that flooded him now were neither hot nor cold. He was numb. He couldn't see, couldn't hear—nothing existed beyond the hacking and slashing of his blade.

Without a sword of his own, Francis raised his still-plated arm to block the blows, spikes bursting from the metal. On one such strike, he managed to catch Julian's blade between two of them, wrenching suddenly enough to dislodge Julian's grip.

His sword went flying, and he recalled Leo's words from the throughway.

Imagine you magnetized your hand—you'd never drop your sword.

It was too late for that . . . or was it?

Despite his uncle's clever counter, a good amount of damage had already been done.

A massive dent bisected the regent's still-plated arm, locking it in place and making it unable to bend or move properly. Cursing in pain and frustration, he peeled back the damaged vambrace and pauldron, tugging fiercely until the whole thing came apart, revealing a *second* iron limb.

"How much practice did *two* limbs take, then?" Julian said furiously.

"Twice as much," the regent said with a grin. Then he threw a piece of his armor straight at Julian's head.

Distracted by the reveal of the second iron arm, Julian only *just* managed to fling it aside with a sweep of his magic.

But the instant the plate veered away from Julian's face, his uncle was upon him with a punch to the jaw that crunched his chin guard and sent him reeling.

He stumbled to the ground. His uncle kicked him in the side of his stomach where his armor was weakest, forcing his hands to drop to protect himself. Taking the opportunity, the regent leapt on top of him, wrenching off his helmet so he could wrap his iron hands around Julian's exposed throat in the exact place where he'd sliced him open mere hours before.

"Better be sure"—his uncle gritted out, teeth clenched and grip tightening, crushing Julian's windpipe—"to finish the job this time. And once I'm done with you, it's on to Rebecca."

Francis was strong. His two iron limbs next to Julian's single iron hand were no match, though Julian tugged and scrabbled against his hold all the same.

He was filled with well magic, but he *couldn't breathe,* and if he couldn't breathe, he couldn't think. And he certainly couldn't use his surplus magic if he was unconscious.

He stopped fighting, releasing his grasp on Francis's wrists . . .

. . . and took hold of his uncle's arm instead. Specifically, the weakened elbow. He clenched with every ounce of strength he had left—and it was enough.

Air wheezed back into Julian's throat as the regent released his grip, yanking his damaged arm out of Julian's reach.

Taking the opportunity, Julian lifted his knee and planted his foot into his uncle's chest, kicking them apart with enough force to send both of them sprawling.

As Julian caught his breath with choking, agonized coughs, his uncle got to his feet, preparing for another strike.

Julian realized with a pang that he would never win this battle. His uncle was the most brutal and ruthless person he knew. Even with the power of the well, Julian couldn't bring himself to choke the life from the man as his uncle had so nearly done to him.

He couldn't win this game of strength and savagery.

But perhaps he could win a different way.

Eyes on Francis, Julian reached for the buckle that held his pauldron in place.

He removed it.

The regent's eyes narrowed as Julian removed the second, then his breastplate and arm guards and every piece of armor he wore.

The puzzlement on his uncle's face turned to amusement. To triumph.

"What's this?" he cried, loud enough for the Red Guard to hear, though they were in no state to appreciate their master's victory, hunched over wounds or unconsciously bleeding out. "Had enough, have you, my boy? I always knew you were weak, but *this*?"

He laughed, the sound like hot pokers being jammed into Julian's ears. "You could remove yours as well," Julian said. "Fight me man to man."

Francis shook his head ruefully. "Not this *fair fight* nonsense again, Julian. Without your armor, without that hand that I *gifted* you with, you'd be no match for me at all, and you know it. With or without that well of magic."

Julian ignored him, finishing the job.

He'd stacked his plate in a pile, and when he summoned his sword—his uncle's amusement flickered momentarily—he placed it in the middle, hilt upright, blade embedded into the earth.

Then he went to his knees before the symbolic effigy, the offering, the visual representation of his surrender. But while he lowered his head in a show of submission, he also pressed his metal hand to the ground, reaching, seeking, until he found what he sought.

A vein of iron.

"This is for the best, you know," his uncle said smugly, striding forward. "This way, Rebecca does not have to suffer for your mistakes. Rest easy, knowing you did the right thing in surrendering—in embracing your true, inferior nature."

He came to a pause before Julian and his forfeited weapons and armor. Smirking, Francis reached for the sword, intending to pull it from the earth and claim it for himself.

It was the ultimate shame for an ironsmith's sword to be claimed by another in battle, and some said that the iron would actually change allegiance if taken by a superior warrior.

But the instant the regent's hands took hold of the hilt, Julian's body started to glow. His uncle's face swam before him, his expression shifting from fierce self-satisfaction to confusion.

Julian imagined his eyes were pools of black, just as Wren's had been awash in pale white and sickly green.

Drawing upon every ounce he had left, Julian pushed the well's magic deep into the ground, into the vein of iron below him. The instant it absorbed the power, he sent the magic back up again, into his sword's point. The weapon absorbed the charge and quickly passed it to the pieces of plate that surrounded it.

The magnetization happened at once, the regent wrenched forward by his hands. He pulled tentatively, but neither the sword, magnetically connected to the armor, nor his hands, magnetically connected to the sword, would budge. And all of it was held fast to the ground thanks to the vein of iron below.

"What've you . . . ?" he muttered, but he had taken a step closer as he spoke, walking into the magnetic field, and before he could even get the words out, he was yanked to his knees by the armor that remained on the rest of his body.

Julian felt the pull as well, but just in his hand—the only piece of iron that remained on his body.

It was a small price to pay to see his uncle humbled. Julian had even given him the chance to remove his armor, but he'd refused. Strength over all else.

Francis was starting to panic now, pulling and pulling, but it only seemed to make the magnetization hold him more strongly. His face was as red as his armor and covered in sweat as he yanked and tugged and dragged his feet in the dirt.

"Yield," Julian said.

The regent ignored him, still trying to find purchase, to find some way out. "Help me!" he barked at the Red Guard, who were still gravely wounded and scattered around them. "Get over here and *help me*!"

A few of them lifted their heads or tried half-heartedly to get to their feet, but none of them came to his aid. Julian wondered if he'd wield that Hand of the Queen scepter now if he could.

"You can't fight it," Julian said, reclaiming the man's attention. "Surrender, and I'll—"

"Never!"

Then his uncle clenched his jaw, gathered his strength, and heaved with every scrap of energy he possessed. He pulled his arms so forcefully, so insistently, that with a shocking *crack* they tore free from his body, one at the damaged elbow and the other at the shoulder joint.

Stunned, Julian released the magnetization and stood.

His uncle lay there, broken and defeated, spitting venom as blood oozed from his shoulder and the stump of his other arm flailed and attempted to gain him purchase.

"What have you done to me?" he snarled.

Julian stared down at him. "I didn't do anything, Uncle. You did this to yourself."

He made quick work of Francis after that. Despite his fury, the man was pale-faced and clammy with shock, and no immediate threat, but Julian knew he'd recover eventually. He removed every scrap of iron, including Francis's broken limbs and the Hand of the Queen scepter, and tied his uncle up with rope from the saddlebags. He gave the wounded members of the Red Guard the same treatment, leaving them in a pile along the road. Luckily for them, they were inside the palisade; otherwise roaming revenants might come upon them.

Pity.

He made sure to tie up the horses as well, to ensure they didn't wander into trouble they didn't deserve.

Julian would have preferred to bring the regent and the Red Guard with him to ensure they were properly imprisoned, but there wasn't time. He may have cut off the head of the snake, but there was still an iron revenant army marching on the Dominions, and Julian knew they'd need all the help they could get.

So, after strapping on his armor and sliding the scepter into his belt, he mounted the nearest horse and rode like hell to the Breachfort.

THIRTY-SEVEN

The exchange between Wren and Hawke went unnoticed.

Ravenna, seeing Hawke turn his back on his sister and walk toward her, lifted her chin in what Wren interpreted as a look of victory.

Meanwhile, Wren clutched the ring tightly in her hand, the magic within it stirring in her blood, filling her up. The question now was what to do and when. There were dozens of undead ranged around her, ghosts and bones for the taking, but the amplifier ring only provided a limited surplus of magic. . . . If she tried to do too much, she might burn through it and wind up right back where she'd started, magically drained and useless.

Plus, she didn't know what Ravenna was capable of. Could Wren restrain Ravenna, or would she simply abscond and leave her body behind? Would she lash out, killing Vance or Hawke?

Wren didn't want to think too far along the line of Ravenna's future plans, as she had just done some sort of ghostsmith commitment ceremony with Wren's father and now intended to wear Wren's body the way the iron revenants wore their armor. But what was certain was that Wren's body, the body of a ghostsmith who shared her blood, was paramount to her.

Ravenna wanted to resurrect herself—she wanted life, like any undead. But she also wanted power, political and magical, and Wren and Hawke could not let her have it.

He stood next to their mother now, and while Ravenna needed him for what came next, if he refused, Ravenna would punish him. There were ways to hurt someone that didn't involve death, after all.

Shifting her arm so that she could leap free of the manacle at any moment, Wren pictured the place Hawke had reached for the lever so she could quickly unlatch the other one.

"It is time," Ravenna said, turning to Hawke. "I will not ask you again."

Hawke stared at her long and hard before releasing a gust of air. "No."

Ravenna, already unnaturally still since she didn't need to breathe—how had Wren failed to notice that before?—froze in place. "*What?*"

"I won't do it."

"I see," she said, lowering her head. Her gaze landed, almost idly, on the staff she still held. Hawke's staff. She lifted it, and Wren feared she'd strike out at Hawke.

He, too, tensed as if in anticipation of a blow, but then Ravenna twirled the object in her hand, the glowing skull at its top shining brightly.

Hawke stared at it, at his mother, and Wren was confused at the simmering tension. At the dark dread unspooling between them.

"Tail," Hawke breathed faintly, summoning the familiar bound to the staff. The ghost-fox blossomed to life just in time for Ravenna to swing the staff in an arc and smash the skull tip on the ground. A resounding crunch split the taut silence, drowning Hawke's muffled gasp as his familiar trembled and then dispersed in a wash of ghostly smoke.

But it didn't disappear entirely.

Ravenna hadn't reaped the ghost or freed the spirit. No, by crushing its anchor bone before the spirit could be reaped, she had now condemned it to the same existence as those ghosts on the Uprising battlefield. Here but not, worse than undead, doomed to fade into nothing without even a chance at being freed.

Hawke had been willing to do the same to the hundreds of undead inside the well, but now that he saw the truth, Wren thought he might change his tune. Or maybe his hatred for undead humans would remain, but this was no hateful revenant. This was his familiar.

Hawke's chest was rising and falling rapidly, his eyes furiously blinking back tears. It was so casually callous, so effortlessly cruel—yet also calculated, meant to wound him and bully him into submission.

Ravenna took an idle step forward and ground her heel into the bone shards, spreading them across the ground in an excessive display of control.

"Now," she said, tossing the staff aside with a clatter. "I will give you one more chance to—"

Wren had had enough.

She stood, quickly unlatching her other arm and placing Hawke's ring on her finger.

Ravenna looked up at her in surprise, glanced at Hawke, then laughed.

The sound was grating, and Wren didn't know what was so funny.

She looked at Hawke for some indication of what would come next, but he was staring at the crushed animal skull on the ground, utterly lost.

"You cannot compel me!" Ravenna said, still laughing. "I am a *lich*, not some wispy ghost or roaming revenant. I am beyond your reach."

"I may not be able to compel you," Wren said, walking slowly down the steps from the dais and carefully around Vance-Locke's unconscious body. "But I am more than just a ghostsmith." Ravenna's laughter died away. She cocked her head, as if trying to puzzle out what Wren meant. "I am a *bonesmith*, like my father before me, and the best damn valkyr of my generation. I can't command your ghost, but I can break your fucking bones."

Wren lifted her hand, Hawke's ring glowing brightly on her finger, and clenched her fingers into a fist.

Another crack, not unlike the sound of the broken skull, rang out, and Ravenna dropped. Wren had broken the bones of her legs, and caught by surprise, she had gone down with her body.

Seizing the opportunity, Wren took hold of Hawke and dragged him out of Ravenna's reach.

They had barely staggered away when Ravenna's laughter echoed about them once more.

She had collapsed onto her front and now used her arms to raise herself onto her elbows, looking at her children from between strands of dead hair and dried flowers. "You think a couple of broken femurs can stop me?" Her lips peeled back in a sneer, and her eyes flared alarmingly bright. "That it is my *bones* that make me strong?"

Her entire body glowed now, scraps of fabric and clumps of hair whipping around her in an undead wind.

Wren squinted as Ravenna's broken legs—dangling at odd

angles—snapped back together with a sickening crunch. All tier-five undead had the ability to control their bones, to make them walk and reach and stand upright. But they could not *repair* them or make them strong if they were weak. Their mobility relied upon the integrity of their corpse. The worse the shape of the body, the more lumbering and slow the revenant. The more likely the ghost would leave the body behind entirely.

With two broken legs, Ravenna should not be able to stand . . . but she did, her ghost pulling herself upright with virtually no effort. This was the first true evidence of the strength of her ghost—of her special lich abilities.

And Wren feared it would not be the last.

She reached tentatively, trying to sense the bones she had just shattered—but Ravenna's ghost was now wrapped around every fiber and sinew. Every inch of her glowed with her spirit, and Wren's bonesmith magic could not penetrate it.

Ravenna took a step forward. "Your talents are no good here, *bonesmith*."

Wren shrugged, injecting the gesture with seventeen years' worth of arrogant insolence—though she felt anything but. "Then I guess I'll use my blades."

She unsheathed one of her swords; if she was going to go down, she'd go down swinging.

First she tossed Hawke his ring. He caught it, wide-eyed. "Don't just stand there," she snapped, withdrawing the second blade. She jerked her chin at the gaggle of revenants filling the hall. "We need reinforcements."

"Wren, you don't understand. She—"

But Wren had already started forward. Sure, Ravenna could

apparently handle haunted bone—she was still wearing Wren's amplifier ring, after all—but how did she feel about dead bone?

"Help her!" Hawke shouted. "Take hold of the lich."

The nearest revenants lurched forward, two of them, each reaching for one of Ravenna's arms.

And she let them, her gaunt face twisted into a smile.

They gripped her wrists and wrenched her arms wide, exposing Ravenna's chest to Wren's blades. Her ghost glow had shifted, coalescing into a blinding ball of light behind her rib cage.

It was *right there.*

And Wren hesitated.

That was all it took.

Ravenna's smile stretched wider, and the blazing light that was her ghost *fractured,* two smaller pieces breaking off from the whole.

And they settled on the two revenants who held her arms.

Their ghosts flashed brighter than ever before dimming again, though Wren could see the solitary scrap of Ravenna's soul pulsing from within.

They dropped her arms and turned, attention focused on Wren.

She recalled Hawke's words about Ravenna's ghost as a lich.

She can conceal it, shift and reshape it . . . even split *it.*

"No," Wren said, wishing she still had Hawke's ring.

"No! Stop!" Hawke echoed, but the revenants did not waver. "You," he barked, speaking to some of the other revenants. "Protect my sister!"

"You may speak to the vestiges of their minds," Ravenna said, extending her hands. "But I can reach into their *souls.*"

And then, as before, pieces of her ghost fractured, splintering off and landing on the revenants that were attempting to heed Hawke's commands. This was more than magical compulsion. This was *possession.* She wasn't just controlling them; she was a *part* of them, her ghost operating from within.

As her spirit penetrated their bodies, the revenants jerked to a halt. There was a moment of struggle where bones clacked and pieces of fabric swayed. The ghosts battled, but eventually Ravenna won. Her scrap of soul shone brightly, distinguishable within its hosts, but no less potent for it.

Their heads turned as one, away from Ravenna and toward Wren and Hawke.

Their new targets.

THIRTY-EIGHT

"Leo."

A hand landed on Leo's shoulder, making him jump. He wrenched his gaze away from the sight of the iron revenants below to find his brother next to him.

"It's time. Why don't you head to the dining hall with the others."

By *others* he meant the servants and those without any battle training, plus Lady-Smith Svetlana Graven, who had not seen active duty in decades. Leo certainly lacked combat experience, but whatever his brother said, being kidnapped *did* count as seeing action, and he wasn't going to hide from this.

"I'm staying."

Laurent's eyes fluttered closed. "I don't have time to look after you."

"I don't need you to," Leo snapped, annoyed, even if the words also revealed Laurent's affection for him—a rare occurrence.

"I'll keep an eye on him, Your Highness," Inara said.

Laurent surveyed her, clad in bone armor with gleaming eye black, and accepted the offer with a grudging nod.

Then he turned away, shouting more orders. Archers had started to fill the battlements, arrows nocked and ready, while Leo knew that no steel arrowhead would penetrate that iron shell.

The commander stood on Leo's other side, bellowing instructions like Laurent, while Inara crossed her arms over her chest and watched.

The iron revenants had reached the bone palisade . . . and marched past it like it was nothing.

Inara's lips flattened into a grim line, though she said nothing. She might believe Leo, unlike Laurent, but she'd never seen one of these things before. Maybe even she had doubted they were as powerful as Leo had implied.

In fact, some of the iron revenants marched straight *through* the palisade, knocking the towering bones aside until they crunched and cracked underfoot.

The first and greatest of their defenses—dead bone—had just proved insufficient. Leo raked his gaze over the undead soldiers but saw no sign of any bridge-building materials. Now all their faith lay in the second defense.

Leo swallowed.

Finally, interminably tense minutes later, the iron revenants arrived at the Breachfort gate.

They were organized in neat rows and divided into three companies.

From the central column, a single soldier stepped forward.

Laurent frowned down at it, and Leo suspected he was noticing the lack of air or eye holes for the first time. The bizarre, faceless mask that marked these soldiers as unlike any other.

"Take it down!" Laurent shouted, and a volley of arrows pelted the lone revenant.

As Leo had expected, the projectiles ricocheted harmlessly off the iron armor and found no gaps large enough to exploit. The archers ceased their attack, and silence descended.

But then, much to Leo's surprise, the undead reached up and pulled its helmet off.

The face beneath was almost normal looking.

Almost.

The skin was waxen and pale, the hair matted, and the eyes . . . milky and unseeing, with a pale sheen of ghost-green over the surface.

Laurent blanched, but still it seemed he had not accepted the truth. He snatched a bow from the nearest soldier on the Wall, nocked an arrow, and took aim.

He had always been a talented archer.

The arrow whistled through the air and pierced the revenant's eye clean through. A flash of ghostlight burst from the wound, but otherwise, the revenant was unaffected. It didn't stumble or stagger.

It didn't react at all except to tilt its head upward.

Laurent gaped at the thing below, and Leo saw the moment that all the bravado, all the confidence, drained from him.

The revenant pulled the arrow from its eye socket with sickening calm, put its helmet back into place, and then charged straight at the gate.

It tore through the bone portcullis like a cobweb, and a second later there was a resounding impact from below, shaking the very stones beneath Leo's feet as it collided with the massive double doors.

Laurent stared, wordless, as the rest of the revenants followed suit.

"Fire at will!" shouted the commander, taking the reins.

Of course the arrows were useless, and panicked fear started to flutter against Leo's ribs, so high in his chest it made it hard to breathe.

"Secondary defenses!" came the commander's next order, and soldiers bearing great big rocks and broken bits of masonry—helped by the two stonesmiths who had aided Leo earlier—started to drop the heavy items through murder holes above the gate. While they connected with their targets and certainly seemed to make more of an impression than the arrows, they did little damage. They were enough to send some of the iron revenants off course or slow their momentum, but they weren't enough to stop them.

Again, the revenants rammed into the gate, shaking the defenders above and causing people to cry out in alarm.

"It's not working—none of it's working," said Laurent, his words mirroring the expressions on the soldiers that continued to fight on either side of them, though their barrage of arrows and falling debris was dwindling in the face of the obvious futility.

"We have to change our strategy," Leo said to his brother, who was clearly in shock. Leo gripped his shoulders. "Do you hear me? We pivot or we die."

Laurent stared at him, shaking his head wordlessly. "I don't . . . I can't . . . never seen . . ."

Leo shoved him roughly aside and turned around. "Soldiers of the Dominions!" His voice carried despite the repeated heavy thumps as the iron revenants rammed into the gate. "Your arrows won't work; our weapons won't penetrate. We are not stronger than this foe, but we can be smarter." He grinned his trademark grin, hoping to take a few notes about confidence, however false, from his brother's book. "All of you"—he directed his words to the archers on the Wall—"get down there and reinforce the gate. Create a blockade with anything you can carry. Crates, carts, buckets, and barrels. You two," he added, speaking to the pair of stonesmiths. "Help them. Take stones from the fort if need be."

There was a moment of silence in which Leo feared no one would obey him, and then, from somewhere behind: "Do as he says."

Leo whirled to see Laurent standing there, still pale and wide-eyed but seemingly coming back to himself.

Leo smiled gratefully as his orders were hastily carried out.

"Now what?" Laurent asked.

"Come with me."

Leo, Laurent, and Inara dashed down the stairs into the courtyard, past soldiers and craftspeople and servants, too, helping to carry items to shore up the gate's wide double doors. Down here, the impacts were shatteringly loud, sending dust into the air and thumping with the steady inescapability of a heartbeat.

"Hey, you five," Leo said, stopping a group of soldiers with the royal insignia on their chests. "There are barrels of water in the cellars. Bring them to the top of the wall. Commander Duncan will know what to do with them. Hurry."

Once again, it took Laurent's nod of assent before the soldiers ran off. Leo tried not to let their confusion wound his pride. There was no time to be sensitive; Laurent was, technically, in charge here.

They cut through an archway and arrived in the kitchen courtyard next to the cistern. Their work had nearly been complete when the iron revenants had arrived.

"I think one more piece ought to do it," Leo said, sorting through the pile of pipes they'd collected and fitting it to the diverted spout. Laurent frowned at it, tracking its path from the tank to a small metal grating in the wall.

"Is that a drain?" Laurent asked as Leo bent to secure the pipe with Inara's help.

"That's correct," said Leo, giving one final twist and standing. Then he hurried to the tank and took hold of a spoked wheel that was secured next to one of the spouts.

"Where does it drain to?"

Leo smiled. "You'll see. On my mark," he said to Inara, who had moved to stand next to a second wheel. "Ready? Crank it."

Both of them turned their wheels, slowly cutting off the water into the other spouts that led to various places inside the fort. Right now they needed every drop.

Then he and Inara moved to their recently modified spout and the wheel there. Together, they took hold and turned.

The flow came in a rush, rattling the pipe and sending it bouncing as the water streamed through the drain and out of sight.

That done, they ran back to the stairs and up to the top of the fort. Leo bent over the battlements and looked down.

A pool of water had started to form in front of the gate, spewing from the small drain that was situated there. It was meant to flow into a channel that directed it *away* from the road, but with Inara's help, that channel had been redirected to flood the road with water.

To create a barrier between the gate and the revenants.

"I don't believe it," Leo muttered. "It worked."

"Not bad, Gold Prince," Inara said, smiling along with him as the pool of water grew and spread, and the iron revenants reared back from it in confusion and alarm.

"Well, shit," said Laurent, while a cheer went up from the rest of the fort. He looked at Leo. "Nicely done, little brother." He clapped him on the shoulder. "Nicely done."

"I'm not finished yet," Leo said with a grin. "Are we ready, Commander?"

"Ready and waiting," Commander Duncan replied.

Leo watched the churning mass of revenants below, which had lost its cold, inhuman precision for the first time.

But this was where things could get even more dangerous. There were other vulnerable points along the Wall, and Leo suspected they didn't need a gate to get through.

Before they could muster a different attack, Leo looked to either side, then issued another order.

The soldiers who had carried the water barrels to the top of the fort now removed their plugs and emptied their contents into the rain gutters that lined the battlements. Down below, streams of water shot out of their corresponding pipes and into the long, deep channels that Inara and the stonesmith tributes had dug hours earlier.

The water bled away from the Wall in a straight line, hemming the revenants in left and right.

They were about to be trapped like the revenant wolf in Mercy's cage. . . . Only, the third channel that was meant to enclose the revenants to the east wasn't filling as quickly as they needed it to.

Inara spotted it first, pointing. "I think we've got a problem."

Indeed, while the revenants shuffled in place, trying and failing to pass the water barrier, the last channel remained only partially filled. It wouldn't take long for them to find the literal hole in their defenses, and then they'd simply attack the Wall from a different position.

"I'm going out," Inara said, making for the stairs.

"Wait," Leo said, grabbing her arm. He glanced at his brother, who nodded.

"Take some soldiers with you," Laurent said. "As many as you think you need."

"Confuse and distract them, but whatever you do, don't engage," Leo said, anxiety spiking in his veins. Having a front-row seat while people rode out and risked their lives was hard to stomach. *Harder* because it had been his own idea. "See if you can keep them within the water lines."

"Understood, Your Highness."

"Leo," he said with a shaky smile. "Call me Leo."

"Absolutely not," Inara shot back in her usual dry tone, but she squeezed his hand before she departed.

As soon as they rode out through a postern gate, the revenants' attention snapped on to them, suggesting something akin to a hive mind, though Leo suspected it had more to do with the fact that the revenants were undead and they couldn't help themselves.

Already Leo was regretting his decision, and the bubble of happiness he'd felt that his tactics were working was quickly stifled.

The cistern had completely emptied, and while the flooding in front of the gate remained unbreached, it was clear that the water was slowly draining away into the hard, dry earth. The same was true of the channels they had dug, the water barriers growing weaker and weaker by the moment.

And Inara and the other riders were still out there.

Leo wasn't sure if they'd yet noticed, too preoccupied with riding in sweeps back and forth, keeping the revenants' attention and launching attacks when riding alone failed them.

But they didn't have *all* the revenants' attention.

Some were focused on pushing themselves nearer the edges of the channels, the water there growing shallower and narrower as the liquid seeped into the ground.

Their iron boots stomped into the mud, softening the earth; helping the water to leach away.

"Inara! Fall back!" Leo shouted, hands cupped on either side of his mouth, but the words were swallowed in the chaos below.

"FALL BACK!" boomed the commander, whose battle voice had been honed over several decades of service.

Inara's head snapped up, and she started to signal to the others—just as a revenant broke free from the gap in the eastern channel.

It came straight for her, knocking her horse off its feet in a single, iron-fisted swipe, mount and rider sprawling into the dirt.

Leo's heart clenched, but the horse had survived, and it hadn't crushed her. Already Inara was wriggling, trying to get her leg out from underneath the animal, hands scrambling for a weapon as the revenant loomed over her.

It lifted its boot, intending to stomp on her neck, and Leo couldn't watch . . . but he did.

Then, out of nowhere, an iron whip lashed out, wrapping around the revenant's neck and yanking its helmet—along with its head—clean off.

Leo swore the battle went silent, that everyone living and dead alike froze in shock as the suit creaked, swayed, then fell to the ground with a resounding crash.

There, standing next to it clad in iron armor of his own, was Julian Knight.

THIRTY-NINE

"*Shit*," Wren said, stumbling backward, trying to put space between herself and the revenants now controlled by Ravenna.

By her *ghost*.

Corpse Queen indeed.

Just when Wren thought this magic couldn't get any weirder . . . it did.

She shoved one of her swords into Hawke's hands. "Did you know she could do this?" she demanded.

"Yes," he said, gingerly taking the weapon. "How do you think the iron revenants work?"

Wren was in the middle of throwing down a hasty line of bonedust, which would hopefully buy them a second to collect themselves, though her head snapped up at his words. "*What?* I thought that was you—you and that scepter."

Hawke shook his head, flinching when the revenants reached the bonedust, though it did its job and momentarily stalled their attack.

Ravenna, meanwhile, had turned her attention to the other undead inside the chamber, clearly intending to take hold of every single one if need be.

"The iron revenants are too many. Besides, my control cannot span such a distance, no matter how much raw magic I absorb."

"But *hers* can? Her ghost can travel that far from her anchor bone?"

He shrugged helplessly. "She is a lich. As far as I can tell, her spiritual tether knows no limits."

And here Wren had thought the familiars were uncanny. "And the scepter?"

Hawke snorted. "A bit of theater to appease the regent—no more."

Wren considered that as the revenants finally broke through the bonedust circle, plodding ever forward. They couldn't *harm* Wren and Hawke, at least not with deathrot, but they could surround them, pen them in, and keep them trapped. Wield the rusted weapons Wren spotted in some of their hands.

Once they were subdued, Ravenna would *convince* Hawke to finish what he'd started with Locke and Vance. Wren would be just another body for Ravenna to inhabit, a suit of living flesh and bone.

A shudder went through her, and she thought about running, about mowing down the nearest undead and getting the hell out of this place. They'd surely follow her, but not even a ghost could stop her with her ghostsmith blood. She could probably get to freedom if she left Hawke behind. Left Vance behind.

And then what?

It was Ravenna who was controlling the iron revenants. Which meant they had to stop her to stop the army. Without her possessing them, they'd be regular, roaming undead—not a unified force. The well's magic would still make them formidable, but they'd be unlikely to attempt to tear down the Border Wall or attack the Breachfort. In fact, Wren didn't know *what* would happen after Ravenna vacated an undead she had possessed.

It didn't matter. If they stopped Ravenna, they gave the defenders at the Breachfort—however few remained—a chance.

Wren released a handful of knucklebones and hefted her sword. She took a protective stance in front of her brother, while he commanded the nearby revenants who weren't yet possessed by Ravenna to block those that were. It worked—until Ravenna simply split her ghost *again,* taking control of their bodies and turning them around, doubling their foes.

Hawke cursed, stumbling backward, but Wren kept her eyes on Ravenna. Whenever she splintered her soul and possessed a new undead, what remained of her ghost inside her body flickered and dimmed ever so slightly, as if struggling to remain whole.

And how *did* it remain whole? How did Ravenna keep a central sense of self when pieces of her were literally all over the Breachlands?

As Ravenna and Hawke continued vying for control of the undead, Wren noticed there was something *off* about the lich's spine—not surprising since she'd been dead for nearly two decades—except it wasn't bent or broken or rotted away. The *shape* of the bones was off, and Wren knew bones.

A flash of ghostlight cast Ravenna's body into temporary silhouette, and Wren saw it.

Linchpins.

Not one or two, but hundreds.

This must be how she was keeping herself together. Linchpins bound a ghost to its anchor bone; they made the tether stronger and therefore made both spirit and body stronger. If every split of her soul weakened her, then every linchpin counteracted that effect.

Without them, Ravenna would probably be some kind of untethered haze . . . able to permanently leave her remains behind, but weak. She'd lose her connection to the world, to herself and her past life, and eventually all sentience. She needed an intact anchor bone to exist, and by keeping herself connected to it via linchpin, her ghost could protect it.

Usually one linchpin was enough, but with a ghost fragmented hundreds of times? It made sense that she'd need hundreds of linchpins. How an entire spine, which was composed of twenty-four individual vertebrae, could somehow be a *singular* anchor bone was puzzling, but it was not the most pressing of Wren's concerns.

While Ravenna was distracted, Wren surreptitiously extended her hand and reached, but while she could sense the linchpins, she couldn't actually touch them with her magic.

She'd need to get her hands on Hawke's amplifier ring again. Maybe with its power she could remove the linchpins and weaken Ravenna. It might not reap her, but it would surely force her to pull back and reconstitute herself—perhaps abandon the iron revenants entirely.

It was a long shot, but the best idea Wren had.

She hurried to her brother's side, dodging a handful of undead that he'd ordered to stand before him like a barricade. "I need you to keep fighting her," she panted, crouching to speak to him with the hopes that Ravenna couldn't see or hear.

"It's not working," Hawke said tersely, as the revenants before them shook and trembled, fighting off either his or Ravenna's control.

"It doesn't matter. Keep commanding the undead and drawing her out. Make her take on more than she can handle."

He frowned at her. "Why?"

"I'm going to remove her linchpins."

"Linchpins?" he repeated, shocked.

"She has hundreds of them. Look at her back."

He did as bidden, craning his neck to get a glimpse of Ravenna. As she reached for revenants in the darkest corners of the throne room, her back was exposed once more, her spiked spine revealed to Hawke's horrified gaze.

"I didn't—that wasn't me," he said, face pale.

That was interesting. If Hawke hadn't embedded them, then who?

"It doesn't matter. It must be what's keeping her ghost together. Since they're bone, I should be able to get them out, even at a distance, but I need more magic. Which means I need this." She yanked the ring off his finger, then looked at the gathering pool, a mass of undead between them and it. "And *that.*"

Hawke expelled a breath, nodding and sliding his skull mask back into place. "Get ready," he said, and before Wren could ask what he was up to, he had turned his attention toward the wall of undead behind the throne. "Elders!" he cried out, and they flared brightly to life once more.

Ravenna turned at the searing burst of light, but Wren didn't wait to see what would happen next.

She darted between the undead, ducking under reaching limbs and diving between shuffling legs until she landed, sprawled on the floor, right at the edge of the pool. She hesitated for half a second, the memory of the pain from the last time she'd been submerged flashing through her before she plunged her hand into the swirling magic.

It leapt to life under her touch, but the brightness from the Elders kept Ravenna's attention.

Hawke was speaking again, his words echoing loudly in the cavernous space. "Your Corpse Queen is a pretender!"

"Shut your mouth," Ravenna snarled, but Hawke ignored her.

"She is a Nekros, but she is no living ghostsmith. She is worse than undead. She is a lich."

"Blasphemous!" they boomed out. *"The living rule and the dead serve. The dead serve!"*

Ravenna yelled at them to stop, but they did not heed her. They were dead and so obeyed Hawke, the living ghostsmith, alone.

Wren felt a surge of pleasure at that. For all her dark power, Ravenna was still not a ghostsmith. Still not what she had once been.

"The lich is unnatural," the Elders continued. *"The lich must be stopped. It must be destroyed."*

Ravenna marched forward, squaring her skeletal shoulders and gathering her strength. Her ghost flared brightly, and then dozens of pieces of ghostlight burst from her chest like a flock of startled birds.

They descended upon the Elders, whose condemning words were choked off one by one. It took time, though, and effort. The Elders resisted her, their own ancient spirits stronger than most.

But Ravenna won. The Elders fell silent, then—

"Nice try," Ravenna rasped, and the same words echoed from the Elders, reverberating loudly all around them. Pieces of her ghost shimmered among their mounted bones, while her own body sagged slightly, showing signs of exhaustion that matched her flickering ghost.

This was Wren's moment. She extended her hand, Hawke's ring—and the rest of her body—aglow as she reached for Ravenna with everything she had.

But it didn't work.

Ravenna's ghost was still too strong, repelling Wren's magic. It clung to her bones, protecting them and acting as some kind of barrier.

They were *so* close, but Ravenna had possessed every undead in this room . . . and it still wasn't enough.

Hands shaking, Wren fell to her knees, magic and adrenaline coursing through her—along with an overwhelming sense of defeat. Ravenna's lich form was too powerful, and Wren had run out of ideas.

A hand landed on her shoulder, and she nearly jumped out of her skin. A revenant!

She whirled around, and indeed it was a revenant . . . but not one she was expecting.

Starling was staring back at her, so nearly alive that it was alarming, even with the ghost glow haloing her eyes and pouring from the wound on her chest. But her skin, while pale, had not yet started to rot away, and her hair was soft where it wasn't caked with blood. She'd been dead only a couple of days, tops, and already she had risen.

And she had come *here*.

The fact that she had been drawn to whatever living were present in the Breach wasn't surprising, but she wasn't part of the usual violent rabble. She had crept to Wren's side and was looking at her with unnerving intent. Wren glanced down and spotted Hawke's wishbone necklace clutched so tightly in the woman's bloody hand that her fist shook. Wren suspected it was her only tie to her humanity, to her memories, and she feared to let go.

Wren had a sudden, powerful wave of regret over the fact that she'd not been able to give Julian something. That he might rise, angry, afraid, in terrible pain . . . and with no idea who he was or what he'd meant to her.

Swallowing a lump in her throat, Wren looked over her shoulder.

Ravenna hadn't noticed her efforts. She hadn't seen Starling yet either, but *Hawke* had. His eyes flicked Wren's way for half a heartbeat, the pain and regret on his features turning into steely resolve. He faced Ravenna and the wall of Elders.

"Elders!" he yelled. The wall of bones flickered. He was fighting her—fighting her possession and attempting to reclaim them. They were fighting, too. "I am a Son of Death, and you *will* obey me."

Again, the ghostlight quivered, and their mother clenched her hands into fists.

Trusting her brother to keep Ravenna occupied for as long as possible, Wren turned back to Starling.

She opened her mouth as if to speak before remembering that she couldn't—not without throat muscles and vocal cords. It must take time for an undead to be able to form words with their spirit, because Starling shook her head, then gestured toward her chest, to her ghost, which Wren had already touched before. The message, the request, was plain.

Touch my ghost, my memories, again.

So Wren did.

She reached out and was rocketed into Starling's past in an instant. She'd forgotten she was flush with well magic, her ability stronger than it had ever been before.

There was a barrage of images and sounds, and Wren had the sense that Starling was guiding her, leading her to a specific moment in time.

All of a sudden Wren was there. She was in this very room, but it looked different. The Elders were quiet and the crowds of undead were gone, and Ravenna's own powerful ghost was concealed behind her veil.

The only illumination came from the gathering pool.

"Hurry," Ravenna was saying to her.

Wren, who was experiencing the scene from Starling's eyes, glanced down to see that she held a hammer just like the one Hawke used, and next to her was a tray bearing twenty or so linchpins.

As Ravenna turned her back to Starling, she lifted her veil, exposing her rotted corpse and disfigured spine, already pierced through with well over a hundred pins, sticking out at odd angles in a grotesque mimicry of some spiky reptile.

Then, before Starling's borrowed eyes, Wren saw Ravenna peel back her ghost, revealing the raw bone beneath. Exposing herself for Starling's work. Making herself vulnerable.

"There isn't much room," Starling said. Wren felt her unease, her hatred for this task and this woman. She also kept darting glances into the shadows, as if looking for someone. . . . "I think it's time I put these elsewhere on your body."

"No," Ravenna snapped. "I already told you, they must be close together if they are to mimic a proper anchor bone, and the spine is a *connected* series of bones. The pins can't get any closer without occupying the *same* bone, which is, of course, at this scale . . . impossible."

So a lich didn't have a proper anchor bone, then. Instead, Ravenna had to fake it.

Starling didn't argue again; instead, she selected a pin and sought a likely place on a spine as thorny as a porcupine.

As she worked, Starling's gaze flitted to the corner of the room once more—and this time Ravenna noticed.

"He's not here," she said. There was amusement in her voice. "I sent him away on another errand. He's such a good boy. So dutiful. I must thank you for that."

Starling gritted her teeth, interpreting the subtle jab for what it was. "I don't know why you bother with me, then, when he could do this for you." She lined up the pin and raised the hammer. Bone connected with bone, and Ravenna's body shuddered.

"I can't decide who hates these tasks more . . . him or you."

Starling lifted another pin, located another spot. "So you're torturing us both."

Ravenna shrugged, then jolted from the impact of another hammer blow. Wren suspected Starling had used more force than was strictly necessary.

From the look she cast over her emaciated shoulder, Ravenna suspected it too.

"You could say no, of course," she said lightly. "But you know what'll happen if you do."

Starling, who had been reaching for the next pin on the tray, stilled. In her mind flashed a memory of the last time she had refused Ravenna, which had resulted in a younger Hawke cowering in the dark, lip bloodied and cheeks tearstained.

"Besides," Ravenna continued, "I like to keep tabs on you. Just in case . . ."

The memory disappeared.

Wren was blinking it away as she came back to herself, trying to sort through what she'd seen. Starling had been the one to perform the magic that bound Ravenna's powerful lich ghost to her body, but Wren knew that wasn't what the woman wanted her to see.

When Ravenna had peeled away her ghost . . . that was when Starling had been able to puncture the bone. Which meant that Wren needed Ravenna to do the same now if she was to remove those spikes herself.

But how?

"Yes," Wren said into Starling's urgent face. "I understand. But I need her to expose herself, and I doubt she'll do it for me like she did for you."

Starling's hand shot out, and despite the fact that they were on the same side, Wren's instinct was to recoil. But Starling didn't touch Wren—she touched the hilt of a throwing knife attached to Wren's belt. She drew back at once, but the message was clear.

Dead bone. Of course.

But a blade would not achieve the desired effect. Wren needed both precision and range. She needed Ravenna to reveal her entire spine, and for such a task, there was really only one choice.

Wren nodded, and Starling got to her feet. Her movements were stiff, but they were not the rambling shuffle of the rest of the more decayed undead. Back as straight as she could make it, she strode through the tumult, going straight for Ravenna.

Hawke saw her and shook his head in despair. She had already suffered under Ravenna, and Wren knew it would hurt him to see her suffer again, even in death.

But too late.

Ravenna had seen her, had picked her out of the crowd—or perhaps sensed her presence, her ghost not possessed like the others.

She smiled, flaring brightly and turning from the Elders.

"No!" Hawke cried out, but she ignored him.

She turned, extending both her hands wide and forcing the revenants she held in her control to amble forward, creating a circle that trapped both Starling and Hawke within.

"Please, Mother," Hawke said, coming to stand between Ravenna and Starling, heedless of the danger. "You already took her life. Don't take her death, too."

With a nod of Ravenna's head, revenants from the circle stepped forward to take hold of Hawke. He resisted, issuing counter commands, and even breaking a few bones as he kicked and struggled. He'd lost Wren's sword somewhere, but she pushed the thought aside as she edged, slowly, around the outside of the circle.

"I take what I want," Ravenna crowed, turning her attention to Starling. The woman looked at Hawke and pressed her closed hand, the one that held the wishbone, to her chest—to her heart, where her ghost shone brightest.

Tears leaked down Hawke's face, but Starling turned away and met her fate head-on.

Ravenna's ghost surged, preparing for another split, another possession.

It was the perfect distraction.

Wren plunged a hand into her pouch of bonedust. With a downward slash, she unleashed a dense cloud, using her surplus magic to control every particle. It descended upon Ravenna in a rush, whipping up her spine before the lich knew what had hit her.

The instant it made contact, her ghost crackled and peeled away from the bones, leaving Ravenna's back exposed.

With her other hand, Wren reached forward, gripping every last linchpin in her tightest magical hold, and then *yanked* with all her might.

They burst into the air in one vicious, powerful pull—and, after a moment of stunned silence, Ravenna collapsed to the ground.

FORTY

Julian strode over to the fallen bonesmith girl and held out his hand. She stared up at him, and he flashed back to the moment he had first laid eyes on Wren. With a sweep of his magic, his helmet's face guard slid back, revealing his face—not that it would mean much to her. Still, perhaps he'd look less threatening.

She eventually took his hand, her fallen horse scrabbling back to its feet. Somewhere above, applause rang out.

Julian turned, staring up at the top of the battlements. To have Breachfort soldiers cheering *him* was a thing Julian could never have imagined in his wildest dreams.

And there, standing between the parapets, was Prince Leopold.

Julian looked around at the battlefield, at the channels of water and the flooding near the gate. They had trapped the iron revenants in a rough rectangle, with ditches of water along the north and south of the road, with a partially filled eastern channel meant to hem them in. This was where the bonesmith and other riders were attempting to shore up the defenses.

He nodded his approval, and high above, Leo saluted him.

But the battle was not won—not by a long shot. Julian may have just oversold his usefulness in the fight ahead. While he'd made short work of that unsuspecting iron revenant, the truth was, his magic was waning.

Badly.

He had used most of it during the fight with his uncle. What remained was his own usual supply, and he was exhausted. He had almost *died,* for starters, and then he'd run after his uncle as fast as his body would take him, fueled by rage, magic, and adrenaline. After battling with the man, he'd ridden a horse straight here without so much as a break, ditching the animal when the army came into view and proceeding the rest of the way on foot.

It took all he had not to plant his hands on his knees and bend over to catch his breath, but he knew such a sight would undo whatever galvanizing of the troops his previous actions had managed.

A part of him had secretly hoped he'd arrive to see the revenants already disabled, Wren finding some way to stop them, even from afar. But either her attempts hadn't worked . . . or she hadn't yet attempted anything.

That meant it was up to Julian to stop this army in its tracks, to face what he and his family had had a hand in making.

He turned to the bonesmith. "Round up the others and get them back inside," he said, watching as a handful of riders circled the gap in the eastern trench, trying to hold the line and halt any additional revenants that tried to break through. The rest of the water channels were currently doing their job, but it was evident that the protections would not last much longer. The trenches were losing their shape thanks to dozens of heavy iron boots, and the water was leaching away.

Julian would guard the exposed eastern barrier himself. But as he approached, the bonesmith, back on her horse, came with him. She shouted to the others, pointing at what was evidently some sort of postern gate, but she didn't follow them.

"What are you doing?" Julian asked.

"Staying with you," she replied tersely.

Julian frowned. "Why?"

She looked down at him, her pale eyes measuring. "My name's Inara Fell; I'm a valkyr. This is what we do. Besides," she added, "if anything happens to you, I suspect Wren'll kill me."

Julian barked out a laugh, slid his helmet's plates back into place, and reached for the scepter at his belt.

"What's that?" Inara asked.

"It's called the Hand of the Queen," he said, lips tight with distaste as he considered the skeletal hand at its tip. "It's meant to control them."

"That's convenient," she said, with no small amount of doubt.

"That's what I was thinking," he replied. He'd only seen it in action when held by the Corpse Queen, and it had seemed very much powered by her. "But it's worth a shot."

"Now's your chance," she said, nodding at the gap in the trench. With the absence of the other riders, another iron revenant had seen the opening and broken free.

Julian strode forward and raised the scepter between them. "Halt!" he shouted.

The undead stopped in its tracks, and a spark of hope exploded in Julian's chest—only for the revenant to snatch the scepter and crush the bone in a single gauntleted hand. Pieces crumbled to the ground, and Julian was left holding a rod of untreated iron.

The revenant's helmet tilted, its attention latching on to him instead.

"Did you have a backup plan?" Inara asked.

Julian dropped the rod and reached for his sword. He'd been dubious of the scepter's power from the start but hadn't expected it to be proven useless *quite* so quickly.

Before he could draw his weapon, Inara urged her horse forward and reached into a pouch on her belt. He'd often seen Wren do the same, and knew it contained a seemingly never-ending supply of bonedust. She threw an arc of it into the revenant's face.

"But their armor, won't it—" Julian began, before realizing that no matter how seamless their construction, there *must* be gaps in the plate, however minuscule, for them to be able to move.

Forget blades and blunt-force objects, this smallest of weaponry had the potential to do the most damage.

The iron revenant staggered back, swiping ineffectually at its helmet. It wasn't enough to destroy the thing, but it would certainly slow it down. Possibly even weaken it over time.

Inara quirked a brow, seeing that he had caught on. "The neck, elbows, and knees."

Julian nodded, and they got to work.

The iron revenants seemed to have divided their efforts. The majority of them were pushing toward the flooded gate to the west, currently being harried by the soldiers atop the Wall with arrows and other munitions, while the rest were spread around the penned-in space, attempting to breach the watery barriers to the north, south, and east. Given the eastern trench had an actual gap in it, Inara and Julian focused their defensive efforts there.

With his sword transformed into a whip once more, Julian targeted the revenants' weak areas, slashing and yanking, widening the gaps by the barest millimeters, helping make just a little more room for the handfuls of bonedust Inara tossed into the air to penetrate. The clouds of bone swirled and slipped into the openings, causing revenants to stumble and stagger and claw at their own faces.

Some stopped moving outright, their ghosts apparently damaged enough to make moving difficult, but others . . . They seemed completely unharmed by these attacks, their corpses underneath the armor too well-preserved, protecting the soul within.

But something else was happening, too. The iron revenants were becoming more . . . erratic. It was like they were malfunctioning, similar to the way they reacted to Inara's bonedust, except that it was also happening to revenants she hadn't attacked.

They stumbled and staggered, jerking their heads around as if disoriented—nothing like the regimented soldiers they'd seen up until now—and Julian allowed himself to hope. To think that maybe something was transpiring deep in the Breach. That maybe this fight was coming to a close.

Unfortunately, whatever was happening wasn't happening fast enough, and it wasn't happening to all of them. Another revenant broke through their defenses and charged him with a shocking burst of speed, colliding with Julian's chest and taking them both to the ground. The weight of the monstrosity was nearly unbearable, robbing him of breath, the last scraps of Julian's borrowed magic all but spent.

"Ironsmith!" came a voice from above, and Inara rode past, tossing him a weapon—a bone dagger.

With one arm free, Julian managed to catch it by the handle, bringing it down and ramming it into the near-invisible gap between the neck and helmet.

He felt the blade lodge into the flesh beneath, and after the undead shook and trembled a moment, it went still, and Julian wrenched the knife free.

Though the revenant was still shockingly heavy, Julian managed to wriggle out from underneath and get to his feet.

"Here," he gasped as Inara rode up alongside him, holding the weapon out to her, the blade still covered in old blood and filth.

She shook her head. "Keep it. You could use it, and it's not really mine anyway."

Julian frowned down at it, confused, until he recalled the empty sheath on Wren's belt—the family dagger that she had lost. Could this be that same blade?

A loud crashing sound cut through the moment, and both Julian and Inara turned.

There was a cluster of revenants forcefully knocking into one another in something like a frenzy.

The reason for the mad crush? The trench of water that blocked them in on the northern side had fully seeped away. After the revenants had tested and tested the barrier, it seemed the muddy ground was now dry enough for them to pass through, and they all hastened to do so.

All at once a hundred iron revenants were spilling over the nonexistent barrier, and they were coming *straight* for Julian.

FORTY-ONE

The linchpins followed Ravenna, landing on the floor in a cascade after Wren released them with her magic.

While Ravenna's body lay prone, her ghost remained upright, blurred and flickering and in danger of fading away entirely.

And it should have done, if Ravenna were a normal undead. But she was not.

Instead, the scraps of soul she'd embedded around the room returned to her—yanked there by what remained of her lich ghost. As each piece reconnected with the whole, her shape became more distinct, her ghostlight brighter.

But the undead she vacated, on the other hand . . . their spirits vanished entirely. It was the same effect as when Wren pierced a ghost through with her bone blades, eventually damaging them so much they had no choice but to disappear and gather their strength. Even the Elders had gone dark.

This meant that if they could get Ravenna to release the iron revenants, they wouldn't just stop attacking the Breachfort and the Border Wall. . . . They'd stop *existing* at all. Even if it was only temporarily.

Starling had escaped their fate. She remained standing upright, bones and ghost together, watching the scene unfold.

As Ravenna's ghost became clearer, Wren saw a glimpse of her mother in her last moments of life: eyes hollowed, belly still swollen, and a blood-soaked dress.

It caused a pang to pierce Wren's chest. Ravenna looked so young . . . not much older than Wren herself right now. She'd been pregnant and alone, and then she'd had a traumatic birth, forced to give up one child and watch the other slowly dying in her arms as her own life bled out.

Despite reconstituting herself, Ravenna's spirit still appeared weak. Wren would have pegged her as a tier two on sight, though as a lich she defied the revenant scale entirely.

After several breathless seconds hovering, the ghost settled over Ravenna's corpse, which had landed on its back after Wren wrenched the linchpins free. As soon as Ravenna returned to her body, her eyes glowed brightly, and her gaze darted around. Her fingers twitched, but then she grimaced, as if unable to move. Without the linchpins to keep her tether strong, her ghost was too fractured and fragile to control her body.

"Release them," Wren said. "Release the iron revenants."

Drawing back those pieces of her soul might extend Ravenna's existence, but the iron revenants needed to be stopped.

Ravenna didn't respond. Her ghost continued to flicker and tremble, and Wren suspected it was taking every ounce of her focus to hold herself together.

"It doesn't matter," Hawke said, voice dull. "She won't last long now. She's already pushed herself too far, and without the linchpins, she has no true tether."

"But why is she still here?" Wren asked uneasily. Most ghosts, once their tether was cut, disappeared immediately.

"She is a lich," he said simply.

"What?" Ravenna choked out, looking between them. "No tears for your mother?"

Hawke clenched his jaw. "You killed my mother," he said stonily, expression hard—though he couldn't meet Ravenna's gaze. Instead, he looked at Starling, who stood nearby, wishbone still clutched tightly in her hand.

Wren, meanwhile, crouched before Ravenna, meeting her undead stare head-on. "My mother died seventeen years ago. It's time she was gone for good."

Ravenna was the first to look away.

Soon, her chest started heaving, her body mimicking the rising and falling that came with rapid breath, but Wren knew it was her ghost shuddering within her rib cage.

Fighting, even now.

That was the thing about the undead. They always clung to life, to existence, even though what they truly needed was to let go.

After watching her struggle for several painful moments, Hawke reached for Ravenna's hand. She twitched it away.

But despite her contempt for the gesture, something like fear flashed in her glowing eyes.

Wren had never had to reap before, never had to reckon with the last action, the final move that severed someone's connection to the land of the living. Never had to speak with her quarry. And certainly never had to call one of them "mother."

She was suddenly overcome with a strange feeling. Remorse, maybe. Regret. She didn't know this woman and had no love for her . . . but she might have, if she'd had a chance to know her. If her mother had truly lived instead of spending the last two decades clinging to this world, her mind—her *heart*—deteriorating further every day.

And Hawke . . . this would hurt him, however flawed Ravenna was. Wren glanced at Vance-Locke, knowing the pain of an imperfect parent but also understanding that you would love them anyway, because you couldn't help it.

"Was she always like this, do you think?" Hawke asked, barely louder than a whisper. The vast chamber, which had so recently been a battleground, was as quiet as a tomb.

Wren considered—then an idea struck her. "We could find out," she said carefully. She stared down at her hand, then at Ravenna's ghost, still glowing faintly from within her rotted chest. "What she was like. Before. I could use my Vision."

"I doubt she'd—" Hawke began, before Ravenna cut him off.

"Do it," she forced out, the words breathy but distinct. Her eyes latched on to Wren's, and there was panic there. Desperation. As if she had very nearly reached the end.

Wren removed Hawke's amplifier ring, handing it over to him before pulling her own off Ravenna's finger. As soon as they both had their rings on, she plunged one hand into Ravenna's ghost and took hold of her brother's hand with the other. She needed to share this with him in some way, and maybe, with both of them wearing amplifiers and the raw magic pumping through their veins, she could.

It happened quickly, a testament both to the well's power and the fact that Ravenna didn't fight her.

At first it was just flashes of emotion. Ambition, anger . . . and loneliness. The loneliness was most palpable of all. Ravenna had spent years by herself, wandering the ruins and searching for her parents' bodies after the Breach, but she'd been unsuccessful. Wren felt her despair, but all of that changed the day bonesmiths marched on the Haunted Territory.

Wren saw Vance and Locke, young soldiers decked out in bone armor, through Ravenna's eyes—and felt Ravenna's hatred for them burning in her own stomach, Ravenna's desire to make them hurt for what the bonesmiths had done to the ghostsmiths all those centuries ago. She even saw Odile, though Ravenna paid her little mind, noting her unrequited crush on Locke and little else.

Ravenna told her lies and embedded herself with the bonesmiths, but things shifted after that. Her rage burned less brightly, and suddenly lifelong truths warred with new information, and it was an unsettling echo of what Wren herself had experienced with Julian.

The same was true of the desire. Ravenna had desired Locke Graven, had wanted him in a way she never wanted Vance. But with Vance, she could lie more easily, execute her plan more purposefully. With Locke, she questioned everything, including herself.

There was a singular, piercing moment of joy when Ravenna realized she was pregnant, and the emotion washed over Wren like a tidal wave. It brought with it the certainty that Wren had been *wanted,* and that was a balm she had not realized her soul needed.

Confusion soon replaced the happiness, and the feelings and images became more muddled after that—as if Ravenna's uncertainty permeated the memories, forever altering them.

Wren saw the Uprising battlefield, saw hundreds drop dead. Saw Locke Graven fall to his knees, glowing brighter than the sun as the well's magic killed him. Anguish wrenched Ravenna's heart—made it harden for what was to come. What she was to undergo alone.

Ravenna's *will*, her desire to live, was a powerful, palpable thing. Then, in life, and even now in death. She clung to her existence with every scrap of energy she possessed, fierce in her desire to *be*. It occurred to Wren that that's what a ghost's tether truly was: a physical representation of the spirit's will to live.

Interminable darkness gave way to a single ghostlight sconce, and Ravenna, her belly fit to burst, carving one of the amplifier rings while chatting to Locke's bones.

Next Wren saw herself as a baby, crying in Odile's arms. Another wrench of Ravenna's heart. Another hardening.

And then finally the moment at the gathering pool. Her son pressed to her chest, his heartbeat frail and gentle as a baby bird's. Ravenna's head spinning, hands slipping.

She fell, stumbled to the ground. *Protect the baby,* she thought, hurting herself in the process. *Protect the baby.*

She lay on the edge of the glowing pool, trembling and weak, when Hawke's heartbeat slowed. Stopped.

Ravenna was broken and defeated, unable to move—except for a single fingertip. She pulled on the blanket that swaddled Hawke's body, loosening it until a tiny foot sprang loose, plunging into the magic.

Then everything went black.

Wren withdrew with difficulty, imagining how things went after that.

Ravenna died, and though she must have fallen into the pool soon after, it had not been enough to save her.

But she had saved her son.

As Wren came back to herself, she found Hawke across from her, Ravenna's body between them. His expression told her he had seen what she had. He was crying.

Wren knew he was mourning the mother that barely was and not the thing she had become.

So was Wren.

Between them, Ravenna was still holding on.

"It's all right," Hawke said softly, voice choked. This time when he took her hand, there was no resistance. "We're all right. It's over now. It's time to go."

It wasn't a ghostsmith commanding an undead. It was a son speaking to his mother.

And she listened. Ravenna *listened.*

Her soul lifted from her body, and a sensation of intense relief filled the air. A feeling of complete and total calm. Of peace.

The shimmering, fractured ghostlight disappeared, leaving darkness in its wake.

FORTY-TWO

"Go," Julian said to Inara, taking up the bone blade in one hand and his iron sword in the other as a hundred iron revenants marched their way.

"What?" she demanded, trying to keep her horse in check as it bucked and stomped in the face of the coming undead. "I'm not leaving you!"

"They'll need you," he said. "The Dominions. The prince. You can't leave them defenseless. Now go!"

She stared at him hard, and he saw a bit of Wren in her refusal to heed good sense. But eventually she conceded. With a glance up at the fort where Leo watched, she reluctantly wheeled her horse around and made for the postern gate he'd seen earlier.

Leaving Julian standing alone against the onslaught.

He braced himself, knowing this would be his last stand, his last effort in a battle he was never meant to win.

But it wasn't about that.

It was about buying Wren time, about giving her a chance to correct this and save them all.

Julian was living on borrowed time anyway.

But that didn't mean he would go down without a fight.

His whip sword lashed out, knocking two revenants off course and a third onto its knees, but for every undead soldier he disabled or diverted, ten more took their place.

There were shouts from high above, arrows raining down, but Julian didn't have time to give them any attention.

He locked his whip back into a sword just in time to block a blow and then swung the blade around and managed to embed it into a knee, bringing the revenant down—but it took his sword with it.

Julian scrambled, sending his throwing knives pinging off armor left and right, but that was just a stalling tactic, a way to gain a bit of space as revenant after revenant marched their inexorable march.

Somehow he was knocked to the ground. The blow had dazed him; stars danced in front of his vision as he struggled to find purchase on the muddy, trampled ground, crab-walking on hands and feet.

He didn't make it far before a revenant placed an iron-covered boot on his chest. The force of it slammed him to his back, pinning him to the dirt and slowly but surely squeezing the air from his lungs.

If he still had the well's magic, he'd have been able to push the revenant off, but it was too heavy, too much iron for him to displace. Still, he tried, hands shoving and body squirming.

His chest burned, his lungs scraping breath after rasping, wheezing breath, his vision going dark as the revenant lifted its boot for a final, crushing stomp. . . .

Which never came.

Julian braced himself, his entire body tensed and waiting, but nothing happened.

He blinked, his vision clearing enough to reveal the revenant poised above him, boot raised, but otherwise entirely immobilized.

And the sky overhead . . . the steadily falling twilight was alive with glowing, ghost-green scraps of light. It was the same thing he'd seen happen in the Keeper's Cathedral but in reverse. Rather than fall onto the iron revenants' helmets, the scraps of ghostlight rose upward and disappeared, like sparks from a fire.

Julian coughed and caught his breath, pushing himself up on his elbows, stunned to see every single iron revenant scattered before the Breachfort frozen in place.

Horse hooves thundered, and Inara returned, riding up next to Julian and dismounting.

After several breathless seconds, she approached the revenant that had been about to stomp the life from Julian and rapped it hard on the skull. It echoed dully, but there was no response.

Julian got up on shaky legs and stood before the revenant. He considered it for a moment, then pushed.

It landed on the ground with a crash, and from the battlements above rang out a triumphant cheer.

Julian turned east, toward the Breach. Toward *Wren.*

"She did it," he said blankly before raising a fist to the crowd. Inara lifted her sword, and the cheers grew louder. "Wren did it!"

FORTY-THREE

After several silent moments, Wren stood. She sniffed, then closed her eyes, telling herself that somewhere on the other side of the Breachlands, the iron revenants had also departed. That this war was finally coming to an end.

"Come on," she said, speaking to her brother. "We're not done here."

After taking another heartbeat to collect himself, Hawke also got to his feet. Starling remained there, staring at Ravenna's corpse, knowing, perhaps, that her time too was coming to an end. But not quite yet.

First they must tend to the living.

Wren walked over to Vance-Locke, picking a path through all the abandoned bodies.

He was still unconscious, and Wren couldn't tell if that was a good thing or not. With any luck, it would make what came next easier.

"How do I undo this?" she asked Hawke, crouching over her father uncertainly.

He bent down next to her. "You'll need to remove Locke—anchor bone and lifepin together. Then Vance, he'll . . ." Hawke hesitated. "He'll need the well's magic to heal him physically. But his mind . . . I don't know what state it will be in."

Wren blew out a breath. She couldn't allow Locke to continue to possess his body, whatever the outcome.

She swallowed.

Locke was dead and deserved peace, not some unnatural second life. And Vance . . . Wren didn't know what he deserved, not really, but if it were her, she'd choose death over being a prisoner inside her own body.

"I'll need your help," Wren said, hand hovering over her father's chest. "Hold him, and once it's out, get him to the pool. I'll deal with the rest."

Hawke nodded, watching as, with both physical and magical strength, Wren took hold of the sternum and pulled, bringing the lifepin with it. There was a revolting wet slide as the spiked bone came loose and fresh blood started to ooze from Vance's chest, but Wren couldn't focus on that. As Hawke hooked his hands under Vance's arms and dragged him away, Wren turned her attention to Locke.

The sternum glowed with ghostly light, and Wren marveled that her hands could touch it and come away unscathed.

"Locke," she said, and the man's ghost materialized before her, summoned by her voice.

He stared down at her, then at himself, returned to spiritual form. Wren could see enough of his features to recognize him as the same man from the various illustrated histories and painted portraits in Marrow Hall.

Thanks to those images, Wren had already known that Locke

looked a good deal like Vance, though there was always something effortless about him that Vance had never managed to perfect, no matter how he tried.

Even in ghost form, Locke seemed at ease with himself.

"It did not work," he said, more statement than question.

"There's been a change of plans. Ravenna is gone."

"I see," he said. "Is it true? What she said. That I am your father?"

Wren hesitated, glancing at Hawke. Even in Ravenna's memories, Wren had gotten the impression the woman was uncertain who had fathered her children. "I don't know. I'm not sure she did, either. I think she said it was you because she wanted it to be."

His ghost nodded gravely, and Wren was surprised to realize that to her, it didn't matter. She'd had only one father in this life, and he was currently submerged in the gathering pool with Hawke.

As if reading her thoughts, Locke's attention flickered, then drifted toward his brother.

"Was I truly a hero?"

"Yes," Wren said, because according to the rest of the Dominions, he was, whatever the facts had been.

"Be careful with it. That power." He frowned, as if trying to dredge up a memory from deep within. "It killed me, I think."

Wren hesitated. She could show him. Reach out like she had with Ravenna and seek the answers. But she had just told him he'd been a hero, and if he saw the truth . . . Perhaps it was better, kinder—to all of them—not to revisit it. Not to relive it. He was dead already, and it was time he left his life behind.

"It is too much for one person to bear alone," he finished.

Wren considered. "I'm not alone."

He nodded as if that pleased him. "Goodbye, then. Daughter

and son or niece and nephew—children of the House of the Dead."

Wren turned to see that Hawke had wandered to her side. Vance now lay beside the pool, chest rising and falling with breath, though he remained unconscious.

"Goodbye," Wren said, then reached with her magic and yanked his linchpin free. He floated away as if on a gentle breeze, disappearing in a wash of contentment and leaving the chamber darker without his glow.

Wren looked up at her brother. "Are you all right?"

He continued to stare into the middle distance, where Locke had been, his eyes a bit dazed. "Yes, I . . ." He blinked, then glanced around, at Ravenna's remains. "I will be."

"Good, because we've got a well to destroy."

With Ravenna gone, the iron revenants might be no more, but if the well remained, their like could rise again—to say nothing of the other revenants that inundated the Breachlands and made it virtually uninhabitable. A haunted wasteland. But no longer.

"Now, where—"

A surge of awareness inside her chest was quickly followed by a burst of ghostlight as Willow emerged from the wall of the throne room, coming straight for Wren.

She held out her hand, and the ghost-bird fluttered twice around her head before perching there.

Wren recalled, suddenly, the errand she had sent her familiar on.

"Julian," Wren breathed. "Is he . . . ?"

Willow let out a single cry.

Wren's heart leapt and her hand shook; though she was too afraid to take it at face value.

"I sent her to go looking for him," she explained to Hawke, who had sidled up next to her. "I told her that one chirp means he's alive."

"I knew it," Hawke said, and Wren rounded on him, remembering his betrayal in a sudden, piercing flash of anger. "Or I hoped, at least."

"What?" Wren demanded. "You kicked him away from me."

"Only because of Ravenna! And kicking him saved his life. Didn't you see where he landed? In the water."

"And?" Wren's pulse was hammering, pumping her body full of painful, agonizing hope.

"The well leaks into that current. I had to kick him to make it look real," he said, tone apologetic, "and to ensure no one would go looking for him."

"So you think—" Wren swallowed. "You think he might have survived? That the well healed him?"

He dipped his chin at Willow. "She seems certain of it."

Wren lowered her hand, and the familiar took to the air.

She was so relieved, so utterly grateful that she was overwhelmed. She whirled on the spot, seeking some way to release those feelings, and saw Hawke standing there.

First, she shoved him. "You should have told me." Then she threw her arms around him, laughing and crying. He stiffened in apparent alarm at first, then patted her awkwardly.

It would have to do.

Wren drew back, wiping her nose on her sleeve. "Sorry. I'm not really much of a hugger, but . . ."

Hawke smiled shyly at her. "It's all right. Here, I have something for you."

And then he withdrew Ironheart from where it had been tucked into his belt. It had been cleaned of Julian's blood, Wren was relieved to see, and she took it in trembling hands.

"I managed to grab it after the regent left. I thought you might want it."

"Thank you," Wren said.

"You're welcome," he said. "I'm happy for you."

Something in his tone—the forced nature of his words—gave her pause. Wren had received life-affirming good news, but Hawke had not been so fortunate. The two most important people in his life were now dead.

While reaping Ravenna's ghost had been a necessity, there was another undead here who deserved peace. And Wren hated the idea of leaving her behind.

"You know about ley lines?" Wren asked. "Where to find them?"

"Y-yes," said Hawke uncertainly, following her as she strode toward Starling.

"Then you're going to be my reapyr." She held out Ironheart. It was no steel scythe, but it would do in a pinch.

He reared back, unwilling to reclaim the blade. "I don't—I've never—"

"You've used a linchpin," Wren said firmly. "It's the same. Except instead of binding her to her bones, you'll be setting her free."

"But she's . . ." He trailed off, and Wren thought she understood. Starling had been dead only a couple days. She was no ancient sack of bones; her body was well-preserved. It would make everything harder, practically and emotionally.

"Her death wound is in her chest; it's where her ghost detached from. I think you'll be able to reap it, since . . ." Since the flesh was torn open by savage knife swipes. Since Ravenna had been cruel and brutal. "Since you have experience with ley lines."

While Wren approached Starling, Hawke remained where he was, stiff as a statue.

It was difficult to know if Starling would understand, but she still clutched the wishbone. Perhaps she remained tied enough to life that she wouldn't fight them.

"It's time to go, Starling," Wren said gently. "Time to rest."

The woman's head tilted questioningly toward Hawke.

Wren wished Leo were here. He made tact an art form, but she did her best. "She deserves this," she told her brother. "She's already gone."

Though his eyes had filled with tears, he nodded.

And just like that, Starling nodded too.

That is love, Wren thought. *That is trust.*

Starling settled onto the ground, her movements stiff and unnatural.

Hawke got to his knees beside her, examining Starling's bloodied chest. Many of her bones were exposed, including the ribs directly beneath the death wound. Wren was certain one of them was the anchor bone, but it took Hawke a while to find the ley line.

"Got it," he said at last. He held Ironheart, though he hesitated before making the final cut. His eyes lifted to Starling's. She nodded again. Tried to smile. Then her grip tightened on the wishbone. She raised it to her chest—to her heart—once more.

Hawke rested one hand over hers, then, with the other, brought the blade down. The bone cracked, and Starling left her body, the ghost-green eyes dimming, the unnaturally reanimated muscles relaxing.

In the silence that followed, he pried the wishbone necklace from her grip.

"I'm proud of you," Wren said, hoping it didn't sound condescending. "You'd make a fine reapyr."

Hawke lifted his bowed head, surprise on his features. "Really?"

Wren nodded. And he actually smiled, handing over Ironheart again.

At last it was time to deal with the well.

"Do you think it'll work the same as it did with Ravenna?" Wren asked. "That I'll be able to remove the linchpins from the well to reap the trapped undead?"

"There are far more linchpins in the well than what you removed from Ravenna," Hawke said warningly. "Plus, they are scattered and deeply embedded, not sitting before your eyes in a neat row. You would need an immense amount of power and control just to *find* them all, never mind pull them free without shattering the bones in the process. More magic than you can channel on your own."

"Then it's a good thing I have you."

"I'm no bonesmith," he said warily.

"Just like I'm no ghostsmith. I'll do the magic; you'll be my amplifier."

"Still," he said, his expression grave. "It could be too much for us." His attention shifted to Locke's reaped anchor bone.

Wren nodded, but her desire was unwavering. "It won't be. Locke was by himself. We're not."

Hawke smiled slightly. "We're going to need more, then."

"More what?"

He strode over to their mother's corpse, removing several bracelets. "More bones. More magic. As much as we can carry."

Wren found her abandoned sword, and then Hawke led them into an adjoining chamber, more like a storage room, filled to the brim with bones. It looked like a bonesmith armory, except these items were not meant to be worn for protection. They were meant to store magic. There *were* some bonesmith weapons mixed in it as well, and Wren took as many as she could fit in her belt and bandolier. It was bonesmith magic she'd be using, after all.

Hawke was very particular about the items he chose. She assumed it had something to do with their familial bloodline. Surely some of these items had been here for many generations, used by *their* family for countless decades.

They split Ravenna's bracelets between them, then loaded up on other necklaces and cuffs, and Wren even got a face mask. Hers came from a deer, with tall antlers rising over her head, while Hawke donned his ram's head mask once more.

They looked like Wren's worst idea of ghostsmiths, yet oddly, it *felt* familiar. These were bones, after all, even if they were haunted ones. It was like armoring up before a battle.

As they strode from the throne room, Hawke spared a single, sad glance at his broken staff, before they made for the well.

It was deep underground, making the Breach seem practically shallow compared to the cold and murky depths beneath it.

Everything here was raw and uncarved, the stony passage rough and glittering with veins of metal and damp with moisture. They were under Hallow Hall, under the throughway, under the hot spring.

Willow came with them, and Hawke summoned Talon to light the way. They bobbed and weaved between each other, and to Wren's surprise, the glow of ghostlight coupled with their gentle flying movements was soothing to her. Comforting.

Deep in her mind, she started thinking about life *after* this. All she had wanted as soon as she'd learned about her ghostsmith heritage was to erase it—to go back to being a bonesmith and forget everything else. But she knew she couldn't do that now. Not only was her ghostsmith magic a part of her, but it was part of her brother, too, and he needed a place in this world.

And the funny thing? She thought this world could use him. Even without the well, revenants would continue to roam until the magic fully dissipated. Who knew how long that would take? And now that Wren fully understood the pain of undead existence, she didn't think she could go back to fighting them as a regular valkyr. But calming them? Calling them to her side so they could be freed?

That was something she could do.

Perhaps together, she and Hawke could change the way the House of Bone operated. Maybe Ravenna's ultimate wish—to reestablish the House of the Dead—was not an entirely misguided notion. And there were the other ghostsmith nomads to consider. With their help, reapyrs across the Dominions could make short work of unruly undead.

And more immediately, they could make the Breachlands safe again.

Though Talon and Willow continued to illuminate their path, the deeper they got, their light seemed to shrink, as if the darkness were a tangible thing, pressing in on them.

Just when Wren thought she couldn't take it anymore, several wisps of magic floated into the passage ahead, soon turning into a steady glow.

Hawke dismissed his familiar, so Wren did the same, just as an archway appeared ahead, the room beyond it blisteringly bright.

They stepped through, blinking as their eyes adjusted. They were inside a curving round cavern—like the base of a tower—the space filled to the brim with swirling white mist. It rose like steam from a reservoir of molten light at the center of the circular chamber, a vein of raw magic. It bubbled and swirled, surging brighter in their presence, and immediately Wren felt drunk on the power. She squinted at the soaring walls, and the sight robbed her of breath.

Every inch of them was lined with bones.

They appeared to be mostly human, their bodies bent and curved and overlapping to cover the natural stone beneath.

The mist was thick, especially above, obscuring Wren's sense of exactly how high the well went, but if she had to guess, she'd say it was almost as tall as the Breachfort.

While the majority of the illumination came from the vein of raw magic before them, some of it seeped from the very bones, collecting in droplets like water before dripping back into the reservoir or evaporating into the air itself.

And as the light glimmered off the ancient skeletons, it flashed across hundreds of small, smooth pieces of bone embedded within. The linchpins. They bound these undead to their bodies, the haunted bones absorbing magic and drawing it all the way to the top, where Wren assumed it was diverted into the gathering pools.

Hawke was right; there were *far* more pins here than on Ravenna.

Double. Triple, even. Nearly a thousand, if she had to guess.

They were scattered throughout the chamber, disappearing into the haze, but as the magical flare that heralded their arrival dimmed, they continued to reflect what light remained. They looked like stars in the sky, vast and endless and out of reach.

"There are so many," Wren said, her voice warbling around them.

Hawke turned to her. "We don't have to—"

"We do," she cut in. But . . . "If we do this, will *all* the extra magic be gone?"

He frowned. "Our amplifiers should remain charged afterward, until we use them up. And the land will remain seeped in extra magic. But eventually, once *that's* gone . . . that'll be it."

Wren nodded. "Take my hand."

They were both glowing with magic, their various amplifiers shining brightly, but his warm palm was grounding, making Wren feel steady and calm as she closed her eyes and surrendered herself to the power.

She tried to recall how Hawke had done this in the iron revenant chamber.

"Let it fill you up," he said softly, as if reading her mind. He sounded like he, too, had closed his eyes and allowed himself to drift.

"How will I know?" Wren asked as the familiar tingling, near-painful sensation started to take over her body. "When it's too much?"

"You won't," Hawke said simply. "Trust yourself. I think you were right. Locke died because he carried it alone, with no one to remind him of who and what he was. No one to anchor him. Like Starling's wishbone."

Or like Hawke's hand when Wren first tried to use her Vision.

Vance should have done it for Locke, Wren realized. He should have taken his brother's hand and brought him back from the brink.

Wren gripped Hawke more tightly, but in her mind, in her heart, she held on to more than just him. She held on to the Breachfort and Marrow Hall, on to Julian—alive, thank the Digger—and Leo and Inara. She clung to people like Mercy and the commander and maybe even Vance.

She opened her eyes and knew that they shone white as the moon on snow. Then she reached with her other hand and extended her senses. She found the first linchpin, and when she had hold of it, she found the next.

And the next and the next and the next.

Hawke was right that it was different from Ravenna's spine, which had not only been a series of targets she could see, but they had been stacked so closely together that to grab one was to easily grab them all.

Here, she had to be careful. Patient and thorough, lest she miss any. She didn't think she'd get a second shot at this and hated the idea that a handful of undead might linger here, continuing to draw up magic.

One after another she took hold, following the web of their connection, the magical threads that bound them together, like a ghost tethered to its body. Every time she extended herself, she kept her hold on the whole, and while her body trembled and her mind strained, she felt herself grow stronger with each leap.

The magic was surging through her, winding around her body and her bones and connecting them all in a powerful rush.

This, she realized. This was the moment Locke had warned her about. When she would become more than herself, more than a bonesmith and a ghostsmith. When she would become magic itself.

"Steady," Hawke whispered, and Wren realized he was right there with her. But rather than take any of the power for himself, he gave every drop to her—a vessel, just as she had been for him.

And that giving, that togetherness, shook her from her spiraling thoughts. She was here. She was with him.

And she would end this once and for all.

As the last linchpins became a part of her web, held in her palm like a net, Wren took a deep breath and tightened her grip. She pulled them loose, crying out at the exertion.

They burst into the air with such force, with such power, that they exploded.

Wren and Hawke were blown off their feet, landing in a heap at the edge of the reservoir, while shattered bone shards rained from the sky, glittering in the magical light like snow.

Wren feared she'd ruined everything, that she'd destroyed the anchor bones, too, but a second later, the light changed.

A cloud of ghost-green oozed from the walls of bones, telling Wren that she had succeeded.

Just as the linchpins had been freed, so too were the countless undead ghosts that had been trapped because of them. The surge of ghostlight was blinding, and the pulse of magical pressure was enough to make Wren breathless as hundreds of undead were released from their bodies.

There was a flood of sensation, an onslaught of emotion so swift and intense that a sob caught in Wren's throat. Next to her, Hawke gasped.

Then the light, the pressure—the *feeling*—all of it released in a wash of sudden, ringing silence.

But Wren couldn't stop there. The ghosts were free, the bones no longer haunted . . . but these skeletons would still absorb magic, and the vein remained exposed. The source of the magic had to be buried, like it had been centuries ago.

Wren had to tear it all down.

This part, at least, was more in her wheelhouse.

Stepping onto the ledge that surrounded the reservoir, Wren gave a cursory tug. The bones were tightly fastened to the rock behind them, and she suspected that if she dragged down the former, the latter would come too.

"Hawke, get under the archway—back inside the tunnel. And get ready."

"For what?" he asked, sounding dazed as he stumbled to his feet.

"To run."

Then she took hold of the bones and started pulling. As predicted, pieces of stone came with them, large chunks but smaller ones, too, the curved walls crumbling with every magical yank and tug. Once she got it started, gravity did the rest, all of it cascading down and landing atop the vein of magic.

Wren braced beneath the arched entrance, expecting it to splash, to gurgle and react—maybe even explode—but as she edged backward, preparing to run, she was shocked to see an entirely different result. The magic swallowed the debris, piece by piece, with hardly a sound. As it did so, the bits of bone and rock began to dissolve, fusing together and turning the pool solid.

The whole thing was falling apart now, as if the matrix of ghost and bone was all that held these ancient stones together.

When at last the thunderous noise abated and the dust cleared, the ground before them was smooth and devoid of magical light. Wren might think the whole thing had never happened, if not for the odd, bone-shaped bit of earth here or there.

Turning around, she saw Hawke standing behind her, mouth agape.

"That was . . . *louder* than I was expecting," he choked out, swiping at the dust that coated him head to toe. Wren surely looked the same. "And messier."

Wren shrugged, grinning slightly.

She had never been much for subtlety.

FORTY-FOUR

It took a while for Wren and Hawke to come back to themselves, standing there in the gritty detritus of their destruction.

The sharp, shattered mess of their victory.

Already the mist was receding, the evidence of magic being pulled up from the earth. With time, the magic would soak back into the ground to redistribute. Eventually they could fill this in—the entire ghostsmith necropolis—patching the deep wound that had torn their world apart.

Wren pushed the antlered mask off her face and glanced down at her other various amplifiers. They no longer glowed, but they were still flush with power.

She looked to her brother, who removed his mask as well.

"How long will they last?" she asked, her voice hoarse.

He stared at his own amplifiers. "Depends on what we do with them."

† † † †

Back in the throne room, Wren intended to gather what provisions she could and make for the Breachfort.

"I need to see what's happened, to find Julian and Leo and the rest."

"Right, of course," Hawke said, scrubbing the back of his head somewhat awkwardly. "I'll just . . ." He looked around at the utter devastation that was the throne room.

"You're coming with me," Wren said, as if it were obvious. Wasn't it? No way in hell was she leaving him here. Not now, not ever.

His face brightened like the rising sun.

"If you want," she hastened to add, despite his apparently favorable reaction, because it wasn't just about her, as she'd been told several times before.

"I want," he said, almost before she'd even finished.

Wren beamed.

"We keep a wagon and horses for whenever I need to do a supply run," he said. "There's an old stable nearby."

Wren felt a pang of sympathy for the poor horses kept so near a necromantic city crawling with undead, even if their presence was extremely useful right now. And having seen her brother with *ghost* animals, she knew they had likely been well cared for, given the circumstances.

Before they could set out, Wren asked Hawke for a set of manacles and bound Vance's hands while he was still unconscious next to the gathering pool, which was now completely dark.

Though he had spent some time inside it, absorbing magic while the well was still intact, he wore no bones to act as amplifiers, and Wren suspected whatever surplus he had taken had been used to heal him.

Regardless, she'd have to be cautious. Once he awakened and

found himself in chains, he'd likely put up a struggle . . . especially since Wren planned on offering him up to Leo's family. With luck, the crown would be merciful, but she wouldn't allow the lies and deceptions of the last several decades to go on any longer. He was guilty, and he would have to pay a price. Being that he was currently heir of the House of Bone, his punishment would probably be lenient. Or at least would not cost him his head. But she hoped that by handing him over herself, she would ensure her entire house didn't suffer for his actions alone.

As they carried Vance toward the exit, Wren's attention was caught by Hawke's staff, the crushed shards from Tail's skull—his anchor bone—scattered across the ground. The ghost-fox's spirit remained nearby, the barest haze of ghostlight coloring the air.

Hawke followed her line of sight, his expression subdued. "I *did* intend to free him, you know," he said. "But I guess it's too late."

Wren considered the fragments of bone. Even with charged amplifiers, the prospect of reassembling it felt impossible. Perhaps a reapyr could have done it, but not her. Wren was good at breaking things, not piecing them back together.

But there might be something else she could do. . . .

"Hang on. I want to try something." She unceremoniously dropped her father's legs, causing Hawke to stumble before he more gently laid down his upper body.

Wren had managed a powerful connection to Ravenna's memories, even though her ley line had been cut and her anchor bones damaged. Of course, she had been a lich, and her ghost was stronger than most, but Wren had felt it when Hawke had spoken to her. He'd told her to go . . . and she *had*. She hadn't been compelled; she'd just been reasoned with. Somehow, Hawke had gotten through. And it was Ravenna's own will that had seen her tether finally cut. Not a scythe's blade or the removal of the linchpins.

Wren knew it could be different for the others. Ravenna was definitely a special case. But they had to try, didn't they? If they could do this . . . it would change everything.

Kneeling before Tail's ruined skull, Wren considered the pale cloud of vapor that was his ghost. She raised her hand, then glanced at Hawke for permission. He nodded, frowning in confusion, and knelt beside her.

She closed her eyes. The images were faint at first, distant—the swish of a tail, the feel of soft grass and bright sunlight—but they grew stronger under Wren's touch and mental guidance. When she opened her eyes, his ghost solidified before her. It wasn't wholly intact, but stronger and more unified.

"Go on," Wren whispered. "It's your turn."

"My turn?" Hawke repeated. "For what?"

"Tell him," Wren said. When he still didn't speak, she added, "Like you told Ravenna."

Comprehension dawned, along with no small amount of trepidation, but he nodded. "Tail," he said, voice gentle, though Wren felt the magic in it this time. "It's time for you to go. You've done well, and I . . . I couldn't have made it through without you. So thank you. And goodbye."

Withdrawing her hand from the ghost, Wren watched as the blurry shape twitched and trembled, flaring brightly before disappearing in a wisp.

Gone. *Reaped.* Even without an intact anchor bone.

Wren expected Hawke to be subdued, but his expression was one of awe. "I can't believe that worked. That means . . ."

Wren smiled, the haunting sight of the Uprising battlefield flitting into her mind. "That means we can free them all."

It took a long time to get an unconscious Vance up a series of stone stairs and into the stable—*longer* when he awoke and started to struggle against them. After they purposely dropped him on his backside and kicked him when he tried to get to his feet, he finally submitted and allowed them to lift him up and load him into the wagon. He was too weak to stand, and even his verbal assaults were pitiable.

"Come now, little bird, I need you to think this plan through—"

"I have," Wren snapped. "More thoroughly than you thought *yours* through."

He was silent after that. Wren and Hawke rode on the bench as passengers while Vance spent the journey as cargo. Wren did feed him and give him water when he asked, but her kindness extended only so far. This entire mess lay at *his* feet, and it had almost cost Wren everything.

It had almost cost the *Dominions* everything. There was only so much Wren could tolerate.

Only so much she could forgive.

The sun rose as the Wall finally came into view, and the familiar sight of a Breachfort patrol rode upon them. It looked like Vance's soldiers had returned rather than await him as he'd ordered, and Wren was glad of it.

She spotted several bonesmiths in attendance, including Inara Fell, whose mouth fell open at the sight of the wagon with Vance riding as a prisoner in the back.

Wren never thought she'd be so happy to see the girl.

"Took you long enough," Inara said, but there was genuine pleasure in her smile as she rode alongside the wagon. The rest of the patrol circled around to ride with them, their entire party making their slow approach to the fort.

Inara eyed Wren's brother curiously, and Wren wondered just how much she knew about everything that had happened over the past few days. Knowing Inara, *all of it*, but still.

"This is my brother, Hawke," Wren said. "Hawke, this is Inara Fell."

"*Another* Graven?" Inara lamented, and Wren laughed.

It was a shock when they mounted the rise and the Breachfort came into view, line upon line of iron revenants standing there. They were immobile, ranged before the gate like statues in a garden, but Wren still shuddered at the sight.

"I was hoping I'd arrive *after* cleanup," she moaned, and Inara chuckled.

"It's slow going, with only your ironsmith to move them."

Your ironsmith.

As if on cue, Wren saw him standing before the gate, looking their way. She didn't recall making the decision, but the next thing Wren knew, she had leapt down from the wagon and started running.

Julian did the same, his iron armor flashing in the sunlight.

They collided with each other, her ribs bruised and the breath knocked from her lungs in a strange parody of the first time they'd met—but she didn't care.

"You're alive," Wren gasped into the side of his neck. She pulled back slightly, seeing the scar tissue, the evidence of what had happened. Proving it hadn't been some terrible nightmare.

Or perhaps it had been, and she'd just been lucky enough to wake from it.

"I'm alive," he said, drawing back as well so their eyes could meet.

"Thank fuck," Wren said, tears swimming in her vision. Julian laughed.

And then she kissed him. The rest of the world faded away, and there was nothing but his mouth, his lips, the soft noise of surprise he made in the back of his throat, and the way he pulled her closer, kissed her harder, and lifted her off her feet until—

"I see you've *still* got a way with words" came a voice from behind Julian. He startled and pulled away, releasing Wren, much to her annoyance. He stepped aside, face flushed, to reveal Prince Leopold. "*I'm* still alive. Where's *my* kiss?"

Wren wanted to say something clever, but the best she could come up with was "You wish" before she threw her arms around him, too.

Apparently she *was* a hugger.

FORTY-FIVE

There was a lot left to do.

The iron revenants needed to be separated from their suits before their souls could be reaped and the armor taken away. Plus, there were trials to conduct and prisoners to deal with.

As they passed through the gate, Commander Duncan was there directing traffic and taking full control of his fort once more. He took Wren's prisoner off her hands with grim satisfaction, ordering Vance Graven to be put into a cell next to his coconspirators, the regent—who had apparently survived a brutal reunion with Julian—and Galen. Wren would love to be a fly on the wall to hear what those three might talk about as they awaited their fate. Likely cutting deals and shifting blame until the bitter end.

Lady-Smith Svetlana was still in residence, according to Inara, but given her son's recent activities, she had been escorted to her rooms and kept under heavy guard. Ingrid Fell and several other high-ranking members of the House of Bone were due to arrive soon, and the king himself was on his way.

"My father should be here in about a week," Leo said, leading Wren, Hawke, and Julian into the dining hall for food and drink. "Laurent rode to Port Valor to give a verbal account of everything that's transpired, and then they'll return together."

"I'm sure he'll want to talk to all of us," Wren said, sliding onto a bench. They each had family members who'd been involved in the attack, and both Wren and Hawke would have to answer for their part in what had happened.

"But I need to get to the Iron Citadel as soon as possible," Julian said. "I need to make sure Becca's all right and start cleaning up this mess."

"I think there'll be time for you to make the journey there and back," Leo said cautiously. He had waved over a servant, and was now pouring them all cups of mulled wine from a pitcher. "*If* that is your intention . . ."

"It is," Julian said solemnly. "I will face the king and plead my case. For myself and for my people. I'm head of the House of Iron now."

Wren's heart leapt at those words, and the fact that their immediate goals aligned. She schooled her features into a casual expression. "If you're going to make a journey like that, you'll need protection."

Julian's lips quirked. "Know anybody who can help me?"

Wren glanced at her brother. "I know a couple."

They had to deal with the iron revenants before they headed out, but Leo insisted Wren and her brother get some rest first.

"They're not going anywhere," he said, waving a hand at the immobilized army. "And you're about to turn back around and head into the Haunted Territory again. Surely a few hours' sleep can only help things." Wren conceded the point, and the fact that she'd been through the wringer, magically and emotionally. She made for the stairs, Hawke next to her, but Leo halted her steps. "Do me a favor and take this one with you." He shoved ineffectually at Julian's iron-clad shoulder. "He hasn't stopped since he arrived."

Julian did not appear amused, but when Wren slid her hand into his, his expression changed. He allowed himself to be led upstairs.

"Your father's rooms are empty," Leo called out. "As is the room next to them. For your brother's sake."

Despite Leo's less-than-subtle insinuations, once Wren showed her brother to his room and went with Julian into the next, things were decidedly sweet and tender.

They didn't speak, but instead divested each other of their armor. Wren had done this before, when Julian's hand had been threatened by deathrot and she'd needed to get him warm, and of course, she had been known to remove her clothes without much prompting. But it was different this time around.

She moved slowly—not to heighten the suspense, but simply because she wanted to savor the fact that she could. When she moved on to his shirt and fully exposed his scarred neck, something inside her broke.

Tears started falling, though she didn't realize it until Julian swiped one away, his bare skin warm against hers.

His bare skin.

He had removed his gloves, his iron hand bared for her to see. Color was high on his cheeks, and shame threatened at the edges of his features as he stood before her, exposed. She took him in, his lean muscles and pale skin. And his scars. There was the one on his neck, yes, but also the ones on his hand, trailing up his arm all the way to his shoulder.

They were red and angry, interspersed with bits of blackest iron.

They were vulnerabilities; they were strength.

They were *his*, and they were beautiful.

She took his hand in hers, raised it to her lips, and kissed it.

He swallowed, slid his hand along her jaw and cupped her face, leaning his forehead against hers.

They stumbled out of the rest of their clothes and fell into bed. And like they had in that abandoned watchtower in the Breachlands, they fitted themselves together for warmth and stayed that way well into the night. Wren tucked herself up under Julian's chin, her mouth pressed against the scar on his throat, falling asleep to the steady, reassuring beat of his pulse beneath her lips.

The rest of the world could wait.

The next morning at breakfast, Leo was insufferable, smirking at Wren and Julian at every opportunity. Much to her surprise, Julian seemed pleased with the attention, while Hawke looked between the three of them with the same curious expression he'd worn inside the throughway: open interest tempered by mild confusion.

Outside, Julian used his ironsmith abilities to wrench the helmets off the iron revenants one by one, while Wren showed the bonesmiths her father had summoned to the fort how to carefully pull the linchpin free, severing the ghost from its bone. It was strange to show reapyrs how to do their jobs, but since the ley line was already demarcated, both reapyrs and valkyrs could handle the task, and did so as they moved from corpse to corpse. The valkyrs were a paranoid lot, weapons raised in case the revenants tried to attack, but their ghosts were trapped thanks to the linchpin and weakened thanks to

Ravenna. As for their bodies? They were neatly immobilized inside their suits.

Once their souls were reaped, it was a simple matter of removing the armor from the flesh, which Julian piled up in carts, ready to take with him to the Iron Citadel.

As they made their preparations to depart—Wren, Hawke, Julian, and Leopold "I've always wanted to see the Iron Citadel" Valorian—Wren found herself in need of a reapyr. She knew she and Hawke could blunder through, but that simply wouldn't do for what she had planned.

She discussed the issue with Inara, whom Wren had hoped would join them, but Inara had something pressing keeping her behind.

"You want to be here to greet your mother?" Wren guessed as she gathered supplies in the bonesmith temple beneath the fort.

Inara snorted. "Hardly. We aren't all starved for attention from our parents like you." She froze for a moment, as if fearing that by falling back into their old pattern, she had gone too far. Wren clapped a hand on her shoulder and squeezed, smiling softly. Then, because she could—

"Some of us just *get* attention, Fell, whether we're seeking it or not."

Inara rolled her eyes but smiled. Wren was glad for this newfound camaraderie between them. The world was changing, the world of the bonesmiths most of all, and, well . . . she thought the *two* best valkyrs of their generation would probably need each other.

The humor soon left Inara's eyes. "As it turns out, I need a reapyr of my own. It's Sonya's parents I'd like to greet, but hopefully with some comforting news first. They already know about their daughter, but I'm heading out with a small party later today. We'll try to find her and reap her before they arrive."

That was a worthy endeavor, and Wren didn't want to take any bonesmiths from the cause. Luckily, another reapyr would soon arrive at the fort—one familiar with the Breachlands *and* useful in a fight.

Wren was just loading their final supplies into the wagon when a shout went up from the guards atop the Wall. The gate was opened, and Mercy strode through, as strange-looking as ever with her ghostsmith-style bone mask and crossbow slung across her back.

"Mercy!" Wren cried from the courtyard, running to greet her. "What are you doing here?"

"You did it," Mercy said, pushing the skull mask off her face. She glanced to Hawke, Julian, and Leo, who hurried forward as well. "I couldn't believe it, but . . . I could *feel* it. The magic . . . it's leaving."

Wren nodded, looking at her brother. "We destroyed it. Everything should go back to normal soon."

"Normal," Mercy repeated, shaking her head. "Not sure I know what that means."

"Me neither," Hawke admitted, and Mercy grinned.

It didn't take much to convince her to come along on their journey.

"I'm in," she said, shrugging. "Surely the drowned dead can wait a little longer."

Julian was slightly confused by Wren's request—surely a pair of ghostsmiths was enough to keep the undead off their backs?—but Wren had some unfinished business to take care of.

"Leo and I talked to your uncle," she said as they mounted their horses. While Julian, Wren, and Leo would ride horseback, Hawke and Mercy would ride in the wagon.

Julian's face grew stony. "Oh?"

Wren nodded, choosing her words carefully. "I asked him about your father." Julian's eyes narrowed. "Where he was when he was killed. Where they left him."

"And he *told* you?" Julian asked, incredulous.

"Not at first. But . . ." She glanced at Leo, who was already astride his horse behind them.

"I promised him a softer sentence should he cooperate," Leo said. "He obliged. Of course, after he told us what we wanted to know, I told *him* that I held no such sway—being a spare's spare and all—and even if I did, I wouldn't speak a single word on his behalf."

Julian leveled a skeptical look at the prince. "You successfully defended the Breachfort and the rest of the Dominions from an army of undead. I think you can scratch 'spare's spare' from your list of epithets and go with something like 'war hero' instead."

Leo waved a dismissive hand, though when he glanced away, Wren saw that his cheeks were flushed.

"Well," he said, clearing his throat. "Needless to say, Francis got a bit angry after that. He's got quite a temper, you know. Makes Galen look like a kitten."

"And Vance like a spoiled cat that's been declawed," Wren chimed in.

Julian smiled warmly at them both, though his lips trembled.

"We're going to go find him now," Wren said gently. "Finally lay him to rest."

When they arrived, Julian took Wren's hand. He hadn't donned his gloves again since their night together, his skin warm and smooth, with patches of cool metal interspersed. It was just another thing for Wren to learn about him, like the tilt of his brows when he was being judgmental and the way his skin flushed when he was embarrassed.

His hand squeezed hers as tightly as he dared, and he didn't let go.

Not when they found the spot the former regent had described, not when Hawke and Leo started digging, and not when they found a body in ironsmith armor similar to Julian's. Not even when Mercy bent over the corpse in an attempt to locate the anchor bone did Julian release his grip, though Wren had drawn her sword, just in case.

It was unnecessary, though. When Jonathan Knight's spirit rose, Hawke was there, murmuring softly, soothing the ghost and keeping it at bay while Mercy did her work.

The man's death wound had been a slash across the throat, the same as the one dealt to Julian, his ghostly form—still dressed in armor—glowing with sickly green blood around his neck. He looked unnervingly like Julian, from his slicked-back hair to his elegant features, and Wren realized how close she had come to seeing Julian this way.

Jonathan's presence, while soothed by Hawke, still emanated an intensity of focus that made Wren wary. Especially since that focus was on Julian.

"Hi, Dad," Julian said, voice thick. Wren squeezed his hand tighter. Her ghostsmith magic was calling to her, and while she wanted to remain present for Julian, she allowed her thoughts to drift. He was close, the tendrils of his spirit within reach. . . .

"Got it," Mercy said quietly, indicating that his soul was residing in his mandible, the bone nearest to the death wound. What they could see of the body was badly decomposed, thanks to the burial and the fact that the helmet had been removed, and perhaps that was a kindness. Easier to see a skull than a face, Wren thought. Mercy's scythe was at the ready.

Julian's eyes sparkled with unshed tears. "Sorry I took so long," he said to his father's spirit, shuffling his feet uncomfortably. "I'll take care of Becca, I promise. I'll take care of everything." He hesitated, darting a glance at Mercy before adding, "Say hi to Mom for me."

There wasn't much lore in the Dominions about what happened *after* death—after reaping. Inara, who was of Selnori descent, said the people of Selnor believed that the dead became a part of the living world, that they existed in every stick, stone, and snowflake. The Valorians, on the other hand, had brought with them the concept of an afterlife, with rolling green hills and endless blue skies. Wren didn't know what she believed herself, but the idea that the dead could hear the well-wishes of the living, that they might reunite with those they'd lost someday, was undeniably a comforting one.

Finally Julian nodded, and Mercy made the cut. The ghost disappeared, and Julian's shoulders slumped.

To Wren's surprise, it was Hawke who moved to his side first.

"He is at peace," Hawke said. Julian nodded vaguely, Hawke's words coming across as an insincere placation or sympathy delivered by rote. But Julian had forgotten who he was dealing with.

"It's true," Wren hastened to add. "I could feel it."

Julian lifted his eyes to hers. Apparently, they flickered green when she used her ghostsmith magic. Were they green now?

"His death was violent—there should have been anger there, but there wasn't," Hawke explained. "He could have dwelled on his rage. His hatred. His sense of betrayal. But he chose to cling to love instead."

The tears that Julian had been keeping at bay finally started to fall, streaking down his cheeks in silent surrender.

"He was a kind man," Julian said. "A good man."

"So is his son," Wren said.

"Thank you," Julian said quietly. He said it again to Mercy when she put away her scythe, to Leo, who helped exhume the body and load it onto the wagon, and to Hawke, over and over again. *"Thank you."*

FORTY-SIX

They arrived at the Iron Citadel as the sun set.

News had spread of the regent's plot with the undead Corpse Queen and their eventual defeat, thanks in no small part to Leo, who had sent riders along the Coastal Road and urged the information to be spread far and wide. As such, the loyalty of the household guard and locally posted soldiers had rightfully reverted back to Julian.

Or so he believed. Wren was still wary.

"Most of them had no idea of my uncle's plans," Julian explained as they passed under the massive iron gate. On either side stood gleaming metal sculptures shaped like armored soldiers from the infamous Iron Legion that had helped conquer these lands decades ago. The Citadel itself was similarly decked out in slabs of blackest iron, making the whole place look dark and oppressive. "No one here knew about the bounty on my head or that I was in any kind of danger. Only the Red Guard was truly in his confidences."

Despite his assurances, all of them were tense as they entered the main courtyard and dismounted.

Citadel soldiers garrisoned the castle, though Wren saw different uniforms for those posted on the walls and at the gate versus those she recognized as the riders who had been working with the regent on his kidnapping schemes.

Wren recognized some familiar faces, like Jakob, who had helped Leo escape the throughway to safety.

He and the rest of the soldiers, along with every servant, stable hand, and staff member who lived in this place, started to gather before them. Dozens of people.

Then, all at once, they went to their knees before Julian. Asking forgiveness and swearing fealty.

He looked distinctly uncomfortable, Wren thought, by the tightness of his mouth and the way his hands—gloved once more—clenched into fists, but otherwise, he hid it well. His chin was high, his shoulders squared, and his eyes at once forbidding and reassuring.

I will forgive you, they seemed to say. *I will give you a second chance. Do not squander it.*

He opened his mouth, perhaps to say something to that effect, when a cry rang out, and a young girl of around thirteen or so came pelting out of the Citadel and flew right into Julian's outstretched arms.

Becca.

Julian lifted her off her feet, smiling widely as her tangle of brown hair whipped in the wind, while another person entered the courtyard at a more cautious pace. This was surely Becca's mother, judging by her similarly fine clothes and matching hair color, though she looked strained as she approached her stepson. The nearest guards watched her closely, and Wren got the impression she was on house arrest after her brother's actions.

Seeing her, Julian placed his sister back down on the cobblestones.

The woman was beautiful and had a noble bearing that reminded Wren of her brother the regent. But she possessed a quiet confidence rather than outright arrogance. And, like everyone else in the courtyard, she dropped to her knees before Julian. At a severe glance to her daughter, Becca did the same.

"I swear," the woman said, "I had no idea about Francis's schemes. Punish me as you see fit—all I want is for Rebecca to be safe."

Julian reached out a hand, helping his stepmother to her feet. "I know you didn't. Becca will be safe, and so will you." With a gesture, Julian indicated that everyone else should stand as well, including his sister.

Becca did so, her eyes fixed on Wren. "You're a *bonesmith*!" she exclaimed, clearly *thrilled* at the idea and breaking the somewhat tense silence.

"Becca," Julian said, eyes crinkling. "This is Wren."

"I carved myself a bone sword once," she said, speaking lightning fast. "So Mother would let me leave the grounds on my own. She didn't, but I kept it just in case. It took me ages. Do you want to see?"

"Don't you want to meet the rest of my friends?" Julian asked, smiling indulgently. It was an entirely endearing expression on him, and Wren fought the squirming pleasure the sight of it produced in her. "We've got another bonesmith, and a *prince*, and—"

"Nah," Becca said, taking Wren's hand and yanking her toward the nearest doorway. Wren looked over her shoulder for help, but apparently none was forthcoming.

"I thought the *prince* would get her for sure," Becca's mother mused as Wren was pulled out of earshot.

"Another blow to my well-battered pride," Leo said graciously. "Perhaps *you* will allow me to escort you inside, lady . . . ?"

"Please, call me Alanna," the woman said, taking Leo's arm.

"Some girls are more into swords than boys," Mercy said sagely, and both Julian and Hawke nodded.

They didn't stay long. While Julian ensured his sister was safe and his uncle's hold on the Breachlands was broken, the others turned their attention to his father's burial.

The bones were cleaned and prepared by Mercy, with Wren and Hawke helping as best they could. The way her brother watched the woman told Wren he was more than interested in the life of a bonesmith, and she knew she was right to think he'd make a fine reapyr one day. The possibility that he might be *her* reapyr filled her with delight, but the divisions that used to so clearly define her house were blurring. Mercy was a combination of both reapyr and valkyr, and Wren was a combination of both bonesmith and ghostsmith. Hawke was likely the same, and Wren was eager to give him some proper bonesmith training. Together, she knew they'd be capable of great things and was excited to see where the future might take them and their house.

Jonathan Knight was laid to rest in the family crypt next to his first wife, who had received the benefit of a proper burial before the Iron Uprising, when all hell had broken loose east of the Wall.

After, Julian sat outside the marble mausoleum that housed generations of Knights, head bowed as if in thought or silent prayer.

Wren hated to interrupt him, but they had to depart if they wanted to get back to the fort before the king's arrival.

Plus, she had something else she wanted to do on the way back.

As she neared, she withdrew a weapon from her belt.

Ironheart.

Wren settled down next to him and held it out. She'd been wearing it for days and she knew he'd noticed, but there'd been so much going on, she hadn't found a time to discuss it.

He frowned in surprise. "What are you doing? That's yours."

"Julian, I can't. It was your mother's, and—"

"And I've just asked her what she thinks of me giving it away," he said. "I've outgrown it, and I think it suits you."

"What does she say?" Wren asked quietly. This was not the realm of ghosts, of dead existing in *this* world. This was something else.

"She agrees," he said with a smile. "It's yours, if you'll have it."

She took the blade.

"I know how much this means to you, and I . . ."

"Good," he said, not allowing her to reject it—or even pretend to, because of course she wanted it. Of course she wanted a piece of him and his life. Of course she wanted to be worthy of it. "Besides, it seems only fair."

He gestured down at his belt, where a familiar handle poked out from one of his sheaths. Ghostbane. Just as she had been wearing his knife, he had been wearing hers—though again, they'd yet to talk about it.

"Inara let me borrow it during the battle with the iron revenants," Julian explained as he withdrew the blade. Did that count as Inara's blessing? Wren was oddly touched. "When I tried to give it back, she said it wasn't really hers."

"And it isn't really mine," Wren said. "Not anymore." As it was, the blade reminded her of her father and her desperate desire for his approval and attention. Of all the mistakes she had made. But on Julian, its meaning could change. "You should have it. I like how it looks on you." Or rather, she liked how something of *hers* looked on him. His expression had gone very serious, and she laughed uncomfortably. "Or maybe it just makes me feel good to know that you have it. That you have something of mine. Something to make you think of me."

Julian smiled softly. "Same."

Suddenly Wren's throat was tight. She didn't know what this was, exactly—a promise? A declaration?—but it meant something to her all the same.

"You know, I don't need a bone blade to make me think of you," Julian said. "The truth is, you're hard to shake, Wren Graven. You have a way of . . ." He frowned, searching for the words.

"Annoying you?" Wren supplied, grinning.

"Getting under my skin," he clarified, though he was smiling too.

"What I'd like to get under is that armor," she shot back.

She expected him to groan at the feeble line or roll his eyes in embarrassment.

Instead he fixed her with an intent stare. Standing, he took her hand in his—gloves off once more—then whispered, "Prove it."

As they made their way back to the Breachfort, Wren told Julian, Leo, and Mercy that they'd be making a slight detour along the way.

If you could count stopping at a seventeen-year-old haunted battlefield with the intention of reaping the countless lost souls without anchor bones as *slight*.

The Uprising battlefield and its haze of undead was as haunting as Wren remembered as it came into view, a ghost-green glimmer on the horizon. Their party, which included some Iron Citadel soldiers they'd brought with them, took in the sight with a mix of fear and horror.

When they stopped, Hawke approached with open curiosity on his face and Wren with grim resignation. Mercy, too, was clearly interested, but she knew better than to draw too near. The undead in this state were mostly harmless, but if things went the way Wren hoped, that wouldn't be the case for long.

Together with her brother, Wren donned all the amplifiers they'd brought with them, adding to the already chilling atmosphere and causing several of the Citadel soldiers to edge away.

Wren understood, she did—even as she drew her deer-head mask over her face—she just didn't care. This was a part of her, as much a piece of her identity as her twin bone swords and her eye black.

With a nod at Julian, Leo, and Mercy, Wren set to work.

This was all thanks to what had happened in Hollow Hall's throne room. By connecting with both Ravenna's and Tail's ghosts, she had learned something about the undead, about their tethers to the living world. It was all a matter of will, ultimately a choice—the undead just weren't aware of it. But that's what Wren and Hawke were for.

If they could help the undead push past that, they could give them what they truly craved: peace. If they would let go, just as Ravenna and Tail had done, then they could cut their own tethers, whatever the state of their anchor bones.

The primary issue would be getting the ghosts back into a form that could be communicated with. Luckily, Wren had Vision and could use their undead memories—and her powered-up amplifiers—to do so.

She wandered through the ghostlight, allowing each and every particle to touch her skin. Flickers of emotion, of memory, danced through her mind, but she didn't try to take hold of any of them. Rather, she let it wash over her, giving her a sense of the monumental task before her.

Just when she'd started to feel overwhelmed by the seemingly endless souls, a hand took hold of hers.

It was Hawke, lending her his support, his power, once more.

It became easier after that, to sort through the tumult to find connections, patterns, and shared moments. As she made a second circuit of the battlefield, she started nudging the ghosts together, sensing the way they hovered near their abandoned armor or weapons—the closest thing they had to a body.

It took hours. But hunger, coldness, and exhaustion . . . They were distant concepts, her mind awash in the world of the undead, where such things did not matter.

She noted at one point that the others had started a fire, the day having long since shifted into night—but all was not darkness.

The ghosts glowed brighter than ever as they slowly drew themselves together, turning the field from an indistinguishable haze of ghostlight into individual clouds of undead.

But that was only half the job.

"Ready?" she said, turning to Hawke. They were both ghostsmiths, but Hawke was the more powerful and better trained of the two. This was his domain.

He nodded, and together they approached the nearest undead. Wren sensed an audience from their camp as they finally found out whether this little detour of Wren's could even work.

Hawke turned a questioning look at Wren. "Ilya," she said, supplying the undead's name from what she'd pieced together of his memories.

"Ilya," Hawke said firmly, his voice taking on that familiar ghostsmith resonance. "Everything is all right. It's time for you to leave this place. It's time to let go."

The ghost flickered. "So you may rest in peace," Wren added. There was another quiver, a trembling sense of resistance—and then the ghost disappeared in a pop.

Wren looked at Hawke, who wore a matching expression of pleasure and relief. At the edge of the battlefield, Leo whooped, and Julian elbowed him for the inappropriate reaction, though he was grinning. Wren smiled too, happiness swelling within her.

"Come on," Hawke murmured, tugging her hand. "We've a long way to go."

They were at it for most of the night, but by the time dawn stained the eastern sky, they had banished the final undead. The landscape was temporarily dark, the sun's rays not yet reaching the small valley, and Wren took heart from the shadows. From the emptiness. The peace.

While Julian prepared food and Leo forced them to rest next to the fire, Wren and Hawke removed their amplifiers.

Wren lingered on the last of them.

Her ring.

She knew they would have to reap the spirits from all their amplifiers eventually, but this was one Wren did not want to wait for.

She nudged her brother, and he glanced her way, seeing her holding the ring in her hand. Understanding settled on his features.

While the others left them alone, they both summoned their familiars.

Willow and Talon hovered before them, beautiful and sad, comforting and haunting.

"I'll go first," Wren said, knowing this would be difficult for Hawke, who had spent years with Talon as one of his closest companions, but he shook his head.

"Together," he insisted, and they did. They had fine-tuned the words over the course of the evening, and though she was exhausted and magically wrung out, Wren wanted to banish her familiar herself, without the aid of reapyr or scythe. It felt more personal, somehow.

"It's time to let go," they said together, the ghost-birds listening intently. "Your duty is done, and now you may rest in peace."

Their ghosts soared upward, flaring brightly—perhaps in farewell—before disappearing high in the sky, among the stars.

Wren expected Hawke to look sad, and his eyes were bright as they reflected the moonlight. But there was something else there, too. Gratification.

Purpose.

And when he looked at her, she knew they were sharing the same thoughts.

They could do this everywhere. It would take longer, surely, without access to the well and amplifiers to heighten their abilities. But they could amplify each other if need be. They could release the ghosts in Hollow Hall, the Elders from the throne room, the drowned revenants in Laketown, and the rest of the undead throughout the Breachlands.

"This is only the beginning," Wren said, gripping his hand once more. "Only the beginning."

FORTY-SEVEN

Back at the Breachfort, Wren, Julian, and Leo knelt before King Augustus Valorian and told him their story.

Leo's brother Laurent added his account to theirs, as did Mercy, Inara, and Commander Duncan. When Hawke was called to speak, Wren insisted on being there, but her brother did well, and the king was kind.

To him, at least.

He wasn't so kind to the Gravens of Marrow Hall, but Wren couldn't blame him. She'd told him the truth of what had happened, *all of it*, rather than continue the lies that heroized her family or edited their misdeeds. Her father also gave testimony to the king, but Wren didn't want to hear it. She'd lost enough respect for him already. The last thing she needed to hear was pathetic groveling. Svetlana fully renounced her son, but Wren doubted she'd walk away unscathed.

Though he spent days considering, King Augustus eventually

stripped the Graven family of their nobility and gave Marrow Hall and the House of Bone to the Fells.

It was deserving, not that she'd tell Inara that, and honestly, the last thing Wren wanted to do was journey back to Marrow Hall and try to help them rebuild the mess her family had made.

Lady-Smith Ingrid Fell became the new head of their house, and when the king showed mercy by allowing Vance to live—but under house arrest at Marrow Hall under Ingrid's supervision—Wren thought the decrees were just all around. Vance probably deserved the death of a traitor, but living under Ingrid's thumb and seeing his wealth and status stripped away and given to his childhood rival was a far more apt and enduring punishment. Svetlana, too, would remain in the Bonelands, where she could enjoy early retirement and disapprove of Vance for the rest of her days.

Maybe Wren would visit them in the future . . . but not anytime soon.

For now she was to remain at the Breachfort. Not in exile, as before, but rather, to serve as Odile's replacement as head of the resident bonesmiths. Wren felt wildly underqualified at first, but given the task ahead included ridding the Breachlands of the remaining walking revenants and dealing with the aftermath of the destruction of the well, she supposed she was the exact person for the job.

Besides, she'd be close to Julian, who would *also* be busy cleaning up the Breachlands, which meant they'd get to see a lot of each other.

After handing over his uncle—who would be tried and likely executed as a rebel and a traitor—and bending the knee before the king, Julian swore fealty in exchange for reentry for the House of Iron into the Dominions. He had big plans to reopen the ironsmith school one day, but for now he would be focused on hunting down brigands and ensuring his people survived the winter while Wren and her bonesmith tributes cleaned up the undead. Since the ground was still saturated with magic, it would be a while before his lands were truly safe again, but with bonesmiths trained by Wren posted throughout the region, the cleanup would be successful, however long it took. With any luck, they'd enlist some of the ghostsmith nomads to help with the cause.

As for Prince-Smith Leopold Valorian, after he'd successfully defended the Breachfort from an undead invasion, his father had finally given him the respect he deserved—and a rather high-ranking military position.

Which Leo had shot down. Forcefully.

"I want to use my mind to keep the peace, not a sword," he explained over late-night drinks in Vance's—or rather, *Wren's*—chambers. He, Wren, and Julian were seated in cozy chairs before the hearth, taking in the warmth on what had turned into a particularly cold night. The snow had been falling thick and fast for hours, stacking high on the window ledges and making none of them eager to venture back outside.

"Your mind is certainly sharp enough," Julian said, topping off their cups.

"Plus, I don't think he has a sword," Wren added in a stage whisper, to which Leo laughed.

"I told him I wanted a diplomatic position instead. To act as a liaison between the Dominions and the newly reinstated Ironlands. I think I could do a lot of good east of the Wall."

"Diplomatic good isn't *all* you'll be doing east of the Wall," Wren muttered over the lip of her cup. She had seen the way Leo looked at Jakob when they'd visited the Iron Citadel. Leo was a shameless flirt, but there was definitely more to it than that.

The prince wore a scandalized expression and threw a half-eaten roll from their leftover dinners at Wren.

Julian frowned. "I don't get it."

"Of course you don't, darling," Wren said, leaning her head on his shoulder. "That's what makes you so endearing. Just make sure blond-haired, blue-eyed Jakob is a part of your personal guard, or Leo'll have a fit."

"I am a *diplomat*," Leo said, with as much dignity as he could muster in the face of Wren's and Julian's laughter. "Diplomats don't have fits."

"No, but princes sure do."

Leo grinned. "Good point."

As it turned out, Leo *did* have a flair for the diplomatic, and after only a few short days in his new position, he had gotten his father to agree to build another fort along the Wall, called the Golden Gate, where Leo would primarily reside. He hoped to turn it into a thriving thoroughfare between the Ironlands and the capital until the Border Wall could eventually be dismantled.

With Leo as Julian's primary touchpoint with the monarchy, Wren was determined to sit in on some of their negotiating sessions, if only for a laugh. But she knew both would do whatever they could to help make the Ironlands a safe and functioning part of the Dominions again.

Before her new head of house departed for Marrow Hall, Wren requested an audience with Ingrid Fell.

Her palms were sweaty as she was called into Odile's old chambers, though she realized that they would be *her* rooms before long.

One thing that hadn't yet been resolved was her brother—where *he* belonged now that the Corpse Queen was defeated and the Breachlands were no more. The king had left "matters of the undead in the hands of the House of Bone," but Hawke was not a bonesmith. Not officially.

"My brother," Wren said to Ingrid without preamble. She had dragged him with her, and he stood by her side, head bowed nervously. "None of us would have survived if not for him. Not just him but his abilities. *My* abilities. I know that ghostsmiths were exiled centuries ago, and I hated them as much as anyone. But while their magic is dark, there is possibility in it too. Potential. And as for the dark stuff, he never wanted to do the things she—Ravenna, our mother—made him do. He is compassionate and good and only wants to make the world better." She glanced at Hawke, who wore a stunned, grateful expression. She took his hand. "He's been through so much. But together we've done things—miraculous things—that I'd never have managed on my own."

"So I've heard," Ingrid said. She looked like her daughter, sleek and buttoned-up, not a hair or smudge of eye black out of place, but somehow *softer* than Inara. Or maybe it was that she lacked the hard edges and angles, as if all her rigidness had been smoothed out over the years into something that was still firm and resolute but willing to bend.

At least Wren hoped.

"You have?" she asked warily.

"According to Inara, you and your brother defeated the Corpse Queen, destroyed this volatile well of magic, stopped the iron revenants, *and* reaped hundreds of lost souls doomed during the Uprising. Is that correct?"

Wren swallowed. "Yes, lady-smith."

"My husband was on that battlefield," Ingrid said, her pale eyes glittering. "I would have been, too, if I'd not been pregnant with Inara."

Wren gaped. She had known that Inara's father died in the Uprising, but she hadn't yet pieced that particular detail together. It was all such a blur, but her mind flashed back to a ghost with fond memories of a fierce wife, belly swollen with child, doing knife drills with an ancestral blade called Nightstalker.

"So I, along with a great many others in the House of Bone, owe you *and* your brother my thanks."

Wren's heart lurched, hopeful but not yet convinced. Ingrid had given Hawke her thanks, but would she also give him a place?

"We were a single house once," Wren continued. "And while I don't know if the world is ready for that yet, I do think we should open our doors for present and future ghostsmiths. They are few, but if we trained them from the beginning, taught them to use their magic for the good of the Dominions . . . they would be invaluable allies in our fight—our *mission*—to protect the living. I know it might be hard to get people on board, to convince the other smiths that—"

"You think so?" Ingrid cut in. "Because I've had no less than *three* smiths from different houses in my office in the past twelve hours, each pitching a similar case."

"You—what?" Wren spluttered, thoroughly confused.

Ingrid nodded. "Inara was the first. She was quite adamant that *you* remain a member of the House of Bone, despite your father's transgressions. I assured her that would be the case, and then she insisted it only made sense that your *twin brother* also became a part of our house. Only logical."

"Right," Wren said, floored by Inara's staunch support.

"And then I had a rather formidable young ironsmith pay me a call. His speech was short and sweet: he needed both you and your brother—and your ghostsmith talents—to rid his lands of undead. End of story."

Wren found herself grinning a bit at that one.

"And just when I thought I might be able to turn in for the night, I had a prince of the realm at my door. He wined and dined me—if only I were a few decades younger," she added wistfully, "and pleaded your case. He was very convincing."

"Did it work?" Wren asked when silence fell over the room once more. "Are you convinced?"

Ingrid smiled. "I'd have taken the word of my daughter; the others were just gravy. To be frank, we cannot afford to turn away anyone, especially now, when things are so precarious. We must get this undead threat under control, and I think you, Wren and Hawke Graven, will be the ones to do it. So, welcome to the House of Bone," she said to Hawke, whose head snapped up. "And who knows? Perhaps, in time, we will call it the House of the Dead once more."

After days of meetings, testimonies, and signed decrees, a feast was announced to send the king off in style and celebrate the end of the House of Iron's exile and a new era for the Dominions.

It went late into the night, Wren drinking and laughing at the high table with Leo and Laurent, Julian and Hawke, plus Inara and Ingrid, and even Mercy, who ate little but drank plenty—much to Leo's amusement. Mercy had already agreed to help advise Wren in her new role, and in turn, Wren had promised to send stonesmiths to Laketown in the hopes of draining the flooded lands so that bonesmiths could reap the rest of the souls trapped there.

When Hawke passed out at the table, and Leo and Laurent broke into the Valorian royal song, Wren and Julian slipped away together. After a quick word with the guards, the pair of them left through the gate, out into the world beyond. Everything was lit by moonlight, and as Julian took Wren's hand, skin to skin, they crunched through the snow-covered ground, the blanket of white concealing the muddy and churned-up earth—all that remained of the war they'd won.

While the location was familiar, Wren felt she was treading new ground as they walked in silence. Unlike their first meeting, neither of them was armed or armored, the pair of them unguarded and vulnerable before each other.

Wren felt a strange stab of anxiety: She wasn't sure she knew how to be with Julian *without* revenants and undead queens and interhouse politics.

"Do you know when I first realized I liked you?" Julian asked, startling Wren out of her reverie.

"When we kissed?" she guessed. "I'm really good at it."

He rolled his eyes. "Way before that."

Wren rifled through all their memories together—most of them fraught with danger and risk of death, echoing her earlier thoughts. "I have no idea. I was pretty sure I just annoyed you. Still pretty sure of it."

He squeezed her hand, pulling her to a stop so they could face each other. "I first realized I liked you when you asked about my good luck charm. I already knew you were fierce and capable, but that told me you were kind."

Of all the things Wren had been accused of over the years, being kind wasn't one of them. The words filled her with warmth, despite the cold and the snow and the worries that had so recently permeated her thoughts.

Blinking rapidly, she sought something to say. "Hang on—I had just saved your life from deathrot, and that didn't endear me to you, but asking about your *jewelry* did?"

He laughed. "You saved my life because you needed me. You asked about the charm, about my sister, because you cared."

Wren wanted to argue—she had cared before then—but as he smiled down at her, starlight in his inky black eyes, she realized that her fears had been unfounded. She didn't know what the future would hold for them, but she knew she was willing to find out.

ACKNOWLEDGMENTS

As usual, my first and greatest thanks goes to my agent, Penny Moore, and my editor, Sarah McCabe, who are my closest allies through the often arduous process of novel writing. I can't believe we're closing out our second series together!

I have to thank all my publishers, at home and abroad, for believing in the House of the Dead duology and supporting my books—some from the beginning, some for the very first time. Thank you to Erin Files and everyone at Aevitas Creative Management for helping my stories reach new places, and to Simon & Schuster, for giving me the most stunning covers (again!) and hiring *the* Tommy Arnold himself to do the artwork. Thank you to Cayley at S&S Canada for the help with my local events, and to everyone at Hodderscape for making my trip to London so special. And speaking of the UK . . . huge, massive, gigantic thank you to Anissa at Fairyloot. I'm sorry we never got to meet in person so I could bow down before you (and buy you a drink), but I cannot emphasize how grateful I am for your support of *Bonesmith*. I am in awe of what you've built, and so proud to be a part of it.

Deep, heartfelt thank you to my long-suffering friends and family, who take what little I sometimes have to give without complaint, treating me like the outdoor cat that I am: by leaving out food and drink to lure me in and always keeping the light on, just in case. You have supported me and my books from the start, and I love you all.

To my First Riders, my Ride or Dies, and every reader who has ever taken the time to post a review, leave me a kind note, or share a photo of one of my books (or all of them!!): I truly could not do this without you. Thank you for being a part of my worlds. Special shout-out to my Rider Council: Alex, Brianna, and Callum, and super special shout-out to Megan, a real-life warrior tough enough to make Wren Graven jealous.

NICKI PAU PRETO is a fantasy author living just outside Toronto—though her dislike of hockey, snow, and geese makes her the worst Canadian in the country. She studied art and art history in university and worked as a graphic designer before becoming a full-time writer. She is the author of the Crown of Feathers trilogy and the House of the Dead duology, and you can find her online at NickiPauPreto.com.